THE PRISONER

Book Five of The Dark Series

Charnae

Sonder Skookum Publishers, LLC

ISBN: 978-1-962695-16-9 (Digital)
ISBN: 978-1-962695-17-6 (Paperback)
ISBN: 978-1-962695-18-3 (Hardback)

Library of Congress Control Number: 2023923185

Cover Photo Credit: Valua Vitaly/Shutterstock.com
Cover Creation: Canva.com

FIRST EDITION: November 2024

Published by Sonder Skookum Publishers, LLC
Sandy, Utah, U.S.A.
www.charnaesbooks.com

To Matt.
Thanks for the borrowed dialogue.
You're still my favorite.

CHAPTER ONE

Three Days Caged

"Let go of me, you disgusting mole!" I try to pull from his grip, but he sticks to me like cured glue. I hate the mole's amused laughter, which echoes off the stone walls of my new home in the Dark. He refused to give me his name upon my arrival, so I nicknamed him Guard A. His superior attitude has me itching to choose a better name—something degrading to cut him to his core—because I can't help lashing out in the few ways still open to me.

"You're practically a mole yourself," he says, and it's the most I've ever heard from his mouth.

I renounce being called a mole. Even though I'm now living among the light blind—those who can see inside the accursed Dark—I'm far removed from a mole's designation. They're the worst sort of people—cruel, unjust, and uncivilized.

I was born with light sight in the prosperous city of Mirum, growing up beneath the glorious sunshine inside the Adlumen light bubble. I'm a member of the once-powerful Endrack family. My ancestors led Adlumen for over a century from our walled fortress called Ambitus. I'd tell Guard A this if I weren't a prisoner here, if I thought it would make any difference, or if I were still a citizen of Adlumen—because, along with jailing me, they stripped my citizenship. The reminder silences any rebuttal, which is odd since I'm not the quiet type.

It was Captain Rhed, the leader of the Coastal Territory, who made my prison arrangements. He made Dad's as well. Weeks ago, Captain Rhed and three of his guard escorted us from Ambitus. We traveled to Acies, where I saw the

Dark—not visible from Mirum—for the first time since my childhood. Then, inevitably and without fanfare, we entered the void. It was only the second time I'd been inside because Dad preferred to keep his family safely in Ambitus.

Upon entering the wasteland, they separated Dad from me, and we traveled different routes to our Dark prisons. I'm desperate to know what happened to him—at least the basics—and I've tried to drag any bit of information from Guard A. His responses are usually a clanging dish, shuffled step, or mumbled, "Be quiet." I wish he'd just answer. Doesn't he realize a little information would go a long way for both of us? It would keep me… well, not quiet, but quieter. And besides, I ask for very little. I just need my bearings if there's any hope of making this place tolerable.

With so few things to keep my attention, I frequently get caught up in daydreams. Last night, my mind conjured a story to explain Guard A's reluctance to talk—an absurd scenario where he's bound to a magical rule of silence, and each slip costs him a finger. He's down to three on his left hand and a thumb on the right. Unfortunately, Guard A's firm hold on my arm obliterates any idea of him having only four digits. A more general fantasy is envisioning this place as managed by grumpy, troll-like people—taciturn and prone to grunting. It's not an impossible supposition since it is a prison, and grunts and groans are the most common sounds.

"Let go," Guard A says, giving me a heavy tug, and my fingers release their precarious grip on the thin bars. Without my sight, I can't find anything else to grab, so I stumble behind him. Curling my fingers, I try to gather courage I don't have. I hate being at the mercy of others, and it stirs negative feelings inside of me—a mixture of anger and fear. The anger I can manage—it's something I wield as comfortably as a Torquent blade. The fear, though, is new.

Having been in my cell for three days, I've learned a few things about my enclosure: The space is seven feet in each direction. Two sides are rock walls, and two are metal grids. The floor is hard dirt, the bed is lumpy but bug-free, and the ceiling is too high to touch, even standing on the bed. But last night, I climbed the grid and reached it, though my exploration didn't help determine the source of the sweltering breeze that blows through my cage, drying out my skin.

They held Dad in a few different cells back in Adlumen. I visited him in one and later occupied the space with him. The place I'm in now is worse. Just being in the Dark makes it more difficult, but when you add in unidentified smells and tasteless food, my Dark prison is a significant downgrade. Still, I've been inside long enough to develop a sense of safety, and I don't like that Guard A is taking me out.

Curses! I really don't want to go with him.

"Where are we going?" I complain, dragging my feet. I might be afraid, but I refuse to let it show.

Guard A grunts, then mumbles, "Warden."

The warden wants to see me. *How nice.* I wish I could, in turn, see the warden, but that's impossible for someone with light sight in the Dark. Unless the warden has the newly discovered lamlight, which I strongly doubt. First, most people who live in the Dark are light blind, so there'd be no need for using lamlight. Second, it's doubtful they'd provide such luxury for prisoners. And last, I lived an affluent life back in Adlumen and had yet to see the lamlight in action. Such objects won't make it to wherever I am for some time.

No, I won't *see* anyone today. Still, I relax some, knowing I'm meeting the person in charge. But immediately, logic prevails, and the tension returns. After all, there's an equal chance of the warden being unjust as fair.

We pull to a stop. The door clicks before being pushed forward. I'm moved, released, and with another click, it's closed behind me. Guard A is gone.

"Hello," I hear in a moderate voice—not high, not deep.

I pull in a breath and back up against the door.

"Take a seat. Straight in front of you."

After a few unsteady steps, I find the chair and sit, rotating my head aimlessly while looking for nothing but trying to hear everything. It's too quiet.

"I'm Warden Ott, and you're Sharade Endrack. Quite the pot of gold landed in my lap to allow you a spot here."

I sit straighter, staving off the chill running up my spine while I gather my courage. I discover there's not much.

"You have nothing to say about that?" he asks.

"Congratulations?" I keep my face expressionless and my tone flat.

"You're awfully young to be a prisoner in the Dark. Only sixteen."

"What day is it?"

"Condition of your sentence. I'm not supposed to tell you."

"Please," I say, but my request goes unanswered, so I try again. "Please. Just this once."

Warden Ott breathes out heavily. "July eleventh."

The eleventh? My eyes widen. What are the chances?

I shake my head and clear my throat. "I'm sixteen for three more months." *Approximately*. I don't know why I told him. I guess I don't want to be demeaned for my age. Of course, it does no good.

"I'm not accustomed to young people. I forget you have annoying habits."

"We just met. I've barely said a thing. How have I already annoyed you?"

"You have a misguided sense of self and believe you understand the adult world when you clearly do not."

"How so?"

"Well, you're confrontational, though you have no power, and your comments are pointless to your situation."

"Where exactly am I?" We traveled for three weeks in the Dark, but the direction and destination were impossible to determine. I only know we didn't go due west because we'd be in the ocean.

"You'll never know. It's a condition of your sentence." I squint, nettled by his dismissal, then hear the rustle of papers before he continues, "You're female."

"As you see."

"Insolent."

"I find the word a compliment."

"You're full of fear," he says levelly.

"No! I'm full of hate and anger."

A full minute passes—enough time to settle back into my seat. I'm ready to ask if he's still there when the question becomes pointless.

"I think you're right," he says, only inches from my face. I screech, lurching backward. My heart pounds as he adds, "And you're wrong. I'll agree with hate, anger, *and* fear."

His gaze is like a touch—something I feel on my skin as he speaks.

"You have brown eyes, the whites of which will soon be red from tears. Brown hair that's too long for this place. Your scalp will quickly ache from the knots you'll twist into the strands as you spin your nightmares in bed. A pert nose that's high with pride but will be forced to take in breath, and along with air, the surrounding stench. And you have a small, pretty mouth that contains a loud voice. Here, your mouth will only get smaller as each day passes. You'll find the only thing it's suitable for is taking in stale food and murky water. You might lose your voice entirely after a decade with no one to talk to."

I pull my upper lip between my teeth. The dry air already has it chapped, but I suck on it as I ponder the genuine possibilities Warden Ott presents. Popping my lip free, I say, "You're just trying to scare me."

"I'm preparing you for what will be. Should I end it now? Take your life and pocket the money? It seems we'd both benefit."

"No." A random hair tickles my face, and I rub my cheek.

"It seemed a good idea to give you the option." Warden Ott's voice is farther away. "Only sixteen." He tsks.

"Do you give all your prisoners an option?"

"No. I think... hmm, yes, this is only the third time."

"Then why'd you do it?"

"Because someone asked me to."

"My sister? Or Captain Rhed?" They seem the likely candidates—either the one person who might grieve my fate or the man charged with bringing me here.

"Neither."

"Is this one of Captain Rhed's prisons?" It's crossed my mind more than once that I'm in the Coastal Territory.

"I don't just run this place. I own it. I report to no one." He's more than just a warden, making all the decisions himself, but we could still be in the Coastal Territory. Or the Northern, Southern, or Desert Territories. Even the Nomad Lands aren't out of the question. Basically, I could be anywhere.

"So, if it wasn't them, who asked you to give me the option?"

It's silent, except for the shuffle of Warden Ott's pants as he moves back to his chair. I hear him settle, but it's still a moment before he answers, "Your father."

Dad?

"Are you saying my dad is here?"

Warden Ott knocks his knuckles on what sounds like a desk. "You'll never get close enough to speak with him, but yes."

Dad's here. In the Dark. With me. Just knowing we're in the same place releases some tension inside of me. I'm grateful to Warden Ott for sharing the information until he speaks again.

"I didn't tell you that to put a smile on your face." I hear the irritation in his voice. "You're a silly girl. Did you not consider the oddity of your father calmly discussing your death with me? It's becoming clearer how you got into this situation."

"You don't know me well enough to say something like that."

"I never let people inside these walls without knowing everything. After all, who a person is affects the price of confinement." I twist my fingers together, hoping this conversation is done, but I have no such luck. "You're the daughter of Keine Endrack, the former leader of Adlumen. You followed your dad's plan to overthrow the seated rulers."

I wasn't just following a plan. I was doing what was best for Adlumen and my family, but somehow, it all went wrong.

"You went against the wishes of your people."

No. He's wrong about that. I shake my head, pulling in my top lip and sucking on the chapped skin.

"I'm sure you felt justified."

I did and still do. I did the right thing.

"But they all hate you now." Warden Ott releases a light laugh. "Even Keine Endrack."

"No! He loves me."

"What I say is true."

"I was the loyal one," I whisper, brushing a tear from my cheek. I thought him mildly compassionate, but I was wrong —he's eagerly using my situation to hurt me.

"And now you'll serve your time here and probably make us hate you too."

"How long am I here?"

"Condition of your sentence. You'll never know." His chair scrapes across the floor. "Enjoy the walk back to your cell. It will be a long time before you're outside of it again."

The door opens. Guard A's five fingers take my arm and guide me numbly back to my space—my permanent residence until... well, I guess until forever. The thought causes me to freeze in place when we reach the metal entrance. I put my hands on the frame, bracing myself against entering, but he gives me a solid push, and I fly inside, stumbling and skidding to the ground.

"Watch out for the rats," he says, laughing. I scramble across the floor, find a small rock, and throw it at him, but he's already gone.

My hands are wet, and when I settle against the grid bars, I learn it's blood from my fall. I push the wound against my pants to stop the flow. Pressing down, I find a scar from one of the many times I sparred with Chessie. Dad always drove us until we bled, though I always lost the most blood. Still, Chessie tried to make it minimal, but she could only do so much when Dad watched.

I bite my lip and lean my head against the bars. Putting me in this place is the worst thing Chessie's ever done to me. Though, if I look at the situation from another angle, Dad did this to me. But they'd each say I did it to myself. Chessie would claim choosing Dad in the conflict was the catalyst. Dad would condemn my failed assassination attempt.

And it was a failure. I wasn't prepared to take a life and blundered it miserably. I sum it up to being unequipped to succeed in life. Maybe that's why Dad made the request of Warden Ott—he doesn't believe I can survive this place, so why allow me to try?

Maybe I should call Guard A and tell him I'll take the offer—end my life on July eleventh.

It would be poetic to do it today—on my sister's birthday. It shocked me when the warden gave up today's date. It's only been a few months since I sat with Chessie on a Fiducha balcony, discussing her future. Chessie's nineteen today, and Dad had plans to marry her off to Brigadier Siler Pruden. Siler was a perfectly likable guy, but she was organizing her resistance, which I deemed fruitless because Dad would have his way. Like always.

Except he didn't. Because the contenders came, challenging the Succession of Governors and winning Right to Rule. Chessie fared well in the changeover, while Dad lost everything. And I joined him in his descent.

CHAPTER TWO

One Year Caged

When I was ten, I visited Mom's sister in Subsolanus for a week. My brother, Wick, was seven and came with me, but Chessie stayed in Ambitus because Dad insisted she couldn't miss training.

We called Mom's sister Aunty, and even now, I can't recall her given name, though I'm not sure it was ever told to me. Aunty lived in a quirky place that was the polar opposite of Fiducha—the giant home where we lived in Ambitus. Her place didn't look small from the outside—though it would have fit inside of my bedroom—but indoors, you keenly felt the squeeze of the many, many tiny rooms. Aunty liked her divided spaces and filled each with items of little worth but worthy of interest.

We enjoyed exploring the boxes and corners at Aunty's—all except the cellar. My first trip down there for a bottle of canned peaches resulted in unexpected terror. It was a tight, musty, spiderweb-infested space. A second trip never happened because I cried and threw a fit at the mention of it. Aunty talked Wick into going inside—to prove it wasn't scary—but he sided with me, and neither of us ventured there again.

But it became a term we often used. Wick and I referred to anything we didn't like or preferred not to experience as Aunty's Cellar. And it's the perfect way to describe how I feel about my prison in the Dark, so I gave the name to my little cage.

During my first week in Aunty's Cellar, I looked for any opportunity to express myself, aiming my antics at the only target I had: Guard A. I would drink my water—because I'd never waste it—then wait for the mole before throwing my empty cup at him. I wasn't always sure of my aim in the Dark, but I got in a solid hit more than once. But then, I did too good of a job, hitting Guard A on the head. He expressed his displeasure long and loud, making my ears hurt. It was inevitable, I guess, that there'd be repercussions. He didn't return my cup but gave me a new water container—a glass one.

"This is the only thing you'll ever drink from. Throw it at me again, and no matter how small the remnants, it's all you'll have to hold water. I guarantee you'll be sipping blood with every drink you take."

I've willingly spilled my blood before, but it wasn't for a drink of water.

The new container was a bottle with a long, slender neck. I love glass bottles, having collected them back home. When he put it into my hand, I ran my fingers over the shape and imagined it was pretty and green, like one I kept on my bedroom shelf. But after enough time passed, I decided it couldn't look like that. I merely conjured the idea to create a happy thought because there's nothing pretty in the Dark. Without sunlight, everything is ugly.

Guard A is gone now. It was a few months back—or maybe weeks—that he got smart and escaped this place. When Guard B arrived, I didn't have to guess about the patrol change after catching the scent of his unbathed body. Really, it was a boost to my pride because, before he came, I thought I smelled terrible.

As for Warden Ott, I've not spoken to him again. I've asked Guard B about the warden, my dad, and many other things. Each time, I get the same response. "It's a condition of your sentence that I don't tell you."

And so, I exist in uninformed silence during all my waking hours, but I cling to my anger and hate. They're the only things keeping me going. They stoke my refusal to give up, even though there's not much to exist for.

Today, I'm lying on the dirt floor of Aunty's Cellar with my arms spread wide while trying to cool down. There's no breeze, but it's so hot I'm not sure moving air would improve anything. We've had a few days like this, so I know we're heading into the hottest part of the year. We'll have months to suffer in the swelter before fall arrives to give us a break. I survived it once, so I know what to expect, but I'm not looking forward to it.

This existence is so different from what I experienced back home. I was at the top in Adlumen, living with every comfort. It's appropriate to say I've found the bottom in this Dark prison.

Before the governors came to Adlumen, I spent my days tormenting Chessie, punishing Wick, teasing my future brother-in-law, Siler, and making any excuse to go to the training field to flirt with Raden. I ignored Mom, unless I needed something, and tried to make Dad notice me with little success.

And that's it. That was my circle of contact. But now I don't have any of them. I'm without a single friend in the world. One thing I realize hasn't changed: I'm nearly as isolated here as I was in Ambitus. If I could go back, I'd do it differently. I'd insist on more.

I push from the floor—abandoning the direction of my thoughts because there's no use dwelling on unproductive notions—and walk to my bed, retrieving strips of cloth I tore from the bottom of my pants. I wrap my knuckles, find the correct distance from the back wall, and punch. I keep it light—just a quick tap to feel the contact. I mimic what I watched my sister do and repeat what Raden taught me. I hope someday I'll meet someone new and have a worthy reason to punch them.

Tap. Breathe. Tap. Tap.

Part of my purpose is the comfort from keeping a rhythm. Also, it's a reason to move. If Raden were here, he'd insist it's a worthwhile pursuit, and I'd argue the opposite viewpoint just for fun.

I wish it made me happy to think about them, but the pain is too acute to accompany joy. I always thought Chessie was so lucky to have Siler picked out for her. He was solid and reasonable, and all the girls liked him. Dad never talked about me getting married. I hoped he thought about it—that he had someone as good chosen for me. Of course, I always pined for Raden, convinced I was in love with him. Now, I'm not so sure. He's older than me, and though he went along with my flirting, he never returned it. After so much time in the Dark, I wonder if I was blind back in the light. Situationally blind. I don't like to consider it, but there's so much time here and little to do but think.

Tap. Tap. Breathe. Tap.

I'm unwinding the cloth from my fingers when I smell Guard B.

Curses! What's he doing here? It's not mealtime.

"Prisoner. Come to the bars, and then, turn around."

I huff out a laugh. "My name's Sharade, and that sounds like the worst idea I've heard this year." I grin at my joke. It's so seldom I get to be sarcastic.

"I need to check your scalp. We've had an outbreak of lice."

"Lice!" I shriek, dropping my knuckle cloths and scurrying to the metal grid. I turn, leaning so he can check me for bugs, then shudder. But instead of rummaging through the hairs on my head, he grabs my hair and yanks me tight against the bars. "What are you doing?" I screech.

"Hold still, and this will go smoothly."

"No way!" I struggle to escape him, but he has an excellent hold on my locks. They've never done this to me before—mostly, I'm left alone—so I can't imagine what's happening. But after another minute of fruitless wiggling, I hear a strange zipping sound, and I'm instantly free.

"It was getting out of control," I hear in a voice that's not Guard B.

"Warden Ott," I say, reaching back and feeling the shorn strands of hair at my neck. It's a blunt cut—he just held it in place and snipped straight across. Well, not very straight since it's longer on the left. I had so many plans in life. Getting my hair cut by Guard B, who smells like a living corpse, wasn't one of them.

"Why not just tell me you were cutting it? I'd have let you in here to do it right."

"It's not my practice to allow scissors inside the cells," Warden Ott says.

"I would have cooperated even through the grid."

"Eh. The lice story always gets a better response."

"So, no lice, then?"

"Not this week."

Well, at least that's something.

"I'm surprised you're here. I've asked to speak with you in the past. Why come to me now?"

"Because it's a year since we met, and I need to report back your status. I perform the inspections personally. Got to be accurate so that gold keeps landing in my lap."

"It's been a year?" I ask, a little dazed. "Today's July eleventh."

"You remember."

Suddenly, I hear a strange grinding noise, followed by the ping of metal and someone swearing.

"In here, boys," the warden says.

"What is that?" I ask, unable to disguise the fear in my voice. I hate that he hears it. I've spent the entire year proving I'm not afraid—only angry and hate-filled—but one visit from the warden, and I'm a simpering miss.

"It's a bathtub on wheels, being sloppily pushed by a couple of stupid oafs."

"We's not stoopid," I hear in an unfamiliar voice.

The warden chuckles. "If you say so. Sharade, sit on your bed while we get this inside."

A little stunned, I back into my corner. "Does everyone get a bath on their first anniversary?" I ask, taking a seat.

"No. It's a condition of your sentence." It's the only time I've heard that statement and been happy about it. "You get a new set of clothes as well," he adds, and I resist the urge to cheer.

"Can I keep the old ones?"

There's a pause before, "If you must."

I listen to the ruckus of the two moles moving around Aunty's Cellar. They seem to run into everything, and I agree with the warden that they're not too bright. Or coordinated.

"Make sure you lock the wheels," he instructs, and I hear a few clicking sounds. The room is free of them soon after, and the lock on my cage is back in place. I reach over and find the tub. It's metal, and the edges are curled. I lean a little farther, and my fingers touch the water. It's warm.

I'm unsure how the rest of this will go, but I might as well ask. "Are you staying while I bathe?"

I hear Guard B's signature snort. "I assure you, I have no interest in seeing you naked. You're not more than a filthy child."

Warden Ott, however, is less insulting and more informational. "They'll remove the tub in thirty minutes.

Keep track of the time." I want to ask how I'm expected to do that, but they're already gone.

I'm hesitant about undressing but don't dare waste my minutes. It's not until I strip off the last of my clothes that I hear a low chuckle from the adjacent cell. The noise causes me to launch into the tub with a splash.

There's a man over there. He's been housed next to me for a few months at least, but I often forget about him simply because he only makes noise while he sleeps—little whimpers. One time, he reached through the grid and touched me. It was startling, though he did no harm. One thing's for sure—whoever he is, he's not in his right mind. And there's another thing I know—I don't want to think about him while having a vulnerable soak.

Settling into the warm tub, I try to relax. It's a hot day, but the water removes the uncomfortable edge. I lean back, running my fingers through my short hair and letting the water in. I wish they'd left a bar of soap, but I doubt that's a condition of my sentence.

I wonder who made this prison luxury possible. Captain Rhed? My sister? The Adlumen judges or governors? I can't imagine any of them arranging it.

Chessie's twenty today. I wonder if she had a big party in Ambitus. She might have if she's still friends with the governors, but it's more likely she celebrated with Mom and Wick somewhere in Mirum since they planned to move into the city. I imagine Chessie arguing against a birthday party—as she hates attention—but she'd still smile when it happened. If I were in attendance, I'd have lavished profuse attention on her and had her cheeks in full blush, but we'd have laughed about it later.

I twist my fingers into my hair. A moment later, I curl onto my side and hold my breath, dropping beneath the water's surface. Down here, my tears are camouflaged. Down here, only I know the extent of my mourning over the separation from my family.

An hour later, the tub is gone, and I'm wearing clean clothes. Having rinsed out my old clothes, they're now spread out to dry.

Early in my captivity, I gathered small rocks in Aunty's Cellar and piled them in the corner. There are nineteen, and I've devised a counting system to mark my time here. I plan to start from a year ago today—July eleventh—as my day one. There's something important about knowing the date. It helps ignite some hope, though I don't know if there's anything specific to hope for. It's possible there's nothing in my future except a cell in the Dark.

But maybe Diggs—my uncle and another member of Dad's assassination plot—will find us. He's the only conspirator not imprisoned or dead.

Or maybe Dad will liberate me. He's somewhere in this place. Maybe, at this very moment, he's working on a plan to get us out. It's possible. After all, he's a brilliant man, and I'm his flesh and blood. He'd do anything for me. Just as I've proven, I'd do anything for him.

CHAPTER THREE

Two Years Caged

I dip my head below the surface, leisurely blowing bubbles in my yearly bath. It's early morning, and five minutes ago, Warden Ott arrived with Guard B.

"Great. You're alive," Warden Ott said.

"It must be July eleventh." I should have known for sure because I'd been rock-stacking—using a system similar to an abacus—but a few months ago, I knocked them out of place. And, of course, Guard B wouldn't validate anything.

"It is," the warden confirmed, revealing my patched-up rock system was a week off.

"Will you tell me something about my dad? Anything?" I asked.

"No, but have a good year."

And then he was gone while Guard B cut my hair through the bars. He's lasted longer than Guard A, which is impressive since I pester him with questions. He cycles through different response methods. Sometimes he grumbles, sometimes he groans, and occasionally he uses words. Lately, he doesn't do a thing. I'd almost think he's a different person if it weren't for the smell. It seems this place is wearing him down too.

'Have a good year' were the warden's parting words, and they roll through my thoughts. There's no such thing in the Dark. Freedom and association with others are the only things that make anything good—and I have neither.

I lift my head until my lips and nose break through the water. I take a deep breath and go back under. Bathing reminds me of when I was free in Adlumen. I took a bath every day and thought nothing of it. I was a fool about many things—taking my comforts for granted among them.

For two years, I've survived this place. Can I live a worthwhile existence with only one day a year to look forward to?

I don't know if I can.

I surface quickly. My comfortable soak is done, and it's time to scrub off a year's worth of dirt. I lean forward and flick the tub water, listening to the droplets fly, then get started.

I've learned some things during my time here. July is scorching, and January is frigid. The months in between are tolerable, though April and October are best. And September, I discovered firsthand, is fire season.

We could smell the thick and pungent smoke, but there was no sign the guards would move us if the flames turned our way. I was eager to get out of Aunty's Celler, even temporarily, but when I understood they wouldn't evacuate us, I prayed the fire would stay away because I wasn't ready for death—it still frightens me.

The smoke got severe, and when evening arrived on the worst day, I thought I could see smoky sunbeams in Aunty's Cellar. I looked down and was sure my clothes were blue, not gray like I always imagined. The effect was gone after a minute, leaving me clinging to the floor, coughing dirty air. Then I fell asleep or passed out.

It surprised me when I opened my eyes to a new day. My throat ached, but the air was better, and I knew the previous night could have ended all of us prisoners. When Guard B did his rounds, I asked in a scratchy voice if my clothes were indeed blue, but it was during his grunting period, and that's all I got. It was Squatty—the man in the cell next to mine—who answered. "Yes," he said when Guard B was out of earshot.

That was the day I named Squatty because I swore in the smoky sunbeams I saw him squatting against the wall of his cellar. Of course, I know it was a hallucination—something brought on by being near death—but it felt so real. I still have the image burned into my mind.

And now Squatty and I are friends—if one can decide friendship based on the six words he's shared with me. 'Yes' was the first, answering about my blue clothing. In the same conversation, I asked if he whimpers in his sleep because of nightmares. 'Yes' was his second word. Then I asked if his throat hurt like mine. 'Yes' was his third word.

He was a new and exciting source of information, so I asked a more important question, "Do you know where we are?"

"Yes," he said, revealing his fourth word.

"Where?"

But he never answered. I asked more questions that day, but his desire to communicate had dried up.

A few months later, I heard him vomit inside his cell after they'd fed us rancid rice. "You didn't like today's breakfast?" I asked dryly, clutching my aching stomach while he answered with a resounding, "No."

I logged that as number five and became excited because he knew more than one word.

He gave me his sixth word a few weeks back. It was a particularly challenging day—no spectacular reason for it, just the hopelessness of life pressing in on me—and I was against the grid crying when I felt Squatty's hand on my shoulder before he said, "Sharade."

I put my hand on his and turned toward him. "What's your name?" I asked, but all he did was squeeze, and then I cried some more.

"Hey, Squatty," I say, scrubbing my face with bathwater. I

don't know if he's watching me, but he's listening. Unlike last year, he didn't chuckle when I undressed. Maybe it's because he knows me now. I don't think the last time was a lude reaction. I'm sure it was just startling—seeing me strip down—and in this place, anything out of the ordinary is worth a response.

"You want to wash your clothes in my anniversary water?" I ask but don't get a reply. As I'm apt to do, I just keep talking. "Don't be embarrassed. Remember, I'm not a mole like you, so I won't see a thing. Unless there's a random fire in the area and I hallucinate the event." I chuckle and sniff the air dramatically. "But I think you're safe."

I'm met with more silence, which is expected, but he hears me, and that's worth a lot.

Two years ago, I wouldn't have had patience for Squatty. He'd have made me nervous, and I would have avoided him. Now, he's a comfort, and I'm grateful he's here, even if he isn't entirely with it. I was a wholly different person back then and spent a lot of energy declaring I was better than those around me, though I never believed it. I've not accomplished anything worth claiming superiority.

I didn't like myself, and for the most part, my family didn't like me either. Mom sure didn't. Sure, she loved me, but those feelings were an extension of giving birth—a genetic requirement to protect, guide, and love the thing you brought into the world. But nowhere was it required for her to like me.

My sister was my rival, and the thing I fought Chessie for most was Dad's attention. She never had a moment's peace from me, and it's hard to like an irritant. My brother was a different story. Chessie always said Wick was born wise, and sure, he was a keen thinker, but more than that, he was brave—something she never gave him credit for.

It was Wick who persistently told me the things I needed

to hear but didn't want to, and he never worried about how I'd react. The others would give up, but Wick didn't. He'd wait until I stormed off and then come find me. Vicious words and hurled objects didn't deter him. I acted like he was a bother —like I didn't care to listen, but I always did. I wish I'd acted more on his advice. His guidance makes sense to me now.

Growing up, I was always jealous of Chessie but never of Wick. I am now. He was born wise and brave, while I had to get sent to a Dark prison to figure things out.

I lie back in the water, tired of scrubbing, and let out a longing breath. I feel the grit gathered at the bottom of the tub and run my finger through the debris I removed from my hair and skin, wishing it wouldn't be another year before I got to experience this again.

"I'll be in for another few minutes," I say, closing my eyes. "But just come to the bars if you want to wash your stuff." Squatty makes a slight hum in his throat, and it's the last thing I hear before nodding off in the silence beneath a comforting blanket of water. I'm startled awake sometime later by Guard B rattling the metal grid. "You're not out," he states disappointedly.

"I'm sorry!" I surge up, pulling my knees to my chest. "Please! Give me thirty seconds."

He groans, and I hear him move away. I launch from the tub, taking water with me, and discover Squatty's clothes floating on the surface. I smile briefly, but there's no time to waste. Without dressing, I grab my old clothes and throw them in. Quickly, I plunge the items up and down, scrubbing them against the mildly bumpy side of the metal tub. I even wash my shoes. One thing about confinement in a cage is that my footwear will last a long time, which is good since they don't update those each year with my bath.

Guard B ends up giving me five minutes, returning to find me dressed in new clothes with our wet items spread out to dry. I hate thinking of Squatty nude in his cage. You never know—keeping him in filthy clothes may be a condition of his sentence, and I don't want him getting into trouble because of me, so I try to divert the attention from the naked man in the next cage.

"Thanks for waiting. I'm sorry I wasn't on time," I say. Contrition can work to your benefit. I've learned that in the last two years.

No response.

I twist a finger in my hair, again enjoying the shortened locks. I wouldn't care if they shaved it off, but that would probably be too much trouble. Guard B sends the moles in to remove the water while I stand to the side.

"Am I in blue again?" I ask, motioning to my new clothes. Keeping the guard's eyes on me is the plan, but I'm also curious.

The door clicks closed, and Guard B engages the lock on Aunty's Cellar. Then he walks away. I pick up Squatty's shirt, wringing it out again and shaking it to release more water. I do the same to his pants, then take them both to the grid.

"Here are your clothes," I say, pushing them through the six-inch metal squares separating us.

"No," Squatty says, and I pause, then feel the material slip from my hands as he pulls the articles through.

"No?" I ask, confused, and then my face goes smooth in realization. "Ah. My new clothes aren't blue." I run my hand over them. They feel a little different from the last set. "I wish you'd tell me what color I'm wearing. It would be a real comfort to my mind."

I smile in Squatty's direction but don't wait for a reply before moving to the corner to find my rocks. I crouch down, rearranging them to represent the two years I've lived in this place.

It takes little effort to discover the other item Guard B left for me. Breakfast. I know it's here because I hear Squatty enjoying his next door. Though, 'enjoying' is probably too enthusiastic of a word.

Lifting the cold porridge, I pour some into my mouth. I exercise my imagination and pretend it's my favorite cheesecake drizzled with blueberry sauce. Wick's favorite too, and he'd always fight me for the last piece, though Wick's fighting methods differed significantly from Chessie's. The memory makes me chuckle.

Wick preferred the mental game over the physical one, and I was happy to oblige. People would see us arguing and think we didn't get along, but they were wrong. We just enjoyed our game of wills, constantly battling to determine a winner, though we'd never declare a loss or win because we didn't want the contest to end.

I wipe porridge from my chin, licking it off my finger. Chessie's twenty-one today, but my brother turns sixteen this year. I felt so mature at sixteen. How is it possible he's reached that age? I wonder if Dad would be proud of who Wick is at sixteen? More proud than he was of me?

The questions float through my head and prick at my heart, which knows the truth. I always wanted a place in Dad's affections, but he reserved everything for Chessie, the heir, and Wick, the boy.

While Dad made his preferences known, we were given the same opportunities and educated in the same subjects: politics, literature, science, warfare, and fighting. Wick excelled in science and literature, which were mediocre subjects for me. Chessie's skills were warfare, politics, and fighting, which I managed just fine, though they didn't hold my interest. Sure, I had some proficiency with the Torquent blade, mainly because they fascinated me—especially after my sister got cut in a battle against Tyran of Torquent herself

—but my areas of focus were flirting with boys and pleasing my dad.

Ultimately, I chose Dad over everything else. It was easy to do—I didn't even feel like there was a choice. Even so, during our tribunal in Adlumen, he barely spoke to me—only to highlight my failure. Maybe, like me, he's had time to rethink things in this place. Possibly, he regrets his actions and realizes I was a loyal daughter—the only one of his children who tried to see his vision and help him enact it.

I've spent my life getting overlooked. Maybe my chance to get noticed and appreciated is through our separation.

Or maybe they've all forgotten me.

"I wish there were something in this place for me," I say out loud, placing my breakfast on the floor. "Something to look forward to. Something to desire. Something to spark anything but apathy. I feel like I'm losing myself, and I don't know what another year will do to me."

I twist my head to the side, and the tears roll haphazardly across my face. "There has to be something more. Right?"

I listen to the light rustle of the breeze from the still-undetermined source. I pick up a scent in the air—nothing powerful or poignant, just faint and new. I put out my hand and visualize it in front of me. My imagination creates a picture around me, but it's nothing my eyes actually see. I pull in my upper lip, tasting the salt from my tears and rubbing my tongue over the dry, chapped skin.

No. This is it. This is all there is.

My lip quivers when I land on that conclusion. I'm on the verge of releasing great sobbing tears when I hear his voice. It's just a mumbled sound from within Squatty's cage, but I hear the word clearly.

"Orange."

My new favorite color.

CHAPTER FOUR

Three Years Caged

Practice fighting was never my thing unless a violent Torquent blade was involved. I didn't enjoy the drills or endless pounding like Chessie did. I'd watch my sister practice with Raden, but it was out of sheer interest in him. When I got bored, I'd sneak off to the onsite sports facility, going to the tennis courts.

I remember the rhythm of the ball striking the ground and then my racket as I sent it back to my opponent. The beat was cathartic, and in the Dark, I put my fingers in the air, throwing a non-existent ball, keeping the cadence.

Thump, strike. Thump, strike.

When I get bored of it, I stand, wrap my hands in rags, and punch walls—despite the covering, my knuckles are calloused. But I've discovered hitting things makes a noise that takes away my troubled thoughts, even if only briefly.

Tap. Tap. Breathe. Tap.

I've also learned to understand my sister's draw to drills and pounding, as the sounds create a type of music in Aunty's Cellar.

I'm nineteen—the age of my sister when I was taken from Adlumen. I wonder if I look like she did. I haven't seen myself since the day I left, so I couldn't even guess, but I have an image of Chessie in my mind, and I wonder if I have any of her perfection. In the eyes of my family, she was perfect inside and out. They all adored her—even Dad, who adored no one.

I constantly shadowed Chessie because I envied her. I complained about her to anyone who would listen, and I argued with her about her decisions and opinions. I loved Chessie because she was everything I needed in a sister, but I hated her for having it all. I miss her terribly but have no desire to see her. I long to sit on Fiducha's balcony and laugh with her, but I'm furious she sent me to the Dark. Nothing about my relationship with my sister has changed even though miles, time, and circumstances separate us—we're still complicated. We're still devoted adversaries.

I wonder if she misses me. If any of them do. But I'm sure they have it easier with daily events to keep them distracted. They're too busy to miss me, and I shouldn't miss them either. I should hate them all, and I do. I just wish I didn't love them at the same time.

Pressing my fingers against my forehead, I try to stave off a headache. It's this place. There's too much here. Too much silence. Too much isolation. And absolutely too much time with myself. No one should get too involved with Self. In my case, Self is a selfish, stubborn, often volatile individual. Yeah, I should avoid Self at all costs.

Thankfully, my bath will be here soon.

"Be ready, Squatty," I say. I think he's awake. At least I've heard him moving around over there—little noises that don't sound like sleeping—just a purposeful movement here and there, but never anything too loud. That Squatty, he's a quiet one.

Occasionally, his quietness has me wondering if he's disappeared from his enclosure. Indeed, one time, I was so firmly convinced he was gone that I started screaming at him for leaving me, believing he'd escaped our prison and left me behind. It wasn't until he found my arm through the grid that I settled. Another day, I felt every ounce of hopelessness crowding in on me. I was incoherent, listless, and doubted Squatty's existence—convinced I'd made him up entirely. I was relieved when that day passed.

"Squatty," I say again because I need to be sure he's engaged. "Tap if you remember the plan." I hear a faint click, so I nod to confirm his reply.

We have a strategy for today's bathwater. I'll cut my time short, which is, as you'd expect, disappointing. After giving my body a quick scrub, I'll wash our old clothes. Then, using a few old rags, I'll clean some things. I plan to scrub grit off my bed frame and wipe down the metal grid, and I've encouraged Squatty to use some water on himself. Truthfully, this entire plan is to get Squatty clean. It would be good for him, but I don't want to come out and tell him to wash. It would break my heart to hurt his feelings, so I'm lumping his washing in with the other activities. It's hard to tell—since we're in the Dark—but I think he's unaware of my true motives. Then again, it's hard to know if he's on board with any of my plan. He didn't complain—not that he ever really does since he's primarily uncommunicative—but I can't gauge his willingness to engage until we begin.

I lean against the bars, waiting for a sign of Warden Ott's arrival. Mostly, I'm eager to hear the slosh of water in a rolling metal tub. I'm not as eager for the arrival of our guard.

Guard B left some time ago. Guard C lasted only a month. He was ruthless—constantly threatening to enter Aunty's Cellar and beat me, even though I'd done nothing to provoke the punishment. Believe me, I'm an intelligent person and know when to prod and when to shut up. With Guard C, staying quiet was always in my best interest, so I did. I'd never heard Warden Ott yell, but it was a daily occurrence during the month Guard C was here. For that reason, his presence was informative because I often wondered if the warden spent his days here, and now I know he does.

Then, Guard D arrived, and the warden stopped yelling. Things reverted to normal—at least the version of normal you'd expect in prison. While Guard D was a noticeable improvement—threats of physical discipline ended—she's not sunshine and roses. It was clear from the moment we met that Guard D hates me for some unknown reason.

I can tell her approach by the slight drag of her left foot when she walks. It makes a pleasant scraping sound across the dirt floor. She'd be easy to track in the woods with her unmistakable slide.

I hear the sound now and back away from the bars. I've only done this twice, but I know the next steps. The warden will appear, comment on my continued existence, request I approach the grid, and they'll cut my hair. Then, they'll ask me to stand near the bed while they bring in the bathwater before locking me inside with the tub.

I'm so looking forward to getting my hair cut. It's so much nicer than when it's long—like now, in tangles and knots. I'm probably more excited about the cut than the bath.

No, that's not true.

I sit on the edge of my bed, twisting my fingers together, waiting excitedly. Then I hear the mundane sound of a bowl hitting the dirt and Guard D's signature slide.

Curses! She's leaving!

"Hey. What about my bath?" I ask, pushing from the bed.

"Your bath?" There's not an ounce of derision in her tone. She's asking like she doesn't understand. Maybe she's unaware of that condition of my sentence.

"Yes. I should get my three-year bath today."

Guard D just laughs and walks away.

"I don't understand," I say, lifting my breakfast and sniffing the porridge. It has the aroma of craft glue. Sometimes, they put in strange spices and too much salt, and it smells like algae. I'd like to meet our chef someday, though I don't know for what purpose. Curiosity, I guess, because complaining would do no good, and it's not as if I want to applaud their effort. Still, I've learned to like this stuff—

at least the glue version—because it makes my stomach feel better. If I ever had picky sensibilities toward food, they're gone now. Still, I have no appetite for eating today.

Where's my bath?

"Hold tight," I tell Squatty, putting my breakfast back onto the floor. "I'll get this resolved."

And then I wait.

When lunchtime comes, Guard D appears to replace my breakfast bowl—which should be empty but isn't—with my lunch bowl. It smells like a mixture of veggies, beans, and rice—not the worst meal they provide, but it's certainly not my favorite.

"Today's July eleventh, isn't it?" I ask before she can trade out my food. She answers my question with silence. I grab Guard D's shirt, and she smacks my hand, but I don't let go. "Please! Just the date. Just—"

"Let go of me!" she screeches.

"Of course. Of course. I'm sorry. Please, just the date. July eleventh?"

I never ask for the date because I keep it myself with the rocks. I just don't understand. Did I get off on my counting?

Guard D huffs, and I'm not sure she'll answer. I try to think of anything I can offer to tempt her to give me the information, but I have nothing, so I experience immense relief when she finally says, "Yes."

"It's the eleventh?" I ask, surprised I dare clarify.

"Yes."

My stomach sinks. It's the correct day. Warden Ott must have forgotten.

"Tell the warden," I say, reaching for Guard D again but not finding anything with my outstretched fingers. "Remind him of the date."

"I'll do no such thing."

"Please." I scramble along the grid because she's walking away. "Please, just ask him. I won't bother you anymore. I'll be quiet for the rest of the day."

She stops and slides back toward me, saying, "For a month."

"What?"

"You'll be quiet for a month. That includes when I'm not around."

It's not difficult to agree. "Okay. Yes. I promise my silence. After today, of course. Because, well, we need to get this resolved."

"Eat your lunch," Guard D says, shuffling away and closing our negotiation. But I listen to her go with a sense of calm I haven't felt since this morning, knowing we'll fix this mishap soon.

I eat my lunch because I need something in my belly. If I could go back, I'd choose to eat breakfast over this concoction that's nothing to brag over.

Hours later, Guard D arrives with dinner. The wait reminds me of when I was a kid, and Mom would place a wrapped present on the counter, making me look at it all week before finally allowing me to open it on my birthday. I'm not a patient person, and the promise of an exciting gift is enough to remove every other thought from my mind. Such has been my day. I waited anxiously, expecting any moment to hear the squeak of wheels bearing a vessel of water.

Instead, I get Guard D, switching out my bowls—lunch for dinner.

"Did you tell him?" I ask, reaching the grid and gripping the metal bars.

"Yes."

"And?"

In the Dark, my senses pick up on Guard D taking a step back. "And... eat your dinner," she says.

"Eat my dinner?" I ask, listening to her sliding away, dragging her gimpy leg behind her. "Eat my dinner!"

"Yes!" Guard D yells back, not far from me. "I kept my word, and you'll keep yours. It's not my fault things didn't go your way, but if you make so much as a peep tomorrow or during the next thirty days, I'll find a nice springy willow branch and come in there and smack you with it."

I'm so confused.

I twist my hair—long hair that won't get cut today. It's in terrible shape too. I may have to force my fingers into the interlocked pieces and try to braid it.

Abandoning my dinner at the grid, I walk toward Squatty's cage. I need comfort, and he's my best source—admittedly, not much. Clinging to the grid, I lower myself to the floor. I feel the frayed edge of my shirt. Squatty told me it was orange, but it's probably brown now. I thought I'd be trading up today—getting a new color—but I guess I'll be in orange for a while longer.

Did I do something wrong? Am I being punished? I just don't understand.

I lean against the grid, pressing my cheek into the edge of the metal. That's when the first tear falls. I'd kept it together all day, but now, there's no reason. And since I've released one, more want to join the fall—my emotions are out of control.

"Why?" I ask, pressing my fingers into the dirt floor. "Why? Why?" I roll my head back and forth across the grid, the metal digging into the back of my skull. I've tried so hard to cling to hope, but it's harder and harder. With this last pleasure taken from me, what's left to care for? What is there to hold on to?

As if in answer, Squatty appears and slides his hand into mine. It only makes me cry more to know my one support is more ghost than human. Still, I squeeze his fingers and pull his hand toward me.

It's then I realize there's something between our fingers —cold and hard.

"What—" I start, but Squatty's other hand covers my mouth.

"Hide," he says. I've stopped counting his words, but the number isn't high. The one thing I know is that he only speaks when he feels it's vitally important.

I nod, and he drops his hand. Then he leaves me, and I inspect the item in my palm. It's a long chain with a charm on the end—square with rounded edges and a bumpy surface. I can't make it out what it looks like, and there's no point in asking Squatty about it.

I wonder where he got it. I'd guess he's had it this entire time, but how he kept it with him and why he'd give it to me is an enigma—just another of many things I don't understand about Squatty. The mystery of it is enough to snap me out of my sorrow. It's been a bad day, and tomorrow will be more of the same, but I'm done crying.

Crossing Aunty's Cellar, I hide the necklace under my lumpy mattress. I've been so distracted that I forgot about my rocks. I go to the corner and take a seat before moving things around. I add the year-three rock to the appropriate pile and feel around until I locate year one. It has a pointy edge I like to run my finger over. I decided it symbolized the sharpness of my first year—the uncomfortable bump in my life. I thought it would surely be the worst year of my life, but I was wrong. That's how I'd describe this last year, but who knows what the next one will bring.

Huddled in the corner, I don't want to think of the hundreds of rock combinations I'll discover while keeping count of my life here. Still, I let my mind dwell on the rocks because the other thoughts trying to take hold are even less welcome. Like Chessie's voice, echoing something she told me years ago—*I'm here for you, Sharade. No matter what you face, you'll always have me on your side.* I run my finger over the scar she left on my hand.

Where are you now, Chess?

The bath and clothes felt like Chessie's way of keeping her promise—that she was here for me, even in our divided circumstances. But I guess she's abandoned me now. I'm truly alone.

And I'm stuck in this place forever.

I'll never get out because the guards are never lax—always on alert. When I ask questions vital to fleeing, they don't answer, and I've searched every inch of Aunty's Cellar but have found nothing to aid in an escape. Warden Ott has made sure my imprisonment is secure and bears no weakness.

The only weakness is in me.

CHAPTER FIVE

Four Years Caged

I stare at the ceiling, or at least where I imagine the ceiling is located, according to the visual I've created of Aunty's Cellar. It's raining today, which is unusual for this place. The enormous drops hit something metal above me, making a loud echoing ping. It's likely the source of the air I often feel circulating the room.

The rain doesn't help with the uncomfortable heat. It's only warming as the day advances, with stifling humidity infiltrating the air. After four years, I'm used to the wretched summer weather, but this takes it to a new level.

I drink every drop of water from the glass bottle Guard A gave me years ago. Then, lying listlessly, I do the only thing that battles the disagreeable weather and my tedious reality —I talk about better times.

"On cool afternoons in Adlumen-n, I used to walk to the Markets of Mirum-m with Chessie. We'd stop at Meat Madness and share a Reuben sandwich with loads of sauerkraut. Raden-n would beg me to sneak him back a strawberry soda-a, and since I figured it was a great way to gather-r his affection-n, I'd do it. Little did I know, sneaking-g wasn't necessary. Chessie would happily-y have brought him a beverage, and Raden-n held more affection for that drink than he did for me-e."

I turn my head slightly because I don't have the sound quite right. I speak slowly, pausing often.

"I asked Guard F about Dad-d-d. Actually, I ask about him every day now-w-w because why not? Guard F engages more than-n-n the others, though that's not saying much. He cautions me not to worry-y-y myself into a fit. Says a fit won't get me out-t-t of my cage."

I laugh, clutching my waist as I do. "I know you hate it when I laugh about serious things, but you need to get over it." I release a few breathy chuckles, my stomach muscles flexing. "You're not going to join me? You don't think I'm funny?" I huff. "Just because you have no sense of humor, don't ruin my fun. And Guard F getting into a tizzy over my well-being is too funny. I tell him this is Aunty's Cellar-r-r and try to explain about the bottled peaches Aunty keeps, but he gets bored-d-d and leaves. He doesn't understand." I frown, and all my laughter ceases. "No one does. But I need him-m-m to. I need him to stand his ground and argue with me-e-e. I'm not on the verge of a fit—I just like talking-g-g. Simply for the sake of talking-g-g. It calms me to have a conversation-n-n, even a pretend one-ne-ne."

I finally get it right. I moved my bed to this corner where the metal grids meet because I like how my voice sounds echoing off the back wall of Aunty's Cellar. I must put my head just right to get the best sound. Today, I have the added complication of waiting for a lull in the rain before speaking. Still, I've got it down.

The bed placement blocks the door, but they never open it anyway. In January, I would have felt embarrassed lying in this spot—like I was encroaching too much into Squatty's space. In February, it didn't matter anymore.

I sit up and break position for my perfect echo, but I'll find it again.

"Okay, Mom, I'm done talking to you. I want to talk to Wick now. Send him in."

I wave my hand in the air, shooing her away. It's a miracle I got some time with her alone. Mom and Wick are inseparable, but I quickly get bored talking to Mom. Wick's more interesting until he drones on about how Dad's manipulative and deluded. That's when I shut down Wick because I don't want to hear him disparage our dad. I've yet to speak with Chessie because I'm still too mad at her. Maybe one of these days, I'll allow it if she begs for long enough.

"No, wait!" I yell out, calling back my mom. I've always enjoyed rock music and have a wonderfully angry beat stuck in my head. Mom always scolded me to turn the volume down on songs like this, but she has no say here. Not when it's only in my head for me to enjoy. I smile at her and say, "Let's finish this song together, and then you can call Wick in."

"Sharade," I hear and shake my head to figure out what's happening. Is that Mom? Or has Wick arrived early?

"Sharade," I push my back against the grid, and my eyes dart blindly around the cage. "It's been a while, but surely you know who I am."

I put my hand on my chest and let out a relieved breath. "Warden Ott," I say, returning to my actual life and registering that the warden is here to see me again. I drop my hand and turn my head, squinting in his direction. "Is it bath day?" I ask. I wouldn't know, as I gave up on my rocks when there was no real purpose in knowing anymore. But I know by the weather it's summer, so today could be July eleventh.

"No," Warden Ott says. His reply doesn't affect me positively or negatively. It's just an answer, and I enjoy talking, so I don't mind speaking with him before I speak to Wick.

"You missed last year, so I thought you were dead. I imagined Guard D killed you." I tug the ends of my hair—long and in a jumbled mess down my back, though there are a few strands on the side that I smooth out daily. "I also considered you might have as difficult a time keeping track of the date as I do. How do you all keep track of time in the Dark? I find it's practically impossible."

"I'm not dead, but I need to speak with you."

"Is it about where we're located in the Dark? Because I'd still like to know. I thought for a long time it must be Tenebris, but it's not cold enough here. But I'm not familiar with the climate in Labrum, so that's my guess."

"No, Sharade, I came to talk to you about your father."

"Oh!" I lean toward his voice. "Do I get to see him?"

"That's not possible. He died three weeks ago."

I briefly note his somber tone before the full impact registers. "He's dead?"

"Yes."

Dead. Dead.

"What day?" I have to know. I thought I was done with days, but I need him to tell me.

"July second."

"What's today?"

"July twenty-third."

"Three weeks," I mumble, doing the math.

"Yes, that's what I said. Keine Endrack died three weeks ago."

"Why are you telling me?"

"It seemed right that you should know."

"I appreciate that, but it's still strange." The warden keeps me blocked from everything, even basic conversation with the guards. That he would offer anything confuses me.

"I understand," he says, and I believe he does.

"Did Dad try to escape?"

"No."

"Did he take his own life?"

"No."

"Did he ever talk about me?" I pull in my upper lip, rubbing my tongue across the rough, red surface.

The warden lets out a breath. "I only came here to give you the news." *Most unsympathetically.* "I've done that." *Three weeks late.* "Do with it what you will." *Whatever that means.* "But I'm done answering your questions."

"Okay," I reply, not bothering to press for more. That's never gotten me anywhere.

Warden Ott walks away, and I pay attention as he exits. His steps are the only ones I hear. He came alone.

I feel a sudden chill in the humid heat. My skin is clammy, and a shiver runs through me.

My dad is dead.

Keine Endrack is the most powerful man I ever knew, and he had no power in this place. Not even enough to stay alive. How can I hope to survive if he didn't?

I twist on my bed and fall forward, face down. I inhale the old, stagnant scent of my mattress, and my mind returns to another time and place when I was caged.

"Everything's gone to hell, but we still have Diggs on our side."

"What can he do?" I asked Dad. He had so much influence and always seemed indestructible. I didn't think it would get as far as it had, sharing a cell in Ambitus right inside the judicial building.

"You're not listening. Just stay the course, Sharade. Diggs is a conniving son-of-a-bitch, and he won't let us rot in prison. He'll find us, even if it takes a few months."

"Months?" I screeched. "I don't want to be in prison for months."

"It won't be as bad as all that."

Dad said we wouldn't rot in here, but all hope is smothered now. Dad's dead. Word will get back to Adlumen and soon enough to Diggs, wherever he is, and he'll give up his search. Dad's the leader—the one with the plan—and I'm secondary. I'm dispensable.

No one's coming.

I'll be in prison forever. Nothing will ever be better than it is right now. I must accept what I have and learn to be okay with it. Eventually, I'll die right here. In the Dark. With the moles. Whether it's today or years from now, it doesn't matter.

I let the reality of my future settle in and realize it's not much of a surprise. I'm not even angry about it. And there's no one to hate—not even my sister.

Where did they go? The hate and anger.

They slowly leached from me. They faded into the Dark along with everything else about Sharade Endrack—my hopes, feelings, and dreams. There was no point in holding onto hate and anger because I alone felt them. And nothing's worthwhile on your own, not even your emotions.

Who am I now?

I don't even know.

A tear rolls down my cheek, but I stop it with my fist.

No crying!

I won't cry anymore. The only time I'll allow tears is on the day I leave this place, even if that event happens because of my death. On that day, I'll cry again... I'll cry a tear of joy.

"Chessie," I say into the Dark, keeping my voice low and not looking for an echo. "We need to talk." I turn onto my side, so I'm not speaking into the bed. "I'm sorry I've ignored you, but that's what sisters do, right?" I sort of laugh, but Chess doesn't respond. I don't expect her to. "I was angry because you put me here, but I'm beginning to understand why you did it." I touch the grid separating me from Squatty's empty space. "Learning to love someone can be a revelation."

I hear footsteps. It's Guard F. He has a steady clomp that feels like a hammer to my head today. "Dinner," he says, placing the food on the edge of my bed.

"I need to speak with Warden Ott," I say, not touching it. My tone isn't demanding or angry. Not pleading or frightened. It's just a statement from someone who expects nothing to come from her words.

Guard F leaves. I'm unsure if he'll return or if the warden will heed my request.

"What do you think, Self? Is it time?" I ask.

"Yes," Self answers, and I release a defeated breath. "I think we are ready."

"I agree." I've struggled with this before, telling Self she was wrong, but today we're finally aligned. My fingers find the plate—mashed something with carrots. And on the edge, there's an apple.

I haven't had fruit since I came here. Is this from Guard F, or is Warden Ott expressing sympathy? I grip it in my fist and pull it to my chest. I've experienced very little kindness in this place, but this proves someone cares.

Someone.

Maybe Self will change her mind. The surge of hope and emotion doesn't last long. Then my grip softens, and the fruit rolls from my grasp, hitting the floor and rolling away as if it were escaping.

It's so easy for some. Even an apple can get away. Why can't I?

"You wanted to see me?" the warden asks, jerking me from my musings.

I clear my throat. "I wondered if your deal still stands."

"My deal?"

"The day we met, you extended an offer to me."

I have to know. Because apparently, Squatty and Dad found the only way to exit this place, and I'm ready to follow their lead.

"That deal was never on the table, Sharade," the warden says. I drop back, my head hitting the metal grid. "I wouldn't have killed you."

"Because it was a condition of my sentence?" I ask with a humorless laugh.

"Because I don't have the needless desire to take a life."

"It wouldn't be needless," I say, trying to tempt him with how noble it could be, but he doesn't budge. Defeated once again, my shoulders slump as I tell him, "But I know what you mean."

"Do you?"

I think back on my failed attempt at taking Evans Dirby's life. It felt like my actions had a purpose, but did they, really?

"I do. But it's too bad you're so much like me because I'd like to be done now."

CHAPTER SIX

Five Years Caged

I passed the five-year mark, but I don't know precisely when it happened. I sensed it by knowing the seasons, recognizing the summer heat and appreciating the fall coolness. I'm unsure which side of October twenty-first we're on, but either way, I've passed or am nearing my twenty-second birthday.

What a strange milestone to have lived five years in Aunty's Cellar. Before I was banished, my sister challenged Evans, and they fought to determine who between them would be one of Adlumen's three governors. She had no intention of winning, and I planned to step in and challenge him myself. I learned later that a second challenge couldn't be issued for five years.

Five years sounded like forever, but now it's here. I could officially make my challenge. I was so eager then, but now I'm not sure I'd do it. Maybe it's this place twisting things—distorting and confusing right and wrong—or maybe what I value has changed. All I know is I'm not positive what I'd do.

Warden Ott hasn't visited me since he turned me down. I'm glad since our last conversation isn't something I like to think about. I still crave the freedom of that option, but I don't have the courage for it. My existence, bleak as it is, is still something I cling to. Maybe one day I'll understand why.

I asked Guard F about sending a message to my sister. I'd never inquired about the possibility before, mostly because I hadn't wanted to communicate with her. It ended up a moot point because they denied me the opportunity. Likely, she wouldn't respond anyway. She probably doesn't care about me anymore, and I can understand that. This is the direction my thoughts usually take me, circling back around until I'm glad another of my requests wasn't granted.

I hear Guard F tromping down the hall. I hope that, like me, he'll die in this place. It's not that I wish him ill, but he's my favorite guard. While not a pleasant man, he's the best I've had.

Today, he's not alone as he passes Aunty's Cellar, but I don't recognize his companion's gait. My head rotates to follow him, and when he reaches Squatty's cage, his keys clang against the grid.

"I have a present for you," Guard F says. It's funny he'd use that term since I was thinking about my birthday. Still, they've never recognized my birthday before, so I'm pretty sure he's just saying it to be funny.

"What if I don't like it? Will you give me something else?"

Guard F goes on about his business, not addressing my comment. He fumbles with the keys but gets the door unlocked, nudging a new prisoner inside and sealing them in. We won't see Guard F again until lunchtime, so I have a few hours to get a feel for my present.

I listen to the stranger move around in Squatty's cage, getting familiar with the space. I don't like that anyone's in there. I'm accustomed to the quiet and the option to talk to my family or Self whenever I want. I'm not ready to lose that freedom.

Sitting on my bed, I lean against the wall and pull my knees to my chest. I blink with each sound, determining the action that created it.

"What's your name?" the stranger asks—a man—breaking the near silence.

Pulling in my upper lip, I suck, then stop myself. I'm sick of chapped lips. "I don't know that it matters," I finally say. "You'll be gone or dead soon, just like everyone else they put in there."

"Or maybe you'll be the one to go," he says. "In which case, I'd like to have known your name." He doesn't say I'll be dead, which I guess is sort of polite.

"I'm not that lucky," I say, twisting my hair subconsciously. I hear a noise coming from the stranger, similar to the woodpecker in the dead branch outside my window back in Ambitus. "What are you doing?"

"Sorry," he says. "It's just a habit. I click my tongue when I'm thinking."

"Well, you should stop."

He laughs. "Sure. Just like you should stop sucking on your lip. It's bright red."

"You're a mole."

Of course, he is. That's proof of my bad luck right there. I lift a finger in a rude gesture. He laughs again and asks, "What's that for?"

"Just confirming your sight."

"Ah. I won't take it personally then."

"But you should."

"Me being a mole is an issue for you?"

"I have light sight. We're natural enemies."

"I concede there's nothing natural about being light blind, considering your type of sight was the norm for many millennia. However, I don't believe it makes us enemies."

"Then you know little about the world."

"I daresay I know a great deal more about it than you. Age gives me that distinction."

I remember Dad saying that to me and feel the need to set this man straight. "The only thing age does is give the owner of those years more history of making bad choices."

"Hmm. I'd never thought of it that way." He clicks his

tongue. "We should do introductions, and then you can tell me your background so I can better understand your theory."

I put up a hand, shaking my head profusely. "I have no interest in being understood. Or telling you about my life."

"Well, that leaves introductions. I'm called Valore."

"Look. I don't need to make a friend or—"

"Or hear another person's story. Or concern yourself with more worries than your own. I get it."

"Thank you."

"But why not?" he presses.

"Moles always lie," I say, as it's the first thing that comes to my mind.

There's a brief pause before Valore laughs. "You don't believe that."

"Yes, I do."

"No. That's a generalization, and I can tell you're too smart to buy into something so generic."

"People in prison lie," I say, adjusting my words.

"That still feels too broad of a statement."

"Just wait until the warden promises you something and then take it back." He only did that to me once, but it crushed me.

"Well, the desert people aren't traditionally a trustworthy lot. I'll give you that."

"Desert people?"

"Yes. Casmo's citizens aren't who I'd pick as an example of the normally excellent traits of those who are light blind."

My eyes widen. "Casmo? Is that where we are? In the Desert Territory."

"Yes. Didn't you know?"

I shake my head. After all this time, I finally know where

I am, and it's Casmo's domain! The Desert Territory is one of the last places I would have guessed. I barely let it enter my mind as a possibility.

Adlumen isn't friendly with the desert rats. Casmo Junius could be described as reclusive at best, but I've always viewed him as a dictator. His people mingle with no one. His political alliances are few, and even they don't trust him.

They must have paid a heavy price to drop Dad and me here. Casmo would want any Endracks in his territory dead. They likely paid extra to keep our identities quiet. Warden Ott wasn't joking when he spoke about gold landing in his lap. And it's no wonder he's been so particular about the guards not speaking to me.

That my sister sent me to this place says something I never really considered—that my safety wasn't her first concern, that she was afraid of me, that she ultimately didn't care what happened to me, and that she never planned to see me again. Of course, in my trial, they said no one would know my location. But is that really true?

"How long have you been here?" Valore asks.

"Uh." I bite my lip, settling my thoughts after these new revelations. "I just reached five years."

"Five? But you're so young."

I snort, dropping my knees to the bed. "Even the young can cause great offense," I say bitterly.

"You must have done."

"Yeah. That and more." And I'm just realizing how much more in my condemner's eyes.

"I'd like to hear about it," he says, to which I'm more than slightly irritated.

"No. There are many things I don't want to tell you—things I don't plan to tell anyone—and that's one of them."

"Okay." Valore clicks his tongue. "What if we start with

things you don't mind saying? Your name, for one. I can't believe that's a big secret."

Curses! My name.

Yeah, it's a big secret, considering he's a mole, and I'm an Endrack.

"Shar," I say. I hated it back home when people would shorten my name without asking, but it feels right to do it now. I don't feel like Sharade Endrack of Adlumen anymore.

"It's good to meet you, Shar. How old are you?"

"Twenty-two."

"I'm fifty-five," he provides. "Where are you from?"

"Look, it's okay if you want to ask questions, but can we avoid personal stuff?"

"And where you live is personal?"

"For me, it is, yeah."

Valore clicks again, then says, "Okay, let's set up a few guidelines. First, no discussions of where we lived previously, except for knowing I lived in the Dark and you lived in a light bubble. Now, you add one."

I nod, saying, "No last names."

"Okay. And we won't talk about our families. Your turn."

No families. I release a small sigh of relief. "No questions about what landed us in a Dark prison," I add to the list.

"Okay. But if you ever want to know why I'm here, I'll tell you. Uh, let's promise we won't lie to each other, but it's acceptable to say we won't answer a question. Anything else?"

"Not that I can think of. Besides, I'm probably just talking to myself, so why overthink it?" I pick at the edge of my fraying shirt, content with the momentary silence.

"You think I'm imaginary?" Valore asks, breaking it.

"It's possible. I have trouble sometimes knowing what's

real in this place. You'll reach that point too. For all I know, you're just in my head."

"Will you take my hand?"

"What?"

"Come to the bars and take my hand. Unless your other delusions make physical contact." He pauses. "Do they?" I shake my head and hear him reach the grid.

"Come forward. I'm directly in front of you."

I hesitate.

"Please. I want you to know I'm real."

I push off the bed and walk to the bars. I quickly find his outstretched hand and grasp it. It's been almost two years since I touched another person. That thought is still settling in when he speaks.

"See. Now we can be friends, and I could use a friend in here to break the tedium I'm sure will set in."

I pull my hand from his. "I wouldn't call us friends, and I'm accustomed to tedium." I turn in the dirt and make my way back to the mattress.

"You're extremely resistant, even to the slightest overture," Valore observes. "I don't know what you've experienced, but I don't intend to make your confinement more difficult. Truthfully, the deal I'm trying to strike is rather selfish. I've lost a lot, and I could use the support. And I'd like to return the favor if I can."

"I don't want to talk anymore," I say. He gave me an out for when things get too uncomfortable, and I'm taking him up on it.

"Okay," he draws out. "But I'm not one to shy away from tough conversations. Why don't you tell me what's on your mind?"

"You're just another body here to go mad with me in the Dark. You'll keep me up at night with crazy chatter, incoherent mumbling, or loud sobs—I've had it all. You may behave differently right now, but it won't last. Like the others, you'll find that place inside yourself, withdraw, and dwell there away from the living. We all lose ourselves in here."

"You included?"

"Yes. No one is immune."

"You sound fine to me."

"It's a good day," I say with a shrug.

"You look fine too."

"Looks are deceiving."

Valore laughs. "You won't allow me to give you a glimmer of hope, will you?"

"I gave up on hope a while back. Besides, you forget. I have light sight, and I'm in the Dark. I can't see a glimmer of anything."

Valore laughs, and I smile back at him. It feels strange on my lips, and I consider that my mouth forgot how to make the shape.

"You laugh a lot," I say about the deep, throaty sound. "You realize you're in prison, don't you?"

"Would you rather I cry?"

I release a long breath. "You will eventually. I'll take the laughter for as long as you can hold out."

CHAPTER SEVEN

Six Years Caged

"You know what I miss?" Valore asks. "Watermelon."

"Watermelon! Ew, no. That can't be a thing to miss." I shudder.

Valore clicks his tongue while he considers my reaction. The noise means one of two things: He disapproves of something I've said, or it's a placeholder while pondering his response. He does this all the time. The process bothered me at first, but now it makes me smile. While his method always creates a pause—sometimes a long one—today, he's quick to get back on topic.

"Is it the seeds?" he asks. "Is that why you don't like watermelon?"

"No."

"The texture, then?"

"It's just so bland. It's like eating mushy water."

"Apparently, you haven't had the right watermelon."

I shrug. "And I never will."

I say it to be funny—like, haha, I'm never putting that disgusting fruit in my mouth. Instead, it sounds pitiful—like, poor me, I'll never get the chance because we're stuck in this prison forever. The comment chokes out our light mood, which wasn't my intent, so I keep talking, trying to resuscitate it.

"I miss electricity, indoor climate control, hot showers with loads of soap, and breakfast foods that don't slide."

"I'm glad you eventually brought it back to food," Valore

says, smacking his lips hungrily.

"You want to talk about food?" I laugh. "Cherries. Now, cherries are a thing worthy of missing."

"Pits are too big."

"No. They're delectable and worth maneuvering the pit. Avocados too."

"Now, there's a pit!" Valore laughs, and I join him.

Guard F was correct. Nine months ago, he announced he was bringing me a present, and that's an appropriate term for the man in the neighboring cell. I'd even take it further and call him a precious gift.

Today is July eleventh. She's twenty-five, and that sounds so old. I know the date because I'm using my rocks. When Valore arrived, he knew the date, and I decided I felt healthier while keeping track, so I started up again. He doesn't know what today signifies, only that I was counting down to it. And that I feel melancholy now it's arrived. Consequently, he's been talking a lot to cheer me up, and it took little effort for him to do just that.

I'm quite changed since he got here. I hear the peace in my voice and the airiness of my tone. I never considered I could be happy in my Dark prison, but I am. And it's all because of Valore.

He still doesn't know why I'm here. We've never asked for each other's stories, and I've never volunteered mine. The closest I came was a few months back when I was feeling moody and blurted out, "It's awful to do something at sixteen that can never be forgiven."

I didn't tell Valore what I'd done. I didn't tell him who would never forgive me. He just said in return, "Everyone's youth is a cautionary tale. We aren't born wise."

"My brother was," I said while laughing at my declaration, which countered his statement. Valore's a smart man, but he's not perfect.

Valore chuckled, though he didn't believe me, saying, "Maybe. But what I meant is, you'd never be expected to set the example at that age. The example is still being set for you."

At that, I shook my head. "Wrong again. Now you're talking about my sister, who set the example in everything and from an even younger age." Chessie regularly showed me the path to follow by living it herself—I just never joined her there.

That day, I revealed more than I should have, but Valore didn't inquire further, and I was grateful.

"I once grew an avocado tree from seed," he says. "I had a healthy tree full of fruit. I consider it one of the great successes of my life."

"An avocado tree?" I giggle. Sometimes, I don't even recognize myself or the cheerful noises I make. I often wonder if it's Valore's personal mission to get me to make them.

"Yeah. I'm not very good with plants, but I was determined, and in the end, I had a lovely tree with good produce to eat."

"I really don't enjoy talking about food," I say, rubbing my empty stomach while lying on my back in Aunty's Cellar. I'm on the dirt floor because it's cooler down here.

"Tell me about one of your greatest successes, then," he says.

I hum thoughtfully, bending one leg and draping the other over it before bouncing my foot in the air. I recall my youth, growing up in Ambitus with my family. What did I do there that was worthy of being called a success? Something that made a difference that I was proud of? I tap my foot while trying to think of how to answer Valore's question. The problem is, after minutes of silence, I can't think of anything good. In fact, I can't think of anything at all.

"Uh, I don't really have anything," I finally say, turning my head so he can't see my disappointment.

"That can't be true."

"No. I think it is." I pull in my upper lip and suck on it.

"You just need to think harder, but I'll make it easy. Name one time your family praised something you did."

Wrong. That doesn't make it easy, and I bite down on my lip as if it will help me find an answer. It only hurts, like the realization that I've got nothing. I'm tempted to lie, but I made Valore a promise, and so far, I've kept it, so I eventually admit, "They never did that."

"Never?" I hear Valore approach the grid separating us. "Not once?"

"Not that I can remember." Chessie was valued for her fighting skills, though Dad always got after her for lacking diplomacy. Wick was constantly told how intelligent he was. I was told not to start arguments, not to say embarrassing things, and not to incite issues. "Yeah, I can't think of anything."

"Were you good at art or history?" Valore's not ready to give up.

"No."

"Debate?"

"Ha. You'd think so, but no. Debating wasn't my thing because I became too passionate and had trouble arguing a point of view not my own." Wick, on the other hand, excelled in a debate. "They told me I was good at creating trouble. Does that count?"

I guess not because Valore asks, "What about sports?"

"I liked tennis."

"Were you any good?"

"I won more than I lost. Actually, now I think of it, I rarely lost."

"Well, see now! We'll count that as a success," Valore states, but his voice sounds forced, and I'm not feeling too jolly about the discovery either. There's a few moments of silence before he speaks again. "I don't mean to pry, but didn't your family ever congratulate you over your tennis wins?"

"No," I answer. Then, deciding my family doesn't deserve all the blame, I add, "They didn't know I played. I never invited them to watch me." I never shared that part of my life with them, and it's strange to think maybe they didn't know me as well as I knew them.

Valore makes a noise—I'm not sure if it's understanding or disappointment—but he asks nothing more. When we get too close to the subject of our home life, we're always careful to back off, and asking an unrelated question is the most common way to right things.

"Did you ever collect anything?" I ask Valore, picking up my glass bottle and taking a drink. That's one thing I can't complain about concerning my circumstances in prison—Warden Ott has always ensured we have plenty of water. It's warm today, but not the scorching July I'm accustomed to. The weather will change soon, and I'll be choking on hot air for the rest of the month.

"Pocket knives," Valore answers quickly. "My dad gave me one for my twelfth birthday. After that, I was always picking up another one here or there. I probably have thirty back home. What about you?"

"Glass bottles," I say, licking the rim of mine. "Colorful ones. I put lights behind them to show off their shine." I positioned them precisely on my shelf, situating the ones I liked most so they were seen but safe. Valore's like those special bottles, so I'll keep him close enough to experience but far enough from the edge not to break him.

I'm the edge in this scenario. Valore can't get close to my past, or his good opinion of me will shatter. Then I won't be able to enjoy him anymore.

Yeah. Valore must be handled with care. I lost my sister, who was my closest friend—maybe my only true friend—and now that I have another, I'll do anything to keep him.

"What's the best gift you ever received?" Valore asks, moving to a new question.

With my current line of thought, I'm ready to blurt out, "You!" but I keep it under wraps. "I once got a flower from a boy," I say, though it wasn't really a gift, and there wasn't much sentiment behind Raden's gesture. He was goofing off, though I read a lot into it.

"Good for him. Glad to hear the rising generation knows something about how to woo."

"*How to woo*?" I snort and then laugh. What a stupid word. Not at all descriptive of what was happening with Raden. He was likely trying to distract me from something Chessie was up to that she didn't want me to discover.

"Was the boy your age?"

"A few years older. What about you? What's your best gift?"

"That's easy. My wife."

He's mentioned her before. And while he's avoided the details, I know it's not imprisonment causing his longing. His is a permanent sorrow because she's dead. It's strange to be sympathetic to another person's emotions. I thought the feeling was dead in me, but Valore's revived it gradually over the last months.

It's interesting that Valore thought of a person, just as I did before getting nervous and talking about the dumb flower instead. I don't know why I answered that way, sounding childish, but it's still better than telling him he's the gift I thought of.

"I was completely devoted to her," Valore adds.

"I felt that way about someone once," I say, thinking of Dad. "But now, I'm stuck in here." Because of him. "And he's dead. He got the better deal."

"Shar, I—"

"No, I'm sorry. I shouldn't have gone there. Total mood killer."

"Well, I sort of started it."

"You did." I puff out a teasing laugh. "And I don't mind traveling the morose path with you, but let's not do it today. So, if you could have any wish granted, what would it be? And don't say escaping prison because that's too obvious."

"I'd like one more day with my wife."

"Yeah—" I trail off. I want another day with my family too, even though I don't think they'd like one with me. Maybe I'd wish for a day with them before I came here. But, no, that wouldn't work. I have no desire to interact with them like I did back then. I've evolved and would want our relationship to have evolved too.

My family life was unusual—I understand that now. Dad ignored me. Mom feared me. I bickered with Wick and was jealous of Chessie. At this point, a wish involving my family is too complicated.

I've only ever admired two people—my dad and now Valore. Perhaps my greatest desire would be to spend my days with Valore outside of prison, but saying that breaks the rules of the question. And if spending time with him is all I want, then I have nothing to wish for—I'm right where I want to be. How scary is that?

"You ever eat pine nuts?" Valore asks. It's not a surprise we're back to talking about food. He really misses it, and it's an easy segue off the subject of his wife. I'm grateful for the change. I'm thankful for many things where he's concerned.

"No."

"They're pretty plentiful in this area."

"So, you're saying Casmo has the market in pine nuts?" I ask with a smirk.

"You could say that," Valore says, clicking his tongue thoughtfully.

"Where does Casmo live? Is he near where we are?"

"No. He's southeast in Windway. It's a beautiful city. Not the kind of place you'd expect after seeing most of the Desert Territory. Casmo often boasts about all he's done there."

"You've been to Windway?" I can't help but be curious about Casmo's domain since I've heard very little about it. I know Dad visited there at least once.

"That's where I was before I came here," he says as if it's not shocking. "It's lush and green, except now. Everything turns a sickly yellow during July."

I no longer care about the description of Windway. "Wait. You were in Casmo's city before you came to prison?"

"Yes. Actually, I was with Casmo."

"With him?"

With him! Whatever for?

I desperately want to ask about his purpose for being with Casmo. Maybe he's one of his men and got into trouble for some misdeed. I suck in my upper lip, keeping my mouth closed—asking about it will encourage sharing forbidden things, and I can't have that. I'll never be willing to share my past with Valore. It will lower his opinion of me. He fills the roles of all those I loved—the friend my sister was, a companion like Wick, the guide my mom tried to be, a teacher like Raden, and a leader as strong as my father. And I need Valore because he's all I have, so I can't have him thinking badly of me.

“The sunset is orange tonight,” he says after a while. He’s told me how the colors reflect in the hallways through windows that are nowhere near us. I think fondly of the picture it creates in my mind, but it makes me sad since I miss seeing colors. Still, though I have light sight and I’m in the Dark, it’s the best sunset I’ve ever experienced because Valore’s here to share it with me.

CHAPTER EIGHT

Seven Years Caged

Valore clears his throat. "I know we don't talk about family, but I'd like to tell you something if you'll let me." There was a day I would have panicked over the suggestion, but I've known Valore for eighteen months and understand he'll be respectful about what he shares and not expect information in return.

I've been in prison for seven years. I'll be twenty-four in a few months, and I finally know who I am. I'm the daughter who denounced one parent for another, denounced one set of government for another, and both family and government denounced me in the end—discarding me when I didn't meet their expectations, though I don't blame them. Justice was achieved when the denouncer was denounced and abandoned. It's a theme in my life—until Valore.

He's my everything. I'd given up hope of anything good left in life, but he renewed it in me. There's no familial bond between us, but my connection to him is as strong as if we shared blood. I lean on him and pour my heart out to him, and though I haven't told him my past, he accepts my limitations. He accepts me. And his acceptance has allowed me to become the person I want to be—not a version of myself I'm forced into being. It's brought about many revelations.

I'm sorry for what I did. It shocked me when feelings of remorse set in, but I see things differently now. I understand the skillful manipulation my dad wielded and the immense stress he put his family under. Dad spared none of us. He played people expertly. Within our home, he pitted the children against each other, and we vied for position. He even threw Mom into the mix and made her compete with us for his attention. She eventually gave up, which I recognize now, but at the time, I thought it was because she didn't love us. Well, any of us except Wick.

Dad excelled at bringing people into contention, one with another. He pitted groups against each other—positionally, politically, culturally, and geographically. He perpetrated derogatory names—the moles in the Dark and the Torquent trash—corrupting my thinking, and many others' thinking, about entire groups of people.

This new understanding came on gradually, but it began as Valore told me about his home life. Of course, he avoided the details, but in his stories, I recognized how his parenting differed significantly from my upbringing. And now, I wouldn't hesitate to say I grew up in an unhinged, messy environment. And Dad was the one who created it.

I dreamed of my dad valuing me as much as my brother and sister. Every action I took was seeking his approval and no one else's. I loved my dad. I wish he were alive so I could tell him I still love him. But I'd also tell him I'm different, and I wouldn't follow him unquestioningly ever again.

Valore's waiting for my answer. Our mattresses are on the floor, only separated by the grid. We fell asleep like this after talking late into the night, and we haven't moved our beds back yet this morning. The nearness has been necessary since a new prisoner arrived two weeks ago. She's two cells down and has screamed during her every waking hour. Sitting this close is the only way to hear ourselves over her terrified cries. She's asleep now, and my ears are grateful.

Guard F, I'm sure, is grateful too. He's threatened to quit daily since her arrival, and I want to tape the woman's mouth shut to keep him from talking that way. It's not like he's a friend, but he's better than any other guard I've experienced.

I put my hand on the bars, pull myself up, and lean

against the grid.

"Of course, you can tell me," I say. I'm more compliant with Valore than I've been with anyone my entire life. I want to please and make him happy. He's all that matters. It scares me sometimes how much he could ask of me that I'd agree to. I'd tell him about my past if he asked it of me, even though I'm more afraid than ever—petrified, actually —that he'll learn about my history. I couldn't survive his disappointment. Still, I'm optimistic he's not headed for that conversation right now, so I ask, "What's on your mind?"

"I know July eleventh means something to you," he starts, and my skin prickles. "Well, it's a tough day for me too."

"It is?" He's tried to distract me from my sullen mood the last few days, but it appears he needed it just as much. "Why?"

"It's my wedding anniversary."

I say nothing. I know nothing about marriage except what I saw my mom and dad do, and that didn't seem all that special. I watched them get angry and argue more than smile and show affection. I doubt that was my mom's choice. I don't know if Dad was built for love.

"We fell in love while fighting with a Torquent blade."

"Like while you were training?" I can't help but think of Evans and Chessie, making me wonder if anything came of their flirting.

"No. We were on opposite sides of a battle. She was better with the weapon but was injured. I had no problem besting her, but when it came time to deliver the death blow, I couldn't do it. There was something in the soft set of her mouth and the acceptance in her eyes. She didn't feel like my enemy. So, instead of chopping off her head, I gave her my hand and helped her up. It wasn't the typical start of a romance."

I smile to myself because it could be more common than he realizes. Still, I don't want to ruin his story.

"What are you grinning about?" he asks.

Curses! It's so unfair he has the advantage of seeing me.

"It's called a meet-cute," I say to disguise my actual thoughts.

"A meet-cute?" Valore asks, trying out the term.

"Yeah. A unique story about the beginning of a romance... it's a meet-cute."

"I like it." Then he chuckles. "Anyway, I'm sorry if I've been moody."

Hardly. Valore's mood is always temperate—like this place in the fall. Mild with a few climactic hurdles but nothing insurmountable.

I know little about his wife, except he had one, and she's dead, though he's never shared what happened to her. In addition, I'm aware of two sons and a daughter. I'm unsure of their ages, if they're still living, or if he has more children. He was a soldier in the Dark at one time, but I don't know with what group he fought. Since our conversation last year, I've wondered if he was in Casmo's inner court and offended the man. That could be what landed him in prison.

What I do know is he's a mole, as my dad would say, and in the strangest twist, he's become my best friend.

My only friend.

"Today's my sister's birthday," I blurt out. He knows I have a brother and a sister, but that's the extent of it.

"Oh," Valore says, his voice full of understanding.

"I got here three days before she turned nineteen." I suck in my upper lip and pop it out, the skin raw. "Today's not the anniversary of my arrival, but it's the date I use. I don't know why."

“I do,” Valore says but doesn’t explain his theory. I crave his answer, and that worries me. I did the same thing with Dad—wanting his words to give me direction and approval. I sometimes wonder if I’ve replaced one detrimental situation with another, obsessing over Valore’s opinion of me instead of my dad’s. Logically, I understand it’s unhealthy to wrap yourself up in one person. I know this because I did it once, and I’m still riding out the repercussions. But just as reasonably, I ask myself, *Why even care?* In this lonely place in the Dark, Valore’s all I have. He’s it until I die, or he dies —I shudder at the thought—and my attachment, though probably unwise, is inevitable with no compelling reason to prevent it.

“Should we train?” he asks. Breakfast should be here soon, and we should get at it before Guard F shows up with his familiar stomp.

“Sure,” I say, hopping to my feet.

This is a typical start to my day now that Valore’s here. It’s markedly different from my Adlumen mornings, where I’d try to get Dad’s attention over breakfast before following Chessie to the training field, where I flirt with Raden and wish I were my sister. Here, it’s Valore and me working on fighting drills.

And I’m not just pounding walls with wrapped fists. I hadn’t known Valore long before we discovered a shared fascination and skill with the Torquent blade. Valore’s bed had a loose bedpost. He pulled off a second one—putting his mattress onto the floor—and we started doing drills through the grid.

It’s not convenient, but we make it work. The most challenging part is the shape and weight of the bedposts because they don’t have the feel of an actual sword. Still, Valore’s convinced it’s the repetitious movement that counts —that I’m creating an automatic response to call upon someday when the need arises and there's a Torquent blade in my hand. In other words, a day that will never come.

I retrieve the posts kept in Aunty's Cellar—for no particular reason, it just ended up that way. "I envy your posture," Valore says as I cross my small space. I don't know what to say, but the man makes my life easy, as usual, by filling in for me. "My back's bowed from a life of fighting."

"When you were a soldier," I comment, bending to find the edge of my mattress and dragging it back to the frame.

"Well, soldiering is one of many types of fighting I've engaged in. They've all taken an advanced toll on my body."

I don't like to hear this. Any pain or ailment afflicting Valore affects me personally. He needs to be healthy and perfect.

For forever.

"Don't look so upset. I'm fine," he says, reading my expression. "Come over here, and we'll get started."

We begin our exercises. Valore calls out his intention, and I react. And today, as in the past few weeks, we do it quietly to prevent the screaming prisoner from rousing.

Valore uses unique Torquent blade postures—unlike any Raden taught me—and frequently argues the merits of his technique. Early in our acquaintance, Valore explained the style is specific to his family—postures only they use—and it made me wonder if he was a Torque, but the idea was fleeting since the Torques live in a light bubble. But after today's revelation, I'm reconsidering it from a different angle.

Having been steadfast about not sharing our histories, I feel nervous as I lower my arm and ask, "Did you practice the Torquent blade with your wife?"

"I did." His voice is thoughtful and patient.

"Did you create your family technique together?"

"No. She was an artist with a blade. Anything amazing I

teach you came from her."

So, it's possible his wife was the Torque. He said they were on opposite sides of a battle, and that would make sense with him being light blind. There are questions on my tongue, as curiosity tries to take over, but I swallow them down and say, "Thank you. We can continue practicing now."

Valore resumes his training as if there'd been no disruption. "You're doing better, but you keep dropping your wrist."

With a teasing huff, I smile and try again. If I had my sight, I'd be better equipped to decide if he's right about my stance. Then again, without it, I have to pay attention to everything, and I wonder if it actually improves my skills. Regardless, I suck up any complaints and do as he says.

"Remember, a real blade is serrated, so the edge will jump if you slide it like that."

So, don't slide it—that's what he means. I know this, but I can't seem to concentrate today. Valore continues instructing me, correcting the slightest misstep until each skill is perfect. The repetition he demands makes my movement second nature until I can perform on repeat to his satisfaction. Today, I get weary of the effort faster than usual, so I'm glad when breakfast arrives. We stop to eat our runny meal while the female prisoner wakes and shrieks anew.

"Will it ever stop?" I ask, shaking my head in dismay.

"We might have more cause for concern if it does."

I frown. "You're probably right."

"You were tough to connect with—angry and spiteful—but I'm glad you weren't like that," he admits.

"Sorry." I curl my lip. "It was a tough time." I think back on Squatty's death and briefly revisit the aching loss. I spiraled, frequently speaking to Self and withdrawing into my mind while madness crept into the edges of my thoughts.

It frightens me to remember the state I was in.

"I understood, Shar. I was just glad there was someone to spend my days with. I still am. I don't know how well I would have done without you here."

I hold my bowl aloft, frozen. I've relied on others my entire life, but no one has ever said they depend on me. Not until this moment. Maybe that's why my need for him is so strong. I've never vocalized what he means to me—that he saved my life—but perhaps now's the time. Lowering my bowl, I tell him in a voice barely heard over prisoner screams, "I was ready to give up before you got here."

"I don't like the sound of that one bit."

"I had nothing. But you needn't worry. I won't do anything while you're with me."

"And even if I'm not," he states, low and demanding. "Promise me, Shar." I shake my head, feeling sorrow bubble up. The tears try to form, but I resist. There's only one reason I'll cry, and this isn't it.

"You have a lot of living left to do," Valore presses.

"How do you figure?"

"I see it in your every move and expression. You still have things you want to set right."

I pull in my upper lip. What he says is true. I wish I could show those I wronged that I've become a better person—that I'm unwaveringly set on an alternate course in life. It would be life-changing if I could seek redemption and forgiveness, but it has to be enough to know I'd try. "It's a pretty sentiment, but it's not based in reality, is it?"

"Don't underestimate reality. It has a way of changing without notice." Yeah. And usually, for the worse.

We eat in silence. Valore could be right about life opening up someday, but I won't depend on it, hope for it, or even fear it. This is my life, and I'm resolved to survive this world, even if my purposes are mundane. I reach the bottom of the bowl before I ask, “Doesn’t the monotony of this place ever get to you?”

“Sure. I wish I had some wood and a knife to work on something with my hands.”

“You whittle?”

“Yes.”

I smile, visualizing Valore working wood. “What do you make?”

“I carve silly faces.”

“Like, a floating head?”

“No.” He chuckles. “I carve the bodies too, but I enjoy working on faces the most.”

“How big are they?”

“Six inches is pretty standard,” Valore says with a click of his tongue.

“For the face or the entire body?”

“Whole thing.”

“Wow. The face must be tiny. How do you do it?” I can’t imagine producing that kind of detail.

“It’s not difficult. I use a tiny knife.” Valore laughs, and I join him.

Life doesn’t sparkle like I once thought it would. I imagined myself married to Raden with two kids, standing by my sister as she led Adlumen. But I’ve found contentment. After years of loss and loneliness, I have someone I’m devoted to. There’s nothing I wouldn’t do for the man in the next cell. I wonder if he feels the same, but I’m too afraid to ask.

I wish I could tell my family all that’s transpired, though I doubt they’d believe it. Still, it’s comforting for me to know: I am changed.

CHAPTER NINE

Eight Years Caged

It's the middle of the night. While I cannot see so much as a shadow in the Dark, after eight years in the Desert Territory, my other senses know the hour. The temperature is too cool for daytime in mid-August, and there aren't enough prison noises for it to be early morning. The desert bugs are making noise, which will cease when the sun rises. Among the chirp and hum, I hear a separate sound—the scrape of metal.

I sit up in bed, pretty sure it's coming from above—from the vent I long suspected was in my ceiling, which Valore confirmed. The slight rattle increases, and then there's a pop. "Valore!" I whisper.

"I hear it too," he whispers back.

"Is it an animal?" I scoot into a corner to get as far away from the opening as possible. I don't want a critter leaping down on top of me.

"I don't think so." We hear a loud crack, a pause, and then a plume of debris falls into my enclosure. I imagine a dust cloud in Aunty's Celler as I cough, waving a hand in front of my face. Tucking my nose and mouth inside my thin shirt, I turn into the corner. It helps some, and I'm able to catch my breath.

"Winter?" Sue asks, the commotion waking her. We discovered the screaming woman is named Sue. She cries less these days but frequently talks to someone called Winter—someone who's not here. It's a common side effect of this place.

"Winter's sleeping, Sue. You should too," Valore answers,

his voice smooth and unaffected. The dust must have settled before reaching his cell. I'm about to ask what's happening—my lack of sight is a real hindrance in this situation—when I hear an unusual thump followed by a groan. I turn toward the sound.

"What are you doing here?" Valore asks, and it's immediately clear he's not talking to me.

"What does it look like?" comes the reply in a husky whisper only feet from where I'm huddled. My eyes widen from the shock, knowing there's a man inside the cage with me. I'm not used to being close to anyone except Valore or Guard F, so it takes a minute to recover—long enough, the man's on the move, crossing Aunty's Cellar to the metal grid. Then, I hear the unmistakable sound of hinges in motion.

By the Dark! He's opened my cell!

I launch to my feet, but when I reach the door, it's already closed.

"Hey!" I fist the bars and shake.

"Be quiet," he whispers, only inches away.

"Let me out," I counter and shake it again.

"Shh!"

"I'm not making a portion of the noise you did." I point at my debris-covered room.

He grunts. Nothing in the sound makes me believe he's swayed, but then he says, "I'll be back. Your cell is my exit."

"Oh."

And then he's gone.

But he doesn't go far.

After a few clicks, Valore's door swings open. I cross Aunty's Cellar, stumbling over the pile of junk, before reaching the grid. I grip it, looking their way fruitlessly, then hear a slapping sound. "It took me years to find you," the stranger says, and I realize they're embracing. They must be good friends. "Years!" he emphasizes while keeping his voice low.

"I'm well aware," Valore says with a chuckle.

I'm honestly surprised a guard hasn't come our way—the noise when the ceiling crashed down wasn't slight. Valore's friend must have timed it just right, so the patrol wasn't near. Still, it won't be long until someone's back—ten minutes, if we're lucky. I suck in my upper lip, the skin already raw from the day before. The last thing I need is to make it more chapped, but I can't help myself. I'm still in shock over what's taking place.

"By the Dark, we looked everywhere for you. We checked this place twice, but Ott swore he hadn't heard a thing about you. Should have known the bastard was lying." Then there's another embrace with lots of back-smacking. "When I firmed up your location, I dropped everything and came straight away."

"How'd you find me?" Valore asks, his voice muffled, and I lean forward to better hear the answer.

"Tyran."

Tyran of Torquent? This man moves in high circles if she's providing him with information. I'm impressed, but Valore's not pleased. "No! Please tell me—" Valore pauses, then asks with a groan, "What did she want in return?"

"A discussion is all."

"Is all? You make it sound trivial, and there's no such thing where Tyran's concerned. Not even a conversation."

"I'm aware."

"Are you? She likely had a hand in putting me here."

"Yes," the stranger says. The entire conversation has my stomach spinning nervously.

"You should have found another way," Valore scolds, but

the man laughs, saying, "I tried other ways, remember? For years. But we were running out of time."

"Why? What's happening?"

"I'll tell you later. We need to go."

He's right. The guard could arrive at any moment to check the corridor. I cling tighter to my cage, my fingers straining on the bars. Valore's leaving, and I'm so torn. I want him free, but I don't want to be without him. I suck my lip harder as Valore asks, "How many are you?"

"It's just Renegade and me. He's a mile away with the horses."

Valore grumbles. "This is reckless. First, Tyran, and then, using a skeleton crew to do the job of a full team."

"You don't have to worry. I've got a solid plan."

"You have people to care for, and this was too big of a risk. You shouldn't have come," Valore scolds again, clicking his tongue. I can't help but grin since it's a bit late for Valore to give his advice.

"Well, it's too late for that now!" the man says, echoing my thoughts at an uncomfortable volume. He takes it down an octave before adding, "Do you want me to lock you back in and leave?"

I chuckle at the rhetorical question, and the men go quiet. I feel their eyes on me, and my teeth dig into my lip. Then Valore says, "No. I'm done complaining."

"Thank the Dark. Let's go."

Go?

Curses! Valore's leaving!

It was obvious where the situation was headed, but now that it's happening, my stomach twists in anguish. I rub the scar on my hand and remember Chessie's voice from so long ago: *"I'm here for you, Sharade. No matter what you face, you'll always have me on your side."*

I gave up on her hollow promise long ago and put all my hopes on Valore. I remember when it happened—on an especially tough day while I was curled up in Aunty's Cellar, holding the tears back but aching so bad to release them. Valore told me, "I'm here, Shar. I'll always look out for you."

They weren't my sister's exact words but were close enough to snap the brittle thread linking me to her and create a firm connection to Valore. Fear and panic rise in me as I try to figure out how I'll cope in Valore's absence. I can't make anything work—my legs, arms, or voice. I manage to swallow just as Valore says, "We're taking the girl with us."

Hope swells within me.

"The girl?" the stranger repeats as if he's forgotten I'm here. It goes quiet before I suddenly feel their eyes on me again. "Hi," I say and perform a brief wave.

The man laughs. "You're joking."

"I'm not."

I should say something, but my mouth is stuck. I used to have abundant confidence—which feels all but gone—but my conviction toward what is right is more substantial, and I wonder if that's the trade-off.

"Yeah. That's not happening," he spits without pity. The stranger's taking my only friend and has no intention of freeing me. My mouth goes dry.

"I won't leave her," Valore states emphatically.

He's refusing to leave me. I walk the border of my world, clinging to the bars, staring sightlessly in their direction while gathering hope from Valore's statement.

I don't know how to change the man's mind. I'm not sure there's anything I can say to convince him. Valore knows the situation, so I can only wait for the verdict—that is, for Valore to change the man's mind.

"Where's she from?"

"Adlumen," Valore answers without pause. How did he know that? I never once told him or even alluded to it.

"How long have you been here?" the stranger asks me, and I can tell he's closer now, with only the bars and a few inches of air separating us.

"Eight years."

"You're a remnant of the days of Endrack's reign—when your people hated mine."

"Your people?" I ask, still unsure where he's from.

"The citizens of the South T."

There's nothing I can say because he's got it exactly right. My people hated his, and Dad brought me up despising and cursing the existence of the Souther moles. Is that where Valore's from too?

"It's as I thought," he says with a sneer.

"I don't feel that way now!" I say in a rush. It's the truth, spoken with fear coursing through me at the prospect of being stuck in prison without my primary reason for living. I wish I could disguise my terror, but I can't, and he hears it.

"And why would you? It's easy to ignore your prejudice to get what you want—a free ride out of prison." There's disdain in his voice, and it's only getting thicker.

The fear dissipates, replaced with something else—frustration. I've not felt the emotion in years, and it's a reminder of my old self—angry and hate-filled. It's an echo from when I used to throw things to express myself—hairbrushes and dishware—whatever was handy.

The frustration tightens my insides like a screw in my chest. I want to release the pressure and let the man have it, but his open scorn drives me to prove myself.

This place has changed me. Valore has changed me. I'm no longer Sharade Endrack.

I'm just Shar—a twenty-four-year-old girl schooled in

abandonment. A girl who knows what it's like to be unloved but loves others to the point of obsession. If he's going to accuse me of anything, it should at least be the right thing!

"You're not a free ride!" I snap. "You're the means of liberation from this hell. And it is hell. If you don't believe me, spend eight years here and find out."

"Well, I doubt you landed here for choosing the wrong summer cut." My fingers automatically go to my hair. "Or dressing in shorts during pant season."

"You're correct. I deserved to be here, but now I deserve to be free."

"An excellent argument, Shar," Valore says, and my cheeks heat at the compliment. "I believe one of us is acting the dullard, and it's not the lady nor the old man."

The stranger heaves a sigh. "I forget you enjoy confrontation."

Valore clicks his tongue. "You're the same. You'd argue with a pencil writing your own words."

The man chuckles. "You've been telling me that since I was six."

"Eh. Probably three. You were contrary from a young age."

"Look. We don't have time to debate this."

"Agreed. Which means we should all three leave."

"But she's—"

"It doesn't matter what you think of her," Valore says, cutting him off. He's close to the bars now, reaching through to take my hand. "She's my closest friend, and she goes with us."

"Friend?" he asks in defeat. I want to stick my tongue out in triumph, but having Valore label me his friend means the world to me. So, instead of acting out, I validate his declaration by staying silent and squeezing his fingers in appreciation.

"This isn't wise," the stranger states.

"And yet, she's going. Sure, there was a day, not long ago, when her people despised ours. But didn't we hate them equally? She deserves a fresh start, and you don't have the right to heap guilt upon her. She's paid for her crimes, and it's our duty to protect her."

Valore's never spoken like this, and hearing his opinion of me is both bolstering and frightening, especially when he adds, "She's a good girl."

I wince, knowing the description's not always been true. I forget they can see me until the stranger says, "She doesn't look too sure." Shock replaces my wince, and he laughs again while I release Valore's hand.

"What if she kills us on our way home?" the man asks.

"You, perhaps," I say, trying to shock him. "But I'd die before I let a single thing happen to Valore. His life matters more than mine."

"On that, we can agree. But I don't trust you."

"We just met, yet you seem to hate me. Why do you doubt me so?"

"That you're a prisoner isn't enough?"

I shake my head. "No. There's more."

"You're right. I have my reasons. One is that I don't believe a single word coming from your mouth."

"I may refuse to tell you something, but I guarantee anything I speak is true. I made a promise the day I met Valore, and I've never gone back on it. I don't intend to."

"Yeah. I still don't believe you, but I'm done debating. You can come because he insists. And if you betray us or become a nuisance, I'll be justified in killing you."

"Killing me?" I clutch my chest while my heart gives way

to the beat of a horse's gallop.

"He won't kill you, Shar. My son has better manners than that."

Son!

A fierce surge of jealousy roars through me because his title holds infinitely more weight than that of a mere friend.

Still reeling from the revelation, it takes a moment to realize Guard F is approaching—his signature tromp announcing his arrival. I anticipate the noise of metal and fists. I'm ready to beg Valore's son to spare the guard who's been offish all these years but isn't so bad. Instead, Guard F says calmly, if not somewhat annoyed, "You should be gone already."

"Ran into a slight delay."

There's a pause before Guard F says, "Yeah. She's always causing trouble."

"You're helping him?" I ask, surprised. Guard F always seemed so... stalwart.

"I wouldn't call it helping as much as profiting."

Money. Of course. Still, I'm glad we won't have to run from Guard F. Or attack him. At least, that's what I think until I hear a crunch—bone hitting bone.

"What the Dark was that for?" Guard F bellows.

"I didn't hit you well enough the first time. No one would've believed I knocked you out with that slight bruise. But this one—well, it's already purpling nicely."

"Great." Guard F grumbles. "Now, would you get the Dark out of here so I'm not discovered idly chatting with a future escapee?"

"*Escapees*. The girl's coming with us."

"The hell she is. You paid me for one prisoner, not two."

"So, bill me." The lock on Aunty's Cellar clicks, and the

door creeks open. I wait for them to walk inside and escape up the vent, but no one moves. "Well? Are you coming or not?" the stranger asks with significant irritation.

"But, aren't we?" I point at the hole above me.

"I changed my mind."

"Of course you did." I raise my nose into the air. "And you call me untrustworthy."

"It's now or never, little prisoner. Are you coming with or arguing your point until I lock you back in."

I abandon my haughty expression and dart around Aunty's Cellar, collecting my things. Moments later, I leave my cage of eight years with the glass bottle in my grip and Squatty's necklace around my neck. I need them because Valore's son will soon take my best friend away—it's inevitable he'll eventually get his way—and when it happens, they'll be the only things I have left in the world.

Guard F takes the lead, stomping the path we should take. I shuffle my feet as I walk where I'm guided, feeling both Valore and his son directing me with a hand here and a nudge there. The instant we exit the prison, I feel a significant burst of air—more circulation than I've felt in years—and I take a moment to breathe it in.

"Your job is to watch over her," the son says to Valore. "I need to keep my eyes and hands at the ready."

"I promise to be no bother," I say, trying to reassure him of my determination to help, not hinder.

The man snorts. "If only that were true, but those are just the empty words of a criminal."

CHAPTER TEN

One Day Free

Freedom has a scent—leafy trees, wild grass, and blossoms. They're smells I wouldn't normally associate with the Desert Territory, but there's no denying it. If my counting rocks hadn't already told me, the surrounding foliage would do the job—it's definitely late summer. I sigh, missing home—specifically, the warm angle of the sun on the balconies in Ambitus.

And then I release the tear I promised to the occasion—my one tear of joy. I'm finally free. I sigh again.

"You need to be quiet, or we'll get caught."

Valore's son is quite the grouch. Still, he's right. I must remain vigilant—help, not hinder, as promised. It's hard to stay somewhere you're not wanted, but I don't have another option. I'd do almost anything to never return to Aunty's Cellar, including taking direction from this man.

"I'll be quiet," I say, but Valore's already got ahold of my arm, pulling me along. I can't help but take another deep breath, drawing in the surrounding aromas.

"What are you doing?" the son whispers.

"I'm sorry. It's just... I can smell the world, and it's nice."

"How can you smell anything over your own stench?" he asks.

Valore's grip tightens. "Son, this behavior isn't becoming. I taught you better. We had no control over our hygiene."

"And we have no control now... over the dogs finding us. They'll sniff her out before dawn." We must be clear of any immediate danger because he's talking without restraint.

"Me as well," Valore scolds. "If you're worried, we should work on cleaning us *both* up."

"Did you forget we're in the middle of an escape? Cleaning up isn't a possibility at this exact moment. We need to get off Casmo's land."

"Then stop making trouble where there's no solution," Valore snaps, and his son quiets. The men bristle with agitation but keep to the task at hand. Our liberator is alert and cautious while Valore moves me smoothly, keeping me from harm.

We walk for what seems like hours. I'm sure the slow passage of time has everything to do with moving silently in the Dark while Valore walks breathlessly beside me, huffing each exhale with force. I notice his steps slowing, and the hunched back he often spoke of seems more bent. This is the most I've walked in nearly a decade, and I feel winded, but Valore needs a quick rest to keep going at a reasonable pace.

I reach out and find the back of our guide's shirt, pulling him to a stop. "What now?" he utters.

"I need a minute to rest," I say confidently, pressing my left hand to my chest with my index finger aimed—hopefully covertly—at my friend. "Not for long. Just to catch my breath." I tap my finger a few times.

"Are you okay?" Valore asks, his tone worried.

"Yes. Just feeling a little disoriented." It's not a lie. It's strange to be outside of Aunty's Cellar. As much as I revel in this freedom, there was safety in my cage.

"Fine," Valore's son announces. "We'll rest." We take a hard right, and he guides us to where there's tree cover. We've walked among bushes and short grass today, but this new ground is uneven and rocky.

Valore helps me sit on a rock. It isn't flat and jabs me right in the backside, so I don't rest my total weight. Valore, however, plops next to me with a relieved grunt. If his son doesn't recognize the relief in the sound, he really is a dullard.

A minute passes, and the Dark feels like it's closing in on me. There's not a grid of metal or a wall of rock containing me. Instead, there's space all around. There's a slight return of the madness that became my companion for many years. I try but can't bear the silence, so I blurt out, "Can I ask a favor?"

"Another one?" The son grumbles.

"Oh, I'm sorry. Do you have something else to do?"

"Besides watching for Casmo's rats to jump us from the trees? No, not much."

I press a slender fist to my bony waist and scowl in his direction.

He sighs. "What is it you need?"

I reach for the back of my neck, grabbing the tangled strands twisted at my nape. "Would you please cut my hair?"

"What?"

"I need you to cut my hair," I repeat, holding up the mess hanging down my back. It turned into such a disaster that I used to sit in Aunty's Cellar and pull it out. At first, it hurt, and then my scalp became numb. But I didn't eat well during my captivity, and pretty soon, it felt like it wasn't growing back properly, so I stopped. Besides, I discovered I could drape it over my face at night to keep the rodents away.

"I'm not a barber! Do I look like I have any clue how to trim and bob a woman's hair?"

"I don't know how you look at all," I state plainly. "And I don't need a bob. I just need it gone."

"Hmm. Now, where did I put my trimming scissors?"

"No need to be a diva," I say. "Just do what the guards did, and use a knife. You have a knife, don't you?" I know he has one, just like I know he's glaring a hole through my head.

"I have four. And if they were cutting it for you, why'd you let it get so long?"

"They stopped. Probably something to do with the *condition of my sentence.*" I got so sick of hearing that excuse for everything they denied me.

"Condition of... say, what?"

"Just cut it! By the Dark, it's not that complicated. Snip! Snip!" I pop my fingers together in a cutting motion.

Valore's son shuffles around, and then the weight of my hair is lifted from my hand. He pulls it to the side, turning my head with it. "It is rather tangled."

"Now's not the time to be polite. It's a raging disaster."

He chokes out a laugh. "The little prisoner speaks the truth."

"Just take some of the larger chunks. I don't care if I end up bald."

"You likely will," he says but starts working.

He does a messy job of it. I know this because minutes later, when he's finished, I feel the edges. It's not great, but not necessarily worse than what the guards did in Aunty's Cellar. Where they performed a blunt cut, he put the blade close to my head, removing small sections at a time. Some parts are a few inches long, while others are just a nub. In any case, it's an improvement from five minutes ago.

"Thanks," I say, meaning it.

He mumbles something I don't quite hear, only catching the words *gnawing* and *humiliation*. I don't ask for a repeat, choosing to pretend he requested I stand up so we could get moving because that's what I do.

The breeze picks up as we walk. A stray leaf brushes my hand while spiky weeds poke my bare ankles. Once, my pants were long enough to cover them, but that was years ago. I'm lucky they're as long as they are.

Our guide keeps a slower pace. I'm sure Valore thinks it's for my benefit, but his son wouldn't put forth such effort to ensure my comfort. Truly, I don't care about his treatment of me. He's good to Valore, and that's what matters. The rest I can deal with.

The next time we stop, Valore's breathing is even—for which I'm grateful—but his son is on edge. "This is where I left Renegade," he says, keeping his voice low. "Something must have happened. We need to get out of here quickly. And we need to pick up the pace."

"We can manage a faster pace," Valore says, patting my arm while I nod.

Valore does well, breathing heavily but keeping up. Meanwhile, I trip over every minor obstacle. They'd travel faster if they left me behind. Carrying me like a helpless baby would even be an improvement. It's not a surprise the grumpy son mentions both options. I want to be angry at him but can't summon the feeling because he's right.

We don't go far, but we go fast. Ten minutes pass before the son announces, "We're here." I want to cheer, but sanity prevails.

Valore wobbles to a stop and slips away from me. I try to keep him upright but descend with him. Landing sideways on his lap, he laughs. "It's just a log. Scoot over, and you can sit on it with me."

"Oh." One second, I'm imagining cuts, bruises, and broken bones. The next, we're sitting laissez-faire on a woodsy log bench. "Where are we?" I ask, noticing the sun's heat on my back for the first time. I haven't felt it in years and want to melt into the sensation.

"Secondary meeting point. We're pretty secluded, so we shouldn't see anyone. Except, hopefully, Renegade."

"So, we just wait?"

"Yes, little prisoner, we wait. Unless you have a pressing engagement."

"Ornery," I say in accusation, and he doesn't dispute me. I settle onto the log, figuring I'll get comfortable until Renegade shows, but then I hear it.

I straighten, craning my ear. "Do you—" I start but stop again to listen. Oh, yes. There's no doubt about what's out there. I'm on my feet a second later.

"Where are you going?" the son asks.

"That way." I point toward the sound without knowing what's between it and me. "I won't be long."

"Renegade could be back any moment. We'll leave without you. Don't think we won't."

"That's grand," I say, walking away with only one goal in my newly trimmed head. Eight years in the Dark, and nothing could keep me—not even a second longer—from the noise sounding in my ears.

"Dear girl, where are you going?" Valore asks, appearing at my side, and then, "Oh. I hear it too." I take careful but eager steps with my hands before me until Valore grips my arm to help, and we move faster together.

My left foot finds it first. The river water is chilly, even on a warm August morning.

"The water's fast," Valore says, but I don't heed his warning. I pull from his hand and trudge in up to my knees. Feeling the current's drag isn't enough to deter me. In one swift move, I sink in, crossing my legs, the water bobbing under my chin.

And then I lie back, dunking my head under.

I've felt my new freedom in the expanse and smells around me, but this is when my liberation sinks in. It's been six years since I was fully immersed in water. Since then, I've cleaned using drinking water poured onto my hands, but it can't compare, even in the slightest, to this feeling.

I stay under, holding my breath. The water is exhilarating! It's colder now I'm completely submerged, but the satisfaction is overwhelming. I pop my head up and take a breath. And then, I'm crying. I tilt my head to the side, and the water is like a pillow. I could stay here forever.

"Are you insane?" Valore's son exclaims, arriving at my side and finding my upper arm to pull me up, but I wrench away. I dunk my head again, pushing my fingers into my scalp. Some of the longer sections of hair are still in clumps, and I work my fingers inside. It hurts and feels marvelous simultaneously—like an impossible itch.

As I surface, I hear Valore. "Let her be, Son. The water is safer than it first appeared."

"Because she got lucky! It was impulsive and reckless—the last thing we need. This is how it will be with her."

"Let her have this. It's only a few years for me, and I'm nearly ready to do the same. She's been in that pit a long time."

"For good reason."

"Maybe so." Valore's voice turns harsh. "But no matter their crimes, no one deserves to be stripped of all joy and pride."

Along with the river's flow, I feel a wash of guilt. I'm causing this rift between them when I promised I wouldn't be a bother.

"Please, don't argue," I beg. "I'm done. I'm getting out." But no one's listening to me as I rise, dripping river water.

"Renegade could be here already, and we're playing in the water."

"We can spare a few minutes. Let her be, Raider."

I freeze, but it lasts only a second before I blurt out,

"Raider!" The water running down my face flies from my lips with the force of that one word. There's no way it's him. No possible way. Life can't be that cruel.

"Yes. My name's Raider Roil."

"Roil," I repeat, staring in his direction while unsure where my eyes actually land.

Raider Roil. And his dad. I suck in my upper lip, biting hard. Valore *Roil.* The leader of the Southern Territory. We never shared last names, so I didn't know. And when I was young, I never knew his first name—Dad just referred to him as Captain Roil. More often, he just called him horrible names because of how much they hated one another.

My best friend in the world was my dad's worst enemy.

And his son! Eight years and Raider Roil's the one to liberate me from my hell. Why did it have to be him? I find it disturbingly poetic that a person I've wronged is the means of my deliverance.

"You know my name?" Raider asks, not sounding surprised. Gathering my thoughts, I try to figure out what that means. Did he already figure out who I am? No. There's no way. He'd have insisted on leaving me in prison.

Didn't he, though?

"Yeah," I push out, walking from the water and stumbling on the slick rocks. "Many people know your name." I squeeze water through my hair and step from the stream. "They know your face too."

"Ah. So, we've met before," Raider says, a slight edge to his tone.

"I didn't say that!" I yell, twisting my shirt until river water drips between my fingers.

Raider chuckles. "Not quite a lie, is it?"

Curses! What's he playing at?

"You just... have a reputation," I say, evading.

"Yes, but what was I known for in your time, little prisoner?"

I keep it simple. And true. "For having a pleasant face."

"My reputation's changed," he says, keeping his voice low and adding, "Has yours?"

I swallow the hard lump forming in my throat, but it won't go down. "Reputations often do, don't they?"

Does he remember me? If so, I don't know what to do about it. Or what he'll do about it. Drown me in this river, perhaps?

"Dad, would you go back and wait for Renegade?" he asks softly. "I don't want to miss him. I'll get her back."

He won't even say my name. He never has, now I think of it. Has he known since the beginning? I think back to Aunty's Cellar when his attitude transformed from uninterested to hostile. Was it because he realized I was more than a random prisoner Valore wanted to liberate?

No. I'm just creating a story in my head. I need to stay calm. We only met once in my youth, which was a long time ago—nearly a third of my life.

"You should go back for Renegade, and I'll help Shar," Valore says, and I nod at the idea, liking it much better than Raider's proposal.

"No. *Shar* will be fine. You have my word," Raider says before leaning in and putting his lips to my ear, whispering, "And we both know how important someone's word is. Don't we, Sharade Endrack?"

CHAPTER ELEVEN

Two Days Free

Renegade never arrives. Eventually, Raider guides us away from the river, and we walk for hours until we reach another meeting spot where we'll stay the night. The entire time, I feel his gaze on me in the Dark. He knows who I am. And every moment we travel, I expect him to open his mouth and tell Valore my identity. But he remains silent, and I'm equally relieved and confused. The fitful night of sleep that follows only gives a slight reprieve from the stressful day.

Day two of freedom has me walking again, my arm linked through Valore's. Raider says we're traveling toward Sperne, a border city in Captain Rhed's Coastal Territory. They'll feel easier when we're out of Casmo's domain, but for my part, Sperne is still in the Dark. It will be some time before we reach a light bubble.

Raider's worried about his friend. I hear it in every huffed breath and barked order. I comply with his demands and stay quiet, even when he complains about me slowing them down. I would never tell him I could go faster and that it's his dad keeping this pace, but I think he knows. I'm an easier target, and truthfully, I'm fine shouldering the blame.

"We're an hour outside Vernam," Raider announces mid-afternoon. My stomach is throwing a fit in its empty state, and my tongue's so dry it's sticking to the roof of my mouth. There's hope that Vernam means fixing these issues since I can't imagine the others are faring much better than me. "I don't have plans to enter the city, but we'll still see people as they go about their daily routine. There's a chance they've heard of escaped prisoners in the area, so you'd better carry a knife for protection."

Valore releases my arm to take the weapon, and a second later, he tells his son, "Shar too."

"I don't—" Raider starts.

"Shar too," Valore presses, speaking over him.

"Fine. I'll give the little prisoner a weapon." Raider grips my hand firmly, pressing the hilt into my palm. "Though I shudder to think what you're liable to do with it."

I suck in a gasp, then cover my mouth with my free hand.

What I'm liable to do.

He knows my past actions with a knife, but I'm shocked he brought it into the conversation. And yet, I'm also surprised when he doesn't elaborate.

"Stop tormenting the girl and give her a visual so she'll know how to handle it."

"She'd likely injure herself instead of getting any protection against an attacker," Raider says coolly. "Though maybe that's best," he mumbles, clearing his throat and adding, "Some people shouldn't have weapons. Ever. Not when they can't discern when it's the right time to use one."

His judgment is heavy and exact. Yes, I used a knife for the wrong purpose—it's a choice I've lived with for eight years—and while I'm not proud of what I did, I'm done punishing myself for it.

I run my hands over the knife to get a feel for it—gently, so I don't cut myself—deciding it's not long but could do some damage. "I know how and, more importantly, when to use it," I say, wanting to shut Raider up and get on our way.

"Very true," Valore confirms. "Shar's very capable and would do well in a fight."

I smile in my friend's direction while Raider roughly straps a belt around my waist to hold the knife. It's loose on me and hangs lazily on my hip. He grumbles—approval or disapproval, I can't be sure—and we're on our way again.

The sun feels hot on my face as we walk. The phenomenon still amazes me—that the sun can warm me despite the Dark preventing my sight. I should wear a hat—if one were available—to keep my skin from burning in the harsh rays, but after so long without the sun, the thought of a stinging sunburn doesn't sound so bad. I almost welcome it.

"When did you get shaggy?" Valore asks, breaking what has chiefly been a silent trek across the scorching Desert Territory terrain.

I try to remember Raider when we met. I was a lot younger and only have a vague image in my mind. I envision lenses covering his eyes—though he wouldn't be wearing them right now—and black hair cut so close to his head that it's barely fuzz. He had a long nose, a wide mouth, and a smooth voice. He wasn't shaggy—that's for sure—but things change. Like his voice, which back then was beautiful—musical even—but this Raider doesn't sound like that. Truthfully, I find few similarities between the two versions of Raider Roil I've met in my lifetime.

"It's just a beard," Raider answers with salty annoyance. "And I wouldn't call it shaggy."

"If anyone's shaggy, I'd say it's you, Valore Roil," I hear and stop in my tracks, twisting toward the voice. It's unfamiliar, and my hand finds the knife at my waist. I'm ready to withdraw the weapon when fingers land on mine.

"Easy," Raider says.

And then Valore's out of my grip, moving away while laughing. "Renny Dover!" Valore exclaims, and my blood chills upon hearing the name. Not only am I traveling with Raider Roil, but we've come upon another individual I'm not eager to meet up with—Renny Dover, a guard member who accompanied Captain Rhed when escorting me to my eight-year prison stint. I duck my head as Valore continues, "My son's recruiting old men to do the hard work these days."

"Ha! That's because we're better at it than these young bucks." I hear them embrace. "It's great to see you."

"It is, but I'm not happy you allowed Raider to come here without more men."

"Allowed? You think I could have stopped him?" the man asks. "Said he'd leave the task to no one else, and even I can admit it was easier just the two of us sneaking in."

"And now the *four* of us sneaking out," Raider says, the criticism aimed at me. I don't argue because I, indeed, make things more complicated. But the desire to survive is stronger than my willingness to go it alone and improve their odds. *Does that make me a bad person?*

"You had me worried, Renegade," Raider says, and my mind connects that Renny Dover and Renegade are one and the same. Captain Rhed only ever called him Renny Dover while we traveled, speaking his name with venom since the captain's wife was previously married to Renny... uh, Renegade. She even had a kid with him—Geric, her middle son—though there's no love lost between father and son. At least, that was the story eight years ago. Who knows what's happened while I've been locked away?

"I always find my way," Renegade says, untroubled by the circumstances. Meanwhile, I'm gnawing on my upper lip, frustrated about my history with these men who are now my traveling companions for however long this arrangement lasts. My luck is regressing.

Raider was concerned about Renegade, but now that he's appeared unharmed, Raider's focus turns to logistics, and his tone is all-business as he asks, "Where are the horses?"

"Gone," Renegade answers flatly. "You know these parts. I got spotted with a fine pair of horses by some of Casmo's rats, and, well, they insisted they belonged to them. If I'd argued, you'd be rescuing *me* from prison too. Or from a hanging."

"That's just great," Raider says, slapping something—hopefully this Renegade fellow. Maybe Raider will turn the man blind so he doesn't out me to Valore. Unlikely. And unkind. Besides, Raider's more than capable of revealing my identity.

"Sorry," Renegade answers, but there's some amusement in his voice.

"It's fine, I guess," Raider mumbles, but I hear his worry.

"You guess? How magnanimous," Renegade says.

"We need to get to Sperne," Raider snaps.

"The fastest way is to stop in Vernam and resupply. Get some mangy but serviceable animals that aren't so tempting."

"I hoped to avoid Vernam, but it seems our best option."

"Do you have money for animals?" Valore asks.

"I brought the bank," Raider says, and I hear the clink of coins. "Seemed the only way to get done what needed doing."

I think of Guard F, who was likely paid a weighty sum for our release—well, Valore's release. He's probably on the lam now, just like us. I sort of wish he'd come with us. I'd be glad of his company since he liked me more than Raider does.

"Since no one's offering the information, who's the girl?" Renegade asks, and my brows raise. *Does he really not recognize me?*

"Her name is Shar. We shared adjoining cells the last… well, almost three years."

Renegade chuckles. "I've always known you're soft, Valore, but I never figured it of Raider. How'd you talk him into allowing her along?"

But Valore doesn't answer. Raider does, and his reasoning is simple. "He's my dad. All he had to do was ask."

He sounds sympathetic toward his dad's desires but also slightly disappointed in himself.

"Well, it took a bit more than that," Valore counters, and I must agree. Meanwhile, I release the breath I'm holding, knowing only one person here knows my identity. I've never been so grateful for my haggard appearance, though maybe Renegade's ignorance comes from having a bad memory. Or possibly my brief, unimportant role in the man's life. Whatever the case, I'm relieved.

We set off, walking another hour in the blistering heat until my feet feel like they're melting to the soles of my thin shoes. When I've nearly reached my breaking point, I notice the sun is no longer bearing down on my face. I feel a soft breeze, hear the rustle of leaves, and realize we're in the shade of a tree.

"You three stay here. I'm heading into Vernam. Renegade, you know what to do if I'm not back in an hour."

"I do," Renegade says, and I wish they'd share the plan but don't feel it's my place to ask. Besides, it's probably something like disposing of the interloper and regrouping. "There's a nice bench next to that barn. I'll get Valore settled. We *old men* will use any excuse to relax our feeble bones."

"Shar, take my arm," Valore says, but as I reach to find it, Renegade says, "Raider will escort her over. Let's you and I start."

I hear them move away, knowing it's a setup and Raider planned for this, somehow getting Renegade to execute the maneuver. When I no longer hear the shuffle of feet, Raider speaks. "Listen, I don't have time for you, but Dad wants you here. You're along for the ride, and I'm powerless against it. Whatever. I'll deal. But I have three weeks to stop a pointless war, and—"

"War?" I blurt out, startled by the declaration.

"Shh!"

"What do you mean?" I reach out, grabbing his arm. I find it easily, even in the Dark, but I no sooner have him in my grasp than he pries me off.

"I shouldn't have mentioned it. We'll discuss it when we're out of Casmo's domain. Until then, keep Dad happy, and don't ask questions."

"You used to be nicer," I accuse. It's a childish observation but also true.

"Look, *Sharade*. There are only three things you need to know about me: I'm focused, so if you want to survive this, I'd suggest you keep quiet and let me do my thing. I'm logical, so I won't get sucked into any raw emotions you throw at me to get your way. And I hold a grudge. Nothing more need be said on that point. Don't you agree?"

"I don't get emotional," I say rather than answering the question.

Raider snorts. "I saw that tear when we left your prison."

I glare at him before saying, "It was a debt I owed." He doesn't deserve any more of an explanation. Still, I add, "It's paid, so I'm done. No more tears."

Raider grunts and then leaves without another word. He, of course, doesn't escort me to the bench, so I have to shuffle my way there with Renegade's voice as my guide.

My mind runs over Raider's comment about war. Who's fighting, and what's the conflict about? I consider asking Renegade, but it will only anger Raider to learn I've spoken of it. He's angry if I talk about almost anything. I can't imagine his fury if I broached something he specifically ruled out discussing until we're safely outside the Desert Territory.

I've been sitting for what feels like hours with Renegade and Valore, both snoring to my left. Renegade said we're at the back of an old farm, and he described it to me. Randomly, I consider that farms have fruit trees, and there could be a spare apple, peach, or pear lying around unwanted. It's an idea born of hunger and boredom, so I push up and follow the edge of the barn until I find the fence he described, then walk along it. Finding my way back will be as easy as turning around and following the fence line in reverse, so I decide to walk as long as I can, reaching out blindly at random, looking for branches that might hold fruit.

I've been walking for five minutes—no food within reach—when I encounter my worst nightmare.

"Do I want to know what you're doing?" Raider asks.

Of course, he'd find me. "Looking for food," I say, unashamed.

I'm surprised when he responds with no derision in his tone. "Yeah, I'm sorry about that. The food we had was on the horses, but I got some things in Vernam."

"You did?" I can't hide my excitement.

"Yes. And, as luck would have it, eating *purchased* food won't land the little prisoner and her companions in the clink like stealing farmer's crops will."

"What did you get?" I ask, bouncing on my heels and ignoring his dig.

He's close now, right next to me, and I hear him dismount. "A few things. First, however, I got something just for you."

I can't help but be wary. It's probably a chain to tie me to a tree or a mouth gag to keep me quiet while we travel. Instead, I hear a shuffling noise, and then, miraculously, the world appears around me. "Lamlight!" I exclaim, staring at objects within the light's glow. After so long without my vision, it feels like things are crowding in on me, making me dizzy, but I don't even blink my eyes, looking into the distance. I can see a hundred feet or more in every direction, though the barn is beyond the lamlight's reach.

“This is a circlight. You wear it around your neck,” Raider says, and my vision closes in on his face. All I can do is stare as my eyes confirm he’s indeed the Raider Roil I knew during a single weekend when he visited Ambitus. I was sixteen, he was twenty-two, and I thought myself in love. For that brief period, my fascination with Raider Roil even overshadowed my long-standing devotion to Raden Parrs.

Yes, it’s Raider, but he’s changed.

Even before I met him, his good looks were well known in light bubbles and Dark territories alike. He’s still handsome—tall and thin with defined muscles—but he’s not the young man I remember with filled-out cheeks and a ready smile.

My eyes run over him, noting his bull-legged stance remains. His hair is longer—not the barely there fuzz—and Valore described his beard accurately when he called it shaggy. All his features have a hard edge that he once lacked, and there are sad lines around his eyes. Maybe it’s the war he mentioned, or possibly, something else has altered him.

He has a tank top under a thick jacket and wears heavy pants and big boots. How he stands it in this heat is a mystery. I’m barely wearing anything, and I wish it were less. His voice—just like his appearance—has roughened, almost as if it’s unused or he’s averse to speaking. Maybe it’s the words themselves that have adjusted his tone. Where once they were kind, now they’re troubled and impatient—a lot depending on them.

He may be different, but he’s still sure to attract the same attention as he did the first time we met. He’d never make a good spy—he’s too memorable—and I can understand why he was hesitant to go into town.

“I remember you too,” he says, startling me from my thoughts and guessing them too. “You look just like your sister, and I knew the minute I saw you—even under all that grime—that you're an Endrack."

He says my surname like an accusation, and I rub my cheek. The dirt's no longer on my skin, but I feel dirty about our time together in Ambitus. I can only hope he's forgotten the details of what a fool I made of myself.

"Yes, I remember you. I remember everything that happened that night," he continues, ruining my wish and not looking a bit happy about the memory. "There was a brief time when I believed you were more like your sister than your father. But then you proved me wrong."

I wince, looking away.

"And proved me wrong again. And again."

I shake my head, trying to escape the past. I want him to see I've changed, but how can he? He saw me at my worst, and then I descended even lower. I wouldn't have faith in my transformation, either. He's right to doubt me because I did what he's accused me of. And have I really changed, or did a rock and metal cage merely make it seem so? I think I'm different, but what if I'm not?

"Did you think I wouldn't recognize you?" he asks, and I glance up because the question sounds so sincere.

Truthfully, yes. I'm positive I don't resemble the fresh-faced youth I once was. I barely remember the reflection I used to see in the mirror—chestnut hair that was long and moved like silk, brown eyes bright with mischief and energy, and a pert nose tanned from the Adlumen sun. I don't even have to see myself to know I've lost the splendor of my hair. The fullness of life that once lit my eyes has dimmed to a dull glow. Now, I'm pale and frighteningly thin—malnourished—just brittle bones and meager muscle under dry skin.

Raider takes a step forward, rubbing his jaw. "You left a powerful impression at sixteen—one not easily blotted out with time."

A chill runs up my back as if an icy breeze came my way, though the trees don't move. No, the sensation has nothing to do with nature. I'm not a person who typically feels regret or embarrassment, but I feel both at this moment.

"It likely means little, but all I can do is say I'm sorry."

"Well, it's more than you did back then."

Yeah. But back then, I wasn't sorry.

Raider squints like he can read my thoughts. "Dad doesn't know who you are. Is that right?"

I bite my lip.

"Answer me. Does my dad know?"

I shake my head. "We didn't discuss the details of our lives."

"Your idea."

One quick nod, then, "But I never lied to him."

"Best keep it that way if you value your head staying attached to your shoulders. He may be a kind, grandfatherly man, but if he finds out you're the Endrack sister who tried to kill Evans Dirby, that will change."

I suck in my upper lip, my heart plummeting into my gut. I know it will. It's my worst fear spoken by my worst nightmare. "Why haven't you told him about me?" I ask, feeling defeated.

"Maybe I don't want to break his heart."

I let out a relieved sigh. "Thank you."

Raider's laugh is quick and cruel. "I'm not doing it to help you. The thing is, he'll find out eventually. It's inevitable. I'm just letting you sink your own ship and maybe giving you a chance to leave before it happens. It would be better for us all. I guarantee it will be better for you because no one wants to feel Valore Roil's wrath." He pauses while his words enter my heart, and I feel the devastation of that future day. It will destroy me. "Find somewhere to go, Sharade. Sneak away at night and make a life for yourself, but don't stick around."

My hope and happiness are being stripped away with each sentence, and I pray Raider's done talking as he holds out the circlight for me to take. Forcing the bleakness of my situation from my mind, I take the circlight, squeezing it while I ask hoarsely, "Will my identity be obvious, traveling with one of these?"

Raider's reply is even. "No. People travel with them all the time."

I click it around my neck and spin, looking at everything there is to see. I've missed my sight. It's more poignant now that it's back. This feels like a dream, though a clouded one after our conversation, but I try to focus on the marvel of the moment. I've longed to see again, and reality is much better than waking up disappointed, even if it is accompanied by fresh hurt from Raider's words.

Raider starts walking, and my steps join his rhythm. The trees—yellowed by summer heat—are light green from the lamlight's blue tint, and the white fence bordering our path could use a fresh coat of paint. In the distance, the barn comes into view. Next to the door, a flag hangs, bearing the emblem of the Desert Territory—a rat emerging from the shadows with a diamond necklace in its clutches. The visual evidence of where we are is startling, so I look away at more pleasant things.

"Was it expensive?" I ask, feeling like I should acknowledge the purchase.

"They're not cheap, but we'll travel more quickly."

"Thank you. I'll pay you back someday when I'm able."

Raider shakes his head. "No need. You know how you can pay me back." Yes, I do. He's made it clear. *Don't stick around* —the command echoes in my head. "I may not like or trust you, but I can admit you kept my dad sane. He'd say I owe you more than a circlight."

"But you don't owe me anything, and regardless of how much your dad argues that point, we'll insist that's the case."

Raider laughs at my response—knowing it's precisely what his dad would say—and then, remembering himself, his smile fades, and he says, "Yes. That's the case."

"What are you two doing?" Valore asks when we reach where he and Renegade are sitting. Both are awake, and by the jolly look on my friend's face, he's unaware of the depressing nature of my conversation with Raider.

Valore's different from how I imagined him. While his back is indeed bowed, he has a proud nose and a ready smile that's more significant than Raider's. Father and son share the same black eyes and dark skin, but Valore's hair is gray and knotted at his neck. And when he speaks, I connect his soft voice with his physical features. Knowing him on this new level strikes something in my chest, and I struggle to form words as I remember our days together are numbered.

"Raider brought me a circlight," I scratch out, pointing at the metal and glass around my neck. Those who are light blind can't see the lamlight, so it's not something he'd pick up on automatically.

"So he has!" Valore raises his arms enthusiastically. He's disturbingly thin, and I can see the concern in Raider's expression.

Valore clicks his tongue. "I know what you're thinking," he says with a grin, pointing a thumb at Raider. "There's no way I'm his father."

"No, I wasn't—"

Valore holds up a hand. "Keep in mind, Raider's mother was a stunning woman. Achingly so."

It's true that Valore is rather unassuming compared to

his extraordinary-looking son. Still, I couldn't love him more if he were the most handsome man on the planet. I put my arm around his shoulder and pull him in for a hug. "Then she was a perfect match for you."

I'm tempted to cling to him and not let go, but I force my arms to release him and take a step back. "I guess it's time to go," I say, feeling my throat clog with emotions I don't want detected.

"Not quite yet," Raider says, surprising me. "I got this for you too. And these for you, Dad." He holds out two sets of clothing, passing them off to each of us. I look down at what I'm wearing—black and gross—though sections show the original light tan color.

Valore walks off, disappearing somewhere to change, but I have yet to move.

"It's not what you're used to, but better than what you've got," Raider says, misinterpreting my inaction as disapproval. I don't appreciate him putting words to thoughts that were never mine. Yes, back in Adlumen, I wore exotic clothing, and maybe he finds some amusement in my current dress. But these days, wearing something clean and whole would make me feel like royalty.

Renegade clears his throat uncomfortably, then turns and walks away, disappearing toward where Valore went.

I consider Raider's comment and how he used it to snuff out my joy at being presented with the small kindness. His harshness makes me bristle, and I take an aggressive step forward.

"What I'm used to?" I ask, holding out my hands to show off my rat-eaten, dirt-infused attire. "Not to disabuse you of old notions, but *this* is what I'm used to. I've spent a third of my life in exactly three sets of clothing. I'm not the Adlumen princess you remember, Raider Roil."

To which he tilts his head, saying, "We'll see."

CHAPTER TWELVE

Four Days Free

I share a horse with Renegade, and Valore rides with Raider. We leave Vernam, sticking to overgrown trails off the main path. We see few people and barely speak a word as the men keep alert for signs of trouble.

I've never traveled in the Dark and been able to see my surroundings, so the lamlight is quite fascinating. The distance of vision is limited, but that restriction changes on my fourth day of freedom when we cross into the Coastal Territory, arriving in Sperne. Here, my range of my vision expands to include all other lamlights in the area—the sheer number of people wearing circlights is staggering.

I mention this to Renegade, and he chuckles before telling me, "Made Adlumen quite wealthy—the circlights did —among other things."

The man is very slim—though not prison-thin like Valore and me—with blond hair that needs a wash and blue eyes that need sleep. Renegade rubs his weathered chin with bony fingers as I ask, "What other things?"

"The advanced lenses they manufacture for the light blind, for one, but mostly, the cars."

"Cars?" I ask, and as if summoned, one rolls up alongside us.

"How long were you in that prison?" he asks, his eyes inspecting the side of my face.

"A while," I admit, but I don't give him a number because I'm afraid it will jog his memory. Also, I'm still interested in the car driving away from us. It looks just like the one my sister had while growing up, but hers was the only car I'd ever seen operating. Apparently, that's changed.

It's exciting that Adlumen has prospered. It was my home, and my family led those citizens for generations, so I can't help feeling an abundance of pride that the people are doing so well. "That's great for Adlumen," I tell Renegade.

"It is, but it's also a problem."

"Problem?" I ask, but Raider flashes him a look, and he falls quiet. My mind wanders to Raider's comment about war, and I wonder if that's where Renegade's remark was going.

The horses clomp along the paved roads of Sperne. The crude beat grates on me, unlike the soothing sound their hooves make on dirt. It's late when we arrive at the Hunny Bunny, where we hope to stay the night. It's two floors and made of brick. Inside, the wood floors are scuffed, and the paint is peeling, but the surfaces appear clean. We're exhausted but relieved to be outside of the Desert Territory. The relief is enough to bolster our mood. Even Raider wears a grin while inquiring about lodging. Of course, that could have more to do with the cheerful woman with big brown eyes behind the desk than anything else. While the small establishment only has a dozen rooms, she winks at him while explaining an early departure made a two-room suite available.

Valore stays in the lobby while the rest of us gather our belongings from the horses. My eyes droop, and my limbs feel heavy, but I put my hands out to take the supplies Renegade is unloading. "You okay with taking another?" he asks.

"Sure." As I prepare for more weight, I notice a shadow moving in the narrow space between two brick buildings. The glint of a circlight reflects above bulky shoulders, but it's the thick curve of a nose that startles me.

On reflex, I step back just as Renegade places the last bundle on my batch. Instead of balancing on top, it tumbles down and hits my foot.

"Oh! I'm sorry!" My eyes fly to Renegade.

"No. I should have been more careful."

I try bending to pick it up but can't manage it while holding the other bags. A second later, Raider's at my side with the bundle, but he doesn't stack it on my arms.

"What's wrong?" he asks. I'm upset he noticed my distraction. Still, I can't help glancing into the gap. The man is gone. Was he really there, or was my tired mind making things up? I can't imagine running into someone I know —especially him—in this place after only a few days of freedom. No, the chances are slim—nearly impossible. It was just my imagination.

"It's nothing I want to talk about," I answer, putting my hand out to take the bundle.

Raider tilts his head. "Your evasion is as good as a lie, little prisoner."

"But it's still not a lie. And until you can trust me, it's all you'll get."

"We're at an impasse then because I'll never trust you."

"That's fine," I say, lowering my voice. "Because my only goal is to depart your company as swiftly as possible. Wouldn't want to *stick around* where I'm not wanted."

"We're agreed then," Raider says, walking away.

"Agreed." I look into the gap again. The man's indeed gone. Or maybe he was never there to begin with.

"War," Raider says, and it's like the word rumbles through our connected rooms, bouncing off the walls in a heavy echo. Even in my tired state, it's enough to rally me to the waking world. "That's why we had to get you out of the Desert Territory. It's coming, and when it does, the borders will be secured. I had a small window of opportunity, and I took it."

"Who's the conflict between?" Valore asks, and I nod since it's the very question on my tongue.

"Torquent and Adlumen."

Adlumen! The Torques are at war with my people?

Though, technically, they're not my people. Still, my tongue goes dry, thinking of Adlumen's last conflict with the Torques. My sister almost lost her arm, battling Tyran herself. Dad came back with a limp that took years to settle.

"Allies?" Valore asks.

"The Desert Territory and Hamo aligned with Torquent against Adlumen and the Coastal and Southern Territories."

"So, the usual then," Valore muses, then scolds, "You should have come to me after you resolved this dispute."

"I couldn't risk it. It might have been years before I'd have another chance." Valore nods, clicking his tongue and seeming to understand Raider's reasons for quick action. He might disagree with his son, but the logic is sound. "Besides," Raider continues, "we've got a few weeks before anything starts, and I have a plan for how to stop it."

"How?"

"We'll discuss the details tomorrow. For now, you need some sleep."

Before Valore can argue, Raider helps his dad to his feet. Our lodging is a great room with a table, chair, and couch. Off from it are three doors—two bedrooms and a bathroom. Something marvelous is the electricity—they likely had electric lights in prison, but I received no benefit. Something terrible is the lack of air circulation—the room is a hot box, and a bead of sweat trickles down my back in protest.

Raider guides his dad to one door. "Shar should have this room," Valore says as they walk inside.

"She'll be fine," Raider answers, closing the door to help his dad prepare for bed. I'm glad he's getting him settled.

Valore's exhausted. I feel tired too, but the fatigue is painfully evident on the older man's face.

"I just checked the other room," Renegade says, dropping onto Valore's vacated chair. "There are two small beds."

His meaning is clear. If I'm in a bed, I'll have to share the room with Raider or Renegade.

"You two take the room," I say.

"I'd be fine on the couch," Renegade continues. "But Valore's room is the only single."

I dip my head, scratching my forehead. "I'm fine out here." He doesn't understand the couch is the most luxurious bed I've had in years.

The door clicks, and Raider emerges, lines of worry etching his face. "I wish we could take him straight to the South T. He needs to recuperate." His distraught black eyes land on me. "What were they feeding you in that place?"

"Nothing that builds muscle or hope."

Raider slams his hand on the table. "If I'd only found him sooner."

"We tried," Renegade says, rubbing the bristle on his sun-wrinkled cheeks. "We got him out as soon as we were able."

"It wasn't soon enough!" He stops at the nearest wall and kicks it, startling me and loosening my tongue.

"Look, he's going to be fine," I tell them, irritated when they talk like he's unsuited for the task at hand. "Stuck in that cell, he hasn't walked a long distance in three years. His legs were tired, but he managed. Maintaining his seat on a horse wasn't easy, especially when he hadn't eaten in a few days, but he did it. Now, he's getting rest, shelter, and a steady diet of nutritious food. Give him a week, and he'll jog circles around us. Give him a month, and you'll wish he'd slow down. Just give him some *time*."

Raider stares at me while Renegade chuckles, saying,

"You remind me of a schoolteacher I had at thirteen. I was scared of her but also sort of in love."

"By the light, not you too," Raider complains, running a hand over his scruffy face.

I smile at the man who's old enough to be my dad. "Better watch out, Renegade. I just might be your type." I punch my fluffy pillow a few times to feel it give under the pressure of my fist. "So, bedtime then?" I ask, waiting for them to retreat to their room so I can get comfortable in mine.

"Unfortunately, no. I just told Dad that so he wouldn't fret. We have a few more hours of work ahead of us."

"Oh." I can't help sounding disappointed. I was ready for some shut-eye.

Renegade laughs. "What Raider means is that *we* have things to do."

Raider's brows lift. "Oh, yeah. Nothing she needs to worry about," he says, aiming the comment regarding me at Renegade.

I remember how handsome I thought he was when we met at the reception for the governors. I was so upset about being there—the occasion itself was disgusting to me—but I forgot all of my anger when he walked into the room. I danced with him because I was forced to—the general of Adlumen pushing me into Raider's arms before I could object about dancing with a mole—but the truth was, I didn't want to object. I was instantly enamored of him, and he got an instant opinion of me as well—it wasn't love. I wasn't on his radar in the slightest, so my pride got the better of me, and I pushed and pushed, making sure he'd never forget me. And he hasn't, but my behavior that night wasn't anything I want to be remembered for.

He's still that way—an impressive figure, trying to keep me off his radar—but the situation is different now. He's Valore's son, and while I only want to be supportive, all

Raider wants is to be my enemy. He doesn't understand I no longer want enemies, and it's been a long time since I was in a situation to have one. Part of that is because—after what happened with the governors—I became my own enemy and was full up. The other part is I learned how pleasant life is without negativity draining away everything good.

It's unfair the person I love most in the world should have a son who hates me. I don't want to hate or feel hate directed at me. My only recourse is to move forward despite the hostility.

"Well, what do you have left to do? I can help if needed."

"Renegade's selling the horses and getting food for the trip. I'm getting a car and information from Captain Rhed's guard, so we're prepared for tomorrow's drive." The unspoken message is there's nothing I can do to be helpful.

"But it's so late. Who will be awake for all of that?"

"Sperne's a rather interesting place," Renegade says. "There's always stuff happening, day or night. Not only are there places open for business, but they'll be busy."

"It's well past midnight," I press.

"Yep, and yet, it will still be crowded," Renegade says, hopping to his feet.

The men leave, and I decide to clean up before sleeping. After removing the belted knife from my waist, I head into the bathroom and marvel at the tile, glass, and sleek metal fixtures. There's a mirror too, though I avoid my reflection. Removing my clothes, I wash, rinse, and hang them to dry before entering the shower. Eight years I've gone without this, so I turn up the heat, letting the water beat on my back until my skin goes red. I wash my hair with shampoo. Then, I do it again, creating even more suds because the lather is lovely. I spread it all over, using the complimentary razor for a shave.

By the time I step out, I've shed layers of dead skin and body hair. I dry my short hair and wrap up in a towel to leave the bathroom—with only one set of clothing, mine must dry before dressing again, so the towel must suffice for now.

Reaching the couch, I pull a blanket off the back, gathering it around me. I'm just getting settled when Renegade returns. "How'd it go?" I ask, snuggling into the clean, warm blanket.

"Good. Just back for a quick second before heading out again," he says, disappearing into his room. It's not long—seconds, really—before I go under, barely hearing Renegade exit a minute later.

CHAPTER THIRTEEN

Five Days Free

Opening one eye, I discover Raider at the table, scratching pencil on paper. I struggle to open the other eye, then spot my bare shoulder, and they both pop open. Upon further inspection, the towel has sunk to my waist, but the blanket is under my chin.

I release a relieved breath, and Raider looks up, seeing I'm awake, before returning to his paper. His hair is short—nearly shorn off—and his face is smoothly shaven. It seems the barbers, too, keep late hours in Sperne.

"I was wondering about my sister," I say, sitting up and tucking the blanket under my arms. "Is she married?"

Scratch. Scratch.

"Yes."

I shake my head, a little bewildered. She struggled against marriage so fiercely, and yet, she did it. Though maybe it was the partner she struggled against. Siler was one of her best friends, but she didn't want him as a husband. I always sensed she felt differently about the Coastal soldier turned governor.

"To Evans?" I ask, nervous to speak his name.

Raider nods.

Huh. Chessie married the Lordly Prince.

I almost smile, recalling how much she hated me calling him that, but Raider's pencil—frozen in place—stops my grin. His expression is sour like I have no business even thinking about the two of them. Still, I press on, asking, "Is she happy?"

He looks up. "You can ask her yourself."

Slightly dizzy, I clutch the blanket closer to me. "What do you mean?"

"Tonight, we'll be in Hamo. Then, we have a few more stops that won't interest you before going to Adlumen."

To Adlumen.

I suck in my upper lip, pinching my eyes closed while my head falls back onto the couch. Staring at the darkness behind my eyelids takes the edge off of this discovery and the fear it brings. I learned how to battle my demons in the Dark. Removing my eyesight helps me focus, dispelling the terror trying to grow within me.

But it's not enough, and the panic gets a foothold, taking over. We're going to Adlumen, and that's not a place I should be again. Ever. They might kill me on sight. Exile is assured. Imprisonment is likely, and I can't do that again. I won't survive it a second time. And I can't possibly face my family. Raider's disgust at my presence is only a glimpse of what I'd experience with them. If I can't convince him I've changed—someone who's nearly a stranger—how could I ever hope to convince them?

I'll have to leave the group before we get to Adlumen—there's no way around it. I only have a few days left with Valore and must make good use of our remaining time.

I open my eyes, having nearly forgotten Raider's in the room. He's staring at me, watching me process his news. "I admit, I wanted to see your reaction," he says.

"Did I live up to your expectations?"

"I thought you'd be more vocal. Maybe throw something."

"Sorry."

Raider waves his hand dismissively. "It's fine. You looked sufficiently scared."

"I'm petrified!" I blurt out, then wish I hadn't.

I expect him to gloat over the admission. Instead, he frowns. "I never know when to believe you."

Does he think I'm pretending? That I'm manipulating his emotions? I lift my chin. "I don't care if you believe me or not. I don't care what you think of me, and I'd appreciate it if you'd stay out of my business."

"I'd gladly ignore you and your intentions if you didn't have my dad so tightly invested in your welfare."

"We went through a lot together. He helped me in ways you'd never understand."

"That I believe, but what have you ever done for him?"

"I was his friend."

"I don't know if you're capable of being a friend to anyone but yourself."

"This conversation is pointless. We'll just argue in circles."

"Here's a question for you. If you're as changed as you claim, why are you so desperate to avoid your family?"

"Who says they'd even give me an audience? And if they did, they may want to imprison me again. But regardless of what they'd *do* to me, it's worse considering how they'd *react* to me. I couldn't bear their hatred." It's scary to voice my fears. Life outside of Aunty's Cellar is too real.

"They're not jaded about the world like I am. They'd probably be silly enough to welcome you back with open arms."

"Whereas you're ready to jettison me at the next curve."

"Yes." Raider smiles. "I like that visual. Could we attempt it today on our way to Hamo?"

"Look, you're doing your best to push me away, and it's working. I'm already thinking through my options, and as soon as possible, I'll leave."

"Good. It's best for the little prisoner to find her own way. Best for my father. Best for my mission. And, ultimately, best for you. I know you don't want to go back to Adlumen."

"I'm surprised you're not insisting I go back so they can imprison me again."

"Eight years in that place," Raider says, shaking his head. "I don't trust you or want you around my dad, but I won't campaign to send you back."

"You're too kind," I mock, clutching my chest dramatically. "It's so great hearing your negative opinion of me. Again. But you know what? You know nothing about what I went through since leaving Adlumen, so you can go ahead and shut up about it."

"No problem," Raider says, gripping the edge of his paper. "But whether you visit your home or not, after leaving Adlumen, we travel to my home, and you're not welcome in Caelum."

"I have no interest in going there."

"Good."

"Fine." Hopping to my feet, I grip the blanket around me and shuffle to the bathroom. I squeeze through the door, slamming it shut, but my blanket's in the door, so it makes an unsatisfying thud and reverberates back to hit me. I yank the blanket inside and push it closed with both hands—the towel and blanket dropping to the floor.

My clothes are mostly dry, so I get dressed, simmering in a stew of sadness. I'm so upset about losing my friend, but it's inevitable. He has his family to dote on him. He no longer needs me to make sure he's taken care of.

I wet my hair to take care of the flyaways and turn my head, inspecting the haphazard cut. Then, figuring there's nothing to be done about the mess, I reach for the knob.

Before I can give it a turn, I hear voices.

"You shouldn't have left Caelum," Valore says. "You have duties to your family there."

"I was leaving anyway to take care of this mess between Adlumen and Torquent," Raider answers. "Besides, you're my family, and I also have a duty to you. It's over. Let's not discuss it again."

"Because there's something else you want to discuss," Valore says. "I can see it in your eyes."

"I don't trust her. She's taken you in. You don't see her for what she is?"

"And what is that?"

Curses! Here it is. He's going to tell him about me!

"A fraud."

"Son, I don't understand your attitude. You never used to be this negative. Or unkind."

"Life changes us all."

"You're the best man I know, but you need to work on your compassion."

"It might be best to curb your criticism until our circumstances improve. Give me a few weeks—we'll be back in the South T, and you can lay into me all you want."

"I'm not criticizing. I'm trying to help you see your judgment is clouded."

"Funny. I think it's your judgment that's fuzzy."

"You're only talking this way because you're hurting. Some pain lasts a long time, but you can't let it change who you are. If you step back, you'll see that Shar has much to give."

"You're wrong. She's a criminal, and people like her don't change."

"You act as if you know her better than me. I can

guarantee you don't."

"Give it time, and she'll prove her duplicity. I'm telling you, she has secrets."

"As do I. As do you." Valore pauses. "People are equally capable of changing from bad to good as from good to bad. You've demonstrated the latter proficiently."

"You're saying I'm *bad*?"

Valore sighs. "No. That wasn't the right choice of words. I'm saying you're hardened. You suffered a substantial loss and let it change you fundamentally."

"Name one person who's lost someone they love and not been changed by it," Raider argues.

"Changed. Damaged. Yes. But you've never allowed yourself to heal. You're blocking out every tendency for compassion or forgiveness."

"Dad—"

"Listen, Son. It does us no good to argue. Would you just agree to think about what I've said?"

There's silence on the other side of the door. If I stay here any longer, they'll know I'm listening. I push, and the hinges squeak on their frame. The men look over as I exit. Then Raider ducks his head, but not before I see tears in his eyes.

Valore's facing me, and he looks almost worse than Raider. His eyes are moist, and his face is pale. He still looks tired even after getting nearly twelve hours of sleep.

"I'm done," I say, walking out and leaving the door open.

"Raider says we're going to Hamo," Valore announces. "You ever been there?" I shake my head, looking between them. Valore's still recovering from their argument, and Raider seems content to stay quiet. "Are we meeting with Chadd?" Valore asks, drawing Raider out of his funk with logistical questions.

He must be talking about Chadd Conch—an emissary of

Hamo. I met him several times but was better acquainted with his brother Chett. He was at the governor's reception the day I met Raider and entertained me the second part of the evening after I'd made a fool of myself with Valore's son.

I wish I could forget that night. The frown on Raider's face matches my own, but I soon learn it's for a different reason. "No, Dad. We're not meeting with Chadd," he says. His voice drops an octave as he adds, "Chadd was killed."

Valore's eyes widen. "When did that happen?"

"We learned of it soon after you disappeared. Chett still doesn't know who did it or why."

Valore nods sadly. And while I know he's sad about Chadd's death, it's more than that—a reminder of everything he missed during his three years in prison. I can't imagine what happened during my eight, and I'd just as soon not know.

"I put fresh clothes on the chair," Raider tells his dad, nodding at the pile he prepared. My friend picks them up and passes by me with a smile.

"Looking forward to a shower," Valore says, closing himself inside the bathroom with a click.

Raider waits a few seconds, then asks, "You hear all that?"

"Some of it," I admit, walking to the window. I love being able to see the world again.

"My dad thinks I'm a brute—negative and uncouth," he says, dismayed. They're harsh descriptors, but haven't I thought similar things? I'm sure Valore's never said those exact words—he never would—but I feel bad Raider thinks his dad sees him that way. It's hitting him hard, and I'm opposed to piling more on his current distress.

"I told you before that you don't understand what I went through in prison. Well, Valore doesn't know all you went through in his absence. Don't overthink his words. You're family. You'll figure things out."

Raider tilts his head. "Yet you're sure you won't figure things out with your family."

I rub my chin. "Well, being grouchy and being an attempted murderer are two very different things. One of them is much easier to forgive."

I stretch back the curtain and look down at the street below. A single car bounces along the path, along with a dozen horses and twice that many people. Huddled between the buildings—the same ones as last night—is a person. Is it the same man? He's just out of lamlight range, so I can't be sure, but it feels like I'm being watched. I turn to beckon Raider to the window just as Renegade walks from their room.

"Afternoon, all. Does it look like sun or rain out there?" he asks me.

I glance outside again, unable to see the sky but noting the light reflecting off the shiny surfaces. "Sun," I answer, then look back between the buildings, but the man is gone.

Raider arranges for lunch to be delivered to our room. Thirty minutes later, we have food, and Valore finishes his shower and exits the bathroom, wearing more of Raider's clothing—a button-down shirt and a pair of thick pants he holds gathered in a fist at his waist. "Things have sure changed, Son," Valore says with a laugh, then looks at me. "I used to have a belly."

I hop to my feet, abandoning my food and grabbing a belt belonging to one of the men—it's lying over the back of the couch, and I'm not sure who it belongs to, but Valore obviously needs it the most. Rushing to his side, I help him thread it through the loops. Even the belt's too big, so we tie it in a knot at the front. I laugh when I catch Valore's finger in the loop. "Hey! You're not part of this belt," I exclaim, giggling as I straighten the back of his pants.

Raider watches me from the table. He doesn't trust my motives, but I refuse to stop talking to his dad just because he doesn't like the idea. His suspicions are outdated, and I won't cower to his prejudice. Instead, I give him a bright smile and pull my friend into a big hug. Petty? Yes.

But I refuse to care.

CHAPTER FOURTEEN

Six Days Free

Issues delay our departure an entire day. Car troubles are to blame, and Raider's on edge, slamming doors and swearing whenever the desire strikes. He's even more irritable when Hunny Bunny's suite isn't available a second night, and we end up in a room with one bed. We all insist Valore take it, and the rest of us sleep on the floor, where I discover Renegade's a restless sleeper, kicking throughout the night.

The next afternoon, we're groggy from a sweltering, mostly sleepless night, but the car's functioning properly, so that's an improvement. Raider drives, and Valore rides up front with him. I sit in the back with Renegade. There's a glass windshield, but the sides are open to the outdoors. I reach up to feel the material stretched over the rollbars. It looks like oilskin—the same material those from the Dark use to make their longcoats. When the car moves, the edges of the roof whip slightly, creating a soft rhythm. One thing's for sure—the cover will be more helpful in blocking the sun than protecting us from any August rain. For that reason, it's good it's been a dry season.

We leave Sperne with a list of warnings given to us by members of Captain Rhed's guard, easily recognizable by the circular emblem on their boots, picturing a wave curving over a mountain peak. The road we'll drive borders the Desert Territory the entire way. Therefore, our days of traveling while watching for trouble are far from over.

"What's worse than a rat in your lunch sack?" Renegade asks, sporting a grin as he anticipates revealing the punchline.

“I don’t know,” I say, already laughing. He’s been at this all morning—telling rat jokes that are beyond stupid. Still, their lunacy, combined with Renegade’s enthusiastic delivery, makes them funny.

“Rats hanging from trees bearing weapons.”

I smile but wrinkle my nose in confusion. “I don’t get it.”

“Well, even though we need to watch for natural roadblocks—felled trees and the like—often the danger comes from above,” Renegade yells over the engine’s growl. “If we stop, we’ll get overtaken because they’ll drop on us. But it’s not only Casmo’s rats that pull that trick. We’ll also pass the Cliffs, and the cliff dwellers aren’t opposed to venturing from their buildings, looking for an easy payday.”

“Oh. I see.” I stare past the edge of the oilskin roof at the trees zipping past us.

“Not to worry,” Renegade continues. “Captain Rhed’s guard are stationed randomly in groups of ten, though their locations change daily.”

“Then how do we find them?”

“Uh… today it’s blue flags in the trees. Then we take the first right.”

“That seems rather obvious,” I say.

“Yeah, that’s why they frequently mix things up. Previously, it was pine branch arrows. Before that, rock piles. They use them until compromised. I’m sure it won’t be long.”

“What do we do if we’re caught?” I consider the knife strapped to my waist. I could help in a skirmish, but we’d all be better off if I had a Torquent blade.

“We’ll turn you over to them and pray it’s enough,” Raider yells over his shoulder, grinning while Valore smacks him on the arm.

“Oh, Raider,” I yell back, wearing a smile and crossing my arms superiorly. “We both know you’re the bigger prize.”

◆ ◆ ◆

Renegade insists we remove the oilskin roof for better visibility. We pull over, and he climbs out. Raider follows him, and they get to work untying our roof.

"Who's better at tying knots?" Renegade asks. "A desert rat or a Souther mole?" Raider shakes his head, grinning.

I'm rather surprised by him casually using the term mole, but I ignore that aspect and answer, "Well, the Souther, obviously."

"Huh. That's right. How'd you know?"

I laugh. "Because Casmo's rats will never be superior to your friends in the South T."

Renegade pauses on the knot, then chuckles. "Your deduction skills are stellar, but that's not the punchline."

"Fine, then, tell it to us."

"The Souther mole because moles have opposable thumbs." Renegade leans in. "You know, because you need thumbs to tie knots."

"Huh." I purse my lips and nod. It's not necessarily funny, but it is an interesting fact. Renegade clears his throat in the silence after his humorless joke, then returns to roof removal.

An hour later, we see our first sign of trouble—three desert rats lurking in the bushes—though they don't bother us. Still, it has my companions reevaluating our defense.

"Slow down a sec," Renegade yells to Raider. The engine's roar halves, and the wind dies down. A second later, Renegade digs in our supplies before flipping back around with a sword in hand. Then he gets situated, perched on the seat so his feet are where his backside should be, sitting tall with the wind tossing his long hair. He rests his elbows on the rollbar but holds the weapon vertically so it's in plain sight.

Within the lamlight's limited reach, the leafy tree branches create a dark shadow, blocking out the sunlight, and the dust rising off the road impersonates a heavy mist lurking in the trees. With that backdrop, Renegade creates an intimidating picture, even with his thin frame. In no time, his hair's knotted on the sides. Tonight, he'll be painfully combing it out or shaving it off. Either way, I'm grateful for his sacrifice because we travel the border road without any fuss, having no trouble with rats or cliff dwellers.

We reach the outskirts of Tribus, where the border road meets the Noctis Trail—the delimit trading route between Adlumen and Hamo. It supported trade between the two light bubbles for many years before the lamlight. From Tribus, traveling the Noctis Trail for six days on horseback would take us to Subsolanus within Adlumen's borders. After eight years in prison, it's strange to have such precise knowledge of my location.

"A desert rat and a Souther mole were on the Noctis Trail. One traveled west to Subsolanus. One traveled east to Tribus. Which one reached their destination first?"

"The Souther," I say, sticking with my belief that, in Renegade's jokes, any bad trait or lack of skill belongs to the rats.

"Right you are. The rat arrived days later, but infinitely richer, having robbed every trader he passed on his way."

I snort, rolling my eyes while Renegade plops onto the seat next to me, rummaging in the back to store away his sword.

Much has changed since the discovery of lamlight. I noticed it during my brief time in Sperne, but it's more noticeable the closer we get to Hamo. Cars looking like Chessie's CJ are everywhere with lamlight headlights guiding the way.

While technically in the Coastal Territory, Tribus is a diverse place, butting up against the Hamo light bubble, Casmo's Desert Territory, and the South T. My first impression is that it's a boisterous town full of mistrust and confused energy. They fly no emblems here, where so many cultures converge. Where Sperne felt organized in its complexity, Tribus is a whirlwind.

The interaction between the light blind and those with light sight is seamless. The light blind wear the superior Adlumen lenses, preparing to enter the Hamo light bubble. Those with light sight wear circlights around their necks and conduct business without issue. It's truly a new world!

The dirt roads transition to pavement the closer we get to the heart of Tribus, and the roadways are lined with lamlight posts to guide our way. We arrive at The Woven Branch, where we'll spend the night, and I climb from the back of the car, twisting at my waist to stretch my muscles. It's good to be on solid ground, not bouncing down primitive roads at high speed.

"A desert rat, a cliff dweller, and a Souther mole are in a fight," Renegade says, hopping out of the car to stand beside me. "One's without an eye, one's without an arm, and one's without a weapon. Who wins?"

I shake my head, trying to figure out how any of that is supposed to give me a clue as to the outcome. "I truly have no idea."

Renegade chuckles. "The stealthy Coastal guard member hiding in the bushes, of course." Then he grabs a few bags, loading them into my arms before getting a few for himself.

The Woven Branch has four floors with perfectly spaced windows facing the road on every level. The building is large —maybe ten times the size of Hunny Bunny—and we ascend a dozen steps to the black double doors. The slat siding is crisp white, but the door and window frames are deep red.

We enter, scraping our feet on thick rugs before reaching the main desk where Raider arranges our lodging. Then he pens a message for Arrick—the leader of Hamo—requesting an audience. We anticipate a response in the morning.

Our hotel, we quickly discover, has an active nightlife—people feeding their appetites in the restaurants and betting on chance in the game houses. A thrill runs up my back at the prospect of exploring their offerings, but Raider's in a mood, insisting we stay in. I bite my tongue and don't complain, though I cast him an aggrieved glance, unable to help myself.

As usual, he ignores the look. And me.

CHAPTER FIFTEEN

Seven Days Free

On my seventh day of freedom from Aunty's Cellar, the men don their lenses, and we enter the Hamo light bubble, where I see actual sunshine for the first time in eight years. The colors are brilliant, and the sky reminds me of a bottle back in Ambitus—a milky-blue one Chessie gave me on my thirteenth birthday that became my favorite.

We're destined for Brevis—the capital city of Hamo—and Raider insists, even though they're militarily unaligned, that we're safe to cross their land. Hamo and the Southern Territory normally have a good relationship—indeed, Arrick and Raider are old friends—but Tyran pressured Arrick to side with her, putting the alliances in turmoil. And I guess that's what Raider's here to fix. So, while I continue to form my opinion of him and his actions, I try to allow for the stress he's under.

Yesterday's pace was grueling, so I'm glad the drive to Brevis is only thirty minutes. Unfortunately, our travel time is lengthened the moment we enter the light. "Pull into that warehouse," a member of Hamo's border security says, pointing us to a large structure off the roadway. Raider turns the wheel and goes where instructed. Inside, there's a giant flag bearing Hamo's emblem—a gold, upside-down crown on a gray background. The symbol's always intrigued me as I've never learned its meaning.

Their inspection starts by patting us down, and then they move to the car. For over an hour, they search everything, looking for weapons or other items deemed harmful. They confiscate Raider's knife collection—

including the one that's decorated my hip—plus Renegade's big sword. Sitting on a bench, I watch them empty the entire vehicle, exploring every hiding place—surprised they don't deflate the tires and look inside those. When we're declared a non-threat, they allow us to leave, and thankfully, we're not detained again.

Arriving in the governing seat of Hamo, Arrick greets us at the door of his modest but stately home. Modest in that it's smaller than Hunny Bunny in Sperne—not a soaring edifice like Fiducha in Adlumen—and stately because the outside is a pristine white stone with regal columns at least forty feet high.

Arrick is much like his home—sharply dressed and trimmed with strict stature and politeness. I'd guess he's in his early forties, though the energy in his movements and the confidence in his step make him seem more youthful.

"This is an interesting group," Arrick says, giving us a once-over, though he looks twice at my hair. Besides being windblown, the cut is so uneven it's worth extra attention. I need to fix it, but it's hardly been a priority.

"Valore! Is it truly you?" Arrick advances on my friend, greeting him with a hearty handshake.

"It is. I'm feeling more myself each day." Valore still has the insufficient strength of a recovering prisoner, but his pallor has improved. Raider's cleaned him up a lot—made sure he shaved—though dressing him in fit clothes would improve his appearance even more.

Arrick continues, "You always said you'd find him, Raider, and you did." Raider shakes Arrick's hand, nodding his agreement while wearing a frown. He's bothered he didn't liberate Valore sooner, and it's one thing I admire about Raider—the search took time, but he didn't give up.

"Renegade," Arrick says, nodding at the man with a mass of tangled hair who's hovering in the background. Renegade returns Arrick's gesture but, like Raider, says nothing.

"And who's this?" Arrick appraises me with blue eyes bordering on arrogant. "I'm guessing a neglected house servant you rescued or the victim of a lice infestation."

My nose crinkles, and I take a step back.

"She's my friend and guest," Valore says in a brutal tone.

Arrick raises a brow and follows my step, closing in on me. "I think there's a pretty woman under there."

"Yes, and she's a pretty woman with a brain, so she knows to stay clear from the likes of you," Raider says, surprising me with every word. Then he nudges Arrick away from me.

Arrick laughs, putting up his hands. "I see how it is."

I huff at the absurd assumption, and the two men turn in unison, watching me chew my upper lip. Arrick smiles. Raider frowns.

"You have light sight like me," Arrick says. "So, I can't help but wonder what you're doing with this group. Where are you from?"

Raider insists I look like my sister, but apparently, I'm not that much like her. Or maybe Arrick hasn't seen her in a while. Regardless, I'm not prepared to answer, but I'm saved when Valore steps in, diverting the question with ease. "As I said, she's a family friend—eager to reunite with my daughter, Imily. They were inseparable as children."

"Really?" Arrick looks again at my chopped hair, skinny arms, and gaunt face.

"You know that Southers, more than the other Dark territories, mix with those living in light bubbles."

"If you say so." Arrick pulls up a shoulder, unconvinced, especially since Valore maneuvered the conversation, so I didn't reveal my origin—an origin my friend doesn't even know. But Arrick's attention moves from me to our group's leader. "Raider, let's talk. The rest of you head up the stairs, and my people will get you cleaned up for dinner." He points at me and looks at his servants. "Give her some extra attention." I don't know whether to be pleased or insulted, so I bite my lip lest the wrong response escape.

"Arrick, my dad could also use a physician," Raider says, lifting Valore's sleeve and showing him a welt there. "Do you have anything that needs a doctor's attention?"

It takes a moment to realize Raider's addressing me. I barely hear him because my eyes are so focused on the painful mark on Valore's skin. "Shar?" Raider presses, and I quickly shake my head, turning away to follow my guide. The truth is, I have similar marks, but I'm not ready to admit it. Besides, they're disappearing as my diet improves and movement increases.

While the outside of Arrick's home is white, the inside is filled with color—wooden floors stained a deep brown with navy runners and wallpapered walls in bold patterns. The entryway has thick stripes in gold and gray. The stairwell has a blue and silver diamond pattern. And my guest room has giant white flowers on a champagne background.

They direct me to a shower with a green stone surround and a matching countertop. I'm left to scrub and wash before wrapping in a thick black robe. Then, Arrick's staff shines me up suitably, even trimming my hair—with proper scissors this time.

I dress amid the luxurious surroundings where I'll sleep tonight. The room contains an oversized bed with a cream bedcover, a bed frame with six-inch bedposts nearly touching the ceiling, a sitting area with two plush chairs and fabric to match the wallpaper, and a small reading table. I hold the bedpost for balance as they zip the back of my dress before they help me into a pair of black shoes, securing them with a buckle across the top of my feet.

Arriving for dinner, I feel refreshed—scented and hydrated with lotion—wearing a cute butterfly clip in my hair. A simple beaded necklace hangs at my throat with a matching bracelet around my wrist, and I'm wearing eye makeup. My dress is a lovely foamy green. It's not overdone or stuffy but light and pretty. I've never felt this happy in any clothing I've worn my entire life.

Arrick meets me at the dining-room door wearing a black suit and white dress shirt, greeting me with pandering words regarding my appearance. I don't know why he's putting so much effort into the task. I'm not anyone worth impressing, and ultimately, he's just making me uncomfortable, gushing about my brown eyes.

I recall Dad's opinion of Arrick—a reluctant leader with a cautious approach. Not bold or revolutionary. I used to think that was a bad thing, but now I'm not sure. He aims to avoid creating enemies. How is that wrong? I don't believe it is. But his reluctance and caution make the current situation intriguing. Tyran forced him to choose a side—which must vex him—and although he declared for her, he still hobnobs with Raider. I wonder if he realizes the luxury won't last. If Tyran doesn't demand an end to his waffling, the first South T death at the hand of one of Arrick's people will do the job.

"Would you like to see my knives?" he asks, already taking my arm and leading me to his wall display—handcrafted cases with polished wood and gleaming glass—while pointing out the virtues of each blade.

"Valore collects knives too," Raider says, appearing on my right, dressed in a deep green suit coat and pants with a pale yellow button-down shirt and a black necktie. His shoes are black too, and a brief glimpse of his belt shows the same.

"I know," I say, and then, because the memory of our time in Aunty's Celler comes so vividly to my mind, I add, "I collect bottles."

"Ah." Raider nods. "I wondered what that souvenir was about." I crane my head to watch him retreat across the soft red carpet, wondering why he bothered to stop in the first place.

Minutes later, we sit to dine. I run my finger along the precisely placed plate, sparkling under gleaming chandeliers. It's been a long time since I had to employ table manners. I'm grateful I still remember them, though being polished like crystal helps maintain the appearance of deportment.

Renegade sits across from me, and I barely recognize the man. He's wearing a dinner jacket sans necktie, and the top two buttons of his dress shirt are unbuttoned. But the drastic measures he took to fix his hair are most startling. Instead of hanging a dozen inches down his back, the strands are cut close to his head—maybe an inch on top.

"Your kin might recognize you again," Arrick says with a laugh, to which Renegade replies, "Sure. If I had kin who cared to put forth the effort." Arrick's smile wanes while Renegade forks his chicken, lifting the entire breast to take a large bite, a bit of juice running down his chin and neck.

We finish the first course as Chett Conch arrives, looking remarkably changed from the seventeen-year-old I met when I was sixteen.

At twenty-five, he's a large man. Not as big as Ronen, one of Captain Rhed's sons, but thick and muscly in his own right. His suit with the padded shoulders makes him look even larger. I would hate to go against him in a fight, but when he takes the empty seat next to me, I admit his large presence is comforting.

Raider greets him like a long-lost friend, and the two men fall into easy chatter, but it's not until the main course arrives that the real conversation begins.

"My people depend on me to keep the peace," Arrick says. "I must preserve relations with Torquent."

"By declaring war on Adlumen and the Southern and Coastal Territories?" Raider asks. His question carries his passion, but he's not pushy. Not yet.

"Breaking my alliance with Tyran won't get any of us what we want. Hamo is nearest to Torquent, and we must stay in good standing with them to survive out here."

"Technically, we're the nearest to Torquent since the Southern Territory surrounds it," Raider corrects.

"I was speaking of light bubbles," Arrick clarifies with a frown.

"And we've done plenty to keep the peace with Tyran, *lending* her large chunks of our land, though I don't know how we'll ever get it back. Still, it's allowed the expansion that has appeased her thus far."

"You've done your part, but we've also got Casmo to contend with."

"As do we. You know the Coastal Territory has history with the rats."

"Yes. The two Dark territories understand what I'm facing, but what about Adlumen? Your third partner seems far removed from the encroaching danger."

"Adlumen's no stranger to conflict with Torquent."

"At one time, but not since the governors came into their positions."

"Well, they're experiencing the conflict full-force now since Tyran wants to start a war to seize their land. That the South T has already given up land for Torques to live in using lamlight isn't enough."

"They *are* overcrowded," Arrick says, placing his fork on the edge of the plate—tines down.

"And have been for some time. Does that mean you invade another person's home and kill their citizens? Come on, Arrick, that's not right."

"I've discussed that point with her, Raider. She's determined."

"So, you're going to send your people to kill mine?" Raider asks, then points at the wall. "You're going to get your pretty knives dirty, using them against us." Arrick releases a long breath but says nothing in his defense, so Raider continues, "Why not remain neutral?"

"I've tried. Tyran won't allow it."

"Arrick, I feel quite desperate to resolve this without bloodshed."

"I feel the same desperation. I implored Tyran to find another way, and she mentioned a few things—a list of demands—that, if met, might induce her to withdraw her war declaration, but I doubt they'll be acceptable to you."

"Well, what are they? Let's hear it," Raider says, rolling his hand impatiently.

"She wants Adlumen's beacon."

"What beacon?" Renegade asks. "Adlumen's not even on the water."

"Not that kind of beacon," Raider says morosely.

I grab the end of my short hair, twisting a lock in my fingers. Beacons were a myth in my youth, and then I learned there was a real one in Adlumen—a person who can see in both light bubbles and Dark territories without the aid of lenses or lamlight.

Tesha of Harwell.

I wrinkle my nose, knowing what Tyran does to beacons—experimenting on them until their eyes turn white, yet never cracking the code of their gifted sight.

"How did Tyran learn about the beacon?" Raider asks with an appropriate tone of concern. "That's a closely guarded secret. I'd guess my dad doesn't even know there's one in Adlumen." Valore shakes his head, aligning with

Raider's assumption.

"I don't know, but Tyran is sure in her knowledge."

I bite my lip, knowing exactly where Tyran got her information, but only one person in this room knows my history in Adlumen, so it isn't the time to reveal what I know —not with this audience.

"What else?"

Arrick clears his throat. "She wants Periculum."

Periculum is a border town in the southeast of Adlumen. Where Subsolanus is the start of the old Noctis Trail connecting Adlumen and Hamo, Periculum is the starting point in Adlumen of the Talpa Trail leading to Torquent.

"A city inside the Adlumen light bubble?" Raider asks, narrowing his eyes behind his lenses.

"Yes."

"None of the light bubbles have divided their land to be governed by separate groups. It's a complicated prospect."

"She feels the lamlight discovery uncomplicates it. Using lamlight along the Talpa Trail connects Periculum and Torquent, making governing the two areas easier."

"What's easier, *using lamlight*, is fostering the expansion land already granted to her," Raider says, pounding the table with his fist. Arrick jolts in his chair when the silver rattles, and Raider leans toward him. "Periculum is a preparatory move. If the governors were stupid enough to allow it, she'd move in and plot her takeover from *within* Adlumen's borders. Does she think we're that dense?"

"I said you'd find her list unacceptable," Arrick says, rubbing his brows with his thumbs.

"If it's land in a light bubble she wants, why not turn to her ally?" Raider asks, tapping his index finger on the table with his eyes locked on Arrick. "You're keen to support her. Even prepared for your people to take up arms against nonaggressors in a war of her making. If you're really for peace, why not offer her some of *your* land? Donum's a nice city, and it's closer than Periculum."

Arrick moves his mouth, his lips and tongue working together dryly. "She doesn't want my land," he finally says—a quiet response, filled with distress and a bit of shame.

"Ah. So, her requirements aren't based on the logical needs of her people. They're of a personal nature. She wants to harm Adlumen." Raider's chin bounces up and down as he recaps the situation. "Is that the end of her list, or are there more insulting things she's greedy for?" Raider asks, lifting his glass for a drink but pausing for Arrick's answer.

"Just one more thing."

"And?" Raider prods.

"Well... it's you."

"I'm aware I owe her a visit," Raider says with a wry grin before taking his drink.

Curses! How does the man remain so calm? Maybe Tyran wants to hack him in two?

"You can bet it's more than a visit she's after," Valore says, his eyes bouncing between Arrick and Raider. "Tyran always has two aspects to one move."

"Three aspects. Maybe four," Raider grumbles.

"My source says it's just a visit," Arrick says, cutting into his meat, watching the knife slowly saw the cooked flesh while averting his eyes from Raider.

"What source?" Raider asks, resting his knife on the plate.

Arrick's voice lowers. "I have a trusted person monitoring the situation."

"You have a spy in Tyran's court," Raider says, raising his brows—shocked and impressed in one go.

I remember dreaming of being a spy, thinking it would be thrilling to act duplicitous. Of course, it was easy for such things to hold great appeal when safely behind the walls of Ambitus. Now, I'd rather conduct my business in the open, leaving double-dealing adventures to others.

"I wouldn't label them a spy. Rather, a reliable person looking out for everyone's interests." Arrick's eyes flit among the dinner attendees. "But your arrival in Hamo today is perfect. Indeed, Tyran reached out, insisting I summon you immediately, so everything's well-timed to meet her demand."

"You were to summon me, then ferry me off to her? It appears you're solidly in her pocket," Raider says with a disappointed sigh while Arrick clears his throat uncomfortably. "I'll go to her, but not yet." Raider lowers his drink to the table. "There are things to do first."

Arrick shakes his head. "Tyran doesn't like to be kept waiting."

"Well, it's in everyone's best interest that she wait." Raider smiles. "Her interests included." Folding his arms, he drops his elbows onto the table with a thud—a clean slap in the face of etiquette—before leaning sternly toward Arrick. "I have a solid deterrent—something to really make Tyran pause before launching this war. But I need to know if you'll step up and support me in getting this in front of her, providing a better resolution to all our problems. Are you willing to see my idea for ending this madness?"

"See it?"

"Yes. It requires traveling south for a couple of days."

"You're joking. I can't leave Hamo. Not now."

"I can promise you, Arrick, this is more important than anything you have going on in Hamo. We need to prevent a war."

"I don't know." Arrick shakes his head, looking around the table. "I mean, I hate the idea of war, but I don't believe time away from Hamo or anything we present to Tyran will make a difference."

"We've been friends a long time. Based on the years we've invested in each other, I'm asking you for this indulgence."

"If my son says it's important, you know it is," Valore adds. It's strange seeing him in this setting. He has a naturally stalwart demeanor. Combined with his leadership and guidance skills, it's obvious how his talents were underutilized while consoling a young girl in prison. He manages the pleasant dinner conversation and diplomatic debates with equal proficiency. In our Dark prison, I recognized many of Valore's inherent skills, but it's interesting seeing them put into action.

Valore's comment and delivery are quite persuasive, but Arrick turns to me. "What do you think?"

"What?" I lower my fork and grip the napkin on my lap.

"I'm weeks away from going to war with this guy, and he wants to whisk me away to an unknown destination for show and tell. Do I trust him?"

My eyes flash between Arrick and the other dinner participants, though I avoid Raider's gaze as I answer, "I don't know that my opinion matters much."

"It does to me." His intense gaze doesn't leave my face. "Would *you* trust him?"

Curses! How did I get dragged into this?

"Would I trust him?" I repeat while Raider stares at me with disapproving eyes. "Well, you've likely picked up that he has strong objections toward me." For many reasons, though, I'll leave out the main one. "I hinder his speed, and I'm unnecessary for accomplishing his goals. He makes his feelings clear at every opportunity while still effectively leading his team and keeping his focus on preventing your war. Amid the stress and irritation, he has yet to jettison me from a moving vehicle." I grin, remembering our conversation, then look down at the napkin twisted in my hands. "So, I guess I trust him enough for my needs."

Arrick laughs. "That's your endorsement?"

"It's truthful and accurate. I'd take that any day over gushing propaganda." I drop the napkin and pull on the hem of my green dress. All the men watch me, processing my answer and making me nervous, so I continue to prattle. "In the interest of truth and accuracy, I can't help but wonder if your friendship with Tyran is a good thing. I've never met her, but she seems an extremely untrustworthy person. She may be less of a friend than you expect." There's a pause, and then they're all laughing—Raider included.

"Allies. We're only allies," Arrick bellows. "Tyran has no friends. She probably doesn't even allow the word in her vocabulary. She lets no one close."

"If no one has a sincere connection with her," I begin, looking between them, "and if her ruthless behavior is so well established... well, it seems like she'd be easy to put down."

Chett turns to me. "It would seem that way, except her people love her. She's relentless in her pursuits and has made them rich. Additionally, she treats them well. It's the rest of us that have cause for worry."

"She sounds unpredictable," I surmise.

"She is. And calculating," Valore says, lifting his drink and inspecting the sparkle of the crystal.

"Impossible to read," Arrick adds.

"All reasons you remain at her side," Raider says.

"She's done nothing to betray our trust," Arrick insists.

"Except require you to declare war on another of your

allies."

"I still have hope."

Raider lets out a weary breath. "As do I. Which is why I need you to come with me tomorrow."

"I'll give you my answer in the morning," Arrick says, standing without warning. He says a brief goodbye, exiting the dining room and leaving us feeling unbalanced from his abrupt departure, which felt like an escape.

The rest of us slowly disperse, and I wind my way through the hallways to my bedroom. I'm pleased to find a pair of pajamas laid across the bed. I wash my face and put them on, then climb onto the thick mattress and sink into the freshly laundered sheets, rubbing my cheek across the smooth surface of my pillow. The sheer luxury makes me emotional, so I'm glad when there's a knock on the door.

I discover one of the house staff on the other side. "For you," the young girl says, passing off a folded paper before disappearing down the hallway. Flipping it open, I run my eyes over the words.

You pack extremely light for someone spending a few weeks with an old friend, but enough said on that subject.

There's a suitcase in the closet, a couple of outfits, some shoes, and a few sundries. Take them with you, along with the green dress and the pajamas. Hopefully, they'll remind you of your time here in Hamo and that you're always welcome as my guest.

I'd be delighted if you'd join me for breakfast—nine o'clock. The staff will direct you where to go.

It's signed by Arrick in a loopy scrawl.

I tap the paper against my lip, thinking about his kindness, and then an idea strikes, making it nearly impossible to fall asleep.

CHAPTER SIXTEEN

Eight Days Free

My life in Aunty's Cellar follows me into my dreams. I'm in the Dark without my vision, and the desert heat surrounds me. I hear the stomp of Guard F's footsteps and the uneasy purr of Squatty's snore. My throat is dry, and when I cough, it feels like sand is in my lungs. I can't stop the hacking that ensues.

Uncontrolled coughing wakes me while the glow of hallway lights beneath the door brings feelings of relief that the return to my cage wasn't reality. Continuing to clear my throat, I run my dry tongue over my lips. The thirst from my dream is real, and memories surface of all the times I woke in Aunty's Cellar to find an empty bottle.

My bottle!

My eyes flash wide, and I jump from bed, turning on the light. I can't believe this is the first I've thought about viewing my treasures, but now that it's in my head, I'm beyond excited.

I search for my little packet of belongings and pull out my old bottle, looking at it for the first time. The glass has no shine, and it's a ruddy brown color. "Hmm. Not very pretty, are you?" I muse.

Next, I remove Squatty's necklace—a balled-up mess—bringing it close to observe the details. The chain is a common link in yellow gold. The charm is the same yellow gold. The back is solid with a hammered pattern—each divot black with years of prison experiences pressed into the grooves. The front is covered in layers of old dirt, thick like paste, so it's impossible to determine what it looks like.

I make a quick decision. I have no interest in more dreams, and my pajamas aren't inappropriate for wandering the halls at night, so with my bottle and necklace, I leave my room. Ten minutes later—after finding a helpful house staff member—I'm at a kitchen sink with a small brush, gently scrubbing years of pain from Squatty's necklace. It's well worth the effort.

The front is intricate, picturing a sunrise rising over thunderclouds with a clap of lightning striking back at the daylight. Below the clouds are a turbulent blue ocean and a sandy beach.

The sun is a bright orange jewel—previously, a dirty bump on the square charm—and I thought the other colors were enamel, but on closer inspection, they look like gem pieces, meticulously placed like a mosaic.

I dry the necklace and clean up my brown bottle, even using the brush on it, but there's little improvement. Miniscule scratches and dings mar the surface, giving it a mottled, dusty appearance. There's still no shine when I dry it, but at least it's clean. I run my fingers over the surface, closing my eyes to reacquaint myself with the feel of it. I'm so knowledgeable about this one item in my life. I wish I knew other things so well.

After hanging the necklace around my neck, I tuck the bottle into the crook of my elbow before heading back to my room, pleased I remember the way through the dimly lit halls. Well, mostly. I reach one point and turn left instead of right, but it doesn't take long to realize my error. I spin to reverse my path and, simultaneously, hear a set of male voices—those of Arrick and Chett.

I glance down at my pajamas and the bottle in my hand. My hand goes to my head—my hair in disarray. I left my room unconcerned about my appearance, but I don't want to be seen by those two in my present state. And I don't want to explain the bottle or the necklace. I take a dozen steps—keeping my footfalls light—and tuck behind a heavy piece of furniture set into a cove, where I'll wait for them to pass.

It only takes a second before I wish I'd let myself be seen and weathered the embarrassment.

"It's eating me up, Arrick," Chett says. "Every time I see Raider, I want to tell him, but the prospect is terrifying."

"Your fear is moot because you can't tell him. It's the one thing he couldn't forgive."

"You think I don't know that?"

"Look, Chett, I like Raider too, but the circumstances are tricky, and your friendship is not the priority. You're an emissary of Hamo. You need to keep perspective."

"I'm trying. And my position is the only reason I haven't spoken to him."

"Good. Keep it that way." Arrick's voice is light, but I hear the command in his tone. He's been friendly so far, but it's clear he's not someone to cross.

Curses! I shouldn't be here.

Sucking in my upper lip, I wait for discovery. I tuck tighter into the corner, closing my eyes and holding my breath, but they turn before reaching me, walking back the way they came—their voices fading as they go.

I wait five minutes before emerging, hurrying to my room and latching the door before putting away my belongings. It's with some guilt I quickly dress in the casual pants and shirt Arrick arranged for me to have. I shouldn't be listening to his private conversations when he's been so good to me—it wasn't intentional, but still—and now there's nothing to do except be epically curious about what they're keeping from Raider. Well, be epically curious and one other thing.

Slipping back into the hallway, I consider the doors in

this wing. Renegade's in the room next to mine, but across from us, one room is Valore's, and the other is Raider's. I don't remember whose is whose.

Tiptoeing to the door across from Renegade, I touch the handle, then think better of it. Raider would stay close to those he doesn't trust. He'd keep his dad away from danger. So, I make my way to the second door—the one across from my room—and without knocking, I turn the handle and enter.

"Raider," I whisper, but barely a breath of noise comes out. I let the door fall shut—not loud enough to alert the surrounding rooms, but hopefully sufficient for him to hear.

There's a rustling sound, and a shadow emerges from the bed before I hear, "What in the light are you doing?"

I sigh, knowing I chose correctly.

"Oh, hey," I say like it's no big deal I'm here. "Can we talk real quick?"

"What could the little prisoner want now?" he asks, rubbing a hand over his short hair before flicking on the light by his bed. "It's three in the morning."

"Yeah." I move across the room, whisper-quiet, and find the chair identical to the one in my room, only with a teal paisley pattern that matches the wallpaper. I go to sit down but move Raider's shoes before doing so.

"Can't this wait?"

"No. I was an accidental spy!" I tell him, unable to keep the thrill from my voice.

"Accidental?" Raider lifts the edge of his left lens to rub his eye, which is pressed tightly closed. "What?"

"Yes! I didn't mean to do it... it just happened." I repeat the entire conversation between Arrick and Chett. It's easy since I heard it less than ten minutes ago. Still, I'm proud of how well I manage the details. Maybe this is why I craved this activity in my youth. It's sort of a rush.

I await my congratulations, which are sure to come, but Raider only says, "That's why you woke me up?"

I cross my legs and fall back in the chair. "Doesn't it sound like they're up to something?"

"Obviously. Arrick leads Hamo, and Chett's his right hand. Being 'up to something' is a given."

"But they're keeping secrets from you!"

"Again. Given." Raider yawns.

"You are such a pain! I'm looking out for you, and you're acting so... blasé."

"If you want excitement, keep speaking at that volume. Dad will be interested, that's for sure."

He's so annoying. I tuck my back into the corner of the chair and throw my legs over the arm. "Have you considered Diggs was the one who told about Tesha being a beacon?"

Raider scowls. "You know about her?"

"Yes. Chessie told my dad, and he told me. And Diggs." I run my finger over the edge of the chair. "I told no one and can't speak for who else my dad might have informed, but was Diggs ever caught?"

"He's not been seen in eight years. Many think he's dead."

I think of my uncle and his oversized nose. Maybe he is dead and merely a ghost haunting my mind. Or maybe he's very much alive.

"Why didn't you mention this when we were talking about it at dinner?"

"You're the only one who knows I'm an Endrack."

"Are you sure of that?"

"Unless you told someone. Did you?"

Raider glares at me with black eyes through his lenses. "It bothers me you're still hiding your identity. It's deceptive and unkind to those helping in good faith."

So, everyone except him.

"I'm just not ready," I say in a small voice. I don't know if I'll ever be ready, but I'm clearly overdue for getting it done. This can't go on much longer.

While I sit, processing my fears of discovery, Raider stews in his own frustrations, and his feelings come out in one terse statement. "You can leave now."

I stare at the shadows cast by the small lamp and stay silent, trying to figure out where I went wrong with him this time. Even when I attempt to do something good, he gets angry. I just can't win. I'm tempted to pick up his shoe —maybe both—and hit him in the head. How he treats me brings up past feelings—old defense mechanisms—I don't want to feel again. It's best to do as he asks.

My feet fall to the floor with a thud. "I'm not the same person you met at sixteen, but I'm done trying to prove it to you. You obviously don't appreciate the effort. So, consider me out of your hair. I'll make sure not to *stick around.* Not even another day." I surge to my feet. "Your albatross is flying away."

"Sharade, wait," Raider says with a sigh, but I ignore him, shutting his door more quietly than my indignation craves. Returning to my room, one thought permeates my head after what I've just declared—cutting ties without securing new ones is the surest way to plummet to one's death.

I shower—for the pure joy of it—then sit in my room, making a plan. When I'm done considering my options, it's hours later. At five to nine, I leave my room to try my luck at a new life outside of prison. And there's no doubt it will take some luck.

The house staff directs me to Arrick's breakfast room. It faces the sunrise and is decorated in purple and gold—a very cheery place. I'm early, but he's already there and freshly showered—his black hair is short around the bottom and longer on top, with the wet strands clumping. "Apple?" he asks, holding up a shiny piece of fruit and passing it to me.

I remember the last time I held an apple in my hand. I was sure I'd be in prison forever—that there was nothing left to look forward to—and I accepted my fate. Now, I'm in the world again but still imprisoned by my past. Once again, it's time I accept my life for what it is—to stop hiding from it. And so, I take the apple.

He gives me a plate and dishes out food, piling it high. "Are you trying to tell me something?" I ask, squeezing the tight skin at my waist, but he just grins. I expect the others to file in at any moment, but it's ten minutes past nine when we sit at the round table with the glass top, and we're still the only ones in the room.

"I've never met Valore's daughter," I say to start our conversation. I figure this won't work unless he knows the truth.

"You didn't seem like much of a family friend. To Valore, maybe, but not Raider, which cast doubt on your devoted friendship to Imily."

I nod and bite into my bacon. The sensation from strong food flavors still startles me, and I delightfully lick the fat off my lip.

"My name is Sharade Endrack."

"I wondered. When I saw you in that green dress, you made a remarkable resemblance to your sister."

Huh. I guess Raider's observation holds water. I take the revelation at surface value and move on. "So, you know about my past?"

"You were part of Keine Endrack's plan to overthrow the governors and tried to kill Evans Dirby. You went to prison for your crimes?"

"Yeah." I put down my fork, rubbing my forehead and the headache forming there. "I promise you I've changed."

"You have. No offense to your sister, but I believe you've outdone her in your appeal."

I chuckle. "You're kind, Arrick, but I'm not interested in beauty contests. I was speaking of core convictions."

"I know," he says with an amused nod before tasting his eggs.

"I have pressing things to figure out, and I need to know if you can overlook my past mistakes."

Arrick watches me over the top of his fork. "Truthfully, it's hard to imagine you're the girl who did those things."

"For me too, though it took years for the change to happen."

"What made the difference?"

"Valore," I answer without pause. "And discovering myself through my experiences. I was easily led in my youth and cared more about pleasing others than exploring my own thoughts. I don't feel like the same person. Do you think that's possible? To change so completely?"

This time, it's Arrick who doesn't pause, declaring, "I do."

"Then I have a question for you." One that will take me away from my best friend. One that will remove any opportunity of seeing my family. It makes me sad, but it's for the best. And if not for the best, it's a comfortable solution, knowing my family will doubt the sincerity of my repentance more than Raider has. I lay my fork across the top of my plate and continue, "I wonder about the possibility of staying permanently in Hamo. Would you agree to something like that?"

Arrick's been actively eating—while I've been working a lump down my throat—but now he lowers his fork and puts his hand over mine. "You're welcome here."

I take in a long, quivering breath. "Thank you, Arrick. I'm so grateful." I flip my hand so our palms touch, and I squeeze. "I won't let you down." He returns the gesture, then releases me, and continues eating.

"Valore doesn't know about me," I start, feeling duplicitous in the admission. "When he avoided telling you where I'm from, it's because he doesn't know, and he was protecting my privacy. We kept things very basic in prison, but I'm going to tell him soon. Please don't mention it before I do."

"I understand. Sometimes it's hard to reveal the truth even when you want to," he says, and I think about the conversation I overheard. Arrick understands but doesn't know the admission will be a severing knife in my friendship with Valore. Still, now that I have a place to stay, I can delay no longer. I must tell him today.

Unable to think about it anymore, I turn to another topic that interests me, asking, "Is there any way to stop this madness with Tyran? Is there anyone she'll listen to? Someone she admires who could persuade her?"

"Tyran admires no one more than herself. Raider's the only one who might hold any sway."

"Why Raider?" I ask while Arrick's mid-bite.

He pauses in thought for some time before answering, "Opening up other people's business, especially territory leader business, can be messy. If you don't already know the answer to your question, there's probably a reason. So, I'm going to keep my mouth shut and advise you to ask Raider."

"Fat chance of that happening," I say with a snort.

Arrick chuckles. "Valore, then."

"Maybe." I shrug, prodding food with my fork.

"I wonder what Raider has that he believes is compelling enough to dissuade her," Arrick says. "Do you have any idea?"

"No. He's shared nothing with me." Arrick nods while I bite my apple. The juice dribbles over my lip, and I suck it back, continuing to speak while crunching it. "You asked me at dinner if I trust Raider, and I was rather flippant. He knows who I am and considers me a nuisance, but amid all that's happening, he's spent the effort to keep me alive and free. I wouldn't have made it this far without him. So, really, he's given me the most valuable thing—the chance of another tomorrow. How could I ask more of anyone? It seems his goal for all of us is a better future without needless deaths upsetting the path."

"So, you think I should go."

"He's asking for a few days to prevent a war helmed by a greedy leader. It makes sense to see what's so important it could stop Tyran from taking such ghastly action."

"Okay, I'll go," Arrick says, making me smile. I didn't think he'd be that easy to convince. "But I'll hurry back, knowing you're waiting here for me."

"Waiting?" I laugh and dip my chin nervously. "I'm sorry, Arrick, but I won't spend my liberation pining for your return. I'd like something productive to do. It's been a long time since I did anything with my hands."

"What interests you?"

"Would it shock you to hear I've always been interested in construction? I want to learn how things are made. Furniture. Buildings."

"Would you enjoy being an apprentice?"

I grin. "Yeah, I would."

"It's grueling work."

My grin widens into a broad smile. "Sounds perfect."

The click of the door interrupts us, and I look up as my traveling companions enter—Valore first, followed closely by Raider and Renegade.

"Excellent! You made my nine-thirty breakfast invitation."

Nine-thirty?

I blink at Arrick, but he just smiles, saying, "We were here early and got a head start on you." He pushes back and stands, and I notice his plate is nearly empty. "I have some quick business to attend to, but I'll return in five minutes." Arrick looks at me, winks, and then is gone.

"What was that about?" Renegade asks, stacking food high on his plate.

"There's something I need to tell you," I say, looking at Valore.

"Doing more spying?" Raider asks but doesn't glance my way, so I easily ignore his antagonism.

I'd hoped to tell Valore about both my plans to stay in Hamo and my history in one go, but I only feel comfortable tackling one subject with the others here. Knowing I'll find a moment later today to speak with Valore alone, I tell the group, "I've secured a place here in Hamo."

"What?" Valore blurts out, his breakfast plate wobbling in his hands. It hurts to cause him distress, but I press on. "Arrick's graciously allowed me to stay. I've discussed ways to be productive, and I think I'll be happy here."

"But I wanted you to come home with me," Valore says, looking at Raider like he can fix the problem. I want to laugh, considering Raider's the one who led me in this direction. But I can't laugh, not when I hear the anguish in Valore's voice. He's distraught by the news, and I would do anything to keep my friend from this heartache, but the rift between Raider and me is only growing. Over time, Valore will fall into the chasm and have to choose a side. And there would only be one decision to make.

Raider stomps to the table with delicate dinnerware held

tightly in his bruising grip. He drops the plate to the glass tabletop, shaking down his sleeves and rubbing his palm across his head. "You're joking. Or you're crazy. It's got to be one or the other."

"What did I do now?" I ask with an exasperated sigh, dropping my fork and staring up at him.

Taking my elbow, he pulls me from the dining chair to a corner away from the others. "Arrick is aligned against Adlumen, and you want to stay here?"

"Adlumen hasn't claimed me in eight years."

Raider lowers his voice. "Tyran will find you here and use you against your family."

She will? The thought is rather shocking. And absurd. I was nearly dead in prison, so my family clearly doesn't care about my well-being. What could Tyran benefit from using me? I shake my head, discarding his opinion.

"What are you talking about?" Valore asks, appearing at Raider's side.

Raider blinks, clearing his throat. "There's only one thing you should know about me."

"Just one?" I ask with a straight face, but Raider continues as if I've said nothing.

"I hate greedy people, and war is greed. If you stay here and I'm unsuccessful, you'll be right in the middle of it. Is that what you want?"

"It sounds like I'll be in the middle of things no matter where I go."

"No. This will be the center," he replies, causing Renegade to grunt and Valore to click his tongue. Raider's eyes widen, realizing he's revealed more than is wise. It seems they'll be attacking Hamo first if war comes. Raider was right about one thing—the leaders keep secrets.

"Forget I—" Raider starts, but the heavy door swings

open, and they all turn to watch Arrick enter. Meanwhile, Hamo's leader takes in the three tense men circling me.

"Is this breakfast or an inquisition?" he asks with humor, though his eyes are serious.

The men disperse. Valore is the first to sit, but Raider answers the question. "We were just trying to understand why Shar's plans changed overnight."

"I see." Arrick retakes his chair—a thoughtful scowl on his brow. "I must admit, I don't understand the concern you have for your thorn," he says with a knowing look at Raider. Donning a wry grin, he adds, "But you'll want to thank your little nuisance because she's convinced me. I'll leave with you early tomorrow."

"She did?" Raider's forehead scrunches. He's not nearly as happy about the outcome as he should be.

"She did," Arrick confirms.

Raider's eyes meet mine, the confused expression slowly ebbing. "Well, since she's done such a good job convincing you, I insist she goes with us. She can consider it a reward for helping stop a war." My brows pull in as I stare at the man who just turned my perfect plans upside down.

Going with them is no reward, and I'm as confused as ever. He's finally getting what he wants! Me... out of his way. And now he's dragging me along on their show-and-tell escapade. I shake my head, but any argument I have is dispelled by Arrick's giddy response. "Excellent! How pleasant you'll be joining us rather than beginning the apprenticeship I arranged."

Arranged? In the last five minutes?

I sigh, glaring at Raider, who looks bemused. I guess I can survive a few more days with him. I'll get to spend more time with Valore too. And I can put off our discussion for another day, which is something I can definitely get on board with.

CHAPTER SEVENTEEN

Nine Days Free

Raider's already in a tiff, and it's only mid-morning. He's asked me twice to keep quiet about his unintended Hamo comment—the petitions more command than request. I've promised not to repeat what he said—indeed, I have no interest in getting involved in their war—but I understand how difficult it is for him. His opinion of me is low, making it rather disconcerting when I have such critical knowledge.

I'm positive his moody behavior wouldn't fly for the average person. It's his striking looks—the dark eyes and perfect skin—that keep people obliging. If I threw a fit, they'd tell me to suck it up.

And there are more reasons for his foul mood. Arrick promised an early start on our excursion, and with the sun approaching its zenith, we've yet to leave. Arrick insists he has pressing obligations, but I expect at any moment, he'll change his mind about the trip, destroying Raider's plans. The situation has me feeling restless as Raider's frustration reaches new heights. Meanwhile, Valore tries in vain to calm him down.

"I'm sure it won't be much longer," Valore says for what must be the tenth time. We're gathered in his room, waiting for word that Arrick's ready.

Maybe the first time Raider was appeased, but at this point, he stands, shrugs off his heavy jacket, and throws it onto a chair, declaring, "I'm going for a walk."

When the door closes, it's just Valore and me since Renegade's off doing whatever he does when he's alone. I'm still trying to figure out their personalities. I wish I'd paid Dad more attention because he spoke about these people often, but I wasn't interested in anything that wasn't boys, intrigue, or gossip.

"Where's Raider taking us? Do you know what's at the end?"

"Somewhere south. And no, he hasn't said what's there, but I haven't asked." Valore's a patient man, rarely asking more of a person than they're ready to give, willing to wait until they are. It's an admirable trait.

I pull in my upper lip, already raw from overthinking. "Why does Arrick believe Raider is the only one who can change Tyran's mind about war?"

Valore rubs his bristly cheek. He shaved when we reached Sperne but has let it grow since. Mid-stroke, he says, "Because she's his aunt." I lean back, processing this news, while Valore adds, "Raider's mother was Tyran's younger sister, Sivil."

I bet every member of the Endrack family knows this except me. I found history boring, seeing past events as having no bearing on today. And then the heirs appeared, blowing that assumption out of the water. And now, here's another example of a situation I should have paid attention to.

"Sivil was the woman you fought," I say. The one he chose not to kill. The one he desperately misses. The one who taught him advanced skills with a Torquent blade. I was right to guess she was a Torque.

"Yes. Tyran hates me for taking Sivil away. She planned for them to rule together and conquer anyone who got in their way. Instead, Sivil came into the Dark with me."

I pause, not sure if I want to ask. We've kept so much to ourselves, but that seems to be a thing of the past. "What happened to Sivil?"

“She died in a fight between Adlumen and the South T. Raider was ten.” Which means I was only four. “Our marriage created a fragile peace between Torquent and the South T. Raider visited his Aunt Tyran in Torquent every summer. But the accord ended when Sivil died.”

“Relations between Adlumen and Torquent changed too,” I say. Again, any details I learned in my studies are fuzzy, but Tyran is transparent. Her fury would extend far and wide to exact revenge on any person or group who harmed her. In this case, an Adlumian killed her sister, and my dad gained another enemy.

“Yes. Tyran was distraught and made threats. Ultimately, Lord Endrack cut off trade on the heavily used Talpa Trail delimit route between their two light bubbles. It was a decade before he reinstated it.”

Reinstated after a week-long invasion by Tyran’s Torque bravados. Dad reopening the delimit trade route satisfied her for a time, but now, she’s back for more.

I pull my legs onto the couch, folding them under me. There’s so much hurt perpetrated by people with wild ideas. I was part of that cycle—following the example of those before me—and it makes me wonder if Tyran and I are alike. Maybe her parents taught her this is how things are done, and she doesn’t realize there’s a better way. Maybe she was isolated and didn’t learn how to relate to others. Maybe she sees fighting and arguing as the only methods for producing the desired result. Regardless, I see pieces of her in me. I could easily have turned out just like Tyran if things had gone a certain way.

“Why are you choosing to stay in Hamo?” Valore asks, breaking into my thoughts.

I should probably tell him I’m an Endrack and be done with it, but I want one more day, so I hop to my feet and cross over to him. Leaning over, I kiss the top of his head. “It’s best for all of us if I do."

"It's because of my son," Valore says, his eyes behind the lenses holding mine.

"Partly," I admit, but also, a fresh start would be freeing. Besides, I could end up in a much worse situation if I don't take this one. "Truly, though, I think I could be successful here."

I see in his expression he wants to say more, but he doesn't, so I excuse myself, striding down the hallway with purpose. I stop at my destination, rap on the door, and open it without permission—I'm not in a patient or polite mood today.

Arrick looks up. I'm a little nervous approaching him after the conversation I overheard, but he was kind at yesterday's breakfast. And while I'm unsure about his conversation with Chett, I figure I can worry about it or get over it. And if I'm going to live in Hamo, I'd better do the latter.

"Good morning," he says.

"Eh. Afternoon is more like." I make myself welcome, finding the black leather couch next to his grand wooden desk and dropping onto it.

"Is it that late?"

"Does that mean your business isn't a fake delay, causing Raider to develop an early onset heart condition?"

"He's that bothered?" Arrick smiles.

"You've got him stirred into a dither," I admit, bouncing my foot on the floor.

"I'm almost done."

I should stay quiet and let him finish so we can get going. Instead, I blurt out, "You're not Tyran's ally because you respect her."

Arrick tilts his head, considering my statement, then

nods. "I fear her as many do."

"Do you fear Raider?"

"No."

"Does that mean you admire him?" I can't say I do, but I'm in a different situation than Arrick.

"He's always treated me fairly." Arrick rubs his chin. "Yeah, I'd say so."

"Then why are you so reluctant to go against Tyran? Maybe an admired ally is better than a feared one."

"There are many reasons," Arrick answers quickly, thrumming his fingers on the desktop. It's the first sign of nerves he's displayed.

"Name one."

"I have a sibling who's married to a Torque."

"Ahh." I tilt my head. "The spy."

Arrick chuckles, his blue eyes shining. "She's no spy, but she gives sound advice based on what she knows. I'd hate to see her harmed."

"I don't mean to make light of your concerns." I pause. "Still, that's what I'm going to do by pointing out that there are many people in light bubbles and Dark territories with similar connections. They're equally concerned about their loved ones being harmed by you severing your alliance with the Southern Territory. Why not let Tyran struggle through this conflict on her own? Why not declare neutrality and throw her demands back in her face?"

"You're forgetting Casmo. I'd have both of them coming at me."

"But you'd have all three—Adlumians, Southers, and Coastals—to defend you."

"I'm friends with Raider, but I don't know the governors well enough to switch to their side. Chadd always advised me that Tyran was the ally best suited for our form of government. Chett feels the same."

"Would you have sided with Lord Endrack if he'd asked you to?"

"You really want me to answer that?"

I nod.

"Never."

A laugh pops from my mouth. "Very wise," I say, and his eyes widen with surprise before I ask, "So, then, what in the Dark are you doing with Tyran?"

It makes Arrick grin, but then his expression turns sad. "I wish it were an easy choice, deciding whose hands to put your future into."

"Yeah," I say, standing up. "I think I have some experience here. Sometimes, Arrick, you have to choose logic over instinct. That's what I did, and now I've got a home in Hamo."

"Is that what you did?" he asks, not seeming entirely convinced.

"Mostly." I chuckle. "I'll see you in a bit," I say, slipping out the door with a wave.

With a brisk gait, I return to Valore's room, expecting to find him but discovering only Raider. I'm tempted to retreat before he sees me, then decide he shouldn't dictate my movements, so I make a loud entrance, asking, "Do you think you can stop Tyran by taking away her support? Seems rather futile. I think she'll keep going even if she's the only one standing."

"If it becomes necessary, I have something to offer her," he says, and my first guess is he means the item he's taking us to see. But then I consider it again and decide there's something else he'd dangle in front of Tyran. I should nurture the relative peace from his answer, but I can't help myself—he opened himself up for the debate, and I'm too tempted.

"Is it something you'd *offer*? Or would you be giving her something you already *owe*?" He's repeatedly mentioned he learned of Valore's prison location from Tyran and promised her a conversation for the knowledge, but he keeps putting off the meeting. He insists other things are more pressing, and I believe that's partly true, but I also think he enjoys making her wait. "Do you want her to beg you to come to her?"

It seems a valid question since I've wondered if Raider wants the same from me—to make me endure his discourtesy until I beg for mercy. But it was a long eight years in Aunty's Cellar—there's a fat chance of me ever begging Raider, or anyone else, for anything.

He doesn't answer—just stares with those black eyes behind his lenses. I cross the room to stand by him, bouncing in place and jostling him. "So, which is more enticing? Her coveted conversation or the mysterious offer? Or are they the same?"

Raider rotates to face me. "Look, there are only two things you need to know about me: First, I'm dependable. If I commit to something, I'll make it happen." He stops.

"So, you'll give her the agreed-upon conversation." I grin. "Meaning that's not what's on offer to stop the war." He doesn't even blink, unwilling to give away any information regarding the offering mighty enough to stop Tyran's goals. I clear my throat, returning to his comment and asking, "You said there are two things to know about you. What's the other?"

"I don't forgive."

"Never?"

"Pretty much," he says, his words sure and steady. After a long pause, I can't help myself—I laugh. I fall backward, landing on the blue couch cushions and rolling onto my side, hiccuping happy air.

"I can't imagine what you find so funny."

I shake my head. "I'm sure you can't."

And truthfully, it's not that funny. It's just, Raider constantly puts me in my place by listing his attributes—traits he claims are the *only things* I need to understand to grasp his character—and I can't help but notice today's qualities don't include hating greed, being focused, being logical, or holding a grudge. Of course, I could connect grudge-holding and being unforgiving without too much of a stretch. Still, doesn't he realize he has a growing list of *only things*?

I roll onto my back, still breathing heavily, and stare at the ceiling with a smile frozen on my lips. I've come this far. Why not push some more?

"Your dad told me Tyran's your aunt."

"Did you give him your ancestry as well, little prisoner?" Raider parries. "Likely not. You wouldn't be so lighthearted with your family details."

"Why did you insist I go with you on your excursion?"

"It was a foolish impulse."

I watch him closely as he answers, and I come to one conclusion. "That's not the reason."

"You seem to have a way with Arrick. Maybe you can convince him to my side," Raider snaps. "And it's only a few days, so suck it up."

Curses! There it is—the command for us commoners.

Suck it up. Do as I say. Keep quiet.

When I say nothing, Raider presses the point. "Besides, you owe me."

"She doesn't owe us anything." Valore appears, wrinkles

furrowing his brow as he takes in the scene. "It's her life to live as she sees fit."

"No, Dad. *She owes me*, and she knows exactly why." Raider steps forward, towering over me while I lie on the couch. "Tell him what I'm saying is true."

I think about the secrets he holds over me and the governors' reception from so, so long ago. "It's true," I push out in a whisper.

"And there it is. Some of the first honest words from your lips." Raider spins and is at the door before my feet work, but then I'm off the couch and chasing him. He doesn't get to push me into a corner and then walk away.

"I told you, I don't lie!" I yell at his back. I reach him just as he enters his bedroom. I don't give it a second thought and follow him inside. He turns around, looking startled to see me there, and I push the door closed, turning the lock and leaning against the teal door. "I was a stupid sixteen-year-old. Can you admit people do stupid, misguided, and occasionally despicable things at that age?"

Raider lifts his chin. "I never did."

"Well, I wasn't perfect like you!"

"Don't be childish."

"Raider," I entreat, needing him to understand. "I didn't learn the same things from my parents you learned from yours. My dad taught me to despise and control. Mom taught me she didn't trust me. They both taught me they loved Chessie and Wick more. They left me to my own devices, and I did everything wrong."

"You sure did."

"I was boy crazy," I say defensively.

"You knew I wasn't available."

"You're right. I knew you had a serious girlfriend, but I wasn't the only one pushing that boundary. I watched the entire room flirt with you."

"I was accustomed to batting eyelashes. That wasn't the problem. You crossed the line."

"Because I kissed you," I say, finally voicing the issue out loud. "But Raider, was it really that big of a deal? I'm six years your junior. I was just a kid."

"You didn't kiss like a kid," he mumbles, taking a step forward. "What else did my dad tell you?"

"What?" I shake my head, rocking from the topic change.

"What else did he say about my family?"

"Nothing. What else would he tell me?"

Raider's eyes are stormy behind his lenses—wild and anguished. "You're not the only one looking for forgiveness, Sharade. I have things to atone for as well."

"I have a hard time believing you do anything you don't mean to do with perfect clarity. What sin have you committed that holds no promise of redemption?"

"The sin of trusting when I shouldn't. The sin of not being around when I should. The sin of missing the precious moments to be somewhere less worthy." He directs his answer squarely at me, and I can only guess he holds me responsible for at least part of his committed sins. Well, not me directly, but others who don't deserve trust. Others who've acted like me—thoughtless and without consequence.

"Well, that explains everything, doesn't it?" I ask with a resigned sigh. He'll never allow that I've changed because it's not just me he's holding responsible. He's lumped me together with anyone else who has wronged him.

Raider's unresponsive—not even renewing the questions he had for me. It's a relief when, seconds later, there's a knock, and a staff member updates us through the locked door. We stare at one another while we learn that Arrick's finished his business, and we're leaving Brevis within the half-hour. Raider turns from me without a word to gather his belongings, and I flip the lock to escape his censure.

Our car assignments are prearranged, and I'm sharing a backseat with Valore. I'm happy to focus all my attention on him, knowing this is my last opportunity to shower him with love, and selfishly, I want to be near him for as long as I can. Raider takes the front with Renegade. There's a brief, whispered discussion before Renegade rotates to pass out the confiscated weapons. While Valore tucks his knife safely away, I secure the sheathed knife around my waist. Renegade's wide smile shows he's glad to have his sword back, but there's nothing happy about Raider's expression. As we drive, I frequently feel his disapproving stare through the driver's mirror, but there's no purpose in attempting to ingratiate myself with him—that's a pointless pursuit.

There are two other cars in our caravan, both trailing behind us. Chett and Arrick are in one, with Hamo security taking up the remaining seats—Arrick's most trusted people accompanying their leader to ensure his safety. The second car is more of the same.

Besides talking with Valore, I concentrate on the passing world within the lamlight's reach—places and scenes I've never witnessed before. We avoid the Torquent Expansion, where the citizens of Torquent use lamlight to live in the Dark on land the Southern Territory gave them. It would be fascinating to see, but giving it a wide berth is wise.

It's late afternoon when we cross the Talpa Trail. Today, it's no longer a horse and carriage trade route from Adlumen to Torquent. It's a flat path ideal for cars with a steady stream of them before breaking off to their different destinations.

After five hours of constant driving, we stop in the South T city of Quies, where we arrange beds at the Ash Woods Inn—a two-level building with thick rock walls. I'm terribly thirsty after being blasted with hot air for hours in the car, and I down two glasses of water in succession. A few of us aren't tired, so we go to the inn's restaurant and sit around a thick slab table. I tap my toes on the cobblestone floor while the group nibbles on a tray of small bites and plays a card game. It's not one I'm familiar with, but I catch on quickly and enjoy playing. And winning.

"Again?" Arrick asks with a chuckle as I lift my arms and shimmy in victory.

"I've always been good at games, especially those requiring strategy."

"I shouldn't be surprised," Raider murmurs.

I mostly ignore him, though he puts a damper on my good mood, and I beg out of the next game, choosing to talk with Chett instead. He doesn't like games, so he's just been watching us.

"How was your day?" I ask, then chuckle. "I mean, before we drove for many, many hours."

Chett shrugs, giving me another of his forced smiles. I've noticed them a lot. Chett's mouth never agrees with his eyes. His eyes are always contrary to his words. And his words conflict with his body language. His messages are so mixed he could bake a cake with them.

"Did Arrick tell you about me?" I whisper.

"He did. We don't keep secrets from one another, but I understand discretion is necessary."

"Thanks. Do you remember me from our youth?"

"I remember. It was a fun night," Chett says, and I nod, glad one of us has pleasant memories of the governors' reception because Raider's and mine are quite chaotic.

Chett continues talking, filling me in on his day—friendly but sad behind his fake smile. I want to tell him it's okay—to explain he doesn't need to try so hard with me. I want to assure him of the kinship I feel. Instead, I blurt out, "I heard about your brother. I'm sorry." He loses his smile and barely nods in acknowledgment. I soften my tone, asking, "Do you still have your parents?"

"Just my dad, but he's unwell. His health is fragile, and I'm not there for him as much as I should be. But I also need to make a living, so—" He shrugs. I feel sorry for the man. He seems a tormented individual, though I'm not sure what makes him that way. I'm also not sure I want to find out.

"You had a lot of responsibility from a young age," I surmise. "That must make your dad proud."

Chett's dad was the lead emissary eight years ago when Chett came to the governors' reception. His dad couldn't attend, and Chadd had other business, so they sent the third string—seventeen-year-old Chett. With all his accomplishments, it's incredible he's only a year older than me.

"Maybe. Truthfully, nothing in life has ever gone my way."

"I'd never guess that about you," I say, trying to bolster him while considering another aspect of Chett's sad personality—he's a pessimist.

"Most people wouldn't," he says, melancholy taking over his tone. "But it feels like I've spent my life struggling for purchase."

"Would you believe I've felt the same?"

"I would. We're kindred spirits, you and I." I guess we are, though I've come out of my past with more optimism, thanks to Valore.

"Let's just hope you don't end up in prison," I whisper. "I don't recommend it." Chett laughs, but the sadness is always there, and I consider that sometimes your mind is its own prison.

"What are you two talking about?" Raider asks. I'm unsure how long he's been watching, but his expression is not only inquisitive—it's disapproving.

"Why? Does it bother you that *someone* enjoys speaking to me?"

"You haven't changed a bit from that spoiled sixteen-year-old, prancing around gathering attention from anyone willing to turn their eye."

My shoulders bristle, and I decide Raider's right. Maybe I haven't changed so much, so I bring out some of the old me and let him have it. "Tell me, Raider. All these years have passed where you've been angry at me for sullying your reputation. What happened to the girl you were dating? The one you hate me for? What was her name? Kally?"

Raider slams his drinking glass down and surges to his feet, sending his chair into the wall. He doesn't spare me a look, taking the stairs three at a time and leaving us all in awkward silence.

Wow. I surely didn't expect that response. The men stare numbly at me—shocked and confounded—but it's Valore who clears his throat and says, "Kally died."

Curses! I sure know how to step into it.

"She died?" I clutch my throat. "When?"

"Two months before I was imprisoned. They'd been married a few years. But he lost her and then me, right in succession. It hasn't been easy. It's changed him. I could see it the moment we reunited."

Of course, he's changed. Of course, it's been difficult. That would be tragic for anyone, especially Raider. He feels everything so keenly.

"I didn't mean anything by it. He just keeps digging." And so I reverted to my old petty self and dug right back. I really am acting like my sixteen-year-old self, and I hate it. I don't know if it's being around Raider or being free in the world. Whatever it is, I need to get a grip and start behaving with decorum. I squeeze the edge of the table, ready to stand. "I need to go apologize."

Valore shakes his head, putting out his hand to stop me. "Just let it be. It's best not to discuss it with him."

I settle back onto my seat, but my mind is in turmoil. Valore thinks apologizing is unnecessary, but I now realize the depth of my wrongs. An apology is more than necessary. It's critical, and I'll take care of it as soon as possible.

CHAPTER EIGHTEEN

Ten Days Free

I approach Raider at breakfast, but he walks away before I even open my mouth. I figure I'll try again during our drive, but he trades seats with Chett, claiming he has business with Arrick. No one believes him—I can tell by the looks the others give me—and an embarrassed flush runs up my neck.

The drive is hot and relentless, but we eventually reach Bratus and stop for lunch—only no eating takes place as far as I can see. Raider disappears with Chett, Arrick, and their Hamo security team. Renegade goes to do whatever Renegade does. And Valore's tired, wanting to stay in the car. It leaves me on my own with one thought in my head.

I should have stayed in Hamo.

The farther south we travel, the hotter it gets. I'm not used to the sun, so with a bit of money in my pocket, I purchase a flatbread sandwich and sit under a tree to eat. Then I wander the market of the medium-sized town, searching for a breeze and perusing the outdoor shops—not because I can afford to buy anything but because I genuinely enjoy looking, especially after eight years of little to no stimulation.

I never envisioned I'd travel so far into Dark territory. As I watch people maneuvering with their lamlight, I decide they probably felt the same at one time. Still, I've lived among the light blind for a third of my life, so it's not nearly the big deal it would have once been.

Many things in the market are familiar—items available back in my youth—but there are a few surprises. Mainly,

I'm intrigued by the various objects they've infused with lamlight. The ingenuity of it is impressive. There are gaudy rings, heavy bracelets, and clothes emitting light from shirt-front buttons. Even shoelace holes give off the light. My attention runs over children's items—stuffed animals with lamlight eyes to toys with lamlight handles.

"You like that one?" a salesperson asks while I'm inspecting a woman's purse with a lamlight strap.

"It's interesting," I tell him, knowing he'll go for the hard sell if I give a firm answer or make eye contact.

"I know something you might like even more," he says, startling me by taking my arm. I drop the purse as he pulls me to the side, dragging me between two shops and weaving through layers of blankets displayed for purchase which act like curtains.

"Hey! Let go of me," I give one solid yank, but his fingers dig in harder. Then he stops, spinning around to face me, and recognition sets in. "It's you!" I exclaim, and the need to get away drains from me. The growing fear I experienced ebbs, but it's replaced with alternate worries.

"Yes. It's taken me a while to get you alone." I look over my uncle—my dad's brother—who we always called Diggs. He's significantly changed since I last saw him. There's a deep scar on his forehead—healed but puckered. His gray hair is longer, his clothes plain and unfashionable, and he has permanent frown wrinkles on his forehead and around his mouth. He licks his lips before asking, "Do you have all your things?"

"What do you mean?" I ask, spreading my fingers and looking down at my empty palms. My mind wanders to the suitcase with my new clothes—minus the foamy green dress, which I left in Hamo, knowing it would serve no purpose on this trip—and the brown bottle rolled inside them to stay safe, but Squatty's necklace is around my neck. I stop mid-thought, feeling stupid for cataloging material things when Diggs is here, and there are important things to discuss.

"I mean is there anything you need from the car before we leave?" he asks.

"Leave?" I choke out, shaking my head. "What makes you think I'm going with you?"

His brow furrows. "Well, you can't think I'd leave you with them."

I don't know what he's been up to since I've been in prison, but just the look of him says it's not good. He's not my path to a better life—that lies in Hamo, especially if Raider can solve this war issue. No, Diggs isn't the answer.

"I'm not interested in a life on the run," I say, staying calm but remaining firm.

The lines on his face deepen. "Hell's beast! You'd rather stay with the moles? Did things go that well for you chained next to Valore Roil in Ott's prison?"

"Well—" I pause. "Wait. You knew where I was?"

"Of course."

My jaw drops. "But you never tried to get me out," I whisper, my words coated in shock.

"It wasn't a simple prospect."

I put a fist on my hip. "Raider didn't make it look so hard."

"Raider," Diggs says with unveiled disgust. "Is he your hero now?"

"Hardly. I frequently think he'll drop me at the nearest hovel. Still, I expect that of him—seeing as he's got bias toward me—but I don't expect it of you. You're my uncle."

"While you were cozied up to Valore Roil, I was trying to stay alive!"

"Cozied!" I suck in my upper lip, then popping it loose. "Of course. My life's been a breeze. I'm sorry yours has been so rough."

"It has been rough! Your sister took my girl from me."

"I know," I say, turning from sarcastic to sympathetic. Saeva was older than me—closer to Chess's age—though she was my friend more than my sister's. Sure, she was unpredictable and played gruesome tricks on people, but that was when we were kids, though Chessie insisted those traits worsened in adulthood. But I wouldn't know. I spent little time with Saeva after I went boy crazy and she started serving in our army.

When the governors descended on Adlumen, they outlined the antics of Saeva's darker side, but I barely listened. They were the enemy, and I didn't trust what they had to say. But I'm in a different place now. We all did awful things as part of Dad's plan. And maybe Saeva did awful things outside of it. All I know is, while I never would have wished death on Saeva, we all got what we deserved for the crimes we perpetrated.

I feel for Diggs—losing a child is awful, even if my cousin was terrible—but we destined ourselves for pain. Our actions brought it about, and blaming others for our hurt is cowardly. "I'm sorry about what happened, but we were doomed before we enacted Dad's plan."

"We weren't doomed. You fell apart, and my daughter died."

I shake my head. "I'm not responsible for her choices."

"*You fell apart*," he repeats. "If you'd kept it together, they'd never have learned about our plan. "

"You blame me," I say, and he doesn't deny it. In his silence, I tilt my head in thought. "Why did you come here, Diggs? If you believe me responsible for Saeva, why would you hope I'd accompany you?"

His shoulders sink. "I just... You're the only one left."

Dad and Saeva are dead, Chessie and Wick are estranged from him, and Mom never liked Diggs, leaving just me. I guess I can understand his need to connect—maybe even to feel close to a daughter figure like the one he lost. She was my cousin, after all. But things have changed. I can't be what he needs. And I can't go with him.

"You need to go, Diggs."

Immediately, I know I've said the wrong thing. His sad face morphs into an angry one, and the set of his mouth goes hard. "This is your only chance to be on my side."

"Oh, Diggs. Must we have sides?"

"The moles think so. I'm sure they're trying to stop Arrick from aligning with Tyran." He pauses, but I confirm nothing, so he continues, "It's futile. Arrick knows who will win this fight. He knows how to pick a side."

I shake my head. Diggs was overconfident back then too. We were all to blame for what happened and could point out the failures in one another. Too bad we didn't recognize them in ourselves. Too bad we didn't see the uselessness of our plan.

"Is that your decision, then?" Diggs asks with a sort of frustrated acceptance.

I think of my future home and career in Hamo and nod. "Just go."

"Keep an eye over your shoulder," he says as he passes by me, entering the blankets.

"I'm not declaring war on you," I tell him.

"No. I'm declaring it on *you*. You're with them, which means I'll come for you when the time is right. But I'll let you sweat it out a while."

Then he's gone, and the closest blanket falls back into place, brushing my arm. I spin on my heel and set off after him—not because I plan to catch up, but because it's the direction I need to go. I launch through the last blanket, but he's nowhere in sight, so I push forward, keeping a fast pace as I race to the cars. The others are already there, except for Chett.

"The little prisoner has returned!" Raider exclaims. Apparently, I was missed. The others' faces say as much, but Raider says no more. He starts toward our car—not Arrick's, but ours—leaving me behind.

"Wait!" I say, rushing toward him. Raider stops, stiffens his shoulders, and kicks the tire. Then he turns to face me. The look on his face says to keep my distance—that he wishes I were a tire. "We need to talk," I say. About a lot of things, but I must stick with the priorities—he needs to know about Diggs.

Raider puts up his hand. "We're not talking right now. You've already wasted enough time."

"Wasted time?" I was out of sight for all of five minutes, and he's acting like I took a day excursion.

Curses! He's infuriating.

Still, I have priorities.

Stick to the priorities.

"But I have—"

"No," Raider barks.

I take a breath, closing my eyes to keep calm. "Would you just list—"

"What don't you understand? I said *no*." Raider gets up in my face, pointing an unsteady finger at me. I understand this has nothing to do with losing time and all to do with my stupid remark about Kally. I'd apologize if he'd let me. But apologies aren't an option.

"I don't want to hear from you. I don't want to think about you. I don't want to see you until we reach Relicum," Raider bellows. "Not a glance my way. Not a single peep from your lips. I don't want to watch you fawn over my dad or simper and flirt with Arrick or Chett. Just stay quiet. Be a damn ghost!"

Fawn? Flirt? Ghost?

"Fine!" I yell, turning for the car.

I'll keep my eyes down.

I'll not utter one peep.

He's the one who'll remain uninformed—not me.

I climb into the car and strap in, staring at my hands tucked between my knees and keeping that posture until we pull away from Bratus. I stew in anger as we travel, striving to be a ghost and knowing it's wrong. Raider doesn't know I have a warning for him, and he'll be upset when he finds out. It's like I'm back in Aunty's Cellar, suffering through another upsetting condition of my sentence and living under the absurd rules of the guards—only Raider's the rule maker and is choosing my form of torture. Silence.

In the quiet, I think about Diggs. He blames me for what happened to his daughter. And he knew all along where I was, but he left me there to rot. I twist my hair, turning it into knots while I brood.

I catch Valore's sympathetic eye more than once, but he only shakes his head, telling me to stay quiet. Renegade's no help, either. The pleading looks I give them are as unproductive as a fire in a downpour. I feel like they're all against me. This isn't good. No. It's not good at all. Once again, I wish I'd stayed in Hamo.

We travel for five hours, and when we finally stop in Relicum, where we'll dine and stay the night, I bounce from the car as soon as it's stopped.

Simpering and flirting? Curses! There are legitimate concerns to discuss!

I head away from Raider and straight to Arrick and Chett

to release the secret I've held all day.

"Arrick! I need to speak with you," I announce.

"What do you think you're doing?" Raider's at my side, flanked by Valore and Renegade. Well, they're following behind him, but they feel like obedient sentinels in formation.

"I'm opening my mouth." I smile, feeling crazed. "Does that go against your decree? Do you think I care?" I snort, turning back to the men from Hamo. "Be a ghost. Does that sound reasonable to you, Arrick? Chett?" I gesture at the two men who gape at me. "Raider wants this pesky girl to shut up so he can be at peace with his thoughts. Well, I'm not at peace. I have something that needs saying, and I don't care what he wants!"

Raider shakes his head to block out my words, but I just talk louder. In fact, I'm yelling, and innocent people passing us on the street turn to gawk.

"My Uncle Diggs is alive! He pulled me aside in the shops in Bratus." I'm breathing like I just ran a mile, but releasing the words is an immense relief.

"And you said nothing until now?" Raider complains.

"You!" I step into his space, pointing a finger in his face. "Don't you dare say that to me! I tried. Multiple times."

"You should have insisted for something like this."

Curses! I know.

"I know! It's important! And it's been eating at me all day. But you said *terrible* things to me. You locked me down when I *repeatedly tried* to tell you. And sure, I hurt your feelings. I get it, and I would have apologized for being insensitive when I asked about Kally. But, of course, that wasn't allowed either. But you can bet, that's the only thing I'm sorry about! The rest isn't on me. It's on *you* and your mean, stubborn pride."

I turn to go, and Raider's fingers latch onto my arm. "Come with me," he says, pulling me away from the others.

"No. I don't—" I choke out, looking at them to save me.

"Stop sputtering, and come with me," Raider says with some amusement.

"What don't you understand? I said no!" I say, repeating his awful words to me.

"I deserve that, but we need to speak privately, so let's go."

Raider leads me away from the group toward a copse of willows moving gently in the warm evening breeze. I yank from his grasp, folding my arms across my chest, but I continue walking, and he looks back to be sure I'm still with him. I feel like a scolded child waiting for punishment. I hate this dynamic. I'm not a kid anymore! And I'm not in the wrong. And I'm not a young woman pushing a man to notice me when he's engaged elsewhere. I'm a pretty decent person nowadays unless I'm around him.

Raider turns when he finds a spot he likes that's a suitable distance from other people. "You look wary of me," he observes.

Wary? Hardly. I'm disgusted.

"I can't say I'm not a little glad of it," he continues.

"Glad? Why?"

"Because I'm constantly wary of you. I've seen firsthand what you're capable of with a tilt of your head or a twist of your wrist."

"I don't know how I'm supposed to respond to that."

"You're not. I just need you to listen."

I nod, not speaking so I can be the listener he needs.

"Kally was my angel," he starts. "But she had her struggles—like everyone else—and one issue was jealousy.

Girls constantly approached me, and it worried Kal. She thought someone would catch my eye, and I'd stray out of her pasture, so to speak. She didn't realize I was a goner for her and her alone."

I can understand that. I had my struggles too—like never feeling I had the love I needed, which led me to act negatively. And being with someone who looks like Raider—well, it would be a trial to ignore the attention he gets.

"You see, you were just the type of girl she worried about. You were young and pretty, and, I admit, I was curious about you. But then you took it too far. And I was angry because —" Raider wipes a hand down his face. "Because I enjoyed kissing you. So, what kind of person did that make me? And what did that mean for Kal and all the times I assured her I'd never wander? And I wondered briefly if she was right. Did I have it in me to stray?"

I close my eyes, embarrassed and overwhelmed. And sorry. I made him doubt himself, and I was just playing. I hate revisiting the destruction I caused during that period of my life. "I was an idiot," I say. "I would never, *ever*, do anything like that now. I swear to you."

The fire ebbs from Raider's eyes, and his voice softens. "I've watched you the last ten days, and I doubt many things, but I believe when you say that. You were young and inexperienced and didn't understand what you were messing with."

"Did you ever tell her what I did?"

He clears his throat, straightening. "I don't keep secrets from those I love." The softness is gone, replaced with a personal dig aimed at my hidden identity.

I stay focused on Kally, saying, "I bet she hated me."

"She didn't have it in her to hate anyone." Raider smiles —an intense expression full of love and sadness. "Kal told me once that she'd have tried to steal me away if I were with someone else, then insisted she'd have chickened out at the last moment."

"Whereas, I never would have. Chickened out, I mean." I projected my confidence, acting the part to prove my fearlessness.

"No. You wouldn't have." He clears his throat before finishing, "You didn't."

"Can we move past this? I want to forget how stupid I was, and I promise not to simper or flirt—with you or anyone else. My mooning days are over."

"Wow. I've really lost my touch if you're not even slightly tempted to flirt with me," Raider says. And then something between us relaxes, and he chuckles.

Lost his touch? He doesn't know how wrong he is, especially with that smile.

"We won't talk about it again," Raider agrees. "But we need to talk about Diggs. I can't believe you didn't tell us what was happening. It was a dangerous move."

"Don't you dare start with me!" I complain, frowning up at him. "You were unyielding. It was awful."

"Yes, I was. We're both awful people," he says, breaking through my anger because he's smiling as he says it. "Let's neither of us be that stupid again."

I nod in agreement, then do as he asks, giving him all the details, and soon we're walking back to the cars. The air is less strained after talking, and there's an understanding between us, but nothing is settled. Indeed, while Raider and I have maneuvered this difficulty, there are many more obstacles on the horizon waiting for us.

CHAPTER NINETEEN

Eleven Days Free

I hoped my talk with Raider would change our dynamic, but I'm proven wrong. The next day at breakfast, he's as sullen as ever, though he's quiet with the others as well. I wonder if he's distracted—that it's not personal—but then I notice when the others speak, he listens. If I talk, he glares.

As I eat my peaches and cream over toast, sprinkled generously with blueberries, I wonder if jealousy drives Raider's continued reticence. After all, I'm jealous of him—I mean, I grew up with Chessie and Wick, so I'm well-versed in coveting—and it makes sense his jealousy could come from the three years I had with his dad. Three years he missed out on—worried and uncertain—while I benefited from interaction with Valore. I've felt similar emotions, thinking about Evans and the other governors interacting with my family and friends. Do they realize what a gift it is? Or do they take it for granted like I did when it was available to me and unappreciated?

But if Raider is jealous, I can't make myself feel bad for him. He has someone to love and love him back. For three years, I got Valore's focus, and now it's returned to where it should always have been—Raider and the rest of the Roils. It's a repeat of my family experience—the love spreading elsewhere. I'm accustomed to coming in last.

Valore seems especially eager as we prepare to leave Relicum. Even his hunched back is a little straighter. We're nearing Raider's destination, which is exciting, but more than that, we'll stay in Ora tonight, where they'll reunite with Imily—Valore's daughter and Raider's sister.

In Aunty's Cellar, I learned little about Valore's family

—at my request, of course—but over time, he casually mentioned a daughter and two sons, though I never learned their names. Even now, I only know about Raider and Imily. I'm unaware of the other son's name or if there are more siblings. I'm curious about it, but not enough to ask.

And it doesn't matter anyway. Soon, I'll have no place in Valore's life, so there's no purpose in knowing the details. This is the way of things—family sticks with family above all else. Well, except mine. But the point is, I can't force myself to stay inside Valore's inner circle. I wouldn't want to. The thing I can do is exit with grace.

Raider pushes back his chair to stand just as I eat my last bite of peach. "I'll ready the car," he says, heading to the door. The problem is there's nothing to get ready—Arrick's people loaded everything before we ate, so all that's left is to finish our food and drive away.

I dab my mouth with a napkin and squeeze from the bench. Without a word to the others, I follow Raider outside. Sure enough, he's by the car but not actively doing anything. He's just leaning against the hood, staring at the sky. "What are you doing out here?" I ask, and he glances over. "Are you nervous about today?"

"No." His answer is too quick.

"Liar." I grin, unable to help myself.

He sort of grunts and looks back at the sky. With the circlight only covering a couple of hundred feet, I can't see what could interest him up there, but I give him the benefit and decide it's fascinating. He clears his throat before casually telling me, "Calling me a liar doesn't make me one. I told you before, I don't lie."

Curses! He's annoying. And handsome. And especially annoying because of his handsomeness.

I tilt my head, considering his words. "Uh, no. You told me you don't keep secrets from those you love. That's a totally different thing."

This time, he growls. "If there's one thing you should know about me, it's that I'm not a liar," he says, and the comment has me biting back a laugh as he adds, "And I'm not nervous about today."

"Fine. You're not nervous. And I'm sorry I *erroneously* called you a liar. I was mistaken." I grin. "But I have a theory, so if I ask you something, will you answer me honestly?"

"Not a liar," he says, which I guess means his answer is yes—that he'll be honest—though he could always choose not to answer.

"Okay. My theory is you're jealous of me." I fold my arms across my chest. "Are you?"

That gets his attention. His black eyes fall on my face, and he laughs before blurting out, "No!" like it's the stupidest idea ever.

"Well, it seems like you are. You get prickly whenever someone's nice to me, and that includes any time you slip up and are kind to me yourself. I think it's because I got time with your dad that you missed out on."

"I missed Dad, sure. I'm sad about our lost time, but I'm not *jealous*." Raider faces me, leaning his elbow on the hood. "I just don't know how you're doing it. I can't figure it out. We all know you're a convicted criminal. Nevertheless, you weasel your way in and make us forget."

"Weasel? That's rich, coming from a *mole*." I laugh. I haven't used the term in a long time—finding it tasteless after knowing Squatty and Valore—but I couldn't resist since he compared me to a weasel. The opening was too perfect.

Raider scowls.

"Oh, come on. It was a funny comeback." I poke his rib, and the scowl turns frustrated. "You just refuse to have fun, don't you?" I ask and poke him again.

He doesn't move.

"Fine. I'm done," I say, grinning and backing away from him with my hands in the air. "But I'm not doing anything underhanded or tricky to create an impression. This is just me."

Raider shakes his head in disagreement. "You were frivolous. Without shame. I can't imagine that just goes away."

My hands drop. "Raider, everyone grows up. Everyone changes."

He pauses, and I think he may finally agree with me, but then he shakes his head again. "No. There's just no way. It must be a ploy."

I've tried to be patient, but he doesn't want to see it. He wants me to be the bad person, and when my lips turn into a frown, I feel worse than the small expression could ever relay.

"But there is a way, Raider. You could try it yourself. All you need is to spend eight years in a Dark prison. You never know, even you might come out less prickly." The comment sits heavy in my gut, and I don't like it. Sucking in my upper lip, I shake my head and continue, "You know what? I take it back. Don't try it. It's better to stay prickly than to find out what happens in a place like that—what someone turns into. And if it weren't for your dad, I'd still be that person—a shell without cares, fears, or emotions. Spending hours talking to Self." I mumble that last part, then clear my throat and say firmly, "It's existence with a scant desire for death. There's enough longing for a permanent escape to mull over the idea of dying but never enough motivation to act on it. No, because action requires effort."

A sad laugh comes from my lips as I add, "Sometimes you can't even bargain your way into death." I wish the others would come outside, but I've not seen them yet. It's quiet, so I keep talking. "I'm aware I cling to your dad with a sort of... sick desperation. I'm aware the way I feel about him borders on obsession. When you've lived as we did, you learn not to care when your behavior isn't healthy. But in that place, because of people like your dad—" And Squatty—the memory of him has me catching my breath and gripping his necklace. "Well, I learned how to love people, and it was a revelation. I never knew feelings like that existed."

"Your sister is a great person," Raider counters.

"She probably is, but she's my sister. When you're young, do you ever appreciate your siblings the way you should? Or does the natural rivalry get in the way?" I shrug, knowing how it was for me. He doesn't answer, so I assume he agrees or at least understands my perspective. "Don't stress about it too much, Raider. I know my time with Valore is limited, and I'm working to distance myself. I'm withdrawing some each day, and when the time comes, I'll be ready. Then, you'll both be rid of me."

Raider says nothing, so I spin away from him. I've taken my mind to a dangerous place—remembering Self and the years conversing with her—and there's only one person who's ever brought me back from that state, so I go in search of him.

Besides, there's a reckoning coming, and I feel ready to tally my transgressions and count the casualties.

"Shar?" I turn and find Chett standing beside me. "Didn't you hear me calling you?" I shake my head, barely remembering the walk inside. "It should be twenty minutes before we go. Arrick's completing a few tasks."

Twenty minutes. That should be enough time.

"Where's Valore?" I ask.

"In his room, I think."

I nod and stride past Chett, taking the stairs two at a time. I knock on Valore's door, and he calls me inside. He's alone, so I ask, "Do you have a minute?" Or twenty?

"Sure. What's up?" He sounds chipper. Of course, he is. He's reuniting with family today. More and more, I know this is the right time to talk. I shut the door and turn the lock. He hears the click and squints.

"I need to tell you something, and I don't want to be interrupted."

Something that will change everything. Because even if you could ever forgive me, you'll always know what I nearly did. You'll always wonder what I could be capable of. There will always be a niggling doubt in your mind. I'll always be tarnished, even if I turn everything around and attempt to be sparkling clean.

"Take a seat," he says, already dropping onto a chair. I do as he says, scooting close to him. I've thought of all the ways I could do this, and now that the time has come, I still don't know the best method. Maybe because I'm tired of keeping it to myself, or possibly because of the time constraint, I decide on the quick approach.

"I never told you my full name in prison. I'm Sharade Endrack. Many people, including your son, know about me. When we met, I was ashamed of the actions that put me in prison, and I didn't want to talk about it, so I came up with our guidelines to hide my past from you. I'm sorry I wasn't upfront, but maybe someday, you might forgive me."

Valore tilts his head, taking in my words. There's a long pause before he finally asks, "Forgive you?"

I suck in my upper lip. The burn from the chapped skin is appropriate, and I deserve to feel the sting. "I understand if that's not possible, but I'd appreciate it if you'd take some time to think it over."

I push to stand up, but Valore captures my wrist and

nods for me to stay seated. "Shar, I don't need to think about anything. There's nothing to forgive. You needed guidelines to feel safe, and I was happy to go along."

"Yeah, but I hid who I was from you. I consider you my best friend, but—"

"You're my best friend too," he says, interrupting.

"But I can't be. Not with how I handled things! You don't even know the real me."

Valore clicks his tongue. "I knew the real you from the first day."

"The first day when I was half crazy and agitative. Are you saying that's the real me?"

"No. You misunderstand. I'm saying I knew you were Sharade Endrack from the moment I saw you in the next cell."

My mouth drops open, and I shake my head. "No."

"Shar, I led the Southern Territory for decades. I've known everyone in your family—your siblings and parents. I've sat in counsel with them, including your granddad and great-granddad. I marveled along with the rest of the world at Keine's luck in securing your mother's hand. She's a remarkable woman, and her daughters are the same."

Moisture fills my eyes. "You must have wanted to reach through the metal grid to strangle me." My shoulders slump, stunned he knew all along.

"My thoughts were far less brutal. I knew if your sister could see you, she'd agree you'd more than fulfilled your sentence."

No. Valore's too calm. Too understanding. But then, he's that way about everything, isn't he? I duck my head, knowing it's more than I deserve. "But, I tried to kill Evans," I say in a near-whisper.

"I'm well aware of your crime."

"He's your son's best friend!" I add, trying to trigger an intense response. There must be one in there, and I'd rather see it now than later.

"Yes. I love Evans profoundly." Valore leans in and grips my shoulders, waiting for me to look into his black eyes. "But, dear girl, don't you realize I learned to love you too?"

My lip trembles, and I suck it in to make it stop but must release it to say, "You can't mean that."

"But I do. Can't we just be grateful for failed efforts and reformed hearts and move on?"

I lunge forward, wrapping my arms around him and burying my face in his shoulder. "I want that more than anything! But I don't believe it's possible."

"I'll help you believe it," he says, sounding so sure.

"At my tribunal," I start. "I can't believe I'm telling you this." I bite my lip, then start again. "At the tribunal, the look of disgust on my sister's face because of what I'd done to Evans—I've never felt so repugnant. And then, her eyes when they sentenced me with indeterminate prison time—there was no concern or sorrow. It was utter disregard for me or my future. Until that point, I felt scared about what was happening. After, I felt angry because I was confused. Dad taught Chessie right alongside me, but the moment we were tested, she chose a different way, and then she hated me for following Dad as we'd always done. Anger toward my sister kept me going during those first years in prison. If I see her again, I'm afraid it will return, and I'll discover your son's right—that I'm not as changed as I think I am."

"Is that why you want to stay in Hamo?"

I nod and lean back so I can see his face. "That and because I have an opportunity there. I like the idea of learning to work with my hands, and Arrick will help me get started."

"I'd help you do that too," he says, but before I tell him the other reasons Hamo is better, the door handle wiggles.

"Dad?" we hear from the hallway. I stand, striding to the door and pulling it open. "Why was that locked?" Raider asks, and I swear he can't address me without it coming out as an accusation.

"Because I had something private to tell Valore."

Raider looks over my shoulder. "The little prisoner finally tell you?" he asks, and I catch Valore nodding from the corner of my eye. Then Raider looks at me. "Never thought you'd do it," he says, leaning against the doorjamb.

"I told you she'd talk when she was ready," Valore says, and the conversation forms a new picture in my mind.

"Wait a minute! You two have talked about this?"

"Of course we have," Raider says like it's a given.

"But you said you weren't going to tell him. That you'd let me be the one to break his heart!"

"Yeah, but as I so recently explained to you, I don't keep secrets from people I love."

"No. Just from people you hate. Like me." Raider just watches, saying nothing. "You also insisted you don't lie. Well, what do you call that?"

Raider raises a shoulder, answering cooly, "Misdirection."

"It's a lie!" I shriek, his reaction infuriating me.

Raider's jaw ticks. "I had no intention of talking to my dad about you. But then, he brought it up with me. Technically, I kept my word."

"How noble of you! You never make a misstep, do you?" I look for something to throw but settle for kicking a chair leg. "You're so annoying! I hate that I revert to acting like a five-year-old around you."

"At least you know you do."

"What car are you driving in today?"

"Ours. Why?"

"I'll go see if Chett will trade with me. I can't stand to see your face anymore this morning." I push past Raider, swear I hear him chuckle, and go in search of Chett. Luckily, he's easily found and compliant with my plan.

Within minutes, we're en route, and I bounce along in the seat next to Arrick, his black hair whipping in the wind. I tell him Valore's aware of my identity, and he asks how it went. I give him the highlights, leaving out any mention of Raider.

I'm grateful when we change topics, and Arrick tells me everything I'll love about living in Hamo, promising to ensure my safety while living within his borders. I feel guilty listening to his assurances, knowing the fight will start in Hamo, but I keep that knowledge locked inside. I don't do it for Raider. I do it for Valore. And because I promised, and I'm no liar!

It's a mystery why they'd choose Hamo over Torquent to begin the bloodshed. Arrick likely has the location for his first attack planned as well. Maybe it's Raider's hometown. Who knows? I'm trying not to care.

Our destination is two hours from Relicum. The first hour isn't bad, though the landscape turns dusty and desolate. With no other Southern Territory settlements nearby, we don't see another person as we travel. The second hour, I feel restless. The scenery hardly changes, and since it's cloudy, the world within our lamlight is darker than normal. It feels eerie—like being back in Aunty's Cellar—but it's hot and dry, and I'm desperate for shade.

Arrick's prattling on about complications with the trade routes in the event of war when he suddenly breaks off mid-sentence. I observe his frozen expression and his eyes that stare straight ahead. Turning my head, I blink a few times at what has claimed his attention.

Curses! It's the sun! And we're seeing it from inside of the Dark.

"It can't be," Arrick says as all three cars pull to a stop, turning off their engines. Glancing over, I find Raider, Valore, and Renegade wearing their lenses. In the Dark!

"There are no light bubbles in this area," Arrick says, hopping from the back of the car.

"No. There aren't," Raider confirms.

This is no light bubble. The sun is not the same one I saw days ago in Hamo. But it's not the one we've experienced the last few days in the Dark. It's as if there's a filter between it and us. Thick enough, the sun isn't quite right. Thin enough, the light blind must be cautious.

"Then, what is this?" Arrick asks, walking the area, gazing up at the half-image of the sky.

"The abatement," Raider tells him, and my mind turns back to when I was sixteen. The governors arrived and talked about how, with time, the Dark would abate—that sometime during the next hundred years, the darkness covering our world would dissipate. Dad said it was true but that it wouldn't happen soon because he needed time to secure Adlumen's future.

It was another example of how Dad's mind worked—that even nature wouldn't dare contradict his timeline—and yet, here it is, earlier than anyone predicted.

I look up at the phenomenon with wonder. Also, a bit of fear because changes like this alter the world. And not just the physical alterations from the Dark abating but also the psychological shift that will come over the people. Raider hopes this will stop a war, though it has an equal chance of starting one.

I walk beneath the burgeoning abatement and come upon a tree that's lost half its leaves. The remaining ones don't look well—wilted and suffering. I reach out, touching one, and with a bit of pressure, it breaks off in my hand. "Look at this," I say, calling the others over.

"What's wrong with it?" Chett asks.

"Look at all the other plants," Raider says, pointing in the distance. "They're unaccustomed to the sun's intensity and need more water."

Raider's comment confirms my thoughts. Already, living things suffer because of the abatement. And as genuinely miraculous as this development is, it's proof there's more distress to come.

CHAPTER TWENTY

Twelve Days Free

We marvel over the abatement, staying in the area and discussing it at length until the sun goes down. It's dark when we finally start for Imily's home in Ora. My circlight illuminates very little since there's no moon, and just the slim headlights to aid my vision. It makes for an unengaging ride, and I sleep most of the way, only opening my eyes when the electric lights in Ora suddenly come into view.

Minutes later, the drivers of our three cars pull the machines into an outbuilding on Imily's property. We don't disturb the main house, even after learning the family is away for the night, but take up lodging in the guest quarters around the back. Imily's relationship with the leader of the Southern Territory means they have frequent visitors in large numbers, so they built the structure as a comfortable stopping point. And if people overflow the forty available rooms, there's a large section of land for tents. Valore tells me all about it as we lean on each other, exhausted and searching for our beds.

My room is small—just large enough for a bed and dresser—but it's quiet and comfortable, and I don't have to share. The second the door latches behind me, and my head hits the bed, I'm asleep. I don't even bother removing my clothes or circlight.

Morning comes fast. I hear voices and head outside after a quick visit to the attached bathroom. I blink against the morning light—which seems brighter than usual, considering the limit of my lamlight—and pretend I'm more alert than I am.

“Morning,” Chett says with a polite nod.

I nod back, and a drop of water lands on my nose, followed by a tiny trickle streaming down my neck. I dipped my head into the sink to tame the flyaways but didn’t take time to dry my hair, knowing the hot August air would do the job. Bending at the waist, I shake my head, sending droplets flying, then straighten, fluffing my damp hair and asking Arrick, “What’s the plan for today?”

“Breakfast. Then we leave for Hamo.”

“Oh,” I say morosely. This is the day I’ll leave Valore. My eyes go straight to him, avoiding Raider’s gaze, and my old friend’s expression reflects my feelings. Today really sucks.

Seconds ago, food sounded marvelous. Now, I’m not sure I could choke down a grape. Still, I follow the others into the main house—a cute structure with blue siding and cheery yellow accents—and five minutes later, I’m at a table with food, trying to be enthusiastic about it.

“We’re counting on both of you to change Tyran’s mind,” Raider says, pointing at Chett and Arrick with a fork.

One of Tyran’s reasons for declaring war is Torquent’s over-crowded light bubble. She’s not satisfied with spreading into the Dark using lamlight and views the borrowed land within the Torquent Expansion as inconvenient and, therefore, a temporary solution.

But Raider insists fighting for light bubble land is unnecessary when more will be available as the Dark abates. Indeed, the site we inspected is not a singular phenomenon. They’ve found multiple pockets of recovery, notably in the Northern Territory and along the coast.

Additionally, Raider argues that obtaining and studying a beacon is pointless since the coming abatement invalidates the skill in the long term.

But he avoids the main issue: Tyran’s not operating on

logic. This is a personal vendetta against Adlumen based on injuries from the last two decades. It's good we know at least one of her motivations because her purpose for wanting a conversation with Raider is still a mystery—at least, it is to me.

Arrick repeatedly voices doubt about the abatement being capable of swaying Tyran entirely. Raider responds by listing the advantages of the astonishing phenomenon. Still, I must agree with Arrick. "All we can do is give her the facts," he explains. "Tyran will only adjust her plans if she sees a benefit. And if the benefit outweighs the offenses of the past."

"Convincing Tyran will take more than facts," Raider counters. "It will take speaking with conviction. You must impress her with what you've seen. Approach her boldly and with confidence."

Arrick's a sensible man—good with words but sometimes failing to see obvious things. Raider excels at discovering core issues but becomes a bulldog when it's time to explicate. These traits don't suit the situation, angering Arrick and making Raider brutish.

"What in the Dark kind of a leader do you think I am?" Arrick's blue eyes flash, and the arrogance he often displays appears in full force before his tone turns condescending. "Of course, I'll recommend what you've shown me and *dazzle her with the benefits*."

"You may have to break your alliance with her to make her see reason."

"My aim has always been to guide *all of you* to peaceful terms," Arrick argues, narrowing his eyes. "But Tyran's not an easy sell. I know you don't want to hear this, Raider, but you must get more involved. You need to have that conversation you're putting off."

These arguments aren't new—with Raider bringing up the alliance and Arrick pointing out Tyran's unfulfilled request—but they never adjust their position.

Raider bites his lip and looks away, and I watch his expression sour. There's something he's not saying—I've felt his lack of transparency since Aunty's Cellar when he first mentioned Tyran's demand—but he won't engage and discuss it in depth. Instead, he broods in silence, sending Valore's anxiety spiraling—the man picking up on the same things I am. "It's not a good idea to meet with her," Valore says, confirming my thoughts as he clicks his tongue nervously.

"Likely not, but Tyran doesn't forgive debts," Arrick points out. "I'll promote the abatement as the most remarkable event in centuries, capable of solving many of our problems. But even if the promise of new land persuades her in some aspects, the only way to reach a solid outcome—and by that, I mean the number one way to avert this war—is for Raider to talk to her."

Raider sighs, staring at his plate. A second later, he pulls the napkin from his lap, throwing it onto the table. Pushing his chair back, he strides to the staircase, thumping his heavy boot against the thick banister in a drumbeat rhythm. "Do what you can," he growls out. "Just remember all the lives in our hands."

Arrick and Chett nod, but Raider doesn't see it. He's staring at the rungs, looking torn between staying and going.

"We'll leave for home in an hour," Chett says quietly to me, then stands with Arrick, and they slip from the room.

Valore shakes his head, then rubs the gray strands of hair thoughtfully. "I need to talk more with them," he says, pushing back from the table and abruptly leaving. He'll attempt to dissuade a meeting between Raider and Tyran, but I doubt he'll get very far. Still, I can't blame him for trying.

Now, it's just Raider and me in the big room since

Renegade's off doing his thing. With my thoughts on Renegade, I can't help but ask, "Did you tell Renegade who I am?"

"He already knew. Recognized you the first day."

I snort out an unamused laugh. Of course, he did. And for ten days, he's pretended ignorance. He's a good soldier, giving nothing away. I wait for Raider to say more—to dig into my transgressions as he's apt to do—but he keeps his back to me, and I note the tense set of his shoulders, often a precursor to him kicking something. Of course, the banister's already received repeated blows, but I wouldn't rule out another object getting the same treatment.

"The abatement was impressive," I say, resting my elbows on the table. "It could make a difference."

"Do you really think it will?" His eyes fly to mine, locking me in place with his stare.

"I don't know," I say. "I don't know Tyran."

"Neither do I. Not really." Raider releases a breath—heavy and long.

"Why does she want to talk to you so much?" I ask, clinking my fork quietly on the edge of my plate. I'm not sure he'll answer, but I have thirty minutes before I'll never see him again, so I might as well ask my questions.

"I think she's afraid of being alone."

Does she want Raider's company? Though the question runs through my head, it's not what I ask. "Tyran actually fears something?" Everything I've heard makes that seem impossible.

"It seems that way to me. However, she's without compassion, so it's an alarming combination."

"Her people don't view those as unstable qualities in a leader?"

"I doubt they see it. And if they do, well, the Torques

enjoy their light bubble's strength. What reason is there to fight against what works?"

None until their people start dying. Nodding, I stand, and we separate to our respective quarters. Me, to gather my things. And Raider... well, he's got a lot on his mind to sort out.

I secure the latch after packing my few possessions inside my little suitcase. With a deep breath to gather courage, I search for Valore. It's not a long process, as he's right outside my door with Renegade and the men from Hamo.

"I'd like you to stay another day," Valore says as soon as I clear the doorway. "My daughter returns in a few hours, and it's important to me that you meet."

I open my mouth, unsure of what to say. I hate to deny Valore anything, but I feel powerless in this situation. I think of Raider—how annoyed he'd be—and the men from Hamo who are my ride. I can't delay them.

"I'm not sure that's a good idea," I tell him.

"Only one more day," he says. His pleading tone hits me hard, and I want to say yes, but I can't.

"It's not logistically possible. You have places to go, and it's not back to Hamo. Who will get me there if I don't leave now?"

"We'll figure something out."

"That could delay me more than one day." I shake my head. "I'm sorry, but no. I must go today."

Valore frowns, looking at the ground. I'm unsure if he's coming up with another argument or what exactly is happening until I see a tear run down his nose and drop off the end.

Curses! Why's he doing this to me?

It hurts bad enough to leave him. Does he have to make it

so hard?

I put my suitcase on the ground and approach Valore, putting my arms around his neck and tucking my head into his shoulder. "We'll see each other again," I say, hoping the words are true more than believing they are.

His arms tighten around me, and a sob leaves his throat. I squeeze tighter just as Chett says, "I can stay an extra day."

I twist, still holding onto my friend. "What?"

Chett watches me, wearing his forced smile—his eyes never brightening and sadness heavy on his brow. "We can get an early start tomorrow. If we push hard, we can arrive not long after Arrick gets there." He sounds sincere enough, even if the delivery lacks vigor.

"Are you okay with that?" I ask Arrick, who's already accommodated me more than is necessary.

"I think it would work out perfectly," he says with a smile. "Just remember, you have a job and a home back in Hamo." He approaches, reaching up to touch my cheek, but at the last moment, he changes his mind and grips my shoulder. He looks at Valore, whose eyes are still wet with tears. "I promise she'll be safe and productive in Brevis. She'll be happy there."

Safe? That's not assured. Happy? I can't help but wonder if there's such an outcome when it means I'll be separated from Valore. Still, I'm willing to try on both accounts—so I don't remain dependent, leeching him dry with my needs.

"I appreciate that," Valore says, still sounding sad, taking my hand and squeezing it until my fingers ache.

"Well, it sounds like we have a plan," Arrick says with a parting smile. "I'll see you again in a few days."

"Dad!" Imily runs toward Valore, abandoning the people I

assume are her husband and children at the yellow door of their home. She slows just enough before making contact to keep from plowing him into the wall but wraps him in a fierce hug. "I can't believe it's you. You don't look too bad. How do you feel? I can't believe Raider finally found you. We've missed you so much! Are you hungry?"

Imily differs from how I imagined. Her brown skin is lighter than Raider's, and her hair is long, black, and sleek. She has the same dark eyes, but the edges are curved with happy lines, giving her a carefree expression her dad and brother lack. She's tiny compared to them but packs a punch with her personality. She laughs a lot and cries just as much, all with an abundance of enthusiasm. She has twice the energy of anyone I've ever met, with more spirit in her pinky finger than our entire group has combined.

When we're introduced, she draws me in for multiple hugs, then passes me off, demanding I hug her husband next and then her two children. The situation is loaded with awkwardness.

Chett's lucky he already knows the family, so Imily avoids pouring profuse attention on him. But she heaps love on Valore, praises Renegade, and shames Raider at every opportunity—doing it joyfully and with finesse, so the smile never leaves Raider's lips.

"You're in so much trouble when you see Stryke," she says, flitting around the room, tucking pillows under arms, and filling glasses with water and ice. "He was furious when you went for Dad without him."

I've confirmed it's just the three children. Raider's the oldest, Stryke next, and then Imily. Valore says he named the boys after his two best friends growing up, and his wife named their only daughter after her grandmother.

"Stryke gets mad about everything," Raider counters with a laugh. He's been somber much of our acquaintance, so seeing this side of him is surprising. He's more relaxed with his sister, and I've seen genuine delight in his expression more in the last hour than in the eleven days prior. I'm reminded of the handsome, charismatic man I met in Ambitus eight years ago. Life has wounded him and crushed his happiness, but here, among his people, he comes to life.

Imily takes another dig at Raider, and the laughter that follows has him clutching his belly and glancing at me with a happy gleam.

"Still here?" he asked, emerging from his room this morning. Arrick's car was gone, and I was not.

"For the day," I replied, letting him know there was a time limit—a short one.

He seemed satisfied with my answer. More so, he didn't seem surprised I was staying on. I expected more accusations of weaseling, which didn't come. I expected his silent anger, but it didn't happen. No, Raider seems less bothered and more accepting, and I can only guess it's because he's surrounded by the ones he loves.

"Are you a soldier like Uncle Raider?" Imily's daughter Dody asks, climbing onto the couch to sit beside me, her legs tucked beneath her.

"No."

"Then, why don't you have hair?" she asks, looking at me with wide, pretty eyes, her curly brown hair framing her face.

"Dody!" Imily chides, but I shake my head, grinning. The girl's only five, and I'm not bothered by her curiosity or honesty. Indeed, I'm feeling a little like Imily—in the mood to tease.

"I'm glad you asked because that's an interesting story," I say, scooching toward her. "I don't have hair because your uncle cut it off. With a knife!"

The girl's eyes widen, then she twists to look at Raider with a scowl that rivals his.

"She asked me to do it!" he declares, and they all laugh, except the little girl, who reaches out, taking Squatty's necklace in her tiny fingers to inspect it closer.

"Why?" Dody asks, absentmindedly touching the orange jewel sun.

"I wanted to look more like your uncle," I say, and Raider rubs the top of his head with a grin aimed at Dody.

"Which knife?" Imily's boy asks. His name is Harding, and he's seven with the attitude of a brash teenager. While he has his mother's dark skin, he has the round face and freckles of his father.

"My Wendhower," Raider answers.

Harding jumps to his feet, stomping the floor like I've seen Raider do. "You used your Wendhower to cut hair?" he bellows, heavily dissatisfied with Raider's reply. Even I know cutting hair dulls a good knife, but the passion Harding displays is amusing.

"It's what was handy," Raider explains, watching his nephew. There was more to the haircut—me demanding he do it right then—but I don't recall Raider complaining about the knife being an improper tool ever coming into play.

"Well, give it to me, and I'll sharpen it," Harding says, cutting me a dirty look and holding out his hand for the knife.

"I don't have it on me," Raider says. "I gave it to Shar for protection while we traveled."

It's the first time he's called me Shar without dragging out the name distastefully. It's the first time he's acted like arming me wasn't a bad idea. It's the first time I've realized I never gave back the weapon and would have returned to Hamo with it.

Harding's eyes widen. "You let her use your favorite knife?" Then he scowls, switching between Raider and me. Dody's enjoying the show, twisting her little bum until it's pressed against my hip, and her head rests on my arm.

"I wouldn't say it's my favorite," Raider says, watching me. "One of them, maybe."

"Oh, really? You lent me a favorite knife?" I raise my brows challengingly, glancing over and getting a tight smile from Chett.

"Don't read anything into it. It was the smallest one I had on me and, therefore, the best fit for your hand."

"Aw. So, you were looking out for me," I say, batting my lashes.

"Not really," Raider grumbles, pushing the young lad my way. "Go tell the lady you're sorry for losing your temper."

"Wow. Now, I'm a lady too. Your manners are improving by leaps and bounds. What should I expect next? Flowers and perfume?"

Harding spins away with disgust, no apologies administered, while Imily chuckles. "My brother knows how to woo," she says. "Flowers and perfume aren't out of the question. He just needs the moment and the motivation."

Woo? What is it with the Roil family and that word?

"Imily," Raider mumbles while I hope his sister doesn't think I'm pining for a good wooing.

"I know you don't like to talk about it, but everyone needs someone to love," Imily continues.

"I have more than enough people to love," Raider argues.

"Yes, our family is blessed in that regard. But you need someone to love you back," Imily insists. "And not in the way I do or Dad does."

Valore watches, not intervening on either's behalf. I think he agrees with Imily but doesn't dare say the words himself. Chett looks on with despondency, having lost his brother, and it makes me think of my family. I lost them too, just in different ways. At least Chett still has his dad.

"I'm not ready," Raider says, and I can tell he hopes it's the end of the topic.

"You're more than ready," Imily says, not entirely done arguing her case. "But I know you have things that need sorting with Tyran. Though, I'm not worried. You could convince a child to give up their favorite toy."

"It's true," Valore says, slapping Raider's knee. "If there's one thing I know about my son, it's that he's persuasive."

"No! It's that he's an excellent climber," Harding pipes in. "Trees. Mountains. It doesn't matter."

"No," Renegade interrupts, raising a bony finger. "The most impressive thing about Raider is he's as good in hand-to-hand combat as Ronen Wynne. And that's saying something."

"Are you done?" Raider asks and gets a wall of grins in return.

Meanwhile, I lift my hand—a pretend pen scribbling a note in the air.

"What are you doing?" Raider asks with a groan.

"Just taking notes. Adding these qualities to the list."

"What list?"

I chuckle at the confused look on his face, then drop my hand with a pleasant grin. "Some day, I'll tell you. Until then, I'll let you keep guessing."

CHAPTER TWENTY-ONE

Thirteen Days Free

I've never been a superstitious person, but on my thirteenth day of freedom, I wonder if thirteen really is unlucky. The car has a flat tire, and the spare isn't any better. Ora's not a metropolis, and cars aren't commonplace, meaning the nearest tire is miles away, and Imily's husband —I can't remember his name, though she introduced us yesterday—has gone on horseback for it.

"Come play outside with us," Dody says, holding a football.

Harding's got a solid grip on Raider's shirt—having claimed him as his teammate—while I look at the man and ask, "Do you have a ball small enough for my teeny, tiny hands?" I hold them up, envisioning the fingers of a squirrel monkey I once saw at a traveling animal show.

Raider glares, but there's also a slight twitch of his lip. Meanwhile, Dody's considering the size of her hands, so I tell her, "I'm just teasing your uncle about how he chooses knives for ladies." Then, I spring one of her curls before continuing, "But I'm not one for playing football."

"That's too bad," Harding says, not disappointed at all.

"Uncle Raider's the best at it," Dody says. "You'd have a lot of fun. I always come home with grass stains on my clothes."

"And dirt up your nose," Harding adds.

"Your uncle would likely see that as an improvement in my case, but I better let you enjoy it on your own." Harding shrugs and runs out the door.

"You could always just watch," Raider suggests, surprising me.

"Maybe." I lift my shoulder cautiously, and Raider follows the children outside.

Imily walks in just as the others leave, fussing with her black hair—tamed in a braid and rolled into a bun on the back of her neck—as she says, "I'm sure Ballast won't be much longer."

Curses! Ballast! That's his name.

Maybe I'll remember it this time, though probably, I won't. The issue is he's quite forgettable. He's a big man—tall and round with a freckled face and shy eyes—but I've yet to hear him speak, and most times I've seen him, he's ducking from the room. In short, he's the opposite of Imily, and while he's likely a perfectly fine individual, I doubt he'll ever give me a chance to find out.

"It's no problem. Chett doesn't seem bothered."

Imily sits across from me before asking, "Are you involved with my brother?" She poses the question without hesitation or embarrassment—just like Raider would do.

"Me?" I can't contain my laughter. "Oh, by the Dark, no. Is that what all that talk was after dinner yesterday?"

"Maybe a bit."

"Well, let me put your mind at ease. That's not even a remote possibility."

"Why not?" Imily asks, sounding disappointed, which is startling. Then, changing seats, she settles on the chair next to mine.

"Hmm. Is this a reasonable hour to say shocking things?"

Imily giggles. "It takes a lot to startle me."

"Well, brace yourself, Imily. I believe I'm the one to do it."

"Bring it on," she declares.

"The main reason I'd never be involved with your brother is that he hates me."

"That's hard to believe," she says, so I enlighten her, finding some perverse satisfaction in painting myself in the worst possible light.

"I was sixteen and silly, attending the governor's reception when they first came to Adlumen. I flirted with Raider when he asked me not to and forced a kiss on him after he'd told me he was dating someone else. Someone who turned out to be his future wife."

I left a sour impression on Raider that only increased in the days that followed, but Imily's unconcerned, shrugging her shoulder and saying, "We all do dumb things at that age. I know I did."

I bite my lip, holding back a laugh. It wasn't even a week ago I asked Raider to admit young people often do unwise things, and he responded defiantly that he never had. And yet, here's his sister not only acknowledging fallible youth but counting herself among them.

Still, my situation is more than what she's considered, so I ask, "Did you try to assassinate the leader of a light bubble?"

"No! And neither did you!" She laughs but stops when I don't join her. Her expression flattens—her mind working—and I let the information sink in before adding, "Not only that, but it was Raider's best friend, who's now my sister's husband."

"Evans Dirby!" Imily's jaw drops, her eyes widening until the smile lines on the edges disappear. "You're the sister who —"

I nod. "Sharade Endrack, though I go by Shar now. And don't worry, Imily. I won't blame you for keeping your distance now that you know. Any distaste you feel toward me is well-deserved."

Imily sputters—her mouth agape—because I've taken her words, so I push to stand. I'm grateful when Chett opens the door, beckoning me to follow him, and I leave Imily with her new knowledge.

"Is Imily okay?" he asks as we set a leisurely pace across the grass. I'm unsure where we're going, but it doesn't matter.

"Sure. I just told her my part in the assassination attempt on Evans."

"Ah." Chett smiles, but it's like paint covering a bumpy wall—the result not exhibiting as the painter intends—and then he adds, "You are rather shocking for such a small thing."

"I doubt I'm the only one with a disturbing past."

"And I'd agree with you." I watch him, wondering if the troubled look he carries stems from the death of his brother. Everyone deals so differently with death. Losing Kally made Raider angry, while Chett is perpetually sad but pretending not to be. And me, well, I've learned to ignore loss completely since dwelling on the people I miss took my mind to ugly places.

I push my shoulder into his, which takes some effort because he's a big guy and quite a bit taller than me. "I'm just lucky because the most terrible thing I've ever done is extremely well known." I clap my hands, rubbing them together, adding, "It's lovely to be famous."

Ignoring my sarcasm, Chett asks, "What was life like growing up?" Meanwhile, I've just realized our destination —Chett's taking me to the football game, where Raider and Harding are facing off against Renegade and Dody.

"Well, I thought I had everything when, really, my dad made our world very small. But I was mostly happy. I had a lot of energy—like my sister—and Chessie was always up for fun. I miss that about her."

"But you don't think you'll try to reconnect?" I shake my head, knowing a reunion wouldn't be good for either of us, and Chett continues, "Look, Shar, I don't know that you've done anything to warrant a permanent break from your family."

I choke out a laugh. "Are you kidding? I tried to kill a governor, and they sentenced me to a Dark prison indefinitely. My sister married the guy and never tried to contact me. That's pretty telling."

Chett shakes his head. "And yet the opportunity is still there." He stops me by taking my arm and waits for me to meet his eyes. "There are worse things than what you did."

Curses. I can't imagine what.

We continue to the field. Raider sees us approach and raises his hand in greeting. "See," Chett says. "Even Raider's warming up, and he's been formidable before now."

"Maybe Imily's sweetness is wearing off on him."

"Doubtful," Chett says with a chuckle, and we sit. "He's a good guy, though. Lost his wife right before I lost my brother."

I suck in my lip, thinking about loss and willing the thoughts away. "Raider's mom was born in Torquent, wasn't she?" I ask, knowing the answer but needing the distraction.

"Sivil Roil. Yes, she was."

"Tyran's serrated blade tore up my sister's shoulder," I add, just throwing out a random comment.

Chett looks at me, slightly confused, but finally says, "They're a straightforward people, that's for sure. When they're at war, the intent is to kill, and they prepare every advantage."

"No wonder you're glad they're on your side," I say, unable to keep the sting from my voice.

"I'm not glad to be on any side," he returns with his own level of bite.

I'm glad when the footballers appear since our

conversation is on a negative trajectory. The children grab Chett's arms, pulling him toward the field.

"You promised!" Harding yells with no hint of his dad's shyness. No, this little man will not lurk in hallways—he'll be seen and heard.

"But the teams will be uneven," Chett complains, looking at anyone for help—well, anyone but me, making Renegade's eyes narrow as he picks up on the awkwardness from our minor snit.

"I'll sit this one out. I need a breather," Raider says, and Harding opens his mouth to argue, but one shake of Raider's head and the boy's mouth snaps shut.

But Raider doesn't sit for his breather. Renegade herds the children, and as soon as Chett is absorbed into the game, Raider suggests returning to the house. I feel like I'm turning in circles, but I go along for one reason—it seems odd, but for once, I feel more comfortable being around Raider than the other options open to me.

"Thanks," Raider says.

"For what?" I ask, startled by the sincerity in his tone.

"Well, Chett hasn't yelled or rained down punches on me. I assume that means the little prisoner has kept her promise."

Little prisoner. I keep my expression even, but I'm disappointed he's bringing up that nickname again. I'll never get past my well-earned reputation, especially where Raider's concerned.

Equally disappointing are the secrets these men are keeping from one another. It's disheartening that people who usually get along are at odds. All because of Tyran. I rein in my frustration, focusing on the cadence of our footsteps as I say, "Well, you're welcome. I bet that was painful for you to say."

Holding open the house door, Raider grins, admitting, "And you'd win that bet."

◆ ◆ ◆

It's dinnertime, and Ballast has yet to return. Chett's resigned to staying another night, but I grow tired of our delays. I need a clean break from the Roils, but my luck in reaching that objective is nonexistent.

I descend the stairs in the main house since Imily insists we sleep with the family tonight, not in guest housing. I see it as a sign she doesn't hate me too severely.

I've just sat down for our evening meal. Chett's across the table from me, and we're discussing plans for our return to Hamo in the morning. I'm hopeful my troubles are in the past, but then the most significant complication I could imagine shows up in Ora, appearing in the room beneath the cheery yellow doorframe.

It takes a minute for me to catch my breath.

Another minute to process what I'm seeing.

And then I convey to the others what they've already realized for themselves, whispering, "My sister's here."

Chessie Endrack—I guess it's Chessie Dirby now—just entered the dining room. Her walnut brown hair, the same shade as Dad's, has grown out, and she has it up in a ponytail that's braided and hanging over her shoulder. Her olive skin is as golden as ever, setting off the long scar on her cheek. She has a jacket over her arm—so typical for my sister—even though it's a sweltering August night and hardly jacket weather. She's also carrying a bag.

Both jacket and bag drop to the wooden floor. Her dark brown eyes are wide, and her full lips are in an O as she dazedly returns my stare, saying, "It can't be."

For my part, my fork freezes in the air, with a perfectly

roasted square of beef on the end.

Raider's on his feet a second later. "I'll go see your husband," he says, rushing past Chessie, reaching out to squeeze her arm briefly before flying through the doorway.

"It's really you," Chessie says, taking an unsteady step forward.

I drop my fork with a clatter and push back from the table, standing. "It's me. I'll get out of your way."

Chett stands too, and as much as I appreciate the support, I need him to sit back down. I wave off his silent offer for company just as Chessie says, "Wait." I stop, and she approaches. "Will you take my hand?"

"Why?" I ask, drawing my hands away from her. "What for?"

"I, just... I need to know you're real."

She wants to know if I'm *real?* It's a ridiculous comment. After all, she's not the one who spent eight years in a Dark prison having illusory conversations with very non-real people—her included. Still, I guardedly put out my fingers for her to take. She folds her hand around mine and releases a shaky sigh. I look around the room. It's just Valore, Imily, Chett, and me since the children are sleeping, and Renegade's disappeared again.

"Valore can explain things better than me," I whisper, pulling my hand from hers and striding away from the group.

"Shar!" Valore calls out. "It solves nothing to run from this." But I'm already out of the dining room, leaping up the stairs. Chett keeps up, just barely, but when I make it to my bedroom, I slip inside and shut him out, turning the lock.

"I'm sorry, Chett. I need a minute," I say through the door, then turn around and wring my hands.

My sister's here.

Curses! My sister's here!

And Raider mentioned her husband.

Evans.

The unluckiness of my thirteenth day has not only continued but worsened. I suck in my upper lip, running my teeth and tongue over the tender skin. Pressing my back to the door, I close my eyes and slide until I'm on the floor. Then, I focus on my fear, battling my demons in the dark like I've done too many times to count.

I'm searching for something inside of my mind—some strength or determination. I must find a way to face this situation—to come out the other side and not look like a coward.

This wasn't supposed to happen!

I'm avoiding Adlumen for this exact reason, and somehow, they discovered me here.

I should have gone to Hamo with Arrick!

I bang my shoulders on the door just as there's a knock.

"Sharade, let me in." It's Raider. He's been to see Evans, and now he's here for me. Is Evans demanding my head? What's happening out there?

I push harder against the door, ensuring he stays out, because I've changed my mind. They can label me a coward, but I'm not leaving this room. It gets quiet in the hallway, and I'm sure Raider's given up until he appears before me.

Curses! I forgot the adjoining bathroom.

I'm sharing it with Valore, but it was easy enough for Raider to walk on through. "Hey," he says, crouching until we're eye level. "So, that was a surprise." I roll my eyes at the absurd summation. "How about we go down there together, and you get this first meeting over with?"

"Brilliant plan," I deadpan. "At least, for someone who's not *petrified* by that idea."

"Aren't you a little curious?"

"Not really."

"Do you harbor any hope in that cranky container of yours?" He taps the side of my head.

I chuckle shakily. "You're terrible at this."

"Yet all day, my sister's been swearing I'm more than a pretty face."

"Has she? I don't recall." I laugh again, and Raider puts his hand through the crook of my arm and pulls me to my feet. "You think you've convinced me to leave this room?"

"No. My legs are falling asleep." Raider grins down at me, and I don't detect any of his usual annoyance.

"I can't do this," I say, gripping his arm and looking into his black eyes.

"You can," he says with conviction, then adds, "Because we'll be there to help you."

"*We*?" I ask, narrowing my eyes at him. "You're including yourself in that promise?"

"You and I will call a truce for tonight."

"Why?" I ask, not entirely trusting him.

He releases a labored breath. "There's one thing you should know about me," he starts, and it's almost enough to make me crack up, but I'm still too scared about what's downstairs and that Raider could have the right words to convince me to trust him.

"What's that?"

"I'm a sucker for family. And I think you are too." He leans in until he's all I can see. "And you'll regret this day if you don't at least try."

My eyes find Evans first—the Lordly Prince himself—but I

glance away. I can't believe Raider talked me into coming back. He saunters toward his friend with exaggerated casualness, pulling him in for a manly hug. "We barely had a second to catch up with my quick greeting out there."

Yeah. A quick greeting where he alerted Evans that—*Woot! Woot!*—his onetime assassin is in the house.

Curses! Could this day get any worse?

"How's everyone back in Adlumen? What are you all doing out this way?" Raider asks, peppering his friend with questions while Evans stares at me over Raider's shoulder.

His cheeks are fuller than when I last saw him, and he looks different without the lenses he had to wear in the Adlumen light bubble. I hated him so much then—his wide mouth from so much laughter and his confident swagger meant to convince everyone he was the best man in the room and knew it. He wears neither now—the smile nor the swagger—but *Ferrum Pax*, the governor's regalia, is still in the scabbard on his chest.

"I thought you were playing a joke on me," Evans says, disregarding Raider's attempt at conversation. He has a stockier build than Raider but isn't as tall. Hunched over in thought like he is now, he's about the same height as Chessie.

"Yeah, it's no joke," I say with a retreating step. "Look, I don't mind just heading back upstairs. Staying out of your way." I point a thumb toward my room, but Valore appears at my side, escorting me to the table without a word.

"We're just starting dinner if you're hungry," Imily offers the newcomers, her eyes flashing between my sister and me.

Meanwhile, Chett's back in his seat, but he leans across the table to snag the edge of my plate. He pulls it until it's in the spot next to him, and then Valore walks me forward, waiting for me to sit. I look down at my fork, which is still stabbing the meat.

Raider guides the others to the chairs in front of me. It's then I realize he's directing them to three open seats. One for Chessie. One for Evans. And one for the little person clinging to his mom's pants.

Chessie's a mom.

I asked Raider if she was married but never thought to ask about kids. She's twenty-seven now, so kids make sense, but it didn't even enter my mind. I still see her as an eighteen-year-old in Ambitus, sparring and defending her people with every breath.

"It's okay, Hesston," Chessie says soothingly, and I observe the boy who has my sister's walnut brown hair, but the hazel eyes and mouth with the bottom lip bigger than the top are all Evans. "These people are our friends," she continues, prying his fingers off and placing him in the seat across from Valore while she takes the one across from me.

Her face looks different—mature, not old—with a calmness I don't remember. Maybe it's the passage of time or being a mother. Regardless, she soon loses the peaceful expression, her face turning agitated the longer she looks at me. "By the light, you're really alive," she says, shaking her head in disbelief.

"Sorry about that." It's not a joke or even resentment—it honestly seems right to apologize to Chess for continuing to exist.

"No. It's not—" Chessie takes a breath, looking me over. Growing up, my sister had endless energy—could exist on five hours of sleep a night—but she looks tired today. I guess I have that effect on people—wearing them out by merely existing.

"Hey, it's okay. I didn't mean anything by it."

"I didn't either," she says quickly. "It's just... they said you got moved by mistake but weren't sure where you ended up."

"They never moved me."

"Oh." Chessie blinks. "Well, when they sent word that Dad died, that was their update about you. Honestly, I thought you were both dead, and they just didn't want to admit it."

"So, for the last four years, you thought I was dead?"

Chessie's brow furrows. "Dad died two years ago."

"Never trust a desert rat. Dad died *four* years ago." I chuckle dryly, shaking my head. "I guess they got a few extra laps of gold from you."

Chessie just stares while Raider, thankfully, turns the focus on them, asking their reason for visiting Ora. It turns out they're here to see the abating Dark, which launches a halfhearted discussion about the phenomenon. Who knew Sharade Endrack's return would distract from the world's most significant scientific development since the creation of the Dark? I sure didn't expect it, but there's no doubt that's what's happening as I feel their curious eyes on me.

We finish Imily's meal—I even have dessert—and then it feels like as good a time as any to leave. So, I stand and excuse myself, grateful when no one argues for me to stay.

I'm upstairs long enough to change into my pajamas when there's a knock on the door. "Don't make me use the bathroom again," he says, and I smile. At least I can find some humor in this awful day. I open the door, and Raider enters without an invitation, asking, "Are you okay?" with abundant concern.

"Oh, Raider," I say, dropping onto the bed with a dramatic sigh and scooting up on the blue bedcover to lean against the wooden headboard. "You're not playing your part correctly."

"My part?"

I pull my knees up and twist to lean on the pillows. "You're the disjointed, caustic character who makes me look inside and determine to be better. You're not the sympathetic figure who cares about my disappointments and wishes more for me."

"You have me packaged and labeled, do you?"

"Yep. And you've done the same to me."

Raider walks to the bedside chair and sits. His nose twitches before he says, "You're the conniving criminal—murderess and manipulator—undeserving of a second chance."

I grin, dropping my chin onto my fist and resting my elbow on the pillow. "That's better."

"Maybe I miscast you. Maybe you're the misunderstood heroine. Maybe my dad's faith in you has a foundation."

I pull in my lip and release it slowly. "I understand your hesitation. I know what it's like to be disappointed when someone's not all you, or others, imagined them to be."

"You're thinking of your dad," he says, and I don't argue, though I don't want to talk about it.

"It doesn't matter," I say. "And neither does this situation with Chess and Evans. I faced them, and now I can go to Hamo and live my life."

"I don't believe you," Raider says, then goes quiet, expecting a response—wanting me to fight back.

"Oh, dear. You've reverted to your original stereotype," I say tiredly.

"Really?" Raider rubs his chin, his black eyes curious and searching. "Which one is that?"

"The belligerent naysayer, of course. Now, get out of here so I can get some sleep."

CHAPTER TWENTY-TWO

Fourteen Days Free

"Can we talk?" Chessie asks when I open my bedroom door and find her on the other side.

I'm showered and dressed, content to hide in my room—even skip breakfast—until it's time to leave with Chett. With little to occupy myself, I have my brown bottle and Squatty's necklace out on the dresser. When Chessie knocked, I was scraping dirt from a tiny groove in the necklace—since even a good scrub didn't clean everything—and now, she wants to talk.

I sigh. Avoiding my sister is impossible when she's not striving for the same goal.

"Sure," I say, twisting the blunt ends of my hair between my fingers.

I step forward at the same time as she does, and we bump into each other.

"Oh. You want to come in here." My cheeks flush, and I step back.

"Is that okay?"

"I just didn't think you'd want to meet alone." I move to a chair in the corner, allowing her to pick her place in the room. She shuts the door and sits opposite me.

"You're different." The comment is even—not friendly or hateful.

"How so?" I have a few guesses, but I want Chessie to tell me.

"You've lost your conniving expression." She hugs her jacket. "Other things too."

"My sparkle?" I ask, recalling my younger self and how I'd brag about my abundance of sparkle. Chessie frowns as I continue, "You don't put someone in a Dark prison to make them shine. You do it to break them, and it worked. I'm well and truly broken."

"Sharade," Chessie says on an exhale.

"It's just Shar now. Don't confuse me for the sister you once knew." I don't know that it's good to be near Chessie because I feel old traits trying to resurface, and that's something neither of us would be glad about. "Look, I'm sorry. Maybe we should—" I stop when there's another knock on my door.

Curses! Who now?

"Come in," I say, and a second later, Raider's head peeks around the door.

"I didn't know you were busy." He glances at Chessie. "I was just checking on you for breakfast."

I tilt my head and squint. "Since when have you checked on me for anything?"

Raider chuckles. "Yeah. Well, are you coming down or what?" I cross one knee over the other and relax against the padded armchair, settling in. That only makes him laugh outright. "Dody insists on a game before the Adlumians leave for the abatement, but she refuses to play without you."

"No football," I say. "Even for that sweet girl."

"Oh, she knows better than to ask about football. She has a different game in mind. I'll tell her you'll be down in five." Raider grins—a rare sight—and ducks out of the room.

"I never said I'd join them," I say, perplexed by his methods.

"He's good at that," Chessie says. "Getting people to do his bidding." Chessie would know. I'm sure she's seen Raider frequently during my prison years.

"He's good at many things," I say bitterly. "You should see him spit nails."

His laughter echoes in the hallway, penetrating the door —the jerk is apparently eavesdropping. "Hurry down, ladies," we hear, and then footsteps. Chessie smiles at his antics while all I can do is stare at her.

My sister.

Eight years feels like an eternity when we're suddenly sitting together again. She seems so familiar—her usual ticks and expressions—yet she's a stranger to me, both the life she leads and the people in it.

I stand abruptly, grabbing a comb off the dresser. "Should we go down?"

"Not yet." Chessie's suddenly at my side, her body blocking the door. Sure, I could step around her, but she's determined to talk and would likely corner me again downstairs. "I heard you're going to Hamo."

"Is that what's got you worried?" I release a shaky laugh and tug the comb through my short hair. "I haven't perfected my plans, but I'll avoid Adlumen. You can put that troublesome thought from your mind."

"Avoid Adlumen," Chessie repeats. "Like, forever?" She frowns, and it highlights the scar near her lip that looks like a dimple. The scar I gave her—one of many times I threw something at her face. The memory rattles me, as does her fear that I'll ruin her perfect little world.

"Good grief." This time, I laugh out loud. "Do you have nightmares of me turning up and doing something dastardly? You can relax. I'll give you a wide berth."

I take a step, and she grabs my arm. "You misunderstand. I *want* you to go to Adlumen."

"Whatever for?" The residual smile drops from my lips. "That's a terrible idea," I say, my voice raw.

"It's not." She digs her fingers in deeper, keeping me close. "Mom needs to see you."

"Mom?"

"She's mourned your absence for eight years. She needs it."

Mourned. Needs.

I suck in my upper lip, biting the chapped skin.

What about all I mourned? What about what I need?

"No." It's an easy answer to give—the only one I'm capable of.

"You must."

Must?

"I said no." Yanking my arm from her grasp, my elbow slams into the dresser. I wince from the immediate pain, then watch helplessly as my brown bottle teeters, tips, and drops to the floor with a crash.

"Oh, shit!" Chessie says, jumping back, while all I can do is gawk at the jagged carnage. "Pass me that can," she says, pointing past me.

I don't move. I only stare. The circle where my mouth would get water is still whole, as is the bottom. One remnant resembles a tiger's tooth, while another looks like a boat.

"The trash can," Chessie repeats, stacking pieces in the base.

I pull my suitcase across the floor and kneel next to Chessie. "Put them in here," I say, helping to gather the shards.

Her eyes are on me, but I refuse to look at her face. A second later, she pushes to her feet. "Fine. I'll get the can."

I grab her pant leg before she can move. "You have no say in this. It's my bottle, and it goes in here."

She fists her hands, propping them on her hips. "With

your clothes? There will be glass everywhere. You'll cut yourself when—"

"Then I'll cut myself!"

I'm not cautious as I pick up the pieces, feeling the bite of an edge more than once.

"Some things never change," Chessie says. "You're still drawing lines and putting people on the other side."

I don't have it in me to argue. I don't care if she's right. I stay focused and get everything secured, shutting the lid and pushing the suitcase away from me. I should never have taken the bottle out. That's the trouble with fragile things —they should be kept far away from anything capable of breaking them.

"I'm not going to Adlumen, let alone Ambitus," I say, retrieving Squatty's necklace from the dresser and safely tucking it with the rest of my belongings. "I'm an escaped criminal, and the people will detain me without a second thought." I look at my sister. "I understand why you imprisoned me—I even agree with your reasons for doing it —but I'm not going back to prison."

Chessie drops her chin and looks into my eyes. "I don't want you to."

"Yeah? What happens when the governors insist?"

"You forget. I'm married to one."

"Chess," I start, then rub the space between my eyes. "I'll die if I go back to prison, and that's not me being dramatic. If it weren't for Valore, I'd be dead now. I can't... I just can't risk it."

"I swear nothing bad will happen to you. We'll sneak you in and keep everything quiet. No one will know you're there, and you can see our mom."

I laugh. "Nothing stays a secret in Ambitus."

"Well, for the sake of our government's security, I hope

that's not true."

"What would Alfric say if he discovered you'd sneaked me into Ambitus?" General Pruden—who Chessie calls Alfric because of their close friendship—was my Dad's right hand. He was also privy to Dad's misdeeds and instrumental in restoring the governors to their rightful position. His devotion is one hundred percent rooted in Adlumen law, meaning he isn't an ally of mine. He monitors everything that happens in Ambitus. It's folly to think I'd slip in and out without his notice.

"Well, of course, I'd tell Alfric you're there. And the governors too."

"So, only the most powerful people would know. The ones who hate me the most. Brilliant plan, Sis. The answer's still no." I brush past her, deciding there's no point in skipping breakfast now. Food is an escape from this conversation.

"Sharade! Please. Just think about it," Chessie says, chasing after me.

"It's just Shar," I say, whipping around to face her, realizing I've grown taller than my sister. Not by much, but enough that I look down. "I won't make any promises."

My heavy footsteps on the wooden floor announce our arrival. I expect Dody to be there, pulling me away to play, but it seems she got impatient and went to play on her own. Instead, a dozen eyes follow us as we cross the dining room, but the conversation doesn't stop. Hesston's pacing in front of Raider, telling him about his latest antics, and what little I've heard leaves an impression—I never knew a five-year-old could get into so much calculated trouble.

"Then Ma grounded me to my room," Hesston says, glancing at Chessie.

"For dying your cousin's hands purple, is all," Evans states with unconcealed amusement. Hesston chuckles, nods, then cocks his head, strutting around and looking just like his dad.

"He's always trying to impress Raider," Chessie whispers into my ear. "I'll be honest—half the time, I don't know how to keep the reins on that kid."

"Sounds like the grounding was well deserved, Lad," Raider says, pulling my attention away. "Maybe you should give your ma a break and lay off the pranks." Hesston grumbles but watches as I sit with the breakfast food I plated. My stomach still disagrees with an abundance of food, so it's a small amount.

"They've been talking about you," Hesston says to me with a tilt of his head.

"I'm not surprised," I answer, meeting his assertive gaze.

"He says you know the Torquent blade." Hesston nods at Valore but looks at me in disbelief.

"I do."

"She's always been partial to that weapon," Chessie says. My sister thought it was the serrated blade's brutality that caught my interest. I never told her the gnarled scar on her shoulder drove my ambition—fear of ending up with a scar of my own.

"And now she's mastered it," Valore says, looking at me with pride, but I shake my head, wanting him to stay quiet. He's whittling something, and I remember back in Aunty's Cellar, he said it was a hobby he enjoyed. What little I see of his project, he's quite good.

"Mastered?" Chessie asks, her tone unsurprisingly doubtful.

My non-verbal plea for silence goes unheeded as Valore declares, "She'd be a match for Tyran."

Chessie laughs. "I can't imagine that's the case." My hackles rise, and I'm on the verge of challenging her—ready to show off my improved skills—when Raider jumps into the discussion.

"Speaking of Tyran, there are things you need to know." He's speaking to the Adlumians but watching me—stopping me from making a foolish mistake. Because while Chessie's behavior is callous and evokes a decade-old rivalry, I don't want to get into it with her. Raider deserves my thanks, but mostly, I want to get on the road and escape them all.

This latest interaction again highlights why going to Ambitus is a bad idea. During the last two weeks, Raider has teased out bits of my attitude, but overnight, Chessie brought it out in full force.

The conversation that follows is a blur. I don't reengage until the end when Raider tells them Tyran knows Tesha is a beacon and wants her. "How did she find out?" Chessie asks while her eyes beg the gathering to say it wasn't her fault, but Raider and I suspect it was—Chessie told my dad, and he told Diggs and me.

"Diggs is alive," Raider says, answering her question without saying outright who's to blame. An explanation of how he knows Diggs's status follows, which includes my sighting in Sperne and the talk in Bratus.

Chessie's green with remorse, which Evans tries to save her from, saying, "That doesn't mean Diggs sourced the information to Tyran. Historically, she's been creative in her methods to gain governor insight."

"Yeah. Scary Karrie," Chessie grumbles, rolling her eyes. "Remember those stupid interviews we did? And then it turned out the woman was a Torquent spy!"

"I remember," Raider says with little emotion. "It was a rather important day."

There's a pause, and then Chessie gasps. "*Your wedding.* Oh, Raider, I'm so sorry. You must think me completely insensitive."

"Not at all, Chessie." He brushes a hand over his pant leg. "Don't worry about it. I need to take a walk, though. My legs feel tied in knots from days in a car or at this table, and today's schedule only requires more sitting." Raider's up and out of the room before anyone says another word.

"That was so stupid of me," Chessie says while Evans comforts her. None of us leave the room to comfort Raider, though. Not even his dad. I guess some things are better left alone.

◆ ◆ ◆

"Can we talk?"

Curses! What's with that question today? First, it was Chessie, and now...

"Sure," I answer Chett while Valore watches curiously.

Chett leads me away from the cars where everyone's gathered. He's decided to accompany the Adlumians to see the abatement again. It will delay our departure another day —which frustrates me to no end—but he feels diplomacy is worth it. Chett stops when we're by the outbuildings but still within view of the cars. "Your sister wants you to go to Adlumen," he says, and I'm unsure if he's guessing or if Chessie talked to him about it, but it doesn't change my answer.

"Yes, and I've told her it's a bad idea." When he doesn't respond, I ask, "Don't you agree?" I want him to tell me yes—without a doubt—it's a colossally bad idea.

"Not necessarily," he says instead, and I wilt at the flimsy answer.

"I wouldn't do that to you. You stayed here for me, and I'd feel guilty if I didn't return to Hamo with you."

There. That's as good a reason as any.

Chett smiles, and the expression looks nearly legit, but

something still holds him back from genuine happiness. "That component doesn't deserve your consideration," he says. "I was happy to stay, and my time with an Adlumian governor will benefit Hamo, so remove my delay from the equation and do what's best for you."

"And you think going to Ambitus is best?"

"I don't know. But if this war happens and you're in Hamo, it could be many years before you'd have the opportunity to see your family again. Then there are the logistics of your alliance."

"What do you mean?"

"If you come to Hamo, Adlumen will become your enemy. Can you live with that?"

Raider has expressed similar questions, though Chett poses it differently. Could I view my former people, friends, and family as enemies? I don't know. But haven't they considered me their enemy for eight years now? So, maybe automatic reciprocation isn't an outlandish response on my part.

Curses! I thought I was done having enemies.

"I want you to know, whatever you decide, you have a place in Hamo if you need it."

"So, if I go to Adlumen, you'll ensure I'm allowed into Hamo afterward?"

"Yes, and I'll make sure you're protected." Chett pauses, stepping forward and taking my hand. "I'd be honored to give you a place in my home."

I don't know how to take his statement, and he picks up on my uncertainty, saying, "I've confused you." He smiles, and it's his usual conflicted expression. "Do I need to spell out my intentions?"

Intentions. That one word clears up any confusion.

"We barely know each other," I whisper. And having

overheard Chett's private conversation with Arrick, I don't know how much I trust him. Still, while I can't accept Chett's offer, I don't dare refuse it—I'm not in a situation to turn down any extension of kindness.

"True. We don't know each other well, but having you in my life would be no hardship. And maybe we could help each other forget our troubled pasts and move into a brighter future."

"Maybe you could learn to smile again for real?" I ask, surprised I dare mention my observation.

"Maybe." He squeezes my hand, clinging to me like a desperate hope.

"Why bring this up now? Why not wait until we've known each other longer?"

"Because when you return to Hamo, Arrick will make his move."

"Arrick?" I ask, my eyes wide.

"You can't have been blind to his interest."

"As blind as someone with light sight in the Dark. He's old enough to be my dad!"

Chett chuckles. "He's not. How old are you?"

"Almost twenty-five."

"He's forty-one."

"Yeah. And that's too old for me."

"He's quite the lady's man. Methinks if he wants, he'll claim your interest without too much fuss," Chett says with a wink. It's the most playful I've ever seen him. Still, I'm shocked by this subject and shake my head—done with this conversation—stating emphatically, "Methinks not."

CHAPTER TWENTY-THREE

Fifteen Days Free

Knocking my fingers against the door, I hear movement on the other side. I'm at the outbuilding on Imily's property—outside a family guest suite—and after a few more noises from within, the door swings wide.

"Hi," I say to Hesston, who looks up at me with messy hair, a food mustache, and a mischievous grin.

"They were talking about you again, but they'll say they weren't." He leans against the door. "Why do they tell me not to lie when they do it all the time?"

I can't help enjoying his precociousness. Hesston thinks like an adult—much like Chessie did when she was young—but he misbehaves like a child. Similar to Evans, I'd guess. He's an even mix of his parents.

"Adults are funny that way. When you lie, they think you're trying to get away with something naughty. But when they do it... well, they think they're being kind."

"Hmm. Do you lie?"

"Not much anymore, but I used to."

"Because you were being kind?"

"No, I was probably more like you. *Sneaky*." He grins, and I know I've guessed correctly. "But I tell you what, stick to the truth. It's better that way and can be equally entertaining. You'll notice many truths are powerful enough to shock the pants off someone."

Hesston laughs, then calls out, "Ma!"

"What now?" Chessie asks, spilling from the bedroom

door and straightening when she sees me. “Oh. I wasn't expecting anyone.” She clutches her pajamas like she's unpresentable when I've seen her similarly dressed hundreds of times.

“I wanted you to know I've decided to go to Adlumen.”

“You have?” Chessie asks at the same time as Hesston exclaims, “Hooray!” At least I have one fan among the Dirbys. But my sister suddenly looks hesitant. Maybe she regrets forcing the issue. Maybe she's changed her mind.

“Hess, go in with your dad.”

“Aw, Ma.”

“Please, Son. Hurry up.”

“Fine,” Hesston says, stomping out his disapproval as he goes.

Chessie pulls the door shut, steps back, then stares at me.

“Have you changed your mind?” I ask. “I could catch a ride to Hamo with Chett as easily as going to Adlumen with you.”

“No. That's not it.”

“Then, what's the problem?” Because there is one. I can feel it.

“I don't want you to take this the wrong way.”

“Chessie, I've been in prison for eight years. I've experienced a lot of unpleasant things. I doubt you could do much more. Just say it.”

“I'm... uncomfortable with you getting friendly with Hesston.”

Oh. Not what I expected. Not entirely a surprise, either.

“Because I'm a criminal.”

“No. Because I don't want him to get attached and then have you leave. He acts tough, but he's got a soft center.”

And since I'll be in Adlumen a short time before doing

just that—leaving—her concern is valid.

"No problem. I can ignore him. I'll make sure he sees me as unapproachable."

"Oh, no. You don't need to do that."

I squint and scratch my neck. "Well, we should be in Ambitus tomorrow night. I'll stay the following day to speak with Mom, and then I'll get out of your way. I won't be around long enough for him to form an attachment."

"You should stay with us a week, not just a day."

I release a groan, followed by a laugh. "You're not making this easy, Sis. I'm trying to do what you asked, but you keep countering my solutions and conflicting your request. I'm not sure what you want from me."

Chessie pads across the floor, barefoot in her pajamas, and drops onto the couch. "I'm not sure either," she says, pursing her full lips. "But definitely stay for a week."

"I don't enjoy being where I'm not wanted."

"You're wanted. It's just..." Chessie grabs a throw pillow and tucks it under her arms, looking up at me like she needs help finding her thoughts.

"Look. I get it," I say, not fully understanding her struggle but relating to the awkwardness of the situation. "How about we start by not making a big deal out of this?"

Chessie snorts. "Sorry, Sharade, but this is an *enormous* deal."

"Just Shar, Chess," I remind her. "I'm just Shar."

Chessie releases a heavy breath, and her head falls back onto the cushion. "Sorry. I'm doing this all wrong."

"You're not. My sudden reappearance isn't easy. And while I planned to keep a respectful distance, that obviously didn't work out." What a mess. "But I don't want to complicate matters. I'll stay for a week. I'll see Mom, avoid Hesston, and abide by any other rules you have. And when the time's up, I'll go away again. Is that satisfactory?"

"You really have changed," Chessie says, squeezing the pillow tighter. "But I still don't entirely trust you." She shakes her head—like she's coming out of a dream—then looks shocked when she realizes what she's just admitted. She opens her mouth, and I feel an apology coming, but I cut her off before she can start.

"In my Dark prison, I'd wake up to the smell of cooking bacon. It may have been Warden Ott's breakfast. I also wondered if a settlement was nearby, and the inhabitants did it to torture us prisoners. Whatever the reason, I never once had bacon, though they frequently teased me with the scent. It got to where I doubted my memory of the smell itself, and I'd say, 'Self, are you making this up?' and Self would answer, 'Yes, I am.'" I reach for the door handle. "It's best not to trust what isn't proven. That kind of faith in any person or thing can lead to downfall. Or madness." I whisper the last part. "Don't second guess your conflicted feelings about me. I'm the last person to convince you to think otherwise without solid proof."

I open the door and leave her room while a trickle of sweat runs down my back that has nothing to do with the temperature.

Who would have thought that weeks after gaining my freedom, I'd be going to Ambitus—the heart of Adlumen? Not me, that's for sure. But, an hour later, we're in two vehicles with that light bubble as our destination.

"Is it just the two of us?" I ask, taking the front passenger seat with Valore behind the wheel. The other car is at capacity with Evans in the driver's seat, Chessie in the front passenger seat, and Raider and Renegade squeezed around Hesston in the back.

"Yep. Just us. They have updates for Evans about Hamo and Torquent, especially after visiting the abatement with

Chett." There's plenty of room for my sister and nephew in our car, but this configuration makes sense based on Chessie's desire to keep Hesston and me apart.

It burns my heart a bit, but like so many things in life, I can overthink it or get over it.

"More room for us," I say as Valore starts the engine. We pull away from the house, waving goodbye to Imily and the others, with Evans taking the lead.

"If you tire of driving, I can take a turn," I say.

"You know how to drive?" Valore asks over the engine's hum and the whip of the wind.

"I was driving Chessie's car when I was twelve," I say, making Valore chuckle. Then, he revs the engine and catches up to the others, keeping a thirty-foot distance.

"I'm surprised Imily didn't lock you in a bedroom and refuse to let you leave," I say, thinking of his daughter's tearful goodbye.

"She would have if it weren't for Stryke."

"That makes sense." Although, I don't know if I would have given up so easily if I had a familial claim on Valore.

"Besides, she knows I want to see home again. The Southern Territory is my land, but Caelum is where I belong." I suck in my upper lip, thinking about Valore's connection to his home. I envy it, but I don't let the feeling take root because those types of emotions tend to get me into trouble.

"I've been curious about something, and I hope you don't mind if I ask about it," Valore says.

"I can't imagine there's anything you don't know about me, but go ahead."

"What did Chett talk to you about yesterday? Before we left for the abatement?"

"Oh, that," I say, my cheeks burning. I hoped to put that conversation out of my mind for a while. Possibly forever. I grip the metal bar above my head as we bounce along, saying, "Well, he proposed an arrangement of sorts if I go to Hamo."

"What sort of arrangement?"

"A living arrangement." I clear my throat. "With him."

Valore clicks his tongue. "So, a proposal type of proposal," he says, raising his eyebrows.

"Probably. But he didn't get specific about the particulars. He seems to think Arrick might make a similar offer, though he must be wrong. That seems preposterous. I mean, he's much older than me. And while he was accommodating and complimentary, I didn't get that vibe from him."

Valore nods, twisting his hands on the steering wheel.

"I'm sure Chett's seeing things that aren't there. And as for Chett, have you noticed he's a little off? Nice enough, but something is lacking in his expression. I don't think I've ever truly seen who he is. It might be awkward to pair up with him."

"You're considering it?" Valore glances over.

"I'm considering *everything*." Valore purses his lips, facing forward and returning to his silent brooding. "Look. I'm not sold on the idea." I chuckle. "I mean, they must be desperate. I don't even look that good."

I stretch out my pale arms and look down at my skinny legs. Then I push my fingers through my short hair, ruffling it. "I'm like a shorn sheep," I laugh, fingering the lengths.

"They're not desperate," Valore says, not joining me in laughing. "And you're stunning. You just can't see it."

I twist in my seat, looking at the man whose soft kindness became my rock during my most troubled days. "You're as sweet as any grandpa I ever had," I say, though he's my dad's age, but it doesn't seem right to mention Lord Endrack now. I lean over and kiss him on the cheek but straighten quickly and back away from him. I know I'm too attached and can't get drawn in anymore. The day I leave his side is coming fast. I've already avoided it twice, but soon, I'll be without another reason to delay.

"Did you know either of your grandfathers?" he asks.

I giggle. "Fine. No, I never met them." But if I had, I'd have wanted them to be exactly like Valore. "Do you think the abatement's enough to stop a war?" I ask because there's more to think about than my drama—it's best to resolve my personal life later.

"Land greed is a powerful motivator. It could be enough, but Raider's depending on it too much. He needs to consider additional incentives in case of an unwanted outcome."

"You don't think he's already doing that? I mean, he's frequently steps ahead of what I'm thinking."

"Maybe he is. But with the years apart, I don't know him like I once did. He's just so changed, and I worry he won't find his way back to the man he once was. Or maybe that's not even what's best for him."

I recognize Raider's different from our first meeting—not as happy or youthful, having yet to experience the horrors of loss. And these last weeks, I've attributed much of his prickliness to being forced to interact with me—someone he doesn't know or trust. But I'm curious about the differences Valore sees, so I ask, "What changes do you see in him?"

"His attitude is hostile, his kindness diminished, and he's lost his spirit. I know much of it is pain from loss, but he doesn't have the right to treat people unkindly. I know you've felt it."

"I have. Especially at first, but he's been better lately. You don't need to worry about me."

"He's always felt things more keenly than his siblings and never more so than the last few years. He was devoted to Kally—adored her—and they were perfect together. If he didn't have—"

"Wait!" I blurt out. Valore glances over but quickly returns his eyes to the road. "This feels wrong. We shouldn't talk about Raider anymore." I grab my friend's arm, squeezing it. "It would make him uncomfortable, and I shouldn't have pressed you for details. I'm sorry."

Valore's brows dip into a thoughtful scowl, and then he nods, saying no more.

A few hours later, we break for a quick lunch and then shuffle seats before continuing. Raider's driving with Renegade in the front passenger seat and Valore in the back with me. Watching the scenery pass is mind-numbing. The lamlight headlights combined with afternoon sunlight means I can see far into the distance, but I can't see Evans's car, though the light blind passengers insist they can. In any case, Evans is driving fast—something Raider disagrees with because the roads aren't smooth—while Raider takes it slower to keep alert for potholes and avoid jostling his dad.

Raider and Renegade are arguing the merits of cars versus horses—outlining in what situations they prefer which mode of travel—when something catches my eye. I lean up, clutching the back of Renegade's seat for balance, and jerk my head to the side. I catch a final glimpse of what caught my attention before it fades into the Dark, getting just enough of a look to confirm the object's reality.

And then I'm facing forward, grabbing Raider's shoulder. "You need to catch up with them. Now!"

"Who?"

"Chessie and Evans. Go!"

Raider slams his foot on the gas. "What do you know?"

While Raider maneuvers the car, I lunge forward, pressing my hand on the horn. The noise sounds small to my ears, so I grab the bar and pull myself up, waving my arms and yelling for them to stop, but they're too far ahead to hear me over the cars.

"Stay on the left side of the road," I yell to Raider.

My arm freezes mid-wave. What if that's what Diggs wants? Maybe it's better to stay on the right.

Curses! I don't know.

"No! Keep in the middle." Raider follows each instruction without argument and continues honking—the sound is seriously weak—while I'm jumping around, hoping they'll notice me.

"What did you see?" he asks, swerving around a rock. The momentum throws me onto the seat next to Valore.

"An arrow in a tree—two feathers black and one blue. Dad and Diggs created road traps together—usually barbed wire buried to trip and injure horses. The arrow alerts friendlies to travel on the left side."

"But Diggs might target that side specifically in this case," Raider comments, understanding my instruction to drive down the middle.

"Yes. He's playing with us."

"Would Chessie know the meaning of the arrow?" Raider asks, glancing back at me.

"I think so." But she would have told Evans to stop, meaning, "She didn't see it." Their car comes into view, traveling at full speed. "I barely did, so maybe we've passed any trouble," I say, doubting my words as I grip his seat.

It's then Raider notices how close I am to him. "What are you doing? Get buckled in!" he bellows, honking the horn again and pressing harder on the pedal.

I'm about to scoot back and do as he says when I see the commotion ahead.

We all see it.

Raider takes his foot off the gas, coasting, while we watch in horror as the car carrying Evans, Chessie, and Hesston dances all over the road. It twists sideways, dirt blossoming in the air before skidding back the other way. The brakes release a loud whine while loose tire strips slap the underside of the metal wheel well. The car teeters on two wheels before Evans straightens it out, and it lands back on all four, jerking to a sudden stop.

With my hand wrapped in Raider's shirt material, I tighten my fingers and anxiously take in the scene. The front and back tires on the left are flat, bound with a chain of spikes. Chessie's curled forward in the seat, her back heaving with rapid breath, while Hesston stares at us with a tear-stained face.

Raider pulls our car closer, slow on the approach. I'm out within seconds—before we're fully stopped—jumping over the edge and racing to my sister. I grab her arm, and she jolts in her seat, glancing up at me.

She looks fine—shocked and shaken, but I see nothing red and release a relieved breath.

Evans watches the two of us while unbuckling and climbing into the back with Hesston. I undo Chessie's buckle and pull her from the car. She follows without question, and I lean her against the side so she can be close to her family.

"Thank the Dark, you're okay," I say, gripping the edge of the car.

"Weirdest thing... it just blew," Evans says, holding a crying Hesston against his side. "Chessie helped me control the wheel, so we didn't roll."

"It didn't just blow," Raider says, inspecting the tire with the roll of spikes wrapped around it. "This was no accident, and we must get back on the road as soon as possible."

"I don't think we'll all fit in one car," Evans says, running one hand over his dark brown hair that's already sticking up in all directions from the ride.

Raider kicks the flattened wheel before grumbling, "Then someone needs to take the lookout while we change these tires." Ballast got them a few spares when he picked up Chett's tire but made it clear they weren't in the best shape. He insisted, quite emphatically, that they were barely better than nothing.

"I'll be the lookout," I say, releasing Chessie, putting on hand on the knife at my waist, and stepping toward the woods.

"Are you sure that's a good idea?" Raider asks. "We know who's out there."

"You think there's someone better?" I ask with a laugh. "I'd say I'm the most expendable of this group." Valore opens his mouth to argue, so I hurriedly add, "I'm joking." Sort of. "But chances are, if I see him, he won't hurt me. He'll just gloat."

"Who?" Chessie asks.

"Uncle Diggs," I say, already to the trees. "If I'm not back in ten, leave me."

"By the Dark, don't be an idiot!" Raider exclaims, and I admit I am being an idiot, but Chessie's weird rules put me in this mindset. "We're not leaving you, and you're not going out there alone."

"No, she's not. Because I'm going with her," Evans announces, jumping from the car and giving Raider a friendly push. "I'm better in the trees, and you're better with that thing." Chessie's eyes widen as she watches her husband walk toward me. Meanwhile, Raider nods his agreement and spins to join Renegade, who's already started on the tires.

Evans takes the lead while I ask, "You're not afraid to be alone with me?"

"No," he says, eyes scanning the ground.

I glance back at my sister. "Chess looks worried." Her eyes even flash to the knife I have. It makes me want to tear it from my waist and throw it into the bushes, regardless of it being a favorite of Raider's.

"She's a worrier. You know that." She is, though she tries to hide it.

For five minutes, we walk silently in a circuit. I watch the woods while Evans keeps his eyes on the ground. There are few signs of life out here—at most, it's a random bug or chirping bird that catches my attention. I let him determine our path, and it's not long before we're back near the cars, but we keep walking, heading away from them again.

"She missed you," Evans says, breaking the silence but not looking at me.

Chessie. I wait a moment, unsure what to say, before finally answering, "She doesn't act like it."

"This way," Evans says. We're on the road—fifty yards from the parked cars—when he points out where Diggs buried the spikes. They're strategically placed in a section of soft dirt where the road frequently gets washed out. And they're on the left side. That Diggs planned this trap specifically around knowledge my sister and I would have makes me sick. It brings to mind other things equally unsettling.

"Do you want me to go back to prison?" I ask, following behind him, even stepping in the places he does.

"Not unless you commit a new crime." We cross the road and enter the woods on the other side.

"Are you sure?" It seems too simple. He can't really be this relaxed about what happened between us. I mean, I stuck a knife in his back.

"We were different people," he answers. "And it was a different world."

"You don't even know me. How can you believe I'm different?"

"Valore believes it, and I trust him."

Well, Valore is trustworthy, but I could be fooling him. How does Evans know? I feel compelled to force a reaction out of him—to determine if these are his true feelings—so I say, rather callously, "Come on, Evans. I hated you. I wanted to challenge you. I tried to kill you."

That makes him stop, and he moves his attention from the ground he's inspecting to me. "Yeah, and you missed," he says with a chuckle. "You suck at killing people."

I release a laugh, a large smile landing on my mouth unbidden, but I quickly pull it back. "You can't seriously feel so little about this. What I did was deplorable."

"Yeah." Evans crouches, examining a spot under a leafy plant. I join him.

"It probably doesn't mean much, but I'm sorry. I was stupid to follow him." No need to spell out the *him* I'm referring to. "Well, I was stupid in general."

"No worries. We're good," Evans says, waving a hand.

"Just like that?"

He tilts his head and looks over at me. "I don't enjoy holding grudges, is all. It's a waste of energy."

"So, you're not like Raider then," I comment, making Evans laugh.

"No. We're different in that regard."

I push up, straightening my back, and then I see it. "Look!" I say, pointing out another arrow, mere feet from our faces. I want to mention that sometimes the best tracking is performed by looking in front of your nose and not at your feet, but I keep quiet.

The arrow pierces a tree and a flat piece of paper, which we read together.

Congratulations. You found my surprise. Maybe Chessie's dead or that husband of hers, though I doubt I'll get that lucky. Possibly Sharade's the one who didn't make it, or maybe she's reading this letter. You had a chance to pick my side. Do you wish you'd chosen differently? Well, it's too late. I'm coming for you. All of you. And this time, I'll get it right.

Chessie

Evans

Annibeth

Vale

Sharade

You're on my list, and that means one thing: You won't see another year.

I have another list too, created because the Endrack daughters betrayed my family and me. There's only one person on this list... Hesston... and here's my promise: I'll remove one of his fingers for each year I've been without Saeva, but I'll leave his thumbs and spare his life.

I'll see you all soon,

Diggs

CHAPTER TWENTY-FOUR

Sixteen Days Free

Raider and Evans maneuver us toward our destination. The bouncing car and whipping wind are ceaseless as we fly through towns, not bothering to slow down since all the citizens sleep peacefully as we motor by. The grueling drive lasts until morning, with only brief stops for bathroom breaks.

Two things occupy my mind on repeat. First, the note from Diggs. The words of our uncle are more than an idle threat. He means what he says, and even though I'm sure he'll be more covert next time, our eyes scan for arrows, disturbed dirt, or anything else unusual.

Second, I marvel at Evans for giving me a second chance. He seems more willing to move forward than my sister does. I don't feel redeemed from my actions—I'm not sure that's possible—but expressing my contrition felt good. I'm suddenly glad to be going to Adlumen. My family deserves closure, and so do I. So, I'll take a week, make my apologies, and then, I'll leave.

When we reach the border of Adlumen, the boys take a moment to secure lenses over their eyes. I hadn't thought of it before, but watching Hesston slide his on, I realize he's light blind like his dad.

We pass through settlements on the way to Mirum, and my attention catches on the flags, which differ from the version of my youth. The thin black line symbolizing the Dark is gone. There's only a slight breeze, so it's a while before I see one unfurled enough to notice the profile of Fiducha is gone as well. When I finally get a clear view of the entire emblem, the only thing that remains are the sunbeams in yellow, orange, and red, but instead of three bursts of color, there are six. I'll inquire about it sometime, but first, I'll decide who I'm most comfortable asking.

My sister might seem like the logical choice, but the topic is complicated. We used to argue about whether the beams were a sunrise or sunset. I always preferred sunset because the colors after a long day were more brilliant, whereas Chess saw abundant possibility in a sunrise. Posing the question could easily morph into us discussing the meaning and purpose of a life spent—something I have no interest in doing—so I'll choose someone else to ask.

We ascend the steep hill to Ambitus. The western terraces of Fiducha are green and vibrant, with pops of orange, pink, and yellow. The walls are covered by trailing plants with little purple flowers. It's strange seeing it again. I mostly ignored its beauty when I was young, and when I gave it any attention, it was from above in our family quarters.

It's late afternoon when we enter the Ambitus gates. Years in prison have changed my feelings about this place. The walls that made me feel secure now feel like a trap. The soldiers roaming the grounds once kept me safe, but now they'll watch me for indiscretion. My eyes wander to the judicial building where the law determined my fate—carried out by Adlumen's judges and advisors—before moving to Fiducha, the monstrosity that was my home for sixteen years.

"Valore, you're in your usual room with Renegade and Raider," Evans says. "Sharade, you can—"

"Shar's with us," Raider interrupts. "She can have my room, and I'll share with Dad."

"Are you sure? There's plenty of space."

"Yes," Raider answers without explanation. "Renegade, will you help Dad get settled? I'll get Shar where she needs to be." Renegade nods and falls into step with Valore.

"We'll see you soon," Evans says to Raider, and then the group walks away, so it's just Raider and me. I'm not ready to leave the car, but I undo the seat belt, which highlights Raider's knife at my waist.

"I guess I won't need this for a while," I say, loosening the belt and passing it to him.

"Probably not," he says with a tired grin, twisting the wound leather into a tighter coil.

"You gonna go in and grab some sleep?" I ask.

"No. I'm meeting with the governors in the Locus."

"Oh." The Locus—Consilio Locus, to be precise—is where they hold meetings and make critical decisions for Adlumen. It's also where they hold receptions. I spent little time there. It occurs to me, not for the first time, that I had minimal importance in this place.

Staring up at Fiducha, I try to remember which balcony leads to the Locus. How could I forget something like that?

"I have thirty minutes," he continues. "And then we'll be at it for hours, updating the governors on the latest threats."

Threats. I grin. "Bragging about me, are you?"

Raider chuckles. "You're no threat. I know that now."

"Do you?"

Raider's expression doesn't change as he says, "There are *sinister* forces to focus on."

"Like Tyran and Diggs."

"Yes."

"You're being a lot nicer to me," I comment, taking in his smile and relaxed demeanor. This isn't the Raider I met the day I gained my freedom. "When should I expect a return of your former, surly self?"

Raider rubs his jaw, his black eyes watching me. "I still don't trust you completely, but I know you've changed some."

"Just some?"

"Quite a bit," Raider concedes. "Besides, I figure you've got more important people to convince than me." I slump in my seat as his words douse my lighthearted mood and raze any motivation to move. "But I'm glad you chose not to go to Hamo," he continues. "It's not a good place for you."

I roll my head and look at him. "This is just a detour. Hamo's still a possibility."

Raider leans on the frame of the car, scowling at me. "You can still condone living among the enemy and facing off against your own people?"

"These haven't been my people for eight years. And even if my heart still felt linked to them, the judges severed my citizenship with an official decree." I point toward the judicial building before waving at the soldiers milling about the area. "Besides, when word gets out I'm here, they'll protest at the gate and demand I leave."

Raider nods. "It's true. Adlumen might not welcome the little prisoner. But Hamo? Really?"

"I haven't had invitations to stay anywhere else," I point out, directing a stern gaze at him. Valore's made it clear he wants me with him, but Raider's been of the exact opposite opinion. And ultimately, I have to go somewhere.

"Are you nervous about seeing your family?" Raider asks, once again denying an invitation. I want to point out that at least the people in Hamo want me. Instead, I laugh and look up at the balconies. That's where I lived. Who knows where they're housed now? Chessie was looking for places in Mirum before they sent me to prison.

"Nervous is an understatement. Chess isn't too keen on me, while Evans seems unaffected and encouraging. And I'm not mentally ready to see the others, yet here I am."

"Evans has always been easy," Raider muses. "Forgiving and kind. He says I'd do well to be more like him." He rubs his cheek with a thoughtful grin. "And you don't need to worry about seeing Wick. He's not here."

"Where is he?"

"Working. So, it's just your mom."

Mom. Fear and powerful longing build in my bones. I shake my head to shed the sensation.

"It felt good to apologize to the others. I'll spend my week here, do the same with my mom, and then leave."

"You can be satisfied with that?"

I sit up, fire in my eyes. "It's more than I ever hoped was possible, so I have to be. I'll say what I must, and then I can leave. And if I'm lucky, I'll find a piece of my atonement. It will be enough."

Raider shakes his head. "It won't be."

"Are you speaking for me or yourself?"

Raider lets out a long breath. "Yeah, I'm speaking from experience."

"Who do you need forgiveness from?" I ask, remembering him saying that, like me, he had things to atone for.

"From myself."

I tilt my head. "You said you trusted someone when you shouldn't have. Who was it?"

Raider's not as quick to surrender this answer. I don't think he'll tell me, but finally, in a small voice, he says, "I trusted others to protect my family. If something's important, you do it yourself. I'll never make that mistake again. If there's one thing I know, it's that you should never leave matters of the utmost importance to those who aren't invested. You're the one who needs this, Shar. So, you must control how it goes down." Raider leans in, eyes serious.

"Don't be in a rush. Give the process the time it requires. They'll come around, and things will work out, but only if you stick it out."

"How can you be so sure?" I ask in awe of his conviction.

"Because family is the most important thing we have, and families forgive."

"I failed them. I sided with my dad, who never gave me anything in life that was important—only an unachievable goal of making him love me." Raider stares without comment, inspiring me to add, "I'm sure that just adds to your opinion of me—that I was a spoiled and clueless sixteen-year-old."

"I've done nothing like that to my family," he says. "But I know about failing people. I failed my dad and my wife. Dad forgave me, and I'd like to think Kal would too. Still, I feel the weight of those failures every day. Those feelings may never leave you, but if your family decides not to accept you, it's because they're cowards."

I chuckle. "You dare call your best friend's wife a coward?"

Raider grins, rubbing the top of his shorn head as he says, "Well, not to her face. Or his."

"I appreciate the silent support."

We depart the car, and Raider escorts me through the main doors and into the broad stone hallways of Fiducha. We don't ascend to the third floor as was normal in my childhood, but instead, he shows me to our guest suite on the bottom floor. I remember visitors staying in this area. I considered it a place of lesser status. Sure, it was in Fiducha, but it wasn't where the Endracks stayed.

Back then, sleeping in these quarters would have felt like an insult. Today, it seems like a miracle.

He leads me to my room, puts my suitcase at the foot

of the bed, and leaves. Although it's still daytime, I quickly shower, dress in my nightclothes, and climb into bed. The sheets smell the same as they did in my youth. A tear drops onto the pillow, and within seconds, I'm asleep.

CHAPTER TWENTY-FIVE

Seventeen Days Free

I sleep through the evening hours and into the night. When I finally wake—opening one eye like a patchless pirate—it's been fourteen hours, and the morning sun is peeking through my window. I discover clothes in my closet, so after a quick shower, I put them on and leave my room.

"You're awake!" I hear in a cheerful voice, turning to find two ladies, though only one approaches. I take in her long, blond hair, unchanged since my youth. Her guileless face too.

"Do you remember me?" she asks. "Mynk. I was your sister's maid."

"I remember," I say, nodding. I'd forgotten her name but recalled my jealousy over her close friendship with my sister. The jealousy is still there, just a bit, but her warm reception is enough to smother the old feeling.

"I'm glad you found the clothes, but you're smaller than I expected. I'll have the other items exchanged for a different size."

"Please don't bother. Truly, I hope to grow into them."

A pained expression crosses her face, but she quickly disguises it. "It's good you're awake. Your mom is asking to see you."

"She is?" I can't prevent my suddenly increased heart rate or the panicked look on my face. I just woke up. I can't do this now.

"We'll come with you," Raider says, and I turn to see him and Valore on the couch. Were they there the entire time?

"You d-don't need to," I say, my voice quivering

unexpectedly.

"I know, but we will anyway," Raider says, standing.

"Actually, Son, I'm staying here. My head's pounding."

"Are you okay?" I rush to Valore's side. "Do you need anything? I can stay with you." I feel his forehead.

"I'm fine. A little more rest will set me right. But you should go. Get this done so you'll feel more comfortable during your time here." He's so sure that will happen, while I'm not nearly as hopeful.

I exit our room with Raider, entering the enormous hallway. I used to think it was beautiful, but now it seems tacky and overdone. I wonder which of my relatives thought this was a good idea.

I take one step and freeze.

General Pruden's office is across the hall. He's standing outside the door—grayer than the last time I saw him—while a group of people exit his space.

Vale's in the lead—Lady Knowledge—followed by Geric. My eyes stay on the golden-haired man with the stoic expression, wondering if he ever smiles. Evans and Chessie are next. Evans—Lord Peace—pokes his brother Geric's arm, and they look ready to tussle. None of them see me, and I hold even more still, if that's possible. Tesha and Siman are next, holding hands. Tesha sees me, tilts her red head, and lifts her spare hand to wave. I barely perform a nod, sucking in my upper lip and running my teeth over the skin. Ronen and Annibeth are next. My memory didn't accurately record the size of Evans's other brother. He's massive. And Annibeth —Lady Wisdom—looks smaller than I remember, though it's probably just by comparison. However, she hasn't lost her top-notch scowl—a look she's leveling on me now.

"Please don't make me talk to them," I whisper to Raider.

He steps in front of me, blocking their view. "Sure," he

says, taking my arm. I look up at him, and he smiles down at me. "One thing at a time," he says in a soothing voice.

"You're more like Valore than I thought," I say. His eyes widen behind the transparent lenses, and I quickly shake my head, brushing off the unexpected statement. "Which way?"

Raider leads me down the hall. We're announced and enter immediately. Mom's quarters are in the same corner of the building, exactly two floors below where I grew up. The shape of the room is the same. The furniture is placed in the same configuration. When I look at it closer, I realize it's the same furniture.

I envisioned many times walking back into my childhood home. The few differences aside, the feeling is surreal as I enter the space. The mouse and clock cookie jar is in the same spot on the counter. The shelf of books and figurines looks unchanged. Even mom is in her same seat in the center of the couch. She always sat there, with Wick on one side and Chessie on the other. I always sat on a barstool at the counter.

Mom stands, and Raider takes a step back. "I'll leave you to it," he says.

Curses! He's leaving?

I grab his arm. "You said you'd stay with me," I say with frantic eyes. I didn't think I needed him, but when presented with the reality of being alone with her, I want him to stay. I need him to.

"Did I, though?" he asks with a smile, confusing me before adding, "Remember what I said about family."

Family forgives.

I shake my head. They won't forgive *me*. They can't forget what I've done.

He puts his hand on mine, squeezes, then pulls away, and I watch in desperation as he goes out the door.

“I always forget how handsome that man is,” Mom says, and I realize she’s suddenly standing very close.

“How could you forget? That’s all people ever talk about when it comes to Raider,” I say, turning to face her. She looks very much the same. Mom was always taller than me—more Chessie’s height—but now I’ve passed them both, though she has more weight on her hips than either of her daughters. She still wears her chestnut hair in a high bun, but there’s some gray mixed in now. And her skin is the same tone, only with a few more lines around her eyes and mouth. Her clothes are still pristine, and her movements are precise.

Mom tilts her head, her brown eyes studying me. “You don’t agree?”

“About Raider’s looks? Of course I do. But there’s more to him than that.”

“Hmm. Like what?”

“Does it really matter?” I ask, walking past her and finding my way to a barstool. “I feel like you’re stalling.”

“Maybe I am.” She surprises me, sitting beside me and not returning to the center of her couch. It feels strange to see her here alone—no Wick pressed against her side.

“You look different,” she says, noting my short hair and skinny arms. “But you still look so much like Chessie.”

“Too bad for her, huh?” I chuckle, but Mom doesn’t join in, and things get quiet and awkward.

“I want to show you something.” More stalling, but I follow her without comment. She leads me into a bedroom, stopping in front of shelves with dozens of familiar objects.

Items that belonged to me.

I run my finger over boxes and trinkets, but I’m primarily drawn to the bottles. There are more of them than I remembered. “You kept them,” I say, picking up a red one Wick found for me and turning it until the light hits the side, sending color onto the walls and ceiling. "I don't know how this makes me feel."

"I've felt similarly conflicted over the years," Mom admits. "It's just so strange. You're one of the people in the world I know best, yet seeing you here, you feel like a stranger."

I put down the red bottle and lift a sea-green one. It's one of my first—a gift from my dad. "I agree. I know you exceedingly well, and you don't appear to have changed much. Therefore, I expect to get scolded at any moment, but I'll save you the trouble. I've criticized my behavior sufficiently in the last eight years. I've been punished amply. I'm just here to apologize. You were all correct, aligning with the governors and seeing Dad for who he truly was. I behaved badly, and I'm sorry."

Mom smiles sadly. "That's just how Keine would have approached this. Direct and to the point. Expressing his sorrow with little emotion or fuss."

"Is that wrong?" I ask, taking a step back. "Should I prostrate myself on the floor in a puddle of tears?"

"And now his temper emerges." She sighs, walking to the door, and I follow her out.

"I see. It's not contrition you want. Do I need to purge every remnant of him from me? Would that satisfy you?"

Mom drops onto the couch. "You were always more like him than the others."

"Is that why you loved me less?" I ask, sitting on the coffee table. The couch is for my siblings, and I need to be close when she answers—just not too close. She always hated it when I sat on tables, but she doesn't argue now. She just shakes her head, and I see in her expression what I've said is true.

"Did you not love Dad either?" I ask. On our family visit

to see Dad before his tribunal, she told him she loved him, but I always wondered if it was a lie. Mom didn't seem capable of loving and condemning someone simultaneously. It felt like there was room for only one or the other in her heart.

"I loved him a lot," she rushes to say, then adds, "At first."

"And later?"

"I was scared of him."

"You were scared of me too. You still are," I say, putting it together. Even now, she leans away, waiting for me to snap, and she's without Wick or Chessie to save her.

"Yes. And then you tried to kill Evans, and I knew no part of you was mine. You were all his, and I figured you always would be." And there it is—she loved me until she condemned me, and then I was no longer hers.

Why did I ever come back here?

I stand, creating the distance we're both more comfortable with.

"Yes, I acted like him, and maybe I still do, but I'm not Keine Endrack. I don't know if he learned anything in his Dark prison, but I did." I recall clinging to life amid the turmoil, and then my mind goes to Squatty and Valore. "I learned to value my life, independent of my circumstances. I learned to care for people without worrying they'd never care for me in return. But the biggest discovery was that loving someone for the right reasons is life-altering. Equally so, loving someone who returns the emotion is a treasure. It changes people. It changed me."

"I loved you," Mom says. "I still do."

Her words send a chill through me. They're not unwelcome, but they hurt more than they heal. "You just never told me until now. And now, I don't know what to do with it."

"I should have said it sooner."

I laugh bitterly. "That would have been nice."

"Maybe things would have been different."

"Different? Do you mean our relationship, or are you referring to my bad choices?"

"I was thinking of your choices."

I suck in my upper lip, rubbing my teeth across the raw, chapped skin—keeping my mouth occupied as I think through my response. When it's decided, I wipe my mouth with the back of my hand and say, "Don't hold yourself responsible. I own what I did and don't blame anyone else." I take an unsteady breath. "But it would have meant a lot if you'd hoped our relationship had been different. I craved your regard, even knowing I'd never have as much as Chess or Wick. I can't help wondering how we'd have been if you'd pulled me close instead of pushed me away."

"Maybe we can find out now."

"I don't think there's enough time for that substantial of a change."

"What do you mean?"

"I'm only here for a week. Maybe less if the governors or General Pruden intervene." I sound almost hopeful.

"Then where will you go?" Mom reaches back, squeezing her bun as she waits for my answer.

I release a heavy breath, bracing myself. "The current plan is Hamo."

"Hamo?" she blurts out. "They've declared war on us!"

"They haven't declared war on me. Quite the opposite. They're the only ones who've made me feel welcome." I think on Chett's proposal. I haven't decided to accept his offer, but more than making me feel welcome, he's made me feel wanted. I didn't realize until now how much I valued that.

"But they're making war with your people!" Mom presses.

"They're no longer my people. Did you forget the judges stripped me of my citizenship? I belong nowhere and to no one."

"But isn't Valore your friend?" she asks, unwilling to give this up. "Why not go with the Roils?"

Cognizant of Raider's demands, I falter on how to answer without sounding resentful. I settle on, "It's best for his family if I let them reunite without me. And Raider needs all his concentration on what's coming."

"Why not help him?"

"Raider's fight to end this war isn't my fight."

"That statement is proof you haven't changed."

I bite my lip, rubbing the chapped skin with painful strokes before popping it free. "Yeah. And your comment is proof you haven't either."

Mom purses her lips.

I walk to the door, telling her one last thing before leaving. "We needn't rectify things between us. I don't expect approval of my choices or understanding of my future. All I need is for you to hear my apology. I'm sorry for the hurt I caused eight years ago. I was wrong, and I sincerely regret my actions. But I can't worry if you believe me or accept my apology. That's your choice to make, and I'll not pester you toward a conclusion." I unlatch the door and step out without looking back, leaving her with one last comment. "After I've fulfilled my commitment to Chessie, I promise to leave Adlumen and never bother you again."

CHAPTER TWENTY-SIX

Eighteen Days Free

I can't escape the unease from my confrontation with Mom. Telling her I'm sorry should be enough to assuage my guilt. Well, at least some of it. Instead, the finer points of the discussion stick in my head like glue, making it hard to think of anything else.

You were scared of me and still are.

I squeeze out a glob of cleanser and rub circles on the counter. I run the rag over the faucet and around the curve of the sink.

I knew no part of you was mine.

Turning on the water, I rinse and squeeze the rag, then do it again before scouring everything a third time.

That statement is proof you haven't changed.

I spray the mirrors and find a new rag to wipe them down, then wipe the shower door and all the handles.

"We have people for that," Mynk says, startling me, and I bounce back. I glance at my reflection—my disheveled hair, stretched t-shirt, and short shorts—the wet cloth hanging limp in my hand.

"I know," I say, tossing the rag with the rest.

Mynk props her hip against the wall. "I seem to remember you used to take your frustrations out on the training field."

"I did." There and the tennis court, though few knew about the latter.

"There are people out there now," she says, tipping her head in that direction. She doesn't have to say it twice. I give her a grateful smile and put on the appropriate clothes.

It's a cool morning for early September, though the world will heat up soon enough. I trek across the grass, passing familiar trees and bushes eight years matured. It's comforting and confusing that so little has changed.

I have the same feeling when I see him on the field. There was a day I thought I'd marry Raden Parrs. My biggest hope was to make him mine and give Dad a grandchild because it was something Chessie wanted to put off. It's alarming to realize I was willing to marry and have a child to please my dad. But once again, Chessie beat me to the goal that would have made Dad proud.

Raden looks over, and the smile that gave my sixteen-year-old self butterflies shines at me, dissolving my melancholy thoughts.

"Heard you were back in town," he says casually on approach. Chessie said they'd keep my arrival a secret, but it's not a surprise Raden knows. I've never been anyone's favorite. Mom loved Wick the most. Dad's favorite was based on usefulness, so he favored Chessie. And even the boy I liked was best friends with my sister. I never got first place in any of their affections.

"What you doing out here?" he asks.

"Clearing my head." I almost changed my mind about coming—considered going to the tennis court and creating that rhythmic cadence with a ball and racket—but maybe here's the better choice.

He's close now, and I can make out his details. His black hair is longer than I used to like and lighter from hours in the sun. He had more scruff but is now clean-shaven, emphasizing the divot in his chin. He has a few happy wrinkles around his eyes, and his muscles are bigger. Definitely bigger.

"Are you still single?" I ask.

Raden chuckles and asks, "Are you?"

"Well, I was fighting them off," I say flippantly. "There are so many options in prison. Especially a Dark prison. So much easier to hide a gnarly scar or a starving body." I hold out my hand and show him the scar Chessie gave me, then stick out a slim leg and run my hands up and down to highlight my malnourished frame.

"You look good," he says, and even though there's sympathy in his eyes, I believe him. "And, I'm unmarried, though I'm with someone."

"Good for you!" I laugh and, without second-guessing it, pull him in for a friendly hug.

"Damn. I was hoping you'd at least be a little heartbroken." In eight years, he hasn't lost his joyful energy. It makes me happy that some things don't change.

I grin, pushing him away. "If you want your heart broken, bring me a Torquent blade and take up the position."

Raden tilts his head. "Seriously? You still think you've got it."

"I think you've already lost." I wink.

"Hmm," he muses but heads for the weapons shed.

"What are you doing?" my sister asks, appearing at my side in her regular training gear—a loose shirt, thick pants, heavy boots, and a jacket over her arm that she'll never put on.

"Hey, Chess," Raden says, arriving with two Torquent blades. I'm sure the scimitar-style weapons—curved, single-edged, and serrated—explain to my sister precisely what I'm doing. "I brought Fs," he says to me, indicating the weight of the blade. An H is the lightest, so he's barely moved me up from beginner status.

"I could probably handle Ds." I didn't practice with weighted weapons in prison, so starting easy makes sense, but an F feels like an insult.

"Eh. Let's try it for a bit."

Raden's the expert here, so I don't argue, and he seems surprised when I take the F without further complaint. I pass it hand to hand, twisting to feel the balance and trying a few stances. It feels good—the weapon in my hand and the place I go inside my head with it in my grip. I need this.

"Mind if I have a go?" Chessie asks, throwing her jacket to the side and reaching to take the other blade, ready to expend some of her endless energy.

"I'm not sure if Sharade's ready for you yet," Raden says, trying to keep the peace.

"It's just Shar now," I tell him. "And I can manage."

"I'll go easy," my sister says, taking the sword.

I weather the insult, stepping away from Raden and facing my sister. I stretch a moment longer before taking up the Ballantyne posture. She opts for the Van Valen, and I instantly know her move, so when she jumps into action, I toss my sword to the other hand and swing my weapon to the side. The serrated edge catches hers, yanking it free from her fingers and sending it flying across the lawn.

It lands with a soft thud, and I straighten, lowering my sword while Chessie stares—shocked and breathless. Then her brows pull together—tight and thoughtful. Everyone used to tout Chessie's patient demeanor—her most of all—but the trait was useless when it was her and me. A restless energy bounced between us whenever we were together, and I knew how to bend it for my purposes.

"Shall we go again?" I ask airily.

Raden releases a long, low whistle, then chuckles as he heads for the weapon. He places it back in Chessie's hand, and I wait for her to pick a starting posture. She chooses the Lomax, so I crouch, holding the sword two-handed above my head in the Mengele. Her eyes narrow, confirming she's never seen this before. My lips twitch, but I resist smiling.

She chose first posture, so I have first move. I slow my breathing and watch. Wait. After a minute, her arms tire from holding the sword, and the weapon lowers an inch. That's when I strike.

I fake left. She follows. I switch right, but she's already in motion. Rising up, I use my body's momentum to bring the sword down in a powerful arc. I drive her blade into the ground, then kick the handle, popping it from her hand, making it spin across the grass.

She gasps, breathing like she ran a lap around the field. If this were a regular battle, Chessie would have kicked me by now—she enjoys deploying a kick or two as part of her arsenal—but combat with a Torquent blade is refined. It's a system of battle with rules and precise maneuvers. Consequently, she keeps her boots on the grass.

"Where did you learn that?" she asks.

"Valore."

"That was awesome, Aunt Sharade!" Hesston yells, running toward me at full speed. I pass the sword off to Raden just before he connects, surrounding my legs in a strangling hug.

"Thanks," I say, laughing and trying to keep my balance, staring down at his hazel eyes behind the lenses.

"What are you doing out here?" Chessie asks, putting a hand on his shoulder. She gets his attention and pries him off of me, pulling him to her side.

"I wanted to watch."

"I told you to stay inside," she scolds, running her fingers down her braid to smooth it out.

"Why? I'm out here all the time. What's different today?"

Chessie swallows hard, looking guiltily at me.

Curses. The difference is I'm here.

I bite my cheek, spinning away from them and approaching Raden, taking the sword from him and brushing the hilt needlessly. "Should we go again?" I choke out.

Chessie releases a nervous laugh. "I don't know. Will I get to hold the sword for more than a few seconds?"

"Probably not." I twist back to face her. "Sivil Roil was a Torque. She taught Valore postures and defenses only their family use."

"Tyran's sister. I'm sure you learned a lot." Chessie rubs her shoulder, remembering her mangled skin from her only fight with Tyran. There's envy in my sister's eyes, and it shocks me. There was never a time she was envious of me.

"I'd teach you, but it took me years. Almost three, in fact."

"And we don't have that long together. Is that what you're saying?"

"We both know it's best if I don't stay," I answer, looking at Hesston, who's watching us raptly. "We both know you don't *want* me to stay."

Chessie goes quiet. Raden steps up, taking the swords, guessing correctly the brief practice is over.

"But I didn't have my sight when I learned from Valore, so I'm sure you'd pick it up faster. You were always better than me at these things." And then I can't help adding, "You were always better than me at everything."

The Markets of Mirum. It's been a long time since I strolled these streets—perused Market Square, entered Meat Madness for dinner, or slurped a strawberry soda—so I roam for hours. The shopkeepers flash their wares, and a grocer holds out an apple. My mind goes to Aunty's Cellar, making me melancholy, and I wave off the offer of fruit. It's not that I wish for prison, but the simplicity was nice.

The markets have changed—the mood is upbeat, and the people are diverse. The light blind are everywhere, mixing with those who have light sight. There's overall contentment in this place, making it easy to relax. I can't help thinking how appalled Dad would be. Or how wrong he was. Diggs too. Around every corner, I imagine my uncle popping up, wearing a look of disgust.

I'm not ignorant enough to forget I would have aligned with their discontent. I'd have taken offense, made a fuss, told people off, and complained. There's some comfort in knowing I've changed, even if others don't see it. Even if I no longer care to make them see. There's nothing I can do to force acceptance. Their reticence stings, but it's understandable, and I only have a few more days to put up with it.

I find an establishment with a quiet, outdoor corner and order some food. I'm balanced on the back two legs of my chair. My hood's pulled low over my head as I cradle my drink—thick with condensation from the warm air—licking cream off my lips when I hear, "You shouldn't be here."

It appears Raider's finished his latest meeting with the governors, where I'm sure they covered every topic from abatement to war to me.

"Probably not."

Raider stomps his boots, kicking off the dust before sitting across from me. "It took little effort for me to recognize you."

"Well, everyone will see me now you're here. Your pretty face attracts eyes like flowers attract bees."

"I'm serious. You're an easy target for Diggs out here in the markets."

"Oh, Raider, what does it matter?" I ask, pushing my hood back and rustling my unruly hair. "I'm free, but I have nowhere to go. At least, nowhere that makes sense. I have no one. Even your dad. He cares about me but has his own family to worry about. Why bother being safe? It's better to sit here and be an easy target. A very aware, very competent weapon-wielding target."

"You want Diggs to find you. That's your idea? If you're so self-sacrificing, why not let someone else in on your plan? Maybe make it an effective one."

I shrug, lift the soup bowl to my mouth, and take a drink with no consideration for the spoon lying next to it. I've drunk my meals for eight years, and there's no point reverting to manners now—not in the Markets of Mirum.

"You act like you don't care if he ends you," he says, shaking down his jacket sleeves and grabbing the ends.

I lower the bowl and lick my lips. "I don't. Not really. I mean, I'd fight him, and I'd win. But even if something went wrong, everyone would feel better if I were out of the picture."

"My dad wouldn't."

"One out of—" I laugh, thinking it through. "Out of everyone else on the planet. I think the world would be okay."

Raider's foot thumps rhythmically as he listens, but he pauses, his forehead wrinkling with a fresh scowl. "I don't like you like this," he says, leaning in and pushing my bowl to the table until I release it. "You frequently annoy me, but at least you're trying to make headway. This defeatist attitude is beneath you."

"This place is poisonous to me," I say, looking around Mirum but thinking of Adlumen as a whole. "I was aimed at a fresh start before reuniting with Chessie and dear Mom. They're half-sweet, half-sour. Mom's scared of me. And Chess... she doesn't want me near Hesston. Did you know that?"

"She'll change her mind," he says, his black eyes roaming my face.

"I'm not sticking around a few decades for that to happen." I scoop my bowl, sloshing broth over the edge. "I'll get a Torquent blade and find a good cause to fight for. Preventing Diggs from finishing Dad's plan seems a good place to start. And if I survive, I'll find another."

I told Dody I wasn't a soldier like her uncle, but maybe I am.

Raider lifts the edge of the tablecloth and spies the Torquent blade hidden there. I gulp down another warm mouthful of soup, then suck the droplets off my fingers before dropping the empty bowl on the table with a clatter.

"How'd your meeting go?" I ask, showing I'm done being the conversation headliner.

"They're worried." I nod because they should be. "And there's no word from Arrick."

"It's only been six days," I say. "It's not like it's a quick trip."

"I know. I'm trying to be patient, but what if I'm waiting and hoping for something that will never happen? Maybe I should go prepare my people instead."

"It's tough to know," I concede. "But you're still preparing things for them, even if you're not with them. And I think you can give it a few more days before rejoining the troops. You have a small cushion."

Raider nods, rubbing his hand over his mouth and jaw, the short hairs bristling. He lifts a hand, gets the server's attention, asks for a strawberry soda, and scoots his chair around, so we're sitting side by side.

"It was driving you nuts, wasn't it?" I ask with a grin.

"What?"

"Sitting so vulnerably. I was watching your back, you know. No one was going to get the drop on you." I chuckle and take another foamy drink.

"It's a habit to sit so I can see."

"A good habit," I say as the server drops off his drink. "And it's a good thing you found me."

"Why's that?"

"I have no way of paying," I say, then laugh. "I didn't even think about it because I never had to pay before. It was just charged to Ambitus. Isn't that dumb?"

"You're assuming I won't leave you in the lurch."

I consider his statement, then ask, "What would your dad say if you did?"

Raider grumbles. "You've got me there."

He ends up ordering dinner, choosing a hearty stew instead of my brothy soup. "What do you think of Chett?" I ask while Raider selects a gravy-laden carrot.

"In what way?"

"I dunno. I can't figure him out."

"But you want to. I get it. He's a charmer."

"It's not that." I scoff. "He's nice enough, but there's something not quite right."

"Losing his brother messed him up. Loss changes a person." Raider's thinking of Kally while I think of my family. Still, I don't think that's all there is to it, but I put it out of my mind because something infinitely more interesting draws my attention.

"Look at that," I say, pointing to the horizon where the sky has turned a brilliant pink and orange.

"Wow," Raider mumbles around a bite of stew.

"How do sunsets compare in the Dark?" I ask. I've always wondered.

"They're not as vibrant there, though it used to be the opposite. It changed when Adlumen started making these better lenses."

"Well, nature's providing an ample show tonight." I squint against the sun.

"Yeah. Especially since orange is my favorite color, and a stunning sunset is the best thing to showcase every shade of orange."

"Wait." I lift a finger. "What about fall leaves? They run the gambit of orange."

"They come in a close second."

"Hmm. Okay. I can agree to that."

"You speak like an expert."

"Of course! Orange is my favorite color too."

The sunset fades, the shops close, and we spend the evening swapping stories about our favorite things. We walk back to Ambitus, not facing death at Diggs's hands—if he was there, he kept out of sight. I have all my limbs, and my Torquent blade remains untouched.

How disappointing. But there's always tomorrow.

CHAPTER TWENTY-SEVEN

Twenty Days Free

The word is out. All of Mirum knows I'm in Ambitus, and it won't be long until the whole of Adlumen hears about it. It wasn't my careless trip to the markets that did it. Nope. It was my display with Chessie and the Torquent blades on the training field.

And it gets worse. Not only do they know I escaped prison, but rumor is I'm an informant for Tyran, and I'm here to finish the plan Lord Endrack enacted eight years ago, removing the governors from power.

The governors are popular. They've provided fair leadership, enacted laws, and supported products that have made the people rich. In short, they loathe the idea of someone interrupting their bright future. Consequently, they dislike Tyran—most Torques, really—and me. Some demand my execution, others want me imprisoned again, but at the very least, they want me gone with a lifetime ban from entering Adlumen.

Dashed is the slim hope I had of the people forgiving me. Still, I can't help feeling smug over their reaction because I told the others my coming here was a bad idea, and I was right.

It's Chessie who delivers the news after avoiding me for a full day. She promises there'll be no executions, prisons, or bans, but it's hard to trust her assurances. People are unpredictable, and things could turn ugly quicker than rain turns to sunshine. I envision a gathered mob demanding action and Hesston's safety being threatened. What wouldn't Chessie or Evans do to protect him? The list seems small. They'd surely give me up. I wouldn't expect them to do otherwise.

Chessie acts as if she has sway in the decisions pertaining to me, but she doesn't. She may have the ear of the governors, but she's not one herself. And I saw the looks they gave me upon my arrival. They didn't lose a wink of sleep while I was in a Dark prison. No. I can't depend on Chessie or any of the others. I need to get out of Adlumen.

"I'll pack my things," I say automatically, releasing a dark chuckle when I look at my little suitcase—a broken bottle, Squatty's necklace, and a few articles of clothing. That's all I have—not even a coin to my name. I have a closet of clothes here but wouldn't dare take anything. Well, maybe a jacket and some better shoes. And a pair of thick socks. I've missed socks.

"You needn't go anywhere," Chessie says. "The people will relax, and the governors are drafting a statement insisting you haven't, and won't, leave Ambitus."

"Well," I draw out, sucking in my upper lip.

"What?" she asks, immediately on edge.

"I may have gone to the markets the other day."

"Which day?"

"Two days ago. Raider was with me." I pause, then mumble, "Some of the time."

Chessie sighs, rubbing the eyelids covering her brown eyes. "We've heard nothing about it, so it's unlikely anyone recognized you. Still, what were you thinking?"

I lift my shoulders. "I wanted to see home. And I thought Diggs might find me, and I could take care of a problem."

Chessie breathes out a laugh. "I would say you've got a death wish, but after your display the other morning, I admit, I think you could take him."

"I could," I say, straightening my shoulders.

"Wow. That expression. It makes you look more like my

sister than at any other time since we've reconnected. It's all haughty and determined."

Those are nicer words than she means. In our youth, she accused me of other distasteful attitudes—snobbery, acting put out without cause, and, my favorite, inciting issues. Indeed, my entire family accused me of that last one. They told me to stop my entitled behavior—to grow up—and now I have, and they're unwilling to see it.

"Maybe. Except now, I have a foundation for my confidence. I possess foresight, knowing when to use my gifts, and I've learned not to lend myself out as a tool for others. I'm my own person." Chessie crosses the room, rubbing her thumb across the dresser's edge. "But you still don't trust me," I add. She doesn't respond or even glance my way. "It's okay if you don't. I'm sad I'll never know Hesston, but I got to meet him, so that's something. He seems like a great kid."

"I'm sorry. I'm just not ready. I need more time."

"We're out of time. It may take some planning, but I'd like to leave. I promised you a week, and I made it five days. It will have to be enough. Mom hasn't asked to see me, and you avoided me all of yesterday, so there's no reason to stay."

"I wasn't avoiding you." Chessie takes measured steps, crossing the room and sitting in a chair. I thought the conversation was drawing to a close, but her actions indicate otherwise. "There's a lot... If it wasn't..."

"Just say what you're thinking. I won't freak out. I don't even throw things anymore," I say, lifting a brush from the side table and then placing it gently back onto the surface.

Chessie laughs. "I always hated that. I have more than one scar from you."

"It didn't take long to break the habit in prison," I tell her, remembering Guard A and his threat of drinking from a broken bottle. "Go ahead."

"Yesterday was just a bad day. I planned to take you somewhere to show you something, but I couldn't make it happen. And then I thought we'd go today, but the news from Mirum complicates things, so—" Chessie shrugs, not finishing the sentence.

"We're smart people, Chess. How do we uncomplicate it?"

Chessie tilts her head. It takes a minute, but a slow smile spreads across her face. And just like that, my sister has a plan.

◆ ◆ ◆

We're wearing Adlumen soldier uniforms—dark blue with gold trim. Chessie has on light blind lenses, and I'm wearing an eye patch.

An eye patch!

We pile into a car—not the one Chessie's had forever that she calls CJ, but one of the many replicas. I'm in the back with her. Raden's driving, and there's a stranger in the other seat.

"Keep your head ducked," Chessie says as we approach the Ambitus gate.

I do as she says, though I don't know why.

I mean, I'm wearing an eye patch!

Who could possibly recognize Sharade Endrack at twenty-four—shorn and skinny with an eye patch?

No one. That's who.

We exit Ambitus and bounce along the road, not speaking. We drive for five minutes before stopping beside an enormous warehouse. It looks abandoned, but I hear sounds within. Raden helps me out, and I join Chessie, standing by a door to the building. "We'll wait here," Raden says. "Let you know if there's trouble."

Chessie nods at her best friend and pulls the door open. The heat inside is overwhelming, and the commotion within is significant, overcoming the silence on the empty street. We walk in, and I wipe my brow, yelling to be heard. "What is this place?"

"My factory," Chessie screams back. "When I lost my job leading Adlumen, I had to do something with my time, so I started this. I duplicated CJ, started selling them, and it took off. We handle the cars, and Raider's people get us the gas and oil. At first, we got it from Torquent, but that was terrible."

Chessie leads me past the production line, pointing things out.

"This is amazing."

"I've loved doing it, and there's only one downside—it's another reason for Tyran to seek war."

"She's upset about the cars?"

"She's jealous. The cars. The lamlight. The lenses. Our land. You name it. She hates our prosperity."

"Raider said her war motivation is personal, but it stems from more issues than she's outlined."

"Oh, yeah. There's a lot behind this. And we haven't even mentioned her hate of the Endracks since Dad's conflict with the South T killed Tyran's sister."

Sivil Roil. Raider and Valore have moved past the atrocity my family perpetrated against theirs—it's quite remarkable—but Tyran's not nearly so benevolent.

"What about the meeting Tyran wants with Raider? Could that resolve anything?"

Chessie shrugs. "I don't know what it's about, but Evans is nervous, and Raider won't discuss it." My sister sighs. "But even if Raider solves one issue, I'm afraid she'll just line up the next one on her list." My sister gestures below at the citizens working metal, making a marvelous product she developed.

Tyran. Her greed is disgusting—wanting something Chess worked so hard for. I wish I could stop her from hurting good people. Upon my arrival, I told Mom this wasn't my fight, but suddenly, it seems like it might be.

I shake my head, laughing at the stupid notion. It could never be my fight. Before I made a single move, my own people would insist my help was not wanted. Because they're not my people anymore. They don't want me. I must do better at remembering that.

"Hey. Come check this out," Chessie says, pulling me from contemplation. She takes quick steps, guiding me through the action. One wrong move in here could get you hurt or dead, so I'm glad she's taking the lead. All the workers wear yellow, but with soldiers providing security throughout the building, no one notices as we move around the vast space.

Chessie stops to bring my attention to another car. Not a surprise in a car factory, but the sheer size of this one is startling. "It fits twelve people," she says. "We're working on the mechanics and adjusting the design, but can you imagine? It takes more gas to operate, but not as much as three regular ones, so we save when transporting a large group."

"It's incredible."

Chessie beams, nodding, and we continue walking. We enter a hallway, and my ears are grateful to leave some of the noise behind. She guides me up a flight of stairs and into a room, closing the door and shutting out the rest of the sound. My ears hum from residual use.

She leans against a desk, and I join her, facing a wall of windows and looking down on the yellow workers, moving like bees in a hive.

"This is my office," she says.

"Won't they wonder why two mere soldiers are taking a break in here?"

"They know it's me." Chessie glances over. "They know it's you too."

"Oh, so I can remove the patch?"

"Yeah." Chessie giggles, and I lift it to see with both eyes. "I handpicked these people. They're my friends, and they're compensated well. No one will say a word."

"I'm glad you didn't lose faith in everyone." Just me. It goes unsaid, but Chessie knows what I'm alluding to.

She nods. "I want to trust you. I'm just trying to figure you out."

"Time's up," I say, again reminding her of my looming departure and hearing the bitterness in my tone. I release a breath and try to center myself, knowing this could be my last proper conversation with my sister.

"Let's imagine this is it, Chess. That this is the last time we'll ever speak to one another. Let's lay it all out so we don't regret the coming weeks, wishing we'd said the things that need saying. What do you want me to know?"

"I'm pregnant," Chessie says without delay. "That's why I disappeared yesterday. I wasn't feeling well."

"No way," I say, automatically narrowing my eyes on her stomach.

"I hide it well," she says with a laugh.

"You sure do."

"Hesston doesn't know. Well, most people don't. So, don't say anything."

"A test of trust. I can handle that."

Chessie rubs her cheek. "What about you? What do you want me to know?"

"I was a selfish, temperamental fool."

Chessie grins. "I already knew that."

"Yeah. *But I didn't.*" She nods. "I needed his attention, and it outweighed everything else. When he asked me to do something, I was compliant and accessible. Dad persuaded me without me questioning a thing. I was completely under his control—resolute on his goals and loyal to only him. I see it now. I'm not that way anymore."

Chessie folds her arms over her chest before saying, "Except, you sort of are."

"What do you mean?"

"You moved Dad out of that spot and replaced him with Valore. You're the same way with Raider's dad. He's your entire world, and you're loyal to him above everyone."

I shake my head. "Maybe." *Yes.* "But isn't that a good thing? Valore's a great man."

"What if he wasn't?" Her tone is sharp. "When's the time you choose a side based on what you want and not because of the person you're currently obsessed with pleasing?"

"That's not fair. I make my own choices."

"I don't believe you do. Can you honestly tell me you'd have come to Adlumen if Valore wasn't coming here as well?"

"I don't know," I say, trying to consider her question honestly. "All I know is I feel safe with him."

"What about Raider?"

"What about him?"

"Don't you think it bothers him when you cling to his dad?"

"I made a promise to Raider. He knows I'm leaving soon. So, you can put away your misgivings regarding my character because I'm losing Valore too. I'll be well and truly alone, with no one to obsess over or follow their lead. It will just be me."

"That's not what I'm saying. I don't want you to be alone."

"Don't you? It seems the only way you'll believe I've learned my lesson is if I live my life, relying only on myself. Well, guess what? I did that for five years, and I nearly went mad. But I survived the tough choices of that experience—like when all I wanted was to die, but I discovered how to cling to my existence, bleak as it was. But then Valore came, and he brought me back to life. I owe him *everything* for reasons you could never attempt to understand. So, quit judging my relationship with him."

"You're right. I'm holding you accountable for your actions during the transition, not what you experienced in our separation. But you haven't once said you regret what you did. You haven't said you're sorry."

"You've hardly given me the chance! I've already said those exact words to Evans and Mom."

"You did?"

Curses! Why is this so difficult?

"Yes. It hardly phased Evans because he forgave me in a second. And Mom? She barely acknowledged my apology and hasn't asked to see me again."

"Maybe Mom wants you to make the next move."

"The move is definitely hers." I push from the desk and walk to the door. I want this over. "Apologies have seemed pretty pointless so far. I was waiting for the right time to give you yours, but I wonder if any time is right." I pause, tilting my head as I ask, "Will saying I'm sorry really make anything better between us?"

"It might."

"Okay then, I'm sorry. I'm glad I failed. Exceptionally glad. Evans didn't deserve to die, and I was wrong to do what I did. Dad had misguided ideas, which I recognize now, but I wouldn't take back what happened. I'm relieved to be out of prison and don't want to return. But I'm content with who I've become, and I'd rather know Valore than not." I pause. "Did it make you feel better?"

"I'm not sure," she says, rubbing her finger along the length of the scar on her cheek. While she remains thoughtful, I'm just glad she was honest.

I make Chessie take me back to Ambitus. It's a silent ride, and Raden's curious brown eyes take us in more than once. I trade the soldier's clothes for my own and retreat to my room. After removing the brown bottle from my suitcase, I look at the sections. I find the thick bottom, still in one piece, and take it to the bathroom, sliding it under the running faucet. It holds an inch of water, which I lift to my mouth to take a cautious sip.

As I lick blood from my lips, I decide Guard A was right—broken things cause pain.

CHAPTER TWENTY-EIGHT

Twenty-Seven Days Free

It's been a week since I toured the car factory with my sister, and I'm still in Adlumen. Chessie insists she's trying to get me out of here, but amid the threat of war, they can't spare anyone to provide an adequate escort.

Fiducha feels like another prison. Granted, I'm not in the Dark, and I have soap, daily showers, and clean bedsheets—bedsheets, period—but regardless, I'm stuck. Creeping in is the familiar loneliness of Aunty's Cellar, where the conditions of my sentence kept me isolated and uninformed.

I'm reminded not to leave Ambitus, which I agree to, but I'm even discouraged from venturing outside of our quarters because the Ambitus soldiers cast me unwelcome glances. So, I spend hours staring at my bedroom walls, getting angrier and angrier.

Mom hasn't requested another visit, Chessie is busy, and Raider and Valore are in sessions with the governors. Additionally, Renegade's disappeared again, so I don't even have his craggy company. I feel so alone. The temptation to slip into the night and disappear is intense. Yet, I'm still here, and I'm not really sure why.

I roll across the surface of my unmade bed. Earlier, Mynk sent someone to straighten the sheets, but I told them they'd have to make the bed with me in it. They looked affronted—not thinking me funny—so I tried again, saying, "Thank you, not today."

Sliding my tongue over my upper teeth, I find a remnant of lettuce from lunch and suck it off. I swallow, close my eyes, and decide I'll stay just like this for the rest of the day. Such is the excitement of my life.

"Knock, knock," Raider says, standing in my doorway and tapping on the wall. I keep it open since any movement in our quarters sparks more interest than anything happening between my four walls.

"Hey. What's up?" I ask, craning my head.

"Help me with something?"

After noting my boredom this week, they've recruited me for various tasks. I've done everything from sealing envelopes to folding laundry—nothing that requires exertion or leaving the bedroom. "Sure. Leave it on the table, and I'll take care of it," I say, my attention falling away from him.

Raider laughs, rubbing his short hair aggressively as he strides into the room. "Wow. You've really settled in."

"Settling is best when there's no point in pushing. What I want is on hold, and what everyone else wants is for me to stay out of the way. Done." I drop my arms dramatically onto the bed and stare at him.

"It seems my rescue is overdue. Get up." I groan. "Up!" Raider appears at my side, taking my arm and tugging until I sit. He doesn't stop there. Next, I'm standing, and he's dragging me with him. It's not until I've achieved momentum that he lets go, and I continue after him.

We stop at the couch. He loads a couple of bags into my arms and picks up a few for himself, and I follow him out of our quarters. When we reach the main doors, I ask with some excitement, "Are we going outside?"

"We are."

I get strange looks from those we pass, but when the unfiltered sun hits my face, I'm too happy to care. I squint against the abundant light, looking over the vibrant grass and sky, while Raider unloads my arms. It's then I realize he's putting the bags into a car.

"What's all this?"

"Getting us ready to leave."

"Leave?" My mind goes to Valore and the goodbye I'll soon say to him. What's surprising is the sadness of separation doesn't stay focused on my friend but drifts to include Raider and Renegade.

Curses! When did they become significant enough to feel sad about?

"Where are you going?" I ask, feeling empty and crossing my arms over my chest.

"To the South T. Heading home to Caelum."

"And you're leaving today?"

"Hopefully. We need to finish a few things to be ready."

"Well, it seems like you've got everything covered," I say, nodding at the packed car.

"It's a good start," Raider says, grinning at me. "But our departure might get delayed. It depends on how long the little prisoner takes to get her stuff."

"What?" I stare at him, unsure of what more to say.

Raider puts his hands on his hips and faces Fiducha, squinting. "I know you have more clothes now. How long will it take to pack them?"

I grab his arm, turning him toward me. "Are you seriously taking me to Caelum with you?"

Raider lifts a shoulder but never loses the smile. "Unless you'd rather stay holed up in this place, though I figure you've had enough of confinement."

"I don't want to stay here," I say emphatically. "But you've been very vocal about staying away from your Dad."

Raider's hands land on my shoulders, leaning down until our eyes are the same height. "If there's one thing you should know about me, it's that I'm flexible."

A laugh bursts from my mouth. "Flexible?" I've lost track of everything Raider claims as his most important trait, but I'm sure this newest one conflicts with the others. "Are you sure there isn't anything else I should know about you?"

"Yeah. I'm scrappy." Raider winks as Renegade appears, throwing another bag into the car.

"Hey, guys," Renegade greets us, his blue eyes settle on me. "You comin' with?"

I smile, the move nearly breaking my mouth. "Hell, yeah, I am."

"I'm leaving," I tell my mom. I considered packing my things and slipping out silently, but my conscience got the better of me.

"So soon?" Her hair is down and loose around her shoulders. It's strange seeing it not pulled into her tight bun.

"I've been here almost two weeks."

She actually looks startled by the fact but recovers, asking, "Are you going to Hamo?"

"Not yet. I'm going to the Southern Territory with the Roils. Can I leave this here?" I hold up my broken bottle from the Dark prison. I should throw it away, but I can't bring myself to do it. I need it to survive in some capacity, even if it's broken and useless.

She looks at the pile of brown glass, confused, but nods. She doesn't follow me as I enter the room with shelves displaying my bottle collection. I place it with the rest, comparing the dull object to the shiny ones surrounding it. Unbidden, a surge of anger enters me. Without thinking, my eyes narrow on the sea-green gift from my dad. I pick it up by the neck and slam it onto the wooden shelf. It breaks easily.

My mom appears at the door, her brown eyes wide. "I heard a noise. Are you okay?"

I look over the shattered remains. "Yes. I feel much better," I say, exiting the room and leaving the pieces as they lie.

Meeting up with Raider at the car, I note his earlier lighthearted mood has darkened, and I wonder if he's decided against me accompanying his group to Caelum. He glances over as I arrive, takes in my cautious expression, and asks, "What's wrong?"

"That's what I'm trying to figure out."

He grunts, mumbling, "What are you talking about?"

I point at his boot, kicking a beat on the tire. "I'm never sure what that means. At least, not at first. It always takes a minute to figure it out."

Raider's foot freezes. "I didn't realize I was doing it."

"You usually don't."

"It means nothing."

"Wrong. It always means something. Usually that you're pissed off—quite often at me—though it could be a situation has you ruffled. Did you change your mind about me going with you?"

"I want you to come to Caelum." His foot bounces once, unbidden, but then he stops it with a grimace.

"Well, my next guess is that you're thinking things out."

"That I am."

"What has you concerned?"

He lets out a breath. "Everything."

"Tell me. A worry shared is a worry lessened."

"We haven't heard from Arrick, and every day that passes brings us closer to war."

I nod. "It's a valid concern, but you've done all you can."

"I haven't, though," Raider says, kicking the tire again.

His promise to meet Tyran. It's the first time he's mentioned it without prodding from either Arrick or Valore, and for a moment, I'm unsure how to respond.

Arrick insists Tyran won't tolerate being put off for much longer, while Valore maintains it's a bad idea to give her an audience. Raider doesn't argue either point. Indeed, I believe Raider's more aware of what the meeting involves than he's revealed to anyone.

I wonder if going back on his word may be in everyone's best interest. Especially his. Of course, Tyran would be furious, but she's a stubborn woman, and it's hard for me to believe anything will divert her course.

I'm about to express my thoughts when Raider says, "Regardless of what I've done or not done to prevent war, I worry I've neglected to prepare for it. I've been here, idly waiting for word from Hamo while others ready my people. Maybe joining the Souther soldiers would have been more worthy of my time."

"Second-guessing serves no purpose. Move forward unhindered. Decide tomorrow's actions based on today's knowledge."

"With that logic, it's safer for you to stay here." I open my mouth to argue, but he pushes on. "I'm not saying you're not welcome. It's just... Diggs. Your departure might draw him away from Adlumen."

"I come with issues." I sigh. "Do you worry I'll bring harm your way?"

"No. I worry about exposing you. While distancing him from the governors is good, taking you from Ambitus could put you in more danger."

"I'm not scared of Diggs. I can handle myself."

"So my dad repeatedly tells me."

"Especially if you lend me your tiny lady knife."

Raider groans, but then he's smiling, and the easy expression amid his harrowing concerns eases the tension inside me. "Actually, I have something better. I packed Torquent blades."

"Really?" I nearly giggle. "Please tell me they're not Hs."

Raider chuckles. "No. They're Cs."

"Thank you," I drag out.

"Well, they're what I had. But you're welcome to use them for practice. Or, you know, defense, as needed."

I clap my hands in a quick, child-like beat, asking, "Do you think Valore could handle a C?" That weight is a stretch for me, and my friend has had a slower recovery from prison deprivation.

"No," Raider says, confirming my thoughts before adding, "But I can."

There are two cars in our caravan. Raider, Valore, and I ride in the lead car. Renegade, Raden, and another guy are in the other. He has copper hair and is named Mickens. Though he grew up in Ambitus, I don't recognize him or his name. It's just another reminder of how self-absorbed I was back then.

The real kicker is we have as many spare tires as people. They're strapped to the roll bars and bolted to the sides. Raider's not taking any chances of us getting stuck in transit. And they purposely didn't bring more people because in an emergency—though it would be a squeeze—we could all six fit into one car by abandoning our belongings.

We maintain a quick pace while in Ambitus but take it down a level the moment we enter the Southern Territory. It will take longer to get to Caelum, but if there's an issue, we'll fare better if we're not speeding.

It's fascinating passing through the border town of Calor. It used to be heavily monitored, but now the passage is wide open. People come and go between the South T and Adlumen, wearing lenses and circlights, respectively. It's an integrated society—vastly different from the Southers living near Torquent, who give the place a wide berth.

I glance at Valore. He's in the back, purring restfully —the noise barely detectable over the engine—with all our belongings tucked around him. His knee rests against my suitcase, which only contains clothing since my broken bottle is back in Ambitus, and Squatty's necklace is around my neck. It feels right to wear it and remember my friend.

"Did you say goodbye to your sister?" Raider asks, drawing my attention.

"I tried." I went to her quarters, but she wasn't there. She was at the car factory, and truthfully, I was glad. I told Evans to tell her goodbye. Hesston was there too, and when I saw the sad look on his face, I spun away and left. Chessie would disapprove of me ingratiating myself, especially with her not around, so it's better if he thinks I'm unkind.

"I'm still shocked you asked me to come along."

"I'm shocked myself," Raider admits. He's hyper-observant, his eyes scanning the road. I'm trying to help, but the lamlight can only do so much. Renegade and Raider know what to look for from Diggs's last road trap, so it's good they're both driving, though I don't expect arrows in trees to give warning. Still, we all watch for soft dirt in our path.

"Well, in a few days, when you realize you've made a mistake, please drop me somewhere nice." I suck my upper lip, running my tongue over the raw skin. "Of course, maybe it won't take a few days."

"Are you nervous about visiting my hometown?"

"Why would you think that?"

"I kick tires, but you have your own tell," Raider says, rubbing his upper lip while keeping his eyes on the road.

"I'm a little nervous, but it's not a stretch to think Caelum may reject me as Adlumen did."

"Maybe. But have you considered moles are nicer than you light lizards?"

I chuckle, having forgotten his people call us that. It never took hold like the term mole did—maybe because it sounds cool, so it's not much of an insult.

"You've changed since coming to Adlumen," Raider says.

I think back to this afternoon when he found me dead to the world on my bed. "You mean I'm more depressed and moody than ever before?"

He shakes his head. "I see glimpses of the fun girl you used to be."

"Fun?" I can't help myself, startling Raider when I reach to put a hand on his forehead. "Do you have a fever? There must be something wrong. Raider Roil never thought I was *fun*."

He pushes my hand away, laughing. "You were fun when you weren't conniving to break up happy couples or plotting to kill people."

"Oh, so two percent of the time?" I used to would have taken offense at the comment, but now I'm joining in to roast myself.

"I'll give you five percent," he says, not missing a beat. "But you were in there. You just didn't let it show. I don't think you knew how."

The smile slides from my face. I'm unsure of what to say, so I change the subject. "I'm glad Valore will see your brother tonight. Three years is too long."

Raider nods, a residual smile on his flawless lips, and we fall into a comfortable silence.

We drive for hours without issue, leading me to believe Diggs isn't out here setting traps for us. Maybe he's traveling behind us. Or maybe he stayed in Mirum. Nothing's certain. I just hope the Ambitus soldiers remain vigilant in protecting the governors.

It's nighttime when we arrive in Caelum, but not late enough the children are asleep. They pour from the main door when we arrive at Stryke's house. The oldest child goes straight to Valore, along with two adults, but the younger ones fall on Raider, and he dotes on them, touching each of their heads before asking, "Where's Sage?"

"Playing next door with the neighbor girls," an older child says. "They're likely tormenting more than playing with him. I'm sure he'll be home soon."

I catch Raider's shadowed grin as the group encircles them. A moment later, all talk ceases while one adult clutches Valore desperately, crying into a shoulder. It's a private moment—one I'm embarrassed to witness—so I'm ecstatic when Renegade appears, asking, "You hungry? Or would you rather skip dinner and retreat to your room?"

"My room," I say without hesitation, and he nods, feeling the same. It makes sense to let their family have this time without us interfering, and Renegade seems to know the house's layout, so I follow him.

Before entering the door, I glance back and find Raider watching me, the light from inside falling across his face. He tilts his head. At first, I think he wonders where I'm going, but then I realize it's not that. He's grateful to us for letting his dad get all the attention. He's nodding his thanks, and my chest blooms with heat, knowing I'm finally being helpful—making the moves he needs—so I nod back and leave them to enjoy their reunion.

CHAPTER TWENTY-NINE

Twenty-Eight Days Free

Meetings. The only people who enjoy meetings are those who lead them. It's an excuse to vent opinions to a captive audience.

Leading a meeting is a narcissist's dream.

I shouldn't complain—really, I shouldn't—because I was actually invited to this meeting. And let me tell you, no one was more shocked by that fact than me. Still, I'm exceedingly bored. They're currently rehashing what they've twice rehashed. I'm an observer only, nodding my head to corroborate Raider's comments. I decide he's not a bad guy, but I'd like him more if he'd talk faster. Or less.

An hour ago—just as the sun rose—there was a knock on my door. On the other side was a man with a lean build, dark brown hair, and a swagger I associate with his family. He introduced himself, though there was no need. Even after eight years in captivity, I recognized Captain Rhed. Not only is he Evans's dad and a longstanding Endrack adversary, but he escorted me to Aunty's Cellar deep in the Desert Territory. Neither of us mentioned the long-ago journey. He simply requested I join a meeting that would take place fifteen minutes later.

Captain Rhed is a decisive and quick-acting person, having been in Caelum for only ten minutes when he called us together. I wish those attributes would translate to this meeting, but the lengthy conversation has more to do with the others in the room than him.

Stryke is here—Raider's brother—and now that I see him in daylight, I can confirm his features aren't as refined as

Raider's or Imily's. He's the bulkier of the two boys but lacks the bull-legged stance Raider inherited from his dad and the exquisite look of their mom. Stryke's handsome, for sure, but he's not stop-a-thief-in-their-tracks gorgeous. No, Raider alone has looks capable of distracting a criminal from their treasure.

I didn't think it was possible, but Stryke has been less welcoming than Raider. His behavior might not be personal—though he has plenty of reasons for mistrust—but regardless of his motivation, he doesn't like me. And since there's nothing I can do about it, I put it from my mind.

Our introduction was brief, and he's only done two things since. The first was to declare heavy distaste for what's happening. He's extremely bitter at the prospect of war—understandably so—and discussing it is like sour milk on Stryke's tongue. The second thing he does is glare. Not at me specifically, but at anyone who speaks. So, definitely not at me because I've yet to say a word. It's not that they're preventing me from giving opinions—I'm avoiding it. I feel like an outsider and would rather not talk unless asked to do so.

Stryke's fierce aversion to war brings a lot of contention to the room. He argues his viewpoint on repeat, which is unnecessary since he's not at odds with anyone—the others aren't rejoicing over the situation either. I'm well-versed in how Raider, Valore, and Renegade feel about it. The others in attendance are Captain Rhed and a top member of his guard—a woman named Biv with short black hair and a stocky, muscled frame—and they've been clear about their desperation to prevent the conflict. It's just that Stryke is extra agitated. I get the feeling he's led a mostly trouble-free life, and he doesn't want that disturbed. Who would?

Raider detours the topic to Diggs, explaining the situation and answering questions while Valore and Renegade insert occasional comments. Any time Renegade speaks, Captain Rhed tenses, and it's obvious the relationship between the two men hasn't improved during the passing years. There's still an undercurrent of quiet annoyance with Captain Rhed glaring his displeasure and Renegade calmly flaming the captain's irritation. While their contention is unfortunate, they remain professional, and truly, it makes the meeting more interesting. Indeed, I don't take my eyes off them until I hear my name mentioned.

"Sharade's been invited to live in Hamo?" Captain Rhed asks, his attention turning to me.

"She has, but her plans are undecided," Raider answers. His words are measured and calm, but his shoulders tighten as he says them.

"Would she consider living there and monitoring the situation for us?" Biv asks Raider.

"Spying," Raider says. "Call it what it is, Biv."

"Yes. Just to gather information. Not necessarily to take action. At least, at first," she continues, outlining my future without asking my thoughts or looking me in the face.

"You're joking, right?" Raider asks, his tone demanding attention. My eyes snap to his. "Shar's been locked up in the Dark for eight years, and you're ready to put her in that situation? Tempt another round of prison, or worse, execution? Is that what you're asking?"

"We ask that and more of others," Biv says, lifting her chin.

"Yeah, but the thing is, you didn't even ask *her*. You asked *me*." He kicks the leg of the table in complaint.

Biv clears her throat, and her eyes move slowly to me. Her resolve after being reprimanded has her staring me down, not even blinking. "Would you be—"

"No." I look at the others before going back to her. "Arrick and Chett extended kindness to me when others did not. I disagree with their alliances and will help you in other ways, but I won't betray them like that. I'm sorry." Valore clicks his tongue and takes my hand, holding it on the table's surface.

"What was the tone like in the Desert Territory towns?" Captain Rhed asks, looking between the four of us who recently escaped from prison in Casmo's territory. He doesn't address the idea of me as a spy, ready to move on.

And suddenly, I'd be glad if the meeting returned to being boring.

"I spent the most time among the people," Renegade answers, rubbing his slim fingers over the back of his neck, missing the hair there. "They're unconcerned. I barely heard mention of the conflict. Their location removes them from immediate action, and Casmo's over-inflated ego keeps them confident."

Captain Rhed nods, leaning back in his chair. "I should tell you I came to Caelum directly from Windway."

The mention of Casmo's capital city in the Desert Territory has Valore fidgeting next to me. It's where he was before seizure and incarceration—Windway, meeting with Casmo himself.

"I went there to discuss alliances," he continues, then looks at Valore. "And other matters."

"You asked him about me?" Valore asks, reading into the comment.

"Yes. Casmo insisted you were dead. Imagine my surprise at learning otherwise upon arriving here today," Captain Rhed says to Valore. "But my main goal in meeting with Casmo was similar to one of your lesser goals from three years ago."

I look at my friend. While I knew he met with Casmo before his imprisonment, he never revealed the reasons for his meeting. Of course, the guidelines I set upon our acquaintance prevented it. Recently, I considered the meeting with Casmo was a regular thing they did—an annual conference that didn't turn out so well—but Captain Rhed's comment has me rethinking it once again.

"You discussed them becoming an ally of the Southern Territory," Valore says, and when Captain Rhed nods, my friend adds, "I'm surprised you got out of there."

"Your capture weighed heavily on my mind, so I prepared leverage."

"Leverage?" Raider asks.

"I took Mal. Pulled him from his bed and hid him away. Casmo wasn't too keen on losing his best rat," Captain Rhed says, looking at me and rightly guessing I didn't know Mal's identity.

"It apparently worked," Raider surmises. "Since you're here."

Captain Rhed grins. "It did."

"What did you learn from Casmo?"

"His heart isn't in this war. He has no desire to fight and is going along to appease Tyran. I believe it's a show of strength, but he hopes things will get resolved before it gets far. Truthfully, if the fighting starts, I could see him withdrawing his support. He and his people have always been a lazy sort—concerned with their interests and little else. They have plenty of space, and losing their lives for Tyran to gain more land holds no enticement. Still, they aren't amenable to coming over to our side."

Raider releases a defeated breath. "So, it all circles back to Arrick. Everything hinges on him convincing Tyran the abatement fulfills her needs."

Tyran's needs. Vengeance, greed, and jealousy fuel her desires. Does the abatement hold the power to combat all that?

"Sure," Captain Rhed says, though his answer has no conviction. In fact, every face in the room looks unsure.

"No," Renegade says, daring to say what the rest of us don't. "Tyran of Torquent still grieves the loss of her mother and sister. She drafted her list of demands, but the only thing she truly wants is to fill that familial vacancy. And Raider's the only one she'll allow to fill it." Renegade's tone sends a chill down my spine, and his words silence us all, causing Valore to turn a ghostly white. Renegade never takes his eyes off Raider—not challenging him but not letting him forget. Tyran's goals are personal, and family is as personal as it gets.

Raider nods. "Even then, would she be happy?" he asks, pushing back his chair to stand. No one answers, but he doesn't wait for their thoughts, announcing, "I need a break."

◆ ◆ ◆

"Why didn't Raider include me?" Stryke asks, pacing the living room in front of his dad. Stryke's mood hasn't changed since the meeting. He hasn't lost his glare and shares his dissatisfaction with anyone with ears.

"You need to let this go," Valore says. "You were each where you needed to be."

Stryke rubs his eyes, dropping his hands in defeat and stalking from the room.

"Imily called it," Renegade says with a grin while nodding to where Stryke disappeared. Renegade's sitting with me on the couch—an over-stuffed blue thing that's trying to swallow me. We're staying out of the way while the others manage their frustrations. It seems we have the fewest issues that need fixing, which is saying something for me. In Adlumen, my list of concerns is endless. Here, it's relatively peaceful, even on the brink of war. And Renegade, well, he seems to live life following the philosophy of stirring no pot and slinging no mud. Unless he's interacting with

Captain Rhed, of course.

"She did," I agree, and then add, "I get the feeling Stryke doesn't like me."

"Eh," Renegade says—just a noise and nothing else. It's not until I widen my eyes and stare at him unblinkingly that he continues, "Known Stryke a while now. He doesn't care much for me either. Indeed, if you're not a child, he doesn't have much use for you."

"What do you mean?" I ask, confused, but there's no time for an answer because the room suddenly fills with children, running through the space and making a commotion. There seem to be more of them than greeted us last night, but they're moving too fast to count.

Renegade keeps a straight face, saying, "And my point is proven."

A little girl appears on the back of the couch, balancing precariously before jumping and landing on her bottom next to me. With no acknowledgment, she climbs to do it again.

"What's happening right now?" I ask in a daze while Renegade chuckles.

"Stryke takes in homeless kids—makes 'em family. It's a thing."

"Oh."

A child runs by, their toe snagging mine before falling to their knees. I lean forward to help, but they're already up and running again. Another swings a long rope, screaming and charging across the room to chase two others.

"Are any of them his... by birth?"

"Just one." He points out the littlest, who's sitting quietly sucking on her fist.

"Wow."

It takes a bit, but I finally get the children organized in my head. There are eight of them, all under twelve. At least, that's my best guess. I'm horrible with children's ages, having been around very few growing up and none for the last eight years. Children are a mystery to me but not an annoyance. They're sort of funny. And the noise is interesting. I prefer it to the silence of Aunty's Cellar.

"Hey there, little man," Renegade says, putting his fist up for a bump from one kid. This one differs from the others with a serious expression and eyes that see too much. He looks between Renegade and me before finally touching his fist to Renegade's. "This is my friend, Shar," he continues, and the little boy's dark eyes stop and stay on me. "Shar, this is Sage. Raider's boy."

My eyes widen. "Raider's what?"

"Your hair is short," Sage says to Renegade, and then, stepping toward me, "So is yours." What is it with kids and the length of my hair? But he's closer, and I see it now. Among the swarm of little people, I didn't connect this one with Raider, but it's undeniable—those black, calculating eyes and the too-perfect lips.

"Yeah." I thumb the blunt ends. "Your dad cut it."

"He cut yours too?" Sage asks Renegade, and my friend shakes his head. Sage looks at my head even closer, and I wonder if I'm going to have a repeat of my conversation with Dody and Harding, but instead, he leans in and touches Squatty's necklace. "That's shiny."

"For a long time, it wasn't."

Sage looks back at my face. Wow, this kid is intense—like his dad. I feel his inspection as if he were running a finger across my skin. "Your nose is different," he says.

"Oh, well—" I look at Renegade for help, but he's holding back a laugh—his blue eyes twinkling—and Sage is waiting for a response. "Thanks. I haven't been told that in a long time. Yours is different too." He takes another step forward and leans against my knee, looking up at me as I ask him,

"How old are you?"

"Six." Before I know what's happening, Sage climbs onto the couch, moving against me and snuggling into my side. I'm sure my bony ribs don't make a good pillow, but he doesn't seem to mind. Slowly, I place my hand on his shoulder and give it a squeeze. Sage releases a content breath, relaxing against me, and I look at Renegade, needing some direction on how to handle what's happening. It's immediately apparent he'll be no help. The hardened man is no longer holding back laughter but staring at little Sage with a soft expression.

"I'll grab us water," Renegade chokes out, launching to his feet. Sage's need for comfort from a stranger has sent us both into a spin.

Over the last month, I've watched Raider react to all the changes in his world. He's performed his duties with detached professionalism, and I knew, the entire time, he suffered underneath. I believed his pain was a mixture of remembering Kally, concern for his dad, and fear for his people. But this little boy was a hidden piece of his turmoil, likely the most significant part.

Raider left his son behind to complete two important goals: To find Valore and to stop a war. The extra caution he put into every move suddenly makes perfect sense. His frustration with recalcitrant leaders who are slow to listen while clinging to unreasonable politics is clear. It all stems from knowing his son is back home in Caelum, waiting for him.

Sage, like so many others, is depending on Raider to make life safe again. But that's not what his six-year-old mind thinks about. He just knows his dad isn't around. Meanwhile, Raider longs to return to his life. It's not the Southern Territory or even Caelum that binds his heart, but this little boy.

But sitting at home won't improve his son's future. So, he left him with Stryke—a capable brother with a great love for children—and Sage became another parentless child taken in.

It must kill Raider to do it.

A sad tear slides down my cheek—an emotion I've avoided for so long—and I pull Sage closer. No wonder Raider despised my presence so heartily. What if I was genuinely unchanged? What if my spoiled, traitorous ways ruined his chance of returning to this life? He calculated the risks of entering the Desert Territory and chose to face the dangers for his dad. But for me? Logic says he should have left me in Aunty's Cellar.

I run my finger over Sage's ear, making him shiver. So many people depend on Raider—his dad, brother, sister, and son. And me too. Where would I be without his aid?

Right now, I'd be back in Fiducha, staring at the ceiling.

It makes me wonder in what areas I hindered his progress. How could I have lessened his worries?

Curses. I'm so ashamed. I could have done so much better.

Raider appears, looking oddly at his boy, curled into my body. I observe my arm lying over Sage's, startled that mine's only slightly thicker in my current state of health. I really need to bulk up.

"I'm sorry. I didn't have the heart to tell him no," I say, staring up at Raider.

He tilts his head. "Why would you do that?"

"The last thing you want is me getting another Roil in my clutches." I laugh, but the sound is weak.

"That's not what I was thinking," Raider says, reaching down to tussle Sage's black hair. "I'm glad he found a place he feels safe. It's not always easy out here, especially as my son, to feel protected."

"Why didn't you tell me you had a son?"

His hand stills. "It never came up."

Yeah, but Valore never mentioned it, either. Except, maybe he tried during our drive from Ora to Adlumen, when I told him it felt wrong for the two of us to discuss Raider. Then again, maybe that wasn't the direction of our conversation. Regardless, Raider kept quiet about Sage, and there are only two reasons I can think of for that. First, because it's a tough subject. Discussions about his son inevitably would lead to talking about Kally, and he avoids that topic with precision because he loved her terribly. She's been gone for four years, meaning Sage was only two when he lost her.

"Thank you," Raider says, looking between us once more before walking away, leaving me with Sage.

"Did you know my mom?" Sage asks, turning to look up at me.

"No." I pull in my upper lip, sucking the dry skin.

The second reason is Raider didn't trust telling me, which is understandable. Ultimately, Valore respected Raider's need to keep it quiet. They're good men. I only wish I'd lived my life to be deserving of such companions.

Renegade arrives with the water. I thought it was just an excuse to get away, but he's back and brought one for Sage too. He helps the boy sit up, and we all drink together.

It occurs to me that Renegade has a past like mine. His actions weren't as extreme, but he has troubled family relationships, and he's disappointed people. Maybe it's the destiny of people like us to sit on the outskirts, helping the noble ones.

There are worse things.

CHAPTER THIRTY

Twenty-Nine Days Free at 5:00 p.m.

Raider is with Captain Rhed, devising their strategic plans, while the children claim my time, demanding games involving everything from mental astuteness to physical agility. I'm proud to say that even after eight years in the Dark, with little to no mental or physical stimulation, I can keep up with them.

I'm behind Stryke's cottage house on a stretch of land he owns. The house isn't as big as Imily's—although he has more than double the people living here—and the land isn't as extensive, though there's plenty of room to move around, and the children take advantage of it.

No one sticks to me more than Sage, and since Raider doesn't discourage it, I adhere right back. It's a relief not all adults believe I'm a corrupting influence on their child's mind and heart—and it's a surprise Raider's the adult in this scenario. Like other times, I figure I can overthink it or get over it.

"Run that way! That way!" I throw my arms to the left while Lea zigzags across the grass, looking back at me. I'm sure she'll trip on the uneven ground, but instead, a boy runs straight for her, catching her off guard and tackling her to the ground.

I bite back a laugh while jogging to see the damage. The girl's unfazed, turning on the boy, baring her teeth, and preparing to bite his arm.

Curses! It's me as a child.

"Hold up!" I pull them apart.

I've screamed so much in the last hour my voice

is fading. I've run around enough to maintain a steady pant, especially in this heat, though it's significantly cooler now we're nearer the ocean. Overall, I've decided watching children is an excellent endurance exercise.

"I want you to have fun and be competitive," I tell them. "But no tackling. And no biting."

I point at the perpetrators. The boy looks penitent, but the girl is unrepentant. I'm about to double down with the pep talk when Sage rushes to me, taking my hand and tugging me away from the others. In our brief association, I've noticed he doesn't like me giving attention to the other children. He's a little attention hog. I remember being the same as a child, begging my parents for their time and searching for anyone to listen to me. Because of that, I don't hesitate to leave the biters and tacklers. They can resolve their issues independent of me.

I turn Sage so his back is to my front and have him step onto my feet. Holding his hands, I take small steps, and pretty soon, he's laughing while I jostle him around, staggering like a dizzy person. He slips off more than once. Eventually, I lay him on the ground and tickle his belly.

And that's how Raider finds us. "Dad!" Sage calls. "Help!" Then he giggles when I find a sensitive spot.

"I'll save you," Raider says. Expecting him to lift Sage away, I'm surprised when he wraps his arms around me, pulling me to my feet.

"What are you doing?" I ask, looking over my shoulder and finding Raider inches away.

"Giving my son his vengeance." Raider wiggles his brows, then says, "Come get her!"

"What? No!" I struggle to escape, but I'm entertained watching Sage huff to his feet and come at me. He's not the best tickler and mostly pokes his tiny fingers into my skin, but I'm laughing so hard the tears are falling. "Okay, stop.

Stop!" I beg, stomping my feet. But Sage doesn't stop, digging harder. *Ouch*. It kind of hurts, and I jerk my foot again.

"Are you trying to kick my son?" Raider whispers into my ear.

"No! I'd never."

"I know." He chuckles, loosening his grip on me. "Sage, Grandpa's helping with the cows today and wants you to join him."

Sage's mind switches from tickling, and he drops his hands. "When?"

"Now."

"Are you coming with?" Sage asks. I'm not sure who he means. He's looking at both of us. It's then I realize Raider still has me in his arms, so I tap his elbow and get him to open up.

"No. She's coming with me."

"I am?" This is news.

Raider keeps addressing Sage. "There's something important I need to show Shar. We won't be back until after you're asleep."

"Oh." The little man suddenly looks less excited.

"I told Grandpa you know how to handle the chickens, and he wants you to show him that too."

"He does?" His black eyes light back up.

"Yeah. He doesn't know all that's changed since he's been gone. Can you help him?"

"Okay." Sage smiles, and my heart melts at the sight. I'm so grateful Valore is reunited with this little explosion.

"Let's go in and let him know," Raider suggests, and we start for the house, but Sage runs ahead, entering the house before we're even halfway there.

"You need anything before we go?"

"Depends on where we're going."

"A few places. But first, I'm showing you around Caelum."

◆ ◆ ◆

Caelum is a beach city. Stryke's place is removed from the coast, but a trip to the water doesn't take long in a car. Raider drives up and down the streets, pointing out the highlights—the market, the school, and the government buildings. Most things are easily seen with the lamlight, even a six-story hotel. While Raider points out the building's carvings and arches, I'm mesmerized by the gleaming glass and marvel at the phenomenon—being unable to see the sun but seeing clear evidence of it in the reflected sunlight.

The air gets cooler the closer we get to the ocean. Raider turns off the car so we can walk down to the sand, and I marvel at the soft cushion of earth under my feet. No amount of lamlight can give me a full picture of the ocean, and I can't imagine what it must look like, going on forever. It's something those of us with light sight won't ever see since there are no known light bubbles containing a vast expanse of water.

"This is amazing," I say, watching the water roll onto the sand, only to turn heel and run back out. I experience the same curiosity with the water as the hotel glass—unseen sunlight glinting off surfaces—and again, my mind can't quite make sense of it.

"It is a sight," he says, picking up a rock and throwing it. With the sound of the waves, I don't even hear it land.

I sit where the water can't reach me, enjoying the sights and sounds as I ask, "Who's the mother of Stryke's child?" Raider raises a brow, and a vision of the many children in Stryke's home pops into my head. Shaking my head, I clarify, "I mean the one who shares his blood."

Raider chuckles. "I knew what you were asking. Just

surprised you knew about it."

"Renegade," I say, and Raider hums in understanding.

"He had a girlfriend. The relationship didn't last, and neither did her commitment to her kid."

"How does he handle it all?"

"Well, partly because his house operates like a zoo." I grin because Raider's description is perfect. "And partly because he loves them so much he makes it work." I nod. Stryke does his best to roll with the punches, though a household of kids is easier for him than the looming threat of war. "But mostly, it's because he has Ms. Pane."

"Who's Ms. Pane?"

"She's Stryke's do-it-all handywoman. I've seen her manage everything from setting a broken bone to fixing a leaky sink. She lives with him, managing everything, including the kids. But her niece had a baby, so she's gone for a few days. I know Stryke's *anxiously* awaiting her return."

I just bet he is.

I stretch my legs in front of me, leaning forward. "I feel so lazy sitting here, but I don't want to leave. It smells too good."

Raider rocks onto his knees on the sand, leaning toward me with an excited grin. "I know just the thing. Be back in a second." He gets to his feet, and I twist my neck to watch him jog away. He stays within range of my circlight, and a minute later, he returns with a long wooden box in his hand. Placing it in the sand between us, he releases the latch, opening it in equal halves to reveal shining Torquent blades strapped onto each side.

"They're beautiful," I say, adjusting to kneel before them. They're unlike any Torquent blade I've ever seen. They're the common scimitar style—curved with a single edge that's sharpened and serrated—but they're narrower than what I'm used to, and instead of a hilt guard, there's a six-inch crossguard. My brows narrow in confusion as I ask, "You borrowed these from Adlumen?"

"No. They're mine," Raider answers, running a thoughtful finger along the dull side. "They were my mother's. I had them with me when I learned where Dad was, so I left them with Evans. Since I was returning to Caelum, I brought them back home." He pulls on the strap, securing the sword closest to him. "I promised you a bit of practice, and now seems as good a time as any."

I grip the edge of the box. "We can't practice with these!" It's a terrible idea. With a Torquent blade in my hand, I'll want to go full throttle, and I won't be able to, knowing the history of these weapons. They were Sivil's! Valore's beloved wife. Raider's loving mother.

Raider chuckles, reaching over and releasing the strap on the sword closest to me. "My mother would hate to hear that. She believed an idle blade was a wasted blade." He lifts the sword, holding it out for me to take. "You ready to show me what my dad taught you?"

I pause. "Well, if you're sure," I say hesitantly, and he nods.

Another pause, and then a grin spreads across my lips. I stand, taking the weapon from him. Rotating my wrist, I feel the weight and balance of the sword, but something is off, so I ask, "Didn't you say they're Cs?" I twist and jab a few times, testing the feel.

"I did," he answers, lifting his blade. "But I was wrong. Forgot Mom preferred Ds."

"Ah." That makes more sense. I walk away from the box, ensuring I have room to move unhindered. "You mind if we do a few stretches and poses first?" My muscles could use a proper loosening before throwing metal around.

"Whatever makes you comfortable," he answers, not moving to join me. I do as he suggests and find what's comfortable. Facing the ocean—the water twenty feet away—I close my eyes. The circlight allows me to see, but with a sword in my hand, it feels right to go without my sight. This is how I trained for over three years, and it still seems the best way to concentrate on the postures and movements associated with a Torquent blade.

My other senses heighten. I hear birds overhead. I smell the salty waves, ebbing and flowing leisurely. The sand warms my feet, and when my foot sinks below the surface, the grains are cool. I hold the hilt two-handed, raising the blade above my head. Spreading my legs, I twist my hips until the sword is parallel to my feet, and I hold the Weldcall posture, breathing steadily through my mouth.

Releasing the hilt with my right hand, I bring the serrated blade level with the horizon and drop to one knee, keeping still in the Cantinot. I count time with my heartbeat, allowing my body to become the posture.

With both hands on the hilt, I lower my other knee to the sand, tucking the grip against my side with the serrated blade fanning across my chest like a deadly rainbow.

"The Wist," Raider says. His voice—closer than expected—jolts me from my exercise, and I open my eyes to look up at him. "Indeed, my dad taught you everything." I nod, not ready to use my voice. "You look like you're dancing." He squats, pressing his blade into the sand and resting his chin on the pommel while he watches me with black eyes. "You look peaceful now—almost angelic—but serenity will transform into fire when the fight is in you. I'm eager to watch it happen. You think we can give it a go before the sun sets?"

"Sets?" My eyes flash toward a horizon I can't see. "How long do we have?"

Raider grins. "An hour. But you were so lost in your perfect postures I wondered if we might be here until tomorrow morning."

"No," I say, pushing up from the sand. "I would have gotten cold."

Raider chuckles and rises with me, taking his place six feet away and asking, "Who postures first?"

I'm pleased when he asks and doesn't assume to give me the stronger position. "You go ahead," I answer, and Raider raises his brow. Clearly, although he gave me the choice, he thought I'd take the advantage. But I've been at a disadvantage for eight years. There's no reason to get used to anything else now.

He puts his free arm out parallel to his body. The Torquent blade rests with the dull side against his arm. He's chosen the Imtal. It's an aggressive stance—the extra hand meant to push the sword into the air and increase the power behind the arc.

A thrill runs up my spine because Raider's giving me a true challenge. By giving him first posture, I let him know I wouldn't be babied. He's responded in kind, choosing one of few postures that grants first move. It puts the opponent at a complete disadvantage. But the action could hardly be called unfair since I pushed him to treat me with equity.

He's bigger and stronger than me, even without considering years of prison food. There's only one option open to me—a feint. But I must choose a posture first.

I drop my right knee to the sand and lift the blade above my head. My right hand grips the hilt, and my left holds the back of the blade, prepared for Raider's crushing blow.

"The Spall," Raider says approvingly. "Your only choice, really."

I don't reply. He finishes his verbal appraisal, pauses, and then his entire body tenses as he sends the blade toward the sky. My body wants to tighten, but I can't allow it to happen.

The sword reaches its apex, and that's when I feint.

Raider's blade is falling toward me—the serrated edge ready to eat whatever's in its path—but I'm spinning away. He's already in motion, and there's no changing direction with that much force driving the metal down. I'm cleanly away when his blade slices the sand.

Aiming the curved edge of my sword at Raider's throat takes no effort at all. "Dead," I announce while Raider's chest heaves from exertion. I'm no less affected—my heart beating in my ears.

"By the Dark, what was that?" he asks, releasing his weapon and facing me.

"A feint."

"I've never heard of that posture," he says, shaking his head in thought.

"That's because it's not a posture. It's a reaction."

His head continues to shake—more agitated now. "You can't run away from the blade each time I come at you."

I tilt my head. "I didn't run away. I stayed right here and put a blade to your throat."

Raider scowls. "You know what I mean."

"I do," I say with a laugh. And really, I understand I can't use a move like that every time. "But Raider, considering our size difference and my general level of health, what other move would you suggest to gain the upper hand?"

"There was no move. That's precisely why I chose the posture. I had a clear advantage until you used your feint."

"Yep. And then the advantage was mine."

Raider groans.

"If you'd anticipated my feint, you could have performed one of your own and claimed your win." Raider mumbles nonsensically, making me grin. "Are you more upset I used a technique you didn't know, or that you lost? I can't quite tell."

His eyes widen. For a moment, he looks shocked, and then his lips twist as he seriously considers my question. Then he chuckles. "I don't quite know. It's just... Dad said you're great, but I've always known, deep down, I'm better than you. And now..."

"Yes?" I ask after the pause goes on too long.

Raider clears his throat. "It's your turn to pick first posture."

I grin at Raider's reluctance to say I might be better at something than him. Of course, he could still be right. We've not yet fully tested each other—our first attempt at measuring our worth with a Torquent blade was finished with a rather tricky move on my part.

So this time, I pick something basic, choosing the Winslav, which has me standing with the Torquent blade aimed straight at his heart. He could use a few postures to counter this move, and I'm curious which he'll pick. His brow twitches while he judges his options. And while I can adapt to all of them, only one feels natural. And so I must hide my pleasure when he chooses the Mondiel.

I nod, telling him I'm ready whenever he makes his move. He doesn't wait, sending his sword straight for mine. Most competitors would perform a drop move, leaving the opponent's sword with nothing to strike. But the opponent, anticipating the drop, would be ready with a countermove that would surely give them the win.

So, I don't drop. I remain in my perfect posture and merely flatten my sword. The serrated edges catch a few times, drawing the energy from Raider's sword until his blade stops, resting on mine. With a quick flick to the side, my blade is unencumbered and aimed at his chest.

"Dead," I say because he would be dead if I pushed forward a foot. Grunting out a laugh—because I've killed him twice now—I lower the blade, and Raider's follows.

"Shit, you're good," he says, rubbing his brow, then running the same hand over his head. The entire time, he keeps his eyes on me. Likely, he wonders if my wins are an anomaly, and if he has one more go, will it be the end of my streak?

Instead of finding out, he reaches for my sword. "As much as I'd like to try again, we must go."

"Well, as much as I'd like to beat you again, I'm glad we're done." I rub the arm that held a Torquent blade moments ago. "It's good those weren't Cs because Ds were heavy enough. Two rounds, and I'm worn out." I shake my head, disappointed by my low endurance.

I follow Raider back to the box, barely able to see it in the distance. "Is the sun down?" I ask. While I appreciate the circlight making it so I can see in the Dark, it's still limiting.

"Nearly," Raider answers, strapping in the blades before closing and latching the box. Raider pushes to his feet, putting his hand out for me to take. I don't understand the move, but I don't fight it and give him my hand. Then he pulls me along through the sand.

But when we get to level ground, he keeps my hand, and I don't know what to make of it. The problem is I like it, while he's probably forgotten we're even connected. Maybe. I don't know.

"Is there any color yet?" I ask to distract my thoughts, and he finally releases me to get the box into the back of the car.

"Not yet," Raider says, looking back at me with a grin. "But I promise I'll let you know when it happens. Especially if it's orange. Now, let's go. There's something important you need to see."

CHAPTER THIRTY-ONE

Twenty-Nine Days Free at 7:30 p.m.

"Where are we?" This is my first time in Caelum, and since we've not returned to the grid of streets Raider showed me earlier, nor to the quiet beach we practiced on, I'm unfamiliar with our location. We appear to be at a different beach—a noisy one filled with shoulder-to-shoulder people.

"The Southern Territory barracks. We're currently housing Coastal Territory and Adlumen soldiers too."

Raider guides me through the crowd dressed in South T green and gold. It doesn't take long for the whispers to start and then become a commotion as news spreads of who's among them—and it's not me who's got them in a dither. The soldiers push in on Raider, slapping his back and releasing cheerful shouts while he interacts with them. The soldiers flash me impassive glances, too engrossed in their leader's return to give me much notice, and I enjoy the ease of being unimportant.

Reaching the edge of the South T soldiers, we enter the gathered Coastals, wearing boots with their emblem on the side. Though kind, they don't respond as gleefully, and we push through them more quickly. "This way," Raider says, changing our course. We walk another hundred feet before I understand our destination.

Stopping in my tracks, I stare at a group wearing circlights with Adlumen sunrays on their chests. "I can't go over there," I say wide-eyed.

"Of course, you can," he says softly.

"They hate me."

"They don't know who you are." Raider pauses. "Well, one of them does." I follow Raider's finger and gasp, my hand going to my throat, where I find the thin chain of Squatty's necklace. I need it to strengthen me, but it's just a delicate metal chain. The only thing that can give me strength is my resolve, and I have none.

"That's why you brought me here?" I whisper.

"It's one reason," Raider says, nudging my back, but I don't move. "You can't stand here forever, Shar."

"Oh, but I think I can," I counter just as the person looks up.

"Too late. He sees you."

Not only does he see me, but he's walking this way.

Raider turns me to face him, and I release the necklace. Putting his fingers under my chin, I'm forced to look into his earnest, black eyes. "You're ready for this." When I don't respond, he reiterates, "You are."

I nod stiffly.

He runs his fingers lightly across my cheek, and I pull in a breath from the unexpected caress. Raider smiles and releases me. The interaction has me wholly flustered, making every worry flee my mind. It lasts until my primary concern enters my space, snapping me back into the moment.

"Sharade?" My brother Wick's voice is full of wonder as he pulls me in for a strangling hug. I can't believe how tall he is. Or that he has such big muscles. Then I marvel because he's not yelling at me to go away. "I wasn't sure if it was you. Damn, you're tiny. The last time I saw you, you were bigger than me." He squeezes me, running a hand over my back. "Hell, I can feel your bones. Are you eating? Are you hungry? I can get you food."

I chuckle, pulling back. "I'm eating fine."

"She speaks too, so I'm not hallucinating." Wick shakes his head, gazing down at me.

"You're not," I return with a giggle. "And while I don't have a great appetite, I'm getting three meals. Give me a little time, and I'll fill out. I may even get boobs again."

Wick's eyes go big, and he chokes out a laugh. "We don't need to talk about that."

"Okay, let's not." I clutch his arms, looking at his mature face.

Curses! He has scruff.

"By the light, it's good to see you," I say. His chestnut hair—a shade darker than mine—is the same, though the freckles over his nose have faded. He still carries a serious expression in his brown eyes, but there's a lightness too that's new since I last saw him. My brother seems content with life.

"Seeing you feels like a miracle," he says, searching my eyes. "They told us you were dead. How did you get here? Where have you been? Wait until Mom and Chess find out you're alive."

I roll my eyes. "They already know. They're not as happy about it as you seem to be."

"Why?" Wick scowls. "What did they do?"

I pull in my upper lip, not wanting to get into it. Part of my motivation for leaving Adlumen was to forget that situation, but he's my brother and the one person who should know.

"Mom thinks I'm too much like Dad and doesn't trust I've outgrown unacceptable behavior. Chess is a little better, but she's afraid I'll corrupt her kid. She says she doesn't want him to get attached and for me to bail, but it's more than that. She gets nervous any time he's around me."

Wick takes my shoulders, holding me steady. "I don't feel that way," he states while his eyes bore into mine. "We've reconnected for less than five minutes, and I can see in your face and hear in your voice that you're different. What about Evans? How did he treat you?"

"He was forgiving, which only made me feel worse."

Wick nods. "He's a good guy. He'll set them straight. We both know Mom and Chess are slow to accept change, but they'll get there, eventually." I want to believe him, but especially where Mom is concerned, it doesn't feel like she'll ever give me a chance. "You were many things growing up but never a liar. You wanted to be a spy, remember? But you'd have been terrible at it. You're too transparent."

"Yeah, I know." Grinning, he pulls me into another hug. "You were always the wise one," I say, dropping my head to his chest.

"It's a burden." Wick chuckles, and then, he has my arm, pulling me to a nearby rock where the three of us sit to talk. Our spot is hardly private with soldiers surrounding us, but they're caught up in their own conversations.

I'm surprised Wick's in Adlumen's army. Growing up, he was all about books, not combat. But he and Evans got close, and Wick started tracking with him. It wasn't long before he became adept at many things under Evans's tutelage, setting him up perfectly to be a soldier. Dad would be so proud. I don't say it, but then, I'm sure Wick already knows what Dad's opinion would be since he often professed displeasure over Wick's disinterest in military matters.

Raider grabs drinks from a passing soldier, lifting his shirt to wipe the condensation off each bottle before giving them to us. "Keep your shirt on," Wick teases, accepting the drink, while Raider chuckles and drops his shirt, now wet on the edge.

We update Wick on all that's happened since the prison escape. My brother is especially concerned about Diggs and his threat against the governors. Raider doesn't mention

Tyran and Arrick—though I bet he would if we had privacy—and I don't disclose my Hamo job or Chett's proposal. Wick hasn't asked about my plans, and although I won't lie, I'd rather not tell him just yet.

"There's someone I need to speak with," Raider says, standing abruptly. "I'll be back."

Sitting with my twenty-one-year-old brother, whom I haven't seen in eight years, we just stare at one another in disbelief. In our short re-acquaintance, my opinion is that he's pretty marvelous.

Wick's the one who eventually breaks the silence, saying, "We tried to get you back."

I squint. "What do you mean?"

"You'd been gone for two years when Chess came to me, saying she wanted you back. I wanted you back too."

"You wanted me back," I repeat.

"She didn't tell you?" I shake my head. "She got permission from the governors for your release. When we told Mom, she cried. She was so relieved."

"*Relieved*?" I laugh at the absurd thought.

"Yes," Wick says, not laughing. "Mom was miserable, wishing she'd acted differently before you went away. Chessie felt like she'd failed you—that punishing you in Adlumen would have been better. And I… well, I thought two years was more than enough to learn your lesson."

"Two years?" I laugh. "Not even close. Try five."

"Five? Really?" My too-smart brother looks disappointed he missed the mark.

"Yeah. I guess I was more stubborn than you thought."

"Were you angry all that time?"

I pause, thinking back. "No. But that's how long it took to humble me." I reach out, taking his hand. We used to be at each other constantly, and now I have an easier time talking to Wick than almost anyone. "Chessie really wanted to bring me home?"

My sister said she'd be there for me. I thought she let me down, but maybe she tried to keep her promise.

"She did, but we couldn't find you." Wick frowns, and I nod, knowing those who keep prisoners aren't an honorable set. Who knows what motivation Warden Ott had for telling them lies?

"It means a lot. Thanks for telling me."

"They're starting," Raider says, reappearing, and I realize the crowd has thinned out around us.

"What's happening?" I ask as Wick helps me up, walking me in the direction everyone else is going.

"We're observing Ante Bellum," Raider says. "It's a South T thing, but today, a couple legions of Coastal guards, a few thousand Adlumen soldiers, and a former Desert Territory prisoner are joining us." Raider winks, and I snort out a laugh. "It's an unofficial ceremony we do before a coming battle."

Curses. A coming battle. That sobers me.

For the first time, it registers that Wick is here preparing to fight. It's stupid, but I've been so caught up in our reunion I hadn't considered the finer points. Wick and all these young women and men are preparing to defend their homes and families. Tyran is a truly despicable person to do such a thing for her selfish pursuits.

And Arrick too. I've made excuses for him, but is he without guilt?

Wick takes my silence for confusion and leans in to say, "We observe Ante Bellum by surrounding an enormous bonfire and burning away the fear in our mind. Symbolically, of course."

I watch the fire lick the air as Raider says, "I was getting to that."

"Maybe," Wick counters with a smirk. "But you were taking too long."

We stop a fair distance from the flames, but the size of the fire puts off remarkable heat, making it hard to breathe. "I'm going to move back," I tell the boys, and while I'm unsure if they'll follow me, they do.

I find a spot away from the crowd where we can still feel a part of the event. A girl watches us approach, smiling and patting an empty spot on the log she's leaning against. I return her smile, and we join her in the open space, turning to look again at the fiery spectacle, though it doesn't keep my attention for long.

"Where did you get that?" the girl asks, pushing off the log and standing directly before me. She's lost her smile, and her gaze is intense as she points at Squatty's necklace.

I lift it from my chest, holding it out for her to see as I answer, "From a friend."

"What was your friend's name?" The girl has no circlight and wears no other identifying symbols, so I can't tell where she's from.

"I don't know."

She tilts her head while her eyes develop an uneasy glint. "You don't know the name of your friend? That makes no sense."

"It does, from my perspective. Do you know something about this necklace?" I ask, moving it closer.

Her eyes narrow on it, and she drops her accusing finger, settling into a relaxed stance. "It depicts a corner of my family crest and once belonged to my mother. My father commissioned the piece, selecting the jewel personally since the orange sun was Mom's favorite element of the crest, and he needed it to be perfect. There's not another necklace like it in the world, and my brother had it with him when he disappeared."

Her brother.

Squatty.

My throat goes dry as I lower the pendant to my chest, asking, "How long ago?"

"Six years."

Yes. I met him six years ago. "How old was he?"

"Nineteen." He was so much younger than I imagined him—barely older than me, which she confirms by adding, "He's twenty-five now. If he's still alive."

Still alive. I pull my upper lip between my teeth, biting it to keep back the tears. Swallowing hard, I choke out, "You don't know what happened to him?"

"No."

"What's his name?"

"I've answered enough of your questions." The girl straightens while her eyes shine with determination and apprehension. "It's my turn for answers."

"Please. Just his name."

She releases a breath. "Dell. My brother's name is Dell Denita."

Dell. His name was Dell.

I smile. I never tried to guess his name in the Dark. Not after I started calling him Squatty. That's who he was to me. But I like Dell too.

"Please, tell me about his life." My tone is desperate, and despite her insistence on getting answers, she softens and shares the information with me. It turns out my friend was painfully shy—not a surprise—but he was fun and a bit of a quiet jokester who put his whole heart into things. He grew up in Tenebris—a town in the Coastal Territory—and was a member of Captain Rhed's guard. He was on a mission to the Desert Territory with two other guard members when he disappeared. The guard searched for them, discovering one dead but never finding the other two.

I tell her how I met Squatty—though I'm careful to call him Dell—and describe our time together in a Desert Territory prison. "It was February, four years ago, when he got really sick. One day, he stopped breathing."

"And he died," she finishes.

"Yes." And I almost did too.

She puts a fist to her cheek, and in one stroke, she wipes the moisture from her eyes, but more follow.

"What's your name?" I ask.

"Lizz."

"I'm Shar." Without permission, I put my arms around her in a tight hug. "For two years, your brother was my best friend." A cry breaks from her throat, and she sobs into my shoulder. It's a while before we release each other. My sorrow manifests quieter than Lizz's, but my cheeks are equally wet.

She lifts the pendant, looking at it closely. "There was a neighbor girl he liked. He planned to give it to her." Lizz chuckles. "You see, Mom made him promise to give it to the one he loved."

"Unfortunately, I was the only person around." I rub my finger over the top, and my heart breaks even before I get the words out, whispering, "You should give it to her."

"Oh, no. She never gave him a second thought after he went missing. She's married now."

"Then you should take it," I say, reaching to undo the clasp.

"No." She holds my hand in place. "I'll never understand what my brother experienced in that prison, but you lived it with him. I'm positive he didn't give you this necklace without deep consideration. He valued it and the promise attached, which tells me he loved you, even if only as a companion in his affliction. He wanted you to have it, and I want that too."

The tears come again, heavier this time, and I knock them away. I swore I'd only cry for happy reasons, and this is not happy. "If you ever change your mind, just tell Captain Rhed, and I'll get it back to you," I say, my voice watery.

"I won't change my mind." Lizz takes my wrist, squeezing in solidarity.

My gaze falls on Wick and Raider. I'd almost forgotten they were here, but they're watching me with compassion and concern. It's all too much, and I mumble, "Excuse me," before pulling from Lizz's grip and heading away from them. I push toward the tents and trees where I can hide my emotions among the branches and evening shadows. I'm grateful no one follows. I don't want anyone to see me while I completely fall apart.

Tucked among the thick leaves, I gain my privacy and lose my composure, letting it all out. Dropping to my knees and gripping Squatty's necklace, the orange jewel bites into my palm, adding to the anguish I feel over the loss of the quiet boy who meant so much to me.

CHAPTER THIRTY-TWO

Twenty-Nine Days Free at 10:00 p.m.

"You ready to get out of here?" Raider asks. I've been in the trees for twenty minutes with my emotions mostly under control for ten.

"More than ready. I just need to say goodbye to Wick."

"I told him we're leaving. Said he'll come by Stryke's tomorrow for breakfast to visit some more." Raider's made all the arrangements, and I'm relieved, yet part of me thinks he's making this too easy on me. I don't deserve to walk the uncomplicated path, but this once, I'll take it.

Minutes later, we're in the car but driving the wrong way. "Aren't we going back to Stryke's?"

"I want to show you one more place if you're up for it."

"It's late," I say because I don't think I am up for it, unsure I can maintain my composure if social niceties are required.

"We don't have to stay long."

I give in with a nod, and he pushes the pedal so we go faster, probably thinking I'll change my mind. My thoughts return to the hoards of people at Ante Bellum, and something occurs to me. "Were Raden and Renegade at the bonfire?" I've barely seen them since we arrived in Caelum.

"Yes. Mickens too."

"Is that who you went off to see?"

"No. It was someone else." And that's all he gives me. It's not annoying or anything.

"Why didn't your dad come? Wouldn't he normally attend that sort of thing?"

"In the past, yeah, but few know he's returned, and I

want to keep it that way for a while longer. Besides, the crowd would wear him out."

Yeah. It was nearly too much for me—all those people packed on the beach with uncertain futures hinging on what their leaders decide.

"Valore seems older out here," I admit, thinking how unstoppable he seemed in the Dark on the other side of a metal grid.

"Do you think I've pushed him too hard?" The concern in Raider's voice has me reevaluating my words.

"Sorry, that's not how I meant it. It's a lot of stimulation and activity after three years, but he'll adapt. He'll be fine." I lean my head against the frame of the car. "It was my perception of his strength I was considering. He was bigger than anything to me. He was the brightest star in my dark night."

Raider nods as he stops the car. Turning off the engine, he walks to my side and waits for me to hop down. It's nighttime, but the place he's brought me to is lit up. The grounds are highlighted using a combination of regular light and lamlight because I can see everything without issue. A large expanse of emerald green grass is framed by thirty-foot palm trees swaying in the breeze and skirted by lush green shrubs and flowers in every color. I can hear the loud crash of ocean water, though I can't see it because of the building. At first, it appears to be a single-floor dwelling, but I realize a lower level exists below where we stand.

"What is this place?"

"It's my home."

"You grew up here?" My mouth drops open, struck dumb by this impressive place.

Raider chuckles. "No. I was born in a hospital in town. I grew up in the Seclusa light bubble, about fifteen minutes to the south, which was a logical place to live with a light-sight mom and light-blind dad."

"I didn't know there were any light bubbles in this area."

"It's tiny. There's not much to it, except a few buildings." Raider moves away from me, and I assume I'm supposed to follow. "This place has been mine for ten years. I loved it the first time I saw it, but it was really run down. So, I fixed it."

"You fixed it." I look around, and a shiver of excitement runs through me.

"Yep."

"*You* did. Like with your own hands. Not just giving orders to other people."

"With my own hands." He grins, and the shiver increases until it feels like I'm vibrating because it's precisely what I want to do—build things with my hands. I open my mouth, ready to barrage him with questions, but he's directing me along the cobbled walk, and my attention catches on something else.

"It's rather plain," I say, observing the Southern Territory flag, flapping steadily in the ocean wind. "Just a yellow stripe and a green one."

"Gold," Raider says with a furrowed brow.

"Gold, then. I'm not saying simplicity is bad, but the other Dark territories and light bubbles have more complex emblems."

"Complexity isn't required to communicate purpose."

A smile lifts one side of my mouth. "Then tell me, what is the purpose behind green and gold?"

"Posterity and prosperity. Those are the two things that matter."

I look at the flag again. There's no need to ask which color belongs to which purpose, but I grin, telling him, "It still looks yellow."

Raider snorts out a laugh. "You're such a contrarian," he says, and after tapping an entry code onto the door panel, he escorts me through the double doors into a grand living space.

"Yeah, maybe I am a contrarian because, while it looks comfortable, that cream couch isn't meant for sitting." Wiping my dusty palms across the front of my clothes, my eyes wander the room, and I reject the idea of relaxing in this pristine place. It's too clean. It's too perfect. I'll sully anything I touch. Meanwhile, Raider drops onto the couch without pause.

"If you don't want to sit, check out the view." He throws his arm across the top of the couch, and I glance over my shoulder at the far wall comprising floor-to-ceiling windows facing the ocean. Again, there must be a combination of light sources outside because I can see the nearest section of the beach and the accompanying waves. Admittedly, the ocean view is stunning. A few windows are open, and the salty breeze invades my senses. I breathe deep, letting it calm me.

The floors are all hard surfaces, but soft touches are everywhere—vibrant plants, colorful paintings, and plush furniture. The shelves lining the northern wall beckon me, not only the craftsmanship but the objects they contain. "Arrick arranged a construction apprenticeship for me in Hamo," I say, running my hand over the first shelf I reach. There's not a speck of dust, meaning he has someone cleaning it for him.

"I didn't know you're interested in building things." His voice is level, and I appreciate him not talking negatively about my opportunity.

"I was curious in my youth, but I'm more interested now," I say, taking in the shelf lighting and how it highlights wooden bowls, metal vases, and glass bottles.

"But you could do that anywhere. Not just Hamo."

I think of Adlumen before replying, "I guess." I approach a bottle transitioning in color from piercing orange to angry red. It's violent and gorgeous, making me think of the sunset I missed tonight. I pick it up, admiring the skill. Turning it in my hand, I catch a sharp edge, wincing as it slices my pinkie finger. I replace the bottle and lift my hand to inspect the stream of blood while cupping my hand beneath the wound so I don't make a mess.

"What a strange day," I say with a thoughtful laugh, turning around to show Raider, but he's already there. Taking my elbow, he carefully pulls me to the sink, placing the cut under flowing water. Reaching for a towel, he dries it, then procures a kit with medical supplies and bandages me up. I flex my finger, looking at the job he did. "I always consider glass enchanting, but beauty can be quite dangerous, can't it?"

"I've always thought so," Raider says, his voice scratchy as he watches me.

I lift my finger between us. "Are you going to kiss it better?" The minute the words leave my mouth, I want them back. I'm not sure why, but Raider makes me impulsive. He always has.

But if there's one thing I want more than to reverse my clumsy statement, it's never to show weakness in front of him, so I let the comment simmer while I hold his gaze.

Raider glances at my finger, his black eyes returning quickly to mine. "No. I don't think I'll kiss it better."

"Your loss," I say, dropping my hand.

"Yes."

I suck in my upper lip, then think better of it, attempting to disguise it as a simple lick rather than the nervous tell it is.

Raider takes a step closer. "It is my loss, but I'm holding out for something better."

From me or in general?

My heart goes into a double-time beat, and I blurt out, "I never knew Dell's name." I clear my throat, dipping my chin and focusing on my bandaged finger. "He barely spoke, and the warden restricted my information. The guards said it was a condition of my sentence. I heard those words so many times, I learned to hate them." I chew on the edge of my lip. "We had a bad summer with terrible wildfires that nearly choked the life from me, and I swore, through the smoke, I saw him squatting in the corner." I look up at Raider. "It felt so real. After going with you, I've wondered if it was the abatement."

My gaze wanders to the tidewater outside. "After that, I called him Squatty. Lizz said he was shy, and maybe that's the reason for his silence, but I think it was trauma. He was terrified and alone, but I couldn't tell her that." I drop my hands, resting my palms on the counter behind me while releasing a long breath.

"They put my dad into Squatty's cell, didn't they?"

"Yes."

I don't want to talk about Squatty anymore. I should have left those emotions in the woods and not brought it up again, but he embarrassed me when he wouldn't kiss my finger, and I was desperate for a distraction. So, I'm baffled when I say, "I don't blame you for not kissing me."

What the hell?

Pushing off the counter, I step around him and walk to the cream couch, which seems more accepting now in my flustered state. "I was prettier with long hair," I say, my tone flippant as I twist the short length between my fingers and laugh, but it sounds fake. It is fake. I don't know what I'm saying. Or doing.

This is absurd.

"You're lovely as is," Raider's voice echoes behind me. "Do I make you nervous? You're jumping from topic to topic, escaping one by bringing up another." He's figured me out easily, and I don't know how to respond, but he doesn't seem to require an answer, continuing, "Let's not avoid things, Shar. Discussing a difficult past can be a healing exercise. Or so I'm told."

I sit, and so does he—closer than expected, and our knees touch.

"Is discussing your past part of this experiment?" I ask. He's been impressively tight-lipped these last weeks—unwilling to reveal his history—so when he says no, I'm off the hook.

So, imagine my disappointment when he answers, "Yes. Me included. Maybe we'll resolve some things that have us stuck in limbo."

Limbo. Is that my problem? Is it his?

The idea draws me in and has me saying, "Okay. Let's talk."

"You want to ask the first question?" he asks with a grin. I already feel exposed after learning about Squatty tonight, but Raider thinks it's time to delve into the tough subjects, so why not dig into my discomfort fully?

"Okay. Three years ago, Valore met Casmo in Windway. Convincing him to be an ally of the South T was a lesser goal. What was the main one?" The look in Valore's eyes any time it's mentioned makes me think I'm somehow involved.

"You're sure you want to know?"

I bend my knee and rest my leg on the couch, facing him. "We're not avoiding things, Raider. So, yes, I'm sure."

"He was there to arrange Lord Endrack's execution."

My body falls against the couch. I can't move. I can't even respond. I knew there was more to it. Valore was methodically quiet about his purpose in Windway, but even though we agreed not to talk about certain things, over time, information would slip. But never that. He never hinted he was there to organize someone's demise.

"Dad was already dead." He had been for a year.

"Yes, but they were still collecting fees from Adlumen, so Casmo wouldn't admit that, would he?"

"No, they love their laps of gold." I recall Warden Ott's voice saying as much. "Well, you've made clear the Southern Territory's feelings about my dad, but what about Adlumen and the Coastal Territory? Were they set on an execution?"

"They were in agreement."

"Why did their preference change from indefinite imprisonment to death?"

"They discovered more evidence about your dad's indiscretions while leading Adlumen. His crimes were more severe than originally thought. Then we got word of a failed escape attempt—one managed from the outside—so we knew his location was no longer a secret. We considered negotiating a relocation but decided moving him would make an escape more plausible. Arranging his execution turned into the logical option."

"How did Valore end up in prison?"

"Negotiations fell apart when my dad called Casmo duplicitous. You see, Dad suspected Lord Endrack was dead and said as much."

"He has good instincts."

"Yes, but Casmo was angry about being challenged, so he sent Dad to *see Lord Endrack for himself*. And then, he locked him up."

"Seriously?"

"Yeah," Raider mumbles, still frustrated by what happened.

"But that's so... so..." Considering options to finish that statement, I select, "ruthless."

"I can think of many things to call it." Raider turns, mirroring my position. "Are you upset my dad didn't tell you?"

I shake my head. "We had a deal. We didn't discuss personal stuff."

"Are you mad about what we planned for your dad?"

I look down, picking the edge of my thumbnail. "I understand why you settled on that choice." I understand, but I don't want to dwell on it. Lord Endrack did despicable things, but he was still my dad.

"You mentioned the apprenticeship in Hamo, but you didn't sound as sure about it—not like when you first brought it up. You're not going there anymore, are you?"

Dropping my hands onto my lap, I look up at him. "No, which is stupid because it's my only real option." There's no other way to describe it—Raider looks relieved. Meanwhile, I'm frustrated by my diminished choices. "I mean, I can't return to Adlumen, but unfortunately, Hamo's wrong for me too."

"What changed your mind?"

"Something my mom said. And something that happened here." I rub the bandage on my pinkie. "I told Mom your fight wasn't my fight, but I've realized it is. Because of Wick. Even if he's the only family member who accepts me, that's something, and I can pledge my support to him. And I can pledge it to you. If you still want me to go to Hamo as a spy, I'll do it."

Raider leans in, alarmed. "I never wanted you to do that."

"You're right. It was Biv who asked. It feels despicable, but if I can help my brother, I'll do it."

"No, Shar. There are other ways."

"Fine. Whatever they are, I'm telling you, I'm in. Put a weapon in my hand and point me in the right direction."

"You're in absolutely no condition to fight!" Raider leans back and scowls. "You need at least twenty pounds of muscle and ten pounds of fat."

"Whatever!" I say with a laugh. "Just understand, you have my support if you need it."

Raider chuckles, relaxing. "Yeah, okay."

I push the shoes from my feet, pulling them under my legs as a chill runs through me.

"You cold?"

"A bit."

"I'll shut the windows." Raider pads to the wall of glass and shuts out the fresh ocean air. It makes me sad but takes the edge off. Now, give me an hour, and I might feel warm again. He opens a bin next to the couch and lifts out a blanket, wrapping it around me and tucking the edges.

"Thanks," I say, looking up at his handsome face. He nods while concentrating on closing any gaps, then returns to his spot, not bothering to get his own blanket.

"Why didn't you tell me you have a son? The real reason this time."

"Oh, I don't know," he says, drumming his fingers on his knee. "I guess it was too much to think about. I'm out there trying to fix the mess we're all in, and it's a reminder of what I'll lose if I fail." He laughs humorlessly. "Then again, maybe that's a reason to keep Sage at the forefront of my mind."

"He's a great kid."

"He is." Raider smiles, and then the expression drifts away. "He's all I have left of her."

"Kally."

He clears his throat roughly. "I don't enjoy talking about

her."

"You agreed to this," I say, then let out a hard breath when I internalize what I'm asking of him. "But you don't have to. Still—" I stop, looking into his dark eyes, not sure I dare speak my thoughts.

"Go ahead."

"You at least talk to Sage about her, right? We all see the heartache you carry and understand your method for managing it. But your son's different, carrying a similar ache and needing to talk about it. He even asked if I knew her."

Raider shakes his head—whether from failure, resistance, or sadness—but doesn't comment.

"If you can't do it, which I completely understand, ask Valore or your siblings. Maybe have Imily spend some time with him. He's desperate for a mother's attention."

"I noticed." His eyes flash to me.

"I'm sorry about that," I say, but he waves it off.

"Don't be."

Raider stares out at the water, and we get quiet. I rest my head on the couch, watching him. After a minute, he reaches out and rubs the corner of the blanket I'm cocooned in before saying, "Kally made this."

I suck in my upper lip, chewing on the raw skin.

"You really need to kick that habit," he says, and I pop the skin free. Then I pull it back in. I can't help it. It feels strange to be cuddled up in his dead wife's handiwork—a person whose loss haunts him and always will. No matter the passage of time, he'll always feel a segment of pain.

I want to strip off the blanket and return it, but that feels slightly worse than using it, so I stay frozen with it surrounding me.

"She made it for Sage on his second birthday," Raider tells me, and I see my out.

"Maybe he wouldn't want me using it."

Raider shakes his head. "I sort of think he'd feel the opposite. You're right. He wants to share her memory with anyone who'll listen even though he has few of his own."

"How did she die?"

He clears his throat, but the emotion remains in his voice. "It was my fault. I was distracted, inexperienced, and overconfident. It happened before I even knew what was going on." His answer tells me nothing about the situation but so much about Raider.

"So, now you're minutely focused, an expert in everything, and still confident without flaunting the fact?"

He actually grins before answering, "Sure. You could say that."

"How did you meet?" I ask, and he seems to settle into this line of questioning.

"Kally was from Tenebris. She dated Ronen for a while, and I met her through him."

"Awkward," I say with a smile.

"You'd think so, but it wasn't. Ronen could tell I was more than just interested. She was beautiful, but she had a radiant personality. He decided what he felt was friendship and practically forced us together."

"Forced?" I shake my head. "How did that work?"

"Her sister Sazanne died during the attack on Harwell." He says it so calmly. Like it wasn't Lord Endrack who orchestrated the attack. Like my dad's actions didn't cause Sazanne's death. "I was in Tenebris—helping with lamlight distribution—when Ronen arrived with the news about Sazanne. But he didn't go to Kally with the information. He came to me. Ronen said he'd seen my interest in Kally and had noticed her similar interest in me. So, he tasked me with two objectives: Telling Kally what happened to her sister and informing her that Ronen was breaking up with her."

"Now, you can't tell me that wasn't awkward!"

Raider smiles, leaning back in his chair. "It took some finesse, but I presented the good before the bad."

"What do you mean?"

"I told Kally I wanted to date her. Then, I told her Ronen was out of the picture."

"Good before bad." I smile.

"Yep. And then, I explained about Sazanne. Ronen joined us at that point to give his condolences. His dog, Yip, sat in her lap for hours while we reminisced about better times. But after that, it was just her and me."

And if it wasn't for my dad, Sazanne would likely be alive today. Twisting Kally's blanket between my fingers, I say, "Like I needed another reason for her to hate me."

"She wouldn't have hated you. Not even a little." Raider scratches his chin. "Well, maybe I should take that back. She'd have hated you *a little* if I'd told her what you did at the governors' reception."

"But… you said you told her!"

Raider chuckles. "I lied."

"I swear, Raider," I start, shaking my head in dismay. "You lie more than any non-liar I've ever met."

"Yeah." He grins. "I rarely do it. Lies normally just cause more problems, but I was trying to make you feel guilty."

"Well, it worked," I say, sulking.

"I won't lie to you again. I promise."

"Fine. I'll believe you. *Until I don't.*" I'm forcing a scowl, but his promise means more than he could ever understand—I need those kinds of assurances in my life. "And I can't believe you didn't tell Kally what happened. You're disappointing me right and left."

Raider laughs again. "I didn't tell her because that's exactly what you wanted me to do."

I nod thoughtfully. Yes, it was.

"Why put myself under needless scrutiny?" he asks. "The only purpose the truth served was to fulfill your baseless adolescent vendetta against a girlfriend I loved."

"I was a brat," I admit without pause.

"You were. But equally charming in your way. And beautiful too. It's been nice to see some of that youthful shine come back into your cheeks."

"In one month, I'm so changed?"

"You are." Raider sighs, and it feels like he's winding down the conversation. The feeling intensifies when he twists, putting both feet onto the floor and staring at it as he says, "It's a relief because your improvement takes some of the stress off Dad's face." He rubs his chin, then pushes up from the couch. Yep. It seems we're leaving. I stand, folding the blanket and placing it back into the bin.

"It's past midnight," he says. "If we return to Stryke's, we'll wake the house. Half his kids sleep in the living room."

"Oh. What do you suggest?"

"It may be best to sleep here. I have a guest room." He shrugs.

"Whatever makes sense. Point me in the right direction."

But Raider doesn't point. He approaches, stopping in front of me. "I need a favor from you, Shar."

"Sure. What is it?"

"Please be careful with my son."

"You want me to stay away from him," I say, remaining calm but unable to keep the hurt from my voice—it's my sister and her son all over again.

"No. Quite the opposite. But I need you to give him

reasonable expectations. You don't have familial ties to my son, and he's fascinated by you. You're a dynamic person who draws people in. You could inadvertently do some damage."

"How do you mean?" I squint at him, trying to understand. He opens his mouth, then stops, looking toward the staircase. "What?"

"I thought I heard something, but it's just the wind picking up." He shakes his head, putting his attention back on me. "Your plans are undecided, and Sage, well, you said yourself he's looking for something."

"Something." I pause. "You mean a mother's attention."

"Yeah. I've been gone too much, and I just reappeared, bringing people I closely associate with—Renegade, who Sage idolizes, and my dad, who I've kept alive in Sage's mind through grand stories. And then there's you. I see it in his expression. He's placed you in a position of great importance and could easily decide you're the something he's missing." Raider rubs his palm over the top of his head. "I'm not concerned about your influence on him. I'm worried about him caring for another person who drops in and out of his life."

"Oh." I bite my lip. "I'll stay mindful of that." Though, I think Raider's reading too much into my interactions with Sage. "Maybe he just needs a pet," I add, partly to be funny. But also, it might make sense. That seemed to help me as a child. Of course, the pets all were Chessie's, and I merely played with them—when she allowed it.

Raider's gone quiet, a distant look in his eyes.

"So, no pet then," I say, and his eyes fly to mine. "That's okay too."

"We had one. I mean, Kal did."

"Oh." I'm finding all the landmines tonight. "Hey, I'm sure it will all work out. You'll get this issue with Tyran resolved and have more time to spend with him. And while you're here, just try to spend as much time with him as possible."

I think of my dad and even my mom, knowing all I ever wanted was their time and attention. They could have done so much for my well-being if they'd been more involved.

"You think I ignore my son?" he asks, suddenly defensive.

I shake my head. "I didn't say that."

He barely hears me. "I couldn't take him with me to the Desert Territory. Or Hamo."

"I realize that," I say, my voice rising.

"Before then, I was with him all the time."

"Raider, calm down. I meant nothing impertinent. I promise you."

"The quality time he needs... he'll only get that if—" He rubs between his eyes.

"If you stop Tyran's war."

"Yeah." He drops his hand. "You don't think I can stop it, do you?"

"I hope you can, but it's a lot of hope to pin on one outcome. War isn't reasonable. In fact, it's most often caused by one party being completely unreasonable."

"I'm just so tired, Shar. I don't want to lose any more people I love. Tyran and her greed—she doesn't consider the casualties, but the potential disasters are all I can think about."

"And that's why you'll make the best decisions. That's why you'll win, no matter the duration." Raider nods, but none of the stress leaves his eyes.

He walks me down the hallway, pointing out four doors containing a bathroom, Sage's room, Raider's suite, and a guest suite. Raider leaves me in front of my door, going to his. I push it open, flip on the light, and walk straight to the bathroom to rinse off my face. Now that I'm alone, I wonder how to dress for bed. I'm still undecided as I walk to the bed and turn down the sheets. I'm clutching the corner of the bedcover when my hand stills.

Because that's when I see it.

CHAPTER THIRTY-THREE

Twenty-Nine Days Free at 11:30 p.m.

"Raider!" His name flies from my mouth with as much volume as I can manage. It's only seconds before he reappears, his hands braced against the sides of the doorframe.

"What's wrong?"

"He was in your house." I pace away from the bed, a shudder running through me. "He might still be here!"

Curses! What if he's under the bed?

I drop to the floor, crouching to get a look, but there's nothing there.

"Who? What are you talking about?"

"Diggs." I straighten and hasten toward him, pressing the letter against his bare chest.

His bare chest.

I snap my hand back, and Raider catches the paper before it drops to the ground. His state of dress didn't register until I touched him, and now I'm embarrassed, twisting away to ignore the mindless incident.

Curses. What am I even thinking about? Diggs was here!

Raider's all business, reading the letter. Finishing, he goes on high alert. "I knew I heard something when we were downstairs." He glances around the space, fidgeting with the corner of the paper, before instructing, "Get your things. We need to leave."

"These are my things!" I say, gesturing to myself.

"Good. I'll get mine and be back."

"No way! He's probably still here. I'm coming with you."

"Come on, then."

I chase after him. "Where are we going?" I ask, my voice trembling along with my hands. "What should we do?" I feel so defenseless with no Torquent blade or even a Wendhower knife in my tiny lady-hands.

His response is clipped, his tone low, and his message brief. "Three goals. Get our people. Get our cars. Go back to Adlumen."

He pulls on a black shirt and throws one at me. "Put that on." I do as he says. It hangs on me like a dress, and I roll up the sleeves to expose my hands.

"I should never have come here," I say, thinking of the threatening note. It's not just me Diggs named. He mentioned Valore and Raider. Wick and Sage.

Sage of all people!

"I've endangered everyone. I should have gone to Hamo. I need to get out of here."

"Give me another second, and we'll be gone," Raider says, pushing a few things into a bag.

"No! I mean, just me. Besides the governors, my sister and I were his only other targets, but I'm the only one who left Ambitus. I created this problem, and if I go away, the problem goes with me."

"We don't know that. Besides, I don't operate that way. I don't leave people behind to fend for themselves."

"Raider, it's okay. I've been left behind plenty. I'm used to it, and I'd rather keep you all safe."

"We'll be fine."

"Raider! He threatened your son." I yank on the edge of the huge sleeves and release a loud groan. "I can't be responsible for what might happen."

"I'll be responsible then."

"No! Not for this. I won't let you."

"You've nothing to worry about. I can keep us safe. Hell, put a Torquent blade in your hand, and you can keep us safe. The most important thing is to connect with the others because sharing knowledge is our best defense right now. They need to know the situation is developing, and then we'll work to resolve it."

I still think it would be better to separate from them, but I don't argue anymore because he's right—our main priority is to alert the others, and my panic is delaying that.

We sneak into the night in our dark clothes. I'm relieved when the car starts because I feared Diggs would sabotage the engine like I was adept at doing to Chessie's CJ in my youth. Raider takes us straight to the Ante Bellum bonfire. I volunteer to stay in the car amid lingering thoughts of our foe trying to disable our transportation, but Raider won't have it, so we race through the people, searching for the ones we need. We find Wick first.

"What's wrong?" he asks, taking in our unusual clothing, rushed movements, and harried faces. I was so happy about our reunion, but now Diggs has targeted him. Once again, I wish I hadn't come here.

Raider fills him in on the basics, and Wick helps us track down Raden and Mickens. It takes much longer to find Renegade, but we eventually do. After that, it's all military business, with Raider and Wick leaving instructions with the people in charge of the soldiers. Everything takes too long, and it feels like forever before we finally leave the bonfire.

Arriving at Stryke's house, the place is eerily dark. I remind myself it's absurdly early—around one in the morning. A half-moon is our only light, and combined with my circlight, it creates moving shadows barely distinguishable from the night, setting me further on edge.

Raider doesn't want to scare the kids and plans to

enter the house quietly and alone. The rest of us argue against anyone being alone in this circumstance, and Raider concedes, allowing Renegade to go with him.

Five excruciating minutes later, Valore and Stryke come outside. Captain Rhed's behind them, carrying a light and relieving some of my anxiety. Raider and Renegade are in the rear, carrying our bags. I'm glad to see them unharmed but feel terrible about the worried looks on their faces. It's my fault it's there.

"Did you see Sage?" I ask Raider when they're close enough to talk without yelling.

"I did. He's okay," he says, and I release a slow breath. Valore approaches, putting an arm around my shoulder while Raider turns to Captain Rhed, saying. "I'm surprised you're still here."

"I was catching up with Valore. Decided to stay the night." Captain Rhed glances at me, and I understand that most, if not all, of their *catching up* was centered on me. I can't say I blame him for wanting more information. After all, there was a day I tried to kill his son.

"Well, I'm relieved since we need to make some quick plans," Raider says.

"How do you want to approach this?" Captain Rhed asks.

"Raden, Mickens, and Valore will stay here. I've arranged for a dozen Souther soldiers to watch the house. They're not doing much outside of drills, and I don't want our family unprotected until we resolve this. Rhed, I'd appreciate it if you put your guard on alert."

"It goes without saying."

"Thanks. Shar, Renegade, and I will leave tonight for Adlumen. We must alert the governors that Diggs is on the move and increasing his hit list. He could already be traveling toward Adlumen, but if not, I hope we'll draw him away."

"You think it's safe to leave Caelum?" Valore asks.

"He entered my home, where we were relaxed and vulnerable, but instead of taking action, he left a written note," Raider says, rubbing his eyes tiredly. "His primary targets—save one—are in Adlumen. I'd say he wants to keep all his prized apples in one cart." He looks at me. "With Shar back in Ambitus, he'll gather there too. Then, we go on the offensive, getting the trackers involved. We'll look for him instead of waiting for him to find us."

"You don't need to go," I say, reaching out and gripping Raider's arm. "Stay here with your family and help your people prepare. Raden and Mickens can take me back. Raden can inform the governors of what's transpired and organize what needs to happen."

Raider's brows dip into a scowl as he considers me. It doesn't take long, but the expression softens. "I appreciate that, but I planned to return tomorrow anyway. They should have word from Hamo, and I need to know what's happening."

I release him, nodding my acquiescence. I'll not tell Raider what to do, but he needed to know there was another acceptable option. I won't be the reason he's once again divided from his son.

"I'm going with you," Wick announces, his brown eyes serious.

"Oh, Wick. Thank you, but it's not necessary," I say with a headshake. "Diggs targeted you and the others to destabilize me. I truly believe when I'm gone from Caelum, you'll be out of his sights. I think he enjoyed having his prey fearfully gathered in a familiar place, and I disrupted that."

Curses! Can this situation be any more frustrating?

We came here to draw Diggs away from Adlumen and, ultimately, drew more people into danger. It was foolish to leave. No matter how boring, I should have stayed in my room.

"Why does Uncle Diggs have it out for you?" Wick asks.

"He wants to finish Dad's crusade of taking out the governors," I say, catching Captain Rhed rubbing his jaw in frustration. "And he wanted my help. I told him no. He didn't take it well. Can you see now why it's better you stay here?"

"Not really," Wick says with a chuckle.

"Wick!"

"I'm not the helpless little brother you remember. I'm actually superb at being a soldier."

"Okay. But I'm not helpless anymore, either," I say, grinning. "And while I've suppressed my temper, I'm still stubborn, especially when I'm right about something."

"Well, I don't think you are," Wick says. "Right, I mean. And I never thought you were helpless. Just misguided. Though, I'm glad to hear that about your temper." My brother chuckles.

"Tell him, Raider. Valore." I look between the two men who know. "I can handle a Torquent blade and protect myself against Diggs. I'll be fine. And holing up in Fiducha is just a precaution. An added... perk." I wince as I say it, knowing being locked up in my childhood home is no picnic, but it's better than prison and won't last nearly as long, so I can spin this story to get my way.

"I'm still going with you," Wick says, folding his arms firmly.

I groan, unsure how long I can fight him on this, especially when the others aren't helping. "Why are you being so insistent?"

"Well, Raider says he's going on the offensive—getting the trackers involved—and I'm the best tracker there is." He puffs out his chest but then shakes his head, deflating as he continues, "But mostly, it's because I want to spend time with my sister." The emotion behind the statement nearly undoes me.

"You don't have to face this alone," Raider says, and I look at his blurry face through my wet eyes. "You have people willing to surround you with support. You should let them."

"I don't know how," I say, and Valore pulls me closer with an arm around my shoulder. "I don't deserve it."

"Young lady," Captain Rhed says, biting his lip in thought before continuing, "It's about time you realize you do."

The first tear falls. Then the next. And then I can't stop them. I lean into Valore, overcome. I hear movement, but I don't lift my head. I hear them whispering, making plans, but I don't focus on what they say. Valore wraps me in his arms, and I feel the fatherly love I looked for but never found at home.

"I can't believe they mean it," I say.

"But they do," Valore returns.

"It means so much. It means everything," I murmur into his nightshirt, then pull back and stare into his eyes. "Valore, I'm afraid. What if my problems with Diggs bring danger to Raider? Sage already lost his mom. I couldn't live with myself if I caused trouble for his dad."

I say it without thinking—mentioning Raider's immense heartache in front of these people—but I guess if anyone understands his pain, it's this group. Still, I'm sorry I said it, and when I look around, wiping away the tears, I feel even worse because Raider is gone.

My shoulders sink, and I slump against Valore. "I didn't mean to say it. I can't handle him being mad at me again."

Valore shakes his head. "He didn't hear you. He's inside, saying goodbye to Sage. He promised the boy he wouldn't leave without letting him know."

Raider's farewell to Sage takes some time, which works

for me since I'm saying goodbye to Valore. He promises we'll see each other soon, and I welcome every assurance, no matter how outlandish. Nothing is certain, but I'm glad he's surrounded by people to keep him safe.

When Raider finally returns, I'm grateful Sage isn't with him. I can't imagine the depth of the boy's sadness, and with how I'm feeling, I don't know if I could handle witnessing it. And it turns out I'm right to doubt my fortitude because I glimpse the little man in an upstairs window. He waves at me before dropping his head against the paneled glass, his shoulders shaking with sorrow. There's not enough light to see tears, but I know they're there.

Pushing away agonizing thoughts, I jump into the car, keeping my eyes on the floor and waiting for them to drive me away.

CHAPTER THIRTY-FOUR

Thirty Days Free

It's a bumpy ride, flying through the night. I'm grateful Raider and Renegade have sight for the Dark because Wick and I would be worthless behind the wheel at this speed. My brother passes me the apple we're sharing as the dim scenery flashes by, and when we reach the apple's core, Wick throws it out. It becomes hard to maintain focus with nothing to occupy my hands or mouth. It's exhausting—the growling engine, the whipping wind, and my limited vision—so I close my eyes and fall asleep.

Entering the Ambitus gates, I wake with my cheek stuck to the seat. Indeed, any part of me pressed against the vinyl is slick with sweat. Using Raider's large shirt, I wipe away the wetness while Wick gets an update from the gate guards. It's good news—there's been no attempt on the governors. They're safe.

Raider drives inside, turning the engine off once we're parked in front of Fiducha. Lowering his head, he rests it on the steering wheel. Renegade yawns before hopping out to stretch. Wick follows his lead, exiting the car and grabbing our things. But I don't get out. Instead, I lean forward, putting my hand on Raider's back, asking, "You okay?"

He mumbles something, takes a deep breath, then leaves the vehicle. My hand falls away, and I'm alone in the car, but then Raider turns around, holding out a hand for me. I climb over the side with his help, and when my feet hit the ground, I slump against the car, where he joins me.

"I'm exhausted," he says, his black eyes steeped with worry. "And we're just getting started."

Raider plans to go inside, gather the governors, meet in the Locus, and hash out the situation until they have a plan. Of course, the sun's barely up—just reaching over the nebulous Dark, so it must be around seven—which means he has some time to collect his thoughts. Still, it will happen soon, and I understand he doesn't feel prepared. I grab his forearm, and he faces me as I say, "You're going to do great."

Raider grins. "Don't get too excited about sending me away. You're coming with."

"I am?" I ask, scrunching my nose distastefully.

"Yeah." He reaches out, fingering the end of my hair. "Might want to get a shower first."

"I'm not worried about my appearance, but I doubt they'll be happy about me attending your meeting."

"Doesn't matter. You're too entrenched in this to sit it out." Raider breaks our connection and rubs a hand over his shorn head. "Let's get going."

Though our conversation was private, the others waited, so we head inside together. Automatically, I walk toward the rooms I stayed in with Renegade and the Roils, but Wick stops me, saying, "Let's go to the family quarters, Shar." He points down the hallway to where Mom lives while I shake my head in profuse refusal. But Wick merely laughs, fists one of my overly long sleeves, and drags me with him.

"Mom!" he calls as we enter. I'm hopeful she's asleep, but my dream is dashed when she pops around the corner, exclaiming, "Wick! Oh, darling Wick! What are you doing home?"

Curses. Can I gag now, or must I wait?

Her brown eyes light up when she sees him, then dim when she catches sight of me, but she recovers quickly.

"What am I doing home? I'm on guard duty," he says with a grin, shooting a thumb at me.

Mom frowns. “What did she do now?”

“Ha! Thanks a lot.” I grip my suitcase tighter, my gaze turning toward the bathroom. “I’m borrowing your shower. Raider’s orders.” A lot gets done by way of his name, so I’m using it. I take my first step, but Wick stops me.

“Wait one sec,” he says, then looks at our mom. “Uncle Diggs made more threats, and I’m here to keep Shar safe. But she did nothing wrong. Your statement was completely out of line, and you owe her an apology.”

Mom’s mouth falls open as she looks between us. Her face is at odds with her immaculate clothes and perfect hair. Her beloved is calling out her bad behavior. I used to would have loved the drama, but now I just want to clean up and focus on keeping everyone alive.

“It’s fine, Wick,” I say, reaching out with a grateful squeeze on his arm. “I need to get showered, though. Raider’s expecting me.” I walk past, relieved to enter the bathroom and lock them out. I quickly enter the water, lingering under the warm spray. Eventually, I force myself out and get dressed, tucking my dirty clothes and Raider’s shirt into my case. After brushing my wet hair, I close my suitcase and head to the living area.

I walk in on my entire family—Wick, Chessie, and Mom—but they don’t notice me.

“I don’t understand either of you. Mom, you cried for months after Shar went into the Dark. And Chessie, you sent her letters for years.”

Mom cried? Chessie sent letters?

“You wanted her back. You talked about it all the time. And Shar’s become a better person than we ever could have dreamed. So, what’s the problem? Why is the reality you longed for so hard to accept? I don’t get it.”

Oh, Wick. He’s wise—always has been—but a little

clueless.

"I get it," I say, and they all turn, startled to find me eavesdropping, but I don't let their expressions bother me. "Dreams aren't real. Dreams don't disappoint you unless you allow them to. But reality doesn't play by those rules. Reality means there's the possibility of disappointment. Reality whispers that I may never meet your expectations."

"Why didn't you respond to my letters?" Chessie asks, proving my point—expectations weren't met, and she wants answers.

"It's difficult to respond to something you never get." I shake my head. "It was a Dark prison, Chess. Did you think they'd supply me a circlight and let me correspond with home? That's not how those places work."

"See!" Wick says. "You could solve these misunderstandings if you'd just talk to her."

"Well, there's no time for talking now," I say, keeping my voice steady. Maybe that's the issue as much as anything—our timing is off.

"Why isn't there time?" Mom asks.

"Because I'm going to a meeting," I say, tucking my shirt into the edge of my pants. "Because I've made this fight my fight." I don't wait for their reaction but cross the room and pull my brother in for a hug. "I appreciate you, Wick, more than you'll ever know, but leave them be." There's no point in him forcing opinions on them. It's better to let them figure out their feelings at their own pace. "Now let's go. We have somewhere to be."

Consilio Locus is a strange place—at least, I've always thought so. A relative of mine decorated the space intending to intimidate. It worked in my youth. Now, the effect is lost.

It's just a room—a rather overdone one.

It's the place where my dad made plans. It's where he met with his general and spoke to his councilors. It's where the governors discuss the same government business with some of the same individuals. I shake my head at the absurdity of it.

It's also the room where, eight years ago, I suffocated Raider Roil with attention and attacked him with a kiss. But I ignore the events of that day and, instead, note the changes in the room.

The Ideation Board is still in the center. It's really just a table—a gigantic table for sure—but Dad loved titles. Like the Wall of Maps, which isn't very original but descriptive. I notice they've updated quite a few maps to reflect the current world.

And they've changed the chairs. I must say, they're much more comfortable. More notably, a bench that used to sit against the Wall of Maps is now at the head of the Ideation Board. It makes sense. They're a matching set—table and bench—but the bench was for three to govern, and Dad was just one person, so he relegated it to a corner. I'm surprised he didn't destroy it. That was his usual approach, but maybe even he had a limit.

But, no, I don't believe that. He just hadn't gotten around to it yet. Or maybe it reminded him of what our family had so successfully stolen. Whatever the case, it's still here and currently occupied by the reinstated governors: Evans Dirby, Vale Dover, and Annibeth Wynne.

There are others here too. Like General Pruden, the leader of Adlumen's army. The man who, along with Captain Rhed, managed my imprisonment. To say I'm comfortable sitting across from him is to tell a lie.

His son, Siler, is next to him—a good guy and one of Chessie's best friends—though seeing him again is strange.

He has the same dark blond hair, but he's added a mustache. His muscles are still big, his eyes still too small but a brilliant blue, and he still acts like he's stronger than he is wise—but those close to him know he has a mind to match the best thinker. My sister used to complain about his maturity level—especially when our dad was pushing an engagement between the two—but I bet eight years has fixed that.

Of course, Wick is here, and—somewhat diminishing my dramatic exit from Mom's home—so is Chessie. And still, there are more—Evans's two brothers, Geric and Ronen, along with the beacon, Tesha Harcort, and her husband, Siman. And surrounding me, like bread does a sandwich, are Raider and Renegade. It makes me feel relatively insulated from the stares I'm getting.

It's a packed house, making it hard to determine who should take the lead. But then, I've never been in a meeting led by the governors. I'm sure they've got it figured out after all this time. A second later, I'm proven right.

"Since this meeting has to do with military matters, I've asked Evans to conduct," Vale says from the center seat of the bench, turning to Evans while her black hair falls over her shoulder.

Evans doesn't hesitate to address Raider, asking, "How'd you know Chett's arriving today?" My brows lift, knowing this could be what Raider's been hoping for—word from Arrick that Tyran's willing to negotiate.

"We didn't. We came for another reason, but since you brought it up, what's the news from Hamo?"

"We don't have details. We only know he'll arrive this morning. What's your reason for returning to Adlumen?" Evans's hazel eyes flash at me briefly, then stay on Raider.

"Diggs made contact," Raider says, revealing the discovery of the note and expansion of the list. "We hope reuniting his primary targets will remove danger from the secondaries. Additionally, we intend to go on the offensive and seek him out before he can act."

There's a lot of shared anxiety over Diggs's threat, but none feel it more than Annibeth. "Is he as terrible as his daughter?" she asks, reaching for her husband's thick arm.

I ponder her question while considering my history with my uncle and cousin. Saeva tortured Annibeth while she was captive. Chessie relayed the details of Annibeth's story eight years ago, but I wouldn't listen then. Today, I recall it with uncomfortable clarity, accepting the depths of my cousin's depravity. One thing sticks out in my mind: Saeva pulling out Annibeth's white-blond hair—locks that now hang thickly down her back—and wearing it in braids on her head like a trophy. Similarly, Diggs has threatened to take Hesston's fingers. Is it in his character to do something similar? To adorn himself with them like a badge of honor?

I conclude it's not beyond what I believe him capable of, which has me answering, "He might be as bad as Saeva."

A whimper escapes Annibeth's throat while the others stare at me. They're not warm expressions of camaraderie when faced with a common threat. No, they're wary and express the general feeling that I'm an outsider and not wanted here. It further proves Adlumen is not the place for me. I need this situation with Diggs resolved so I can get away from this place—get away from them all.

Before Raider can delve further into his plan, news comes that Chett has arrived in Ambitus. It's not long until the emissary from Hamo enters the room. He's yet to utter a word, but his expression alone leads Raider to say, "We're going to war."

My eyes beg Chett to reject Raider's words. He doesn't.

"The abatement wasn't enough to dissuade her," I say, unable to stay quiet even in a room full of people who don't want to hear my thoughts.

"Arrick's afraid of Tyran," Raider says, though we're all afraid of her to one extent or another. She's a terrifying individual—her unreasonableness makes her so. "I'm sure he cowered. Failed to outline the benefits of the abatement or emphasize the horrors of war," he continues, but I doubt it was Arrick's approach that decided Tyran, even if Hamo's leader did cower. Tyran's not bothered by the savagery of killing—not when there's something she wants, and she has a healthy list of desires. Staring at Chett, Raider finishes, "And now, come dawn, we'll be murdering one another."

Yes. Because Tyran's twisting and dividing us in pursuit of her agenda. While Raider doesn't literally mean to kill Chett come morning—it's the sentiment he's keeping at the forefront of this discussion. Tyran's making enemies of friends with her chosen course, and eventually, it's what will be asked—for Chett to kill Raider and Raider to kill Chett.

Chett maintains Raider's gaze, mulling over his prediction but not appearing rattled by it. "It's not as bad as all that," Chett finally says, approaching the Ideation Board and taking a seat.

"Not today, but give it a month," Raider quips.

"How was she not convinced?" Evans asks. "Did she not believe Arrick when he told her about the abatement?"

"She believed him."

"She just doesn't care," Raider surmises, physically revealing none of the disappointment I hear in his voice. "Or, more precisely, obtaining abated land doesn't ease enough of her hunger."

Chett nods. "You're right. It wasn't enough, and she drafted new options."

"Options?" Raider laughs. "You're a true emissary to present her demands under that label."

"What does she want this time?" Evans asks, cutting

through Raider's snark to get to the heart of the matter.

"She's agreed to give up Periculum if terms for the abated land are to her liking. And she's open to calling off the war, but she wants a few things first."

"What things?" Raider asks, getting impatient.

"Some of her requirements have changed, but one hasn't," Chett says. "She wants her nephew to give her the audience he promised."

Raider groans.

"And what about the beacon?" General Pruden asks, making Tesha cling to Siman, her eyes widening with fear.

"She's withdrawn that request." Chett leans forward, rubbing his eyes. "At least the abatement favorably changed a few things for you."

Yes. Periculum and Tesha are out of Tyran's focus for now.

Some in the room relax in the new, more comfortable chairs around the Ideation Board. But Raider knows his foe and maintains his tense posture. "You still haven't told us her new list of wants," he says. "There's no need to coddle our fears. We know it will be bad, so let's hear it."

"It's just one thing," Chett says, resting his thick elbows on the table. "She requires a new emissary to negotiate terms with Adlumen."

Siman's head jerks back. "Have I offended her?" he asks, looking more discomposed than I've ever seen him—his naturally pale skin looks sickly next to his black hair.

"Not that I'm aware of," Chett answers. "Her preference is definitive. She wants the daughter of Endrack to serve as emissary."

My body stiffens, and a chill runs up my back, wondering what Tyran would want with me, until Evans exclaims, "No! Chessie stays here. She's not a governor nor an emissary."

My eyes fall on my sister. Of course, it's Chessie that Tyran wants, but I had a knee-jerk reaction to Chett's comment since the description equally applies to me.

"Chessie was nearly an emissary," Chett says while my sister mindlessly touches her shoulder that bears the scars from Tyran's blade. "And it's what Tyran requires before she'll retract her call to war."

"There's more to it," Evans seethes. "She's been vocal about wanting a rematch with Chess. This appointment has nothing to do with talking out our issues. It will turn into a fight."

I pull in my lip, bouncing my teeth on the skin while considering what Evans is saying. My sister continues to rub her old wound, soothing the spot with fingers that move in hypnotic circles. Then her hand drops protectively to her stomach. No one else sees it, or if they do, they don't consider what it means. But I know. I know where her real concern lies.

"You're probably right," Chett agrees. "But she insists she'll accept no one except Endrack's daughter." Chett clears his throat. "And she wants a meeting immediately."

"No!" Evans declares.

"It's not a good time," Chessie says more calmly, then glances at me, remembering I know her secret. I give her a slight nod, agreeing that it's a terrible time for her to be in this position.

"We'll figure something out," Raider says, shaking his head in dismay.

"Gah! There's got to be another way to appease her," Annibeth says, reaching a hand toward Chessie in a show of support.

"Yes," General Pruden adds, rubbing his lip where an old scar shines white against his bronze skin. "Tyran's brilliant with strategy, politics, and maneuvering. But so are we."

They all agree acquiescence is bad—knowing the situation is more than Tyran's words reveal—but their solidarity is hollow. Not one person expresses a logical solution to the problem, and that's when something niggles at the back of my mind. The beginnings of an idea.

Evans nods, bolstered by General Pruden's declaration. "We'll look at every angle and outmaneuver her," he says, slamming a fist into his palm.

Raider releases a breath, slumping back in his chair. "I hope you can, but we're running out of time. We could talk for days and come up with nothing. Bottom line, we meet Tyran's demands and timeline or go to war."

"She's my wife, is all. No biggie. But I'm expected to give her up and let Tyran get what she wants?" Evans asks, grabbing Chessie's hand and gripping it hard.

"I'm not suggesting we don't try to get Chessie out of it," Raider says, frowning at his friend. "But we need a solid strategy if we don't intend to do exactly as Tyran asks. Trust me, I've been trying to avoid the same fate. I'm not eager to put myself into her hands, but increasingly, it seems the only way to prevent a war. And if that's the case, I'll do it."

"Me too," Chessie says, her full lips pursed and her voice small.

"Dammit!" Evans slams his hand onto the table, and we all fall silent, looking from one face to the next. I've never seen Evans without his broad smile and confident swagger. It makes the situation that much more frightening when he loses his cool.

Tyran has three standing requests to prevent war: Abated land to her liking, Endrack's daughter as emissary to Torquent, and a meeting with Raider. They seem like innocent petitions, but it's clear they form the sinister underpinnings of Tyran's true intentions.

"Arrick's still with Tyran?" Raider asks with a disappointed set to his mouth.

Chett nods. "I'm sorry it's come to this."

"I know you tried," Raider tells him, and there's a flicker of relief in Chett's eyes. "This would feel impossible if it weren't for your guidance and intercession. It hasn't gone entirely how we wanted, but it wasn't your fault. I'd hate to see you on the other side of this fight if it comes to that."

"I should have done more," Chett says, his chin dropping. For once, his facial expression matches his body language. He's despondent, and it's in everything from the set of his shoulders to the blank expression in his eyes. Chett believes our path is set and is not optimistic about the outcome, which only makes that little idea in my head grow.

Back in my Dark prison, Valore talked to me about his greatest successes in life, and I realized I didn't have any. Maybe this moment can be that for me. Maybe this is how I make things right.

At sixteen, I attempted to take Evans's life. Eight years later, I can make amends for some of the hurt I caused. Because I'm perfectly positioned to step in. I can take someone's place who's not ideally situated to do what's required.

For weeks, I've considered my next move. Staying in Adlumen is out. Disappearing into the Dark is an option, but for how long and to what purpose? I could go to Hamo, but I'd feel unworthy of the trust Valore and Raider have in me, especially after committing to their cause.

Or I can follow my little idea instead. I can go to Torquent in Chessie's place. After all, I'm a daughter of Endrack too. I've made many mistakes in my twenty-four years, but if I can succeed at one thing in my life, I want it to be this.

CHAPTER THIRTY-FIVE

Thirty-One Days Free at 12:15 a.m.

My eyes pop open, and I check the clock—it's just after midnight. My sleep schedule matches my travels of late. I've switched to being a night owl, and consequently, I feel wide awake.

The half-moon is outside my window, giving my blue-wallpapered walls an otherworldly glow. When I lived with my family, my room was decorated in gold and green. It's only two floors above me, and I wonder if it still looks like that. Lying here, my mind flips between the past and present, comparing my two lives. It's exhausting and fruitless, so I push off my covers and leave those thoughts behind.

Taking a shower, I wash, dry, and put on a new set of clothes, stuffing the dirties in my suitcase. I'm unsure how this day will go, and it's best to have them with me.

Scrawling a quick note, I tuck it under the edge of my pillow, then consider my escape. There will be guards in the hallway, and my suitcase is a sign I'm on the move, so I head to the window, propping it open and dropping my belongings outside. Being on the bottom floor has its perks, but it's still too high for me to jump.

Spinning, I head through my room and enter the gathering area. The other bedroom doors are closed—Raider and Renegade must be asleep—so I step lightly across the room, making no noise before slipping out the main door. If my plan works, they won't know I'm gone until morning.

I feel a bit guilty about sneaking around. It would be nice to be upfront about it, but they'd never agree with my idea. They don't trust me, which I get, and I doubt they'd be willing to test my loyalty when it's war they're risking. So, I'll do it before anyone can object. They'll be upset when they discover what I've done, but I don't care because it's the right thing to do.

Pressing Squatty's necklace to my chest, I lean forward, glancing down the hallway to the quarters where Mom and Wick sleep. I wish I could tell my brother my plans—I think he'd understand—but it's better if he finds out with everyone else. The only person who needs to know is Chett. Now, I just need to find him.

I stride down the hallway, approaching three guards monitoring nighttime happenings. "Hi," I say to the first, who just nods. I don't know her and hope she doesn't know me. She's not freaking out, so that's a good sign.

"I was hoping Chett Conch might still be up. Do you know which room he's in?"

"He's not in a room because he's right here." I twist and find Chett standing behind me with a mild smile on his lips.

"He was inquiring about your whereabouts too," the girl says to my back.

"Busted. I guess we should talk, then," Chett says, gesturing toward my room.

"Um. The others are in there. Sleeping, but still." Next, he points at his quarters—part of a bank of lodging for single travelers. I nod and follow him, entering his space which contains a sitting area, a bed, and a door to the bathroom. There are no windows, but when Chett flips a switch by the door, a table light flicks on, mutely lighting the spotless room —the undisturbed bedding indicative of his busy day.

I sit on the tan couch, running fingers through my still-wet hair and asking, "You were looking for me?"

"Yeah. What's going on with you and Raider? When we were last together, you could barely be in the same room.

That no longer seems to be the case." Chett has yet to sit down, and hovering above me while asking questions feels a bit like an interrogation.

"Things have changed," I say, sucking in my upper lip and biting it before quickly letting it go. "We don't hate each other anymore."

Chett tilts his head, clearing his throat. "Did you think about my offer?"

"I did." This is not where I imagined this conversation going. In fact, I hoped to avoid this topic altogether. No such luck.

"But not anymore." Chett's intelligent. Even before I shake my head, he understands I've decided against his proposition. But where he gets it wrong is who he believes is behind my decision. "I'm not sure Raider's the man for you," he continues before I tell him the actual reasons—Wick's unwavering support and realizing I can't be on opposing sides from my family. Then he adds, "Raider's too... pure. He'll never get over what you did."

Most people would find Chett's statement insulting, but he speaks the truth. Raider is pure, especially when compared to an attempted assassin. I can't find fault with Chett's reasoning or Raider for taking his time coming to terms with my past. His hesitancy is understandable after meeting Sage.

Chett believes Raider and I are romantically incompatible, failing to understand that's not my focus with him or anyone. Sure, Raider and I have shared flirtatious moments, but they're fleeting and we've remained centered on what's important.

But more than highlighting my grand errors, Chett's words open up old issues I have with self-worth. He has me second-guessing my plan, wondering why Tyran would find any value in me as a replacement for Chessie. Is this a terrible idea? I'm tricking Tyran by entering her domain on a technicality. I could enrage the woman and single-handedly start the war.

I sigh, recalling my initial motivation for this move and letting it settle over me. Maybe the only thing we'll gain by this maneuver is more time for Chess and the others to make a better plan. I can't help feeling even that has merit. So, amid my myriad doubts, I focus on a reply for Chett.

"Whereas, you're my ideal match because you're not pure either," I surmise. "Is that what you're telling me?" Chett doesn't respond, and I nod. "You don't need to answer. How you see yourself is in your every word and expression. It seems we both have polluted pasts, but I daresay, I've emerged some from what holds me down while you're still engulfed in yours. You're constantly overcome by sadness, even when you're trying your best to be cheerful. It weighs you down, Chett, and I think it's more than Chadd's death, which is what they all assume—that separation drives your melancholy—but there's more to it. I sense fear in you."

Chett licks his lips, finally taking a seat next to me on the couch. Running his fingers across the tan velvet upholstery, his throaty voice rumbles, "There are reasons to be afraid."

I take his comment as confirmation of all I've said and add, "Of Tyran."

He has no response, but I don't need one. Many things remain unresolved—especially his ideas about Raider and me—but we've found a better understanding of one another. It's a solid foundation to work from, making me dangerously hopeful. Leaning in, I grip his hand and say, "I need your help." I'm ready to face my first obstacle—convincing Chett of my plan—so I reveal to him, "I'm going to Tyran in Chessie's place."

He stares at me, then blinks. Then, he laughs—the usual kind where something's missing in the sound—before saying, "You're not serious."

"Just hear me out. Did Tyran specifically say she wants Chessie as emissary, or did she exclusively call her Endrack's daughter?" I keep a grip on him, resisting the urge to cross both fingers while waiting for his answer.

"I only ever heard Tyran request Endrack's daughter," he says, and I release him, leaning back with a relieved sigh. Then I smile because Tyran's ego created a loophole. She spelled out her demand in the most derogatory way possible. To her, Chessie isn't her own person. She's merely Endrack's daughter.

But so am I.

"Perfect. Because that's who I am too."

"It's not perfect." Chett shakes his head. "It's semantics."

"Exactly! A good strategist uses semantics to their benefit. And a good leader doesn't allow semantics to trap them. Does that tell you something about Tyran?" I grin but don't let Chett answer. "Here's what I'm thinking. We should leave tonight. You can explain to the governors that something urgent came up, and I'll leave a note they won't find until morning." A note that's already written and sitting on my bed, but Chett doesn't need to know that.

"And I'll drive you to Tyran in Contund," he says, crossing his muscly arms and hunching his large frame until we're face to face. "And she'll be furious, killing us both on the spot."

"No! You're jumping too far ahead. Chessie's a minor piece in Tyran's plan. Trust me on this, Chett." I grab his sleeve, imploring him with my eyes. "Tyran asked for Chessie to keep the governors nervous. My sister is an entertaining addition to Tyran's court—someone to challenge with a Torquent blade in a bored moment. She's a means for engaging the Endracks in a decades-old grudge that began with my dad."

His hand covers mine, and his eyes are just as sincere as he says, "Or maybe she wants revenge on your sister for their fight."

I blink, shaking my head. "My sister's shoulder got shredded while Tyran came out unscathed. Tyran could hardly want payback after winning the fight. It's a challenge meant to intimidate and keep the governors sweating." Chett looks unconvinced, so I ask, "Did she ever mention Chessie before? Or was she an addition after dropping the beacon? Tyran's trying to keep the governors unbalanced and maintain control of negotiations. It's exactly what my dad would have done. It's the kind of thing he taught me to do. Meanwhile, everyone's losing sight of the one constant in all of this."

"And what's that?"

"Raider. He's her primary goal." Chett's brow lifts in consideration. "Think about it. What is her most repeated demand? What turns her rabid with need? It's meeting with Raider."

"If you're right, your plan will fail since we're going there without him." He leans back, and my hand slips from his arm before he spreads his arms across the top of the couch. "And you should know, tricking and denying Tyran in the same visit will do nothing but guarantee her fury."

"Yeah, but there's nothing to worry about because Raider will be there." Chett's eyes narrow. "He will be. Just not with Chessie. See, the important thing is to get me there first. Then we'll wait for Raider to arrive before meeting with Tyran." I push from the couch and pace before him as I talk. "If I tell them I'm going in her place, they'll say no. But if I'm already gone, they'll play it out and see if it appeases Tyran."

"There's no appeasing Tyran. She wants Chessie to serve as emissary, and you might be her sister, but you can hardly fill the role. You're not even an Adlumen citizen at this point."

Scowling, I snap, "By the Dark, Chett, we both know she doesn't care about changing Adlumen's emissary. Siman was doing a fine job. This is all posturing!"

Chett gives me his sad smile. "You're sort of impossible."

"Yeah, maybe." I try to return his smile, but all I can think about is my sister as I ask, "Can you just accept there's a crucial reason I need to be there and not Chessie?"

Chett nods, saying, "The bun in the oven." My eyes widen as I stare at him, and then his hands drop to his stomach, mimicking my sister in a tight feminine voice, *"It's not a good time."* His hands drop to the couch. "Duh. It was a dead giveaway."

I huff out a laugh. "I thought so too. Anyway, no one knows."

"I figured."

"Look, you can play this off however you want. You can say I tricked you. You can say Chessie said she'd be there, and I showed up instead. I'm happy to take whatever blame you want to place on me. But seriously, Tyran asked for Endrack's daughter, and I am one hundred percent that."

"You're sure you want to put yourself in this position?" Chett rubs the scruff on his chin—hope in his eyes that I'll say no. "It could get nasty."

"I can't let my sister go to Torquent."

"Tyran is frightening on a good day. I don't know what this scheme will make of her."

Chett's right. There's no way to know how she'll react, but I'm willing to face anything if my sister's not there and Tyran aims her wrath at me, not Chett. "I hear what you're saying. This could go horribly wrong, but I have to try. The wording of Tyran's demand emphasizes the emissary's relationship with Keine Endrack. We'll just have to get her to decide one daughter's as good as the other."

"One daughter's better, in my opinion. That's why I hate to see her do this," Chett says, looking up at me with admiration that makes me blush, but I maintain his gaze as he adds, "I can't help but feel this is a huge mistake."

"Whereas, I know it's not." Sure, things could go wrong, but I believe more things will go right, making it all worth it. "Will you trust I know something about the ways of conniving people and help me get my sister out of this situation?"

His reaction is a moment coming, but eventually, a slow nod moves his chin. "It appears an important meeting calls me from Adlumen at this dreadful hour," he says, standing from the couch.

I reach out to take his hand, but the gesture seems inadequate in light of our dangerous collaboration, so I put my arms around him in a tight hug. "Thank you so much," I say, and he fidgets in my embrace, so I release him.

To distract from the awkward moment, I tell him the rest of my plan: He'll leave before me, and I'll meet him in Periculum. He'll mention at the gate that Chessie's going out tonight too, so after I get my things and my ride, I'll see if I'm a good enough actress at pretending to be my sister. People keep saying we look alike. I'm hoping it's enough to get me out of Ambitus and on the road to Torquent.

CHAPTER THIRTY-SIX

Thirty-One Days Free at 2:00 a.m.

Suitcase in hand, I head to the stables, where they keep the horses and Chessie's CJ. My arms feel numb with adrenaline, but my nighttime departure isn't the cause. It's this building which has too much history. It's where Chess and I escaped our parents to work on her car, and where I played hide and seek with Wick on rainy days.

It's where I stabbed Adlumen's governor in the back.

A hard swallow pushes down my throat as I struggle against the memories of that day, but they're too powerful. One whiff of my surroundings, and I feel like I'm there again.

> *My nose is saturated with the smell of horses and hay. The knife is in my hand, sweaty with anticipation and fear. I've never done anything like this, but I'll do it for my dad. I'll do it because Chessie won't.*
>
> *The burn in my chest increases when Evans walks into the stables. He doesn't see me, too focused on Chessie's CJ. He runs a hand over the hood and smiles. I hate him for it.*
>
> *I approach from behind. He's too caught up in happy thoughts to hear me. My arm shakes as I lift the weapon into the air. My hand flies in an arc, and the knife meets his skin. The blossom of blood is instantaneous. The sounds he makes are unexpected—a mixture of shock and pain. I never visualized his response when planning out what I'd do. I thought I'd complete the task and walk away without a fuss.*
>
> *Instead, Evans turns toward me, engaging me in the situation I've created. "Sharade," he whispers, surprised*

to see me. Then he grabs his chest and winces before pushing out a pained, "Why?"

Why? Because of my dad. Because of Chessie. Those are my reasons.

But I don't answer. I don't move.

He stretches a desperate hand over his shoulder, trying for the knife, but it's out of reach, and the motion brings an agonizing howl to his lips. I jolt at the sound.

Evans drops to his knees, his hands landing in the dirt. "You really hate me," he grumbles, crouching like a dog while I stare at the growing bloodstain on his shirt. Coughing, blood and spit spray from his lips, revealing the reality of my actions.

"What in the Dark have I done?" I ask, looking down at my unblemished hands.

"You stabbed me, if you don't know," Evans gets out between panting breaths, and then he laughs. Laughs! Even amid dying, he's making jokes. And then, he crumples to the ground, his face planting in the dirt.

"Evans?" I push him with my foot, and he wobbles a bit but isn't in control of his body. My lip trembles, and I put a shaking finger on the edge as I stare at him.

He's dead.

I killed him.

He's dead.

The protruding knife is too much. I drop to my knees, put my hand on his back, and pull it free. Terror, confusion, disappointment, and fear pool deep in my belly. A low scream escapes my lips as I hurl the knife at the far wall.

And then I flee the site of my shame.

My eyes are locked on the spot where Evans fell. For at least a day, I thought I'd succeeded in his death, but it never brought the pride and contentment I expected. I feel far removed from the girl who caused such hurt, but I recall how she thought—her motivations both distant and familiar. I'm sad for her and the things she was willing to do.

I don't know how long I remain caught in the memories, but glancing at Chessie's CJ, I'm reminded there are important tasks ahead to keep more hurt from my family. Her prized possession is prettier than in our youth. The rusty holes are gone, and it's painted a sleek blue. There's a soft roof attached, perfectly fitted to the bars, and the tires don't look ready to pop. In fact, they're shiny from little use. I hope my sister will forgive me for the many things I'll do tonight, but especially for taking her car.

I throw my stuff into the back and open the stable doors. And that's when I see him.

Jumping back with a startled gasp, recognition has me shaking my head, gritting out, "Please, no."

"No, what?" he asks, holding up the note that's supposed to be tucked under my pillow.

"Please, don't interfere, Raider. *Please*. I'm begging you."

The onslaught of memories inside this barn has made me realize that taking Chessie's place isn't only for my sister. It's for Evans too. He's had enough pain, and I want to prevent him from experiencing more. And so, I'm ready to beg Raider to let me go on my way, but it turns out that's not required.

"I'm not here to interfere," he says, striding toward me and giving me the paper. "I'm here to go with you."

"You're… not stopping me?"

"No. Where's Chett meeting us?"

Us? Curses! What's happening right now?

"You know about Chett?" I ask in a daze, and he makes a grunting sound, which means yes. "The Hearty Badger," I say, thinking of the little guest lodge in Periculum. "But." I hold up the note. "They won't know why I've gone."

"I left my own note," Raider says with a grin, but it falls from his lips. "Did it take much to convince Chett?"

"I talked a lot."

"You didn't promise him anything, did you?" Raider asks with an edge to his voice.

"Like what?" I twist my sleeve between my thumbs, reflecting on my conversation with Chett. "I mean, I told him I'd take the blame if it came to that, but that's all."

"Good." He pauses. Nods. "That's good. Hop in. I'll drive."

Only, it's not Chessie's car we climb into. It's Raider's, and he's already moved my belongings into the back. It's for the best since taking out my sister's prized car wouldn't help my case if we make it through this. Still, I'm disappointed. I was looking forward to driving CJ again.

"How'd you find my note so fast?" I ask as he pulls up to the gate. I'm relieved to be with Raider since no one will think anything of him heading out this late, while my plan to pose as Chessie was iffy from the start.

"It was easy after I watched you tiptoe past me." I pull in my lip, glancing over at him, and he chuckles, waving at the soldiers as they motion him through. "I was sleeping on the couch. In the meeting, I could see on your face you were up to something. It didn't take long to figure it out. First off, you're a loud thinker. Second, every time Chett said, 'Endrack's daughter,' you flinched. And third, if there's one thing you should know about me, it's that I'm awfully good at puzzles."

"Puzzles, huh?" I grin upon learning another of Raider's outstanding abilities. "So, you brilliantly deduced my plan, but what's yours?"

Raider maneuvers the car down the Ambitus hill. "Tyran's intentions are finally rising to the surface. She wants land but is flexible about how she gets it. Of course, embarrassing Adlumen is a bonus, and I think that's Chessie's purpose. But slightly more than her land grab and demeaning the Endracks, she wants an audience with me."

"Slightly more?" I smirk, shaking my head, because her desire is more than slight. But it's just like I explained to Chett, and Raider sees it too. "So, you'll meet with her."

"I always knew I would." Raider shifts the car into the next gear. "But I refused to go in uninformed. Or on her timeline. Tyran values nothing she gets too easily."

I take in his words and demeanor—compare them to his attitude when meeting with Chett—and conclude, "You're not as bothered as you let everyone believe." Raider grins. "In fact, I think everything's gone pretty much how you expected."

"Demanding Chessie as emissary threw me for a minute, but otherwise, yes."

Raider's been elusive regarding this topic, but tonight, on the road to Periculum, he's willing to talk. Maybe it's that he finally trusts me—one can hope—or that we're pseudo-partners in this journey. Whatever the case, I'll not squander the opportunity to find out more, so I ask, "What does she want from you?"

"My attention," he says without hesitation. "She hates being ignored. My allegiance. She likes the idea of a family alliance. She'd call it a collaboration, but really, she wants the South T in her pocket to direct on a whim."

"Are you afraid of her?" Chett is, and I wonder if Raider feels the same.

There's a long pause while the wind whips through our car before he answers, "I'm afraid of what I'll have to give up to prevent a war."

"Like what?"

"I doubt anything is off limits in Tyran's quest to recruit

me. She'll use my citizens, family, and friends."

"You think she'll threaten to hurt them?"

"I know she will."

"That's awful. Raider, you can't support her," I say, gripping the handle on the door.

His lips flatten, and he nods. "She's after more than support. She'll want me to join her, and doing so would shackle my very existence. I don't mean to be insensitive, but I'd hardly be better off than you and my dad in a Desert prison."

I bite my lip, watching his hand flex on the steering wheel as I ask, "What will you do?"

"Make her think she can have it all while maneuvering the situation until the terms suit me." He shrugs. "Meanwhile, I must keep my wits and not promise too much."

"I'm sorry," I say because his plan sounds impossible. "Does she think an alliance with you will work? I mean, you don't exactly have similar mindsets."

Raider runs a hand over his fuzzy head. "She's too focused on what she wants and doesn't realize what she'd actually be getting. It wouldn't take long for her to despise me. And dispose of me."

"Dispose of you!" I exclaim, a chill running down my spine. "What are the chances she'll do exactly that when I show up instead of Chessie?"

"It's possible. But effective leaders give precise direction, and for all her bad traits, Tyran knows how to lead." I shake my head ruefully since I told Chett the opposite not an hour ago. "Honestly, she could be impressed with how you manipulated her words. Either that or—"

"Or what?"

"She could launch into a tirade and kill you."

"That's what Chett predicts."

"Really?" Raider shrugs. "Of course, I'm only considering her reaction if she's in a good mood."

"Lovely. What happens if she's in a bad mood?"

"She'll have me killed too."

I lean over and shove his arm. Not enough to tempt a car crash, but enough to let him know he's not funny.

Even though he sort of is.

"Thanks for letting me do this," I say. I had to convince Chett, but Raider didn't act as if there was any other choice than to let me go. I'm determined to see this through, and while I'm grateful for Chett's help, it's Raider's support making me think this might actually work, and so I add, "I'm glad you're here."

"I could say the same thing to you," Raider says, reaching to take my hand. I feel unworthy of his kindness, but I'm too weak to fight it, so I cling to him, and with our fingers linked, we bounce down the road together. Toward Periculum. Toward Tyran. Toward the unknown.

CHAPTER THIRTY-SEVEN

Thirty-One Days Free at 3:00 a.m.

"You're sure quiet," Raider says as we leave the outskirts of Mirum.

With too much on my mind, it's difficult to concentrate on any one thing for too long. Still, a singular thought keeps returning to me. "I wish I'd talked to Wick. He's been great, and I left Ambitus without a word." Raider fidgets in his seat, making me ask, "What's wrong?"

"Nothing's wrong," he says, tapping his fingers on the wheel. "But would it make you feel better if I told you he's not in Ambitus?"

"Depends." I bite my lip. "Where is he?"

"Somewhere between Mirum and Periculum."

Curses! He's out here too, traveling in the same direction we are.

Raider continues, "We got a line on Diggs. He was seen near Periculum, and since we planned to travel this direction in the coming days—" He pauses and glances at me. "At least, Chessie and I were supposed to." He grins. "Anyway, we figured we should be cautious, and Wick left to scope it out."

"Alone?"

"No."

It doesn't take long to figure out who's with him. "Renegade."

Raider nods. "Renegade has a stellar talent for infiltration. He can blend in and get information without a fuss." He shakes his head with wonder. "I don't know what it is, but he has a way about him, and people spill their guts."

"Yeah," I say, thinking of all the times I told him more than intended. It's impressive and irritating. "Is that why Renegade's with you so much?"

"It isn't his winning personality."

"What are you talking about?" I laugh. "I like him."

Raider chuckles. "I do too, but he's an acquired taste. He's excellent at what he does, so I'm always sending him out to check a situation or gather information."

"I always wondered where he was disappearing to."

"Yeah," Raider says, lifting his water and taking a swig. "Add that to Wick's killer tracking abilities, and you've got an ideal hunting duo."

"Wick's that good?" I ask, pride burning in my chest.

"Evans is the best, and he taught Wick everything he knows. So, yeah."

Hitting a bump, the car jerks to the right. Some of Raider's water flies onto my shirt, and I slam my elbow into the door. "Ouch," I mumble, rubbing where it stings.

"You okay?"

"We in a hurry?" I ask, still rubbing.

"Thought it might be good to catch up with them. But no. Not otherwise." I'm not positive, but I think he slows down. "I'm sort of curious," he starts, looking my way, then quickly returning his attention to the road. "Why are you doing this?"

I suck in my lip, scraping my teeth on the skin. "I thought it was obvious."

"Not entirely." Raider licks his lips and glances over again.

"Why do you want to know?"

He shrugs. "You know I have regrets. I guess, well, I wonder where your mind's at. Like, if you find a way to move forward from your mistakes, maybe it'll give me an idea of what I could try."

Pulling my legs under me, I sit cross-legged while the hot wind tousles my hair. "Back when Chessie challenged Evans, and they fought—my sister was ready to give up her life to save him. I'm willing to do the same thing for her. We both know there's more to Tyran switching emissaries, and when the danger comes, I'll face it and not Chess."

I downplayed the situation when I spoke with Chett, calling Chessie a distraction—a replacement for the beacon—when I believe it's more. Sure, Tyran's primary interest is Raider, but I think she wants to punish my family—severely punish us—and my sister is in no condition to take that on.

"Are you taking her place to prove you've changed?" I barely hear his question over the engine's growl.

"No. I can't force acceptance. Your dad helped me understand I can't own that responsibility," I say, missing my friend. "But I'm positioned to make a difference, and going in Chessie's place is the right thing to do. I've been close to death several times in the last eight years. At least, this time, it will be worth something."

I can be what my sister needs. We share the same blood, so I'll take this burden from her. Doing this for my family gives me more hope for the future than I've had in a long time, regardless of the outcome. This is what I must do.

"Well, that's all noble and beautiful, but there's one problem," Raider says. "I'm not going to let you die."

"Well, that's all noble and beautiful of you, but I have no plans of dying. I'm better with the Torquent blade than Chessie is."

"Yeah, but you're not necessarily better than Tyran."

"Are you sure?"

"You forget my dad learned all his methods from my

mom."

Sivil. Tyran's sister.

"I didn't forget. But not all my methods are of the Torquent variety. Sure, I used those against Chessie because she doesn't know them. It was an obvious advantage. But I had a few surprises for you on that beach, and, well, I'd have a few for your aunt as well."

"Maybe she doesn't want an Endrack rematch."

"Maybe. But the idea might tempt her, and I wouldn't discourage it if it opens a way to get us out of this fix." I turn a quizzical eye on Raider, asking, "Besides, if it's not to embarrass Chessie in a rematch, what do you think Tyran wants my sister for?"

"I don't know, but my aunt is devious. There's something we're missing."

I nod, knowing without a doubt that he's right. There's something significant we're missing, and it's the thing I'm most afraid of—the moment we find out what it is.

We're halfway between Mirum and Periculum when I make Raider pull over so I can drive. He insists he's fine to keep going, but it's better if we take turns. Ten minutes later, I smirk as I say, "It's good you're not driving," before pointing at the anxious up-and-down of his foot.

His foot stills.

"You that nervous?" I ask. He shakes his head and looks away, avoiding the question. "Is it my driving? I'll have you know I was handling cars long before you ever thought of getting behind the wheel." Chessie was fascinated by them, and after she fixed CJ, we drove all the time, mostly just circling Ambitus.

"It's not your driving. I'm just thinking about... things."

I hum thoughtfully. "Things. Yeah, I'm always thinking about those too. Pesky, pesky *things*."

"You're a smartass."

"Ooh! Raider's language gets cheap when he's thinking... *about things*."

Raider chuckles, crossing his arms over his chest. "I'm thinking about how to keep people safe."

"We should figure out how to keep *you* safe."

"Me?"

"Well, yes. You're expecting Tyran to force an alliance with the South T to manipulate your government, but what if there's more? What if her motives are more sinister?" I glance over, and he's shaking his head. "This could be an elaborate plot to capture you. Stick you in prison. I know a little something about that, you know?"

"You've been listening to my dad too much." Raider shoots me a look. "Regardless of what she has planned, she'd love that I'm stewing over her intentions. It would amuse her, and that, in itself, frustrates me."

"She's sort of deranged, isn't she?"

"Absolutely." Raider yawns. "I hate to ask this, but would you mind if I close my eyes for a bit?"

"Are you telling me the invincible Raider Roil is tired?"

Raider snorts. "One of us slept the day away, and it wasn't me."

"Sleep if you must," I say, waving a dismissive hand and holding back a grin.

"You're simply an angel," he returns with a laugh, and I can't hold my smile back any longer, but Raider never sees it. He's already closed his eyes, and I swear, a second later, he's snoring.

Part of me enjoys the silence, moving along at night

with nothing but time to think about what's coming and how I'll approach it. I decide the only way to face Tyran is by abandoning my fear. That's how she operates—moving forward without restraint—and she won't respect anyone who doesn't act in the same manner. I'll be dauntless and confident, knowing I'm Endrack's daughter, and if it comes to it, I'm her equal with the Torquent blade.

Of course, that doesn't mean it's going to be easy. I'll likely not escape unscathed, but scars aren't bad—things that leave a mark are often what we value most. I run my finger over the scar Chessie left on my hand just as there's a flash of light.

I lift my foot from the gas pedal and coast. A second later, thunder rumbles in the sky. And, of course, Raider sleeps through it. Five minutes later, there have been two more flashes, and the wind has picked up. It's not ideal in a topless car—too bad we didn't take Chessie's with the roof—especially when the rain starts. And it's not a gentle patter that graduates to a steady beat. No—one second, the world is dry, and the next, it's a downpour.

Raider sputters, jolting forward. "When did this start?" he asks, wiping his saturated face.

"Just now," I answer, barely exaggerating. A gust of wind hits us, pushing the car to the left. Raider reaches out, grabbing the steering wheel and helping us stay on the road.

Snap! Another streak of lightning shoots across the night sky, instantly followed by the crash of thunder. "We're too exposed out here!" Raider yells while my hands tremble on the wheel. "Look for somewhere to take shelter," he continues, craning his head.

"You look. I'll drive. I can barely see ten feet in front of us." As if in answer to my complaint, the sky lights up. Briefly, I can see all around us, and what I discover in that glimpse has me screaming and slamming both feet on the brake.

Raider clutches the side of the car, holding on until we jerk to a stop.

"What in the light?" he exclaims, but I'm already unbuckling my belt. The headlights create a perfect spotlight, and in seconds, Raider sees what I'm reacting to. "Shit!" he says, going for his buckle too, but I'm already searching the back of the car for what I need.

Without the flash of lightning, there's no doubt I would have hit the car blocking the road. But just beyond the car is something more alarming—my brother engaged in battle with our Uncle Diggs.

They grunt and speak words I can't make out, but I remain focused, throwing two bags onto the muddy ground and grabbing the Torquent blade. It clangs unceremoniously against the back of the car, but there's no time for this to be pretty.

Striding forward, I catalog the scene. Wick's exhausted and bleeding, though I can't tell from where. I locate Renegade twenty feet away. He's on the ground and not moving. I've lost track of Raider, but my mind narrows in on one thing—Diggs. He's in my sights—gray hair wet and shining in the car headlights—and even the rain assaulting my eyes can't break my focus.

This isn't a time to consider starting postures or ponder strategy. It's a time to be bold—to channel the skills of a Torquent blade in battle. With that in mind, I run toward them with the sword held high, screaming for Diggs's attention.

Instantly, I get it.

Diggs pushes Wick off to counter my attack. I charge, bringing the heavy sword down. The crack of the weighted weapon matches another boom of thunder—like lightning parting the sky, my blade slices straight through his sword. The pointed end falls to the ground, leaving Diggs holding half a weapon.

I hold my blade straight at his chest, growling, "Drop it." His chest moves up and down with breath, but he doesn't drop the sword. He merely lowers his arm to hang limply by his side.

"By the light, did that seriously just happen?" Wick asks, but I don't respond. I don't even look at him, preferring to stare at Uncle Diggs, watching for any slight movement. "Serious, Shar, you subdued him in like five seconds."

"Why take ten when five will do?" I ask while adrenaline surges through me. "Is Renegade okay?"

There's a pause, but I don't dare move my eyes from Diggs. "I think so," Raider finally yells over the heavy patter of rain. "Wick, secure Diggs."

"Stay back!" Diggs demands, putting a hand up to keep Wick away. He's not engaging his broken sword, but I don't trust he won't.

Raider appears, leaving Renegade when things with Diggs aren't progressing how we'd like. I keep my sword aimed at him while Wick and Raider flank the man. I don't know where he thinks he's going, but he doesn't relax his posture.

"I'm glad you came upon us," Diggs says, looking straight at me from behind his oversized nose. "Are you going to Torquent?" When I don't answer, he draws his own conclusion. "Of course you are. You've never committed to the right things, always getting caught up in the wrong ones. For what you and your sister did to my Saeva, I wish I could be there when you face what Tyran has in store for you."

"Too bad you'll miss it, then," I say, unshrinking. "But I'll be there when you face what awaits you in Adlumen."

Diggs laughs. "Looks like we'll both miss out," he says, and I shriek as he lunges forward, diving onto my Torquent blade.

Curses! What's he done?

I release the weapon and take staggering steps, backing away from Uncle Diggs. His hands go up to clutch the hilt of the sword. "I'm not weak like you." The words wheeze past his lips. "Not content... to rot away... in prison."

He takes another breath, turns away from me, and crumples sideways to the ground.

And for the first time since we arrived upon the scene, I take my eyes off of him, staring down at my fingers. Though I tried to kill Evans, this is the first time someone's died by my hand. And even though Diggs played a more significant part in the outcome, I can't prevent the revulsion that flows through me.

The rain continues, washing the blood from Diggs's body but not purging the putrid feeling from inside of me. I feel dirty. Distraught.

Sick.

Rushing away from the others, I make it fifteen feet before clinging to a dead tree branch, emptying my stomach while the bark presses into my gut. I cough and cry while the rain cleanses my face. And then I think of Tyran.

The fear I committed to abandon returns in full force. I'm traveling to meet Tyran in Chessie's stead, and none of us know what that will mean. It could be a heated discussion, or it could come to this. Watching my uncle die, I'm suddenly conflicted, not knowing if I can manage a battle with Tyran.

Those around me are much more capable of knowing when and how to take life. It's quite clear I'm a failure where death is concerned—unable to procure it when intended and enabling it without meaning to. And, even though I'm not completely upset by the realization, I'm terrified by it. What if I don't act when the moment is right? What if I rush forward when I should hold back? What if the wrong person dies? And how do I move on if everything crashes down around us, and it's all my fault?

I thought abandoning my fear was the answer, but now it's at the forefront of my mind, casting a shadow over everything.

CHAPTER THIRTY-EIGHT

Thirty-One Days Free at 5:00 a.m.

"Get him into the car!" Raider's panicked voice pulls me from the hum in my ears, and I push off the tree, wiping my mouth with the back of my hand and rushing to where they're gathered around our car.

"Careful of his head."

"There's so much blood."

It's hard to keep track of who's saying what as they scramble, making split-second decisions. I join them in the cacophony. When thoughts pop into our minds, we yell them out, jumping into action before making a consensus. It's a miracle we work as seamlessly as we do.

"Keep pressure on the wound," Raider tells Wick while he presses down on the gas. The tires struggle in the mud but find traction, and we speed away.

"What happened?" I ask, looking back at my brother with his hands pressed to Renegade's body, fingers outlined in blood. The rain falls hard, washing Renegade's life onto the floor where red puddles gather. The sickness rises in my stomach again, so I face forward while Wick talks.

"We tracked Uncle Diggs as planned, but he was waiting for us," he yells over the car and rain. "Looking back, the clues were too obvious. He picked the time and place. The only thing he couldn't plan was the weather, and even that worked to his advantage. If you hadn't come along—"

I squeeze my eyes shut, considering what could have happened if we hadn't arrived when we did. I hate the visions entering my mind and struggle to keep them from overwhelming me.

"He attacked Renegade first," Wick continues. "It happened so fast, there was nothing I could do. Then he was on me, and I had to keep a clear head, so I just left Renegade there."

"You did the right thing," Raider says.

Raider's right. My brother did the only logical thing, defending them both against Diggs, but it isn't easy making those choices when someone's life is on the line. I hear the regret in Wick's voice when he says, "He's got to pull through this. He's just got to."

Raider drives furiously through the rain, wiping his lenses frequently. Anger rolls off him like the moisture beading on our skin, and he pushes the car harder than ever. One misstep on this road, and we'll crash. We all know it but don't tell him to slow down. Renegade's our friend. He's a partner and compatriot. He'd do this and more for us. We must give him everything we have, so I check my buckle is tight and will Raider to go even faster.

It feels like it will never happen, but finally, Periculum comes into view. Wick and Raider are familiar with the town and head straight to the barracks, where there will be people with medical training.

Raider pulls into a tent where we're instantly protected from the rain, and I brush the water from my eyes. For the first time in what feels like forever, the water's not immediately replaced.

The soldiers inside are awake—on the night shift and ready for any calamity. They jump into action, barely uttering a word while taking in the scene and getting background from Wick and Raider. They gently move Renegade to an adjoining room, shouting out their needs and intentions as they go. The three of us stay behind. My brother stares at his red-stained hands until a soldier grips his shoulder. "Let's get you cleaned up," she says before leading him away.

Glancing at Raider, he's blood-free, as am I. That's at least something.

"Are you okay?" he asks. The room was full of commotion, but now, only his commanding voice fills the silent space.

"We just left his body there," I say, thinking of Diggs.

"I'll have someone get him," he says, fixing the problem, even though I didn't bring it up needing a solution. The situation is difficult to comprehend and has me perplexed. Diggs was a beloved uncle and co-conspirator. Then, for eight years, he was a memory. But the moment he reappeared in my life, he became my foe. How did it all come about?

Raider sits down, and I decide to do the same since my legs are barely holding me up. "Is he going to make it?" I ask, dropping next to Raider. The seat is uncomfortable, which seems fitting—everything feels hard, wet, and sad.

"I don't know."

His hopeless words do nothing to improve my mood, and I release a long sigh. "Will you just lie to me about it?"

Raider scoots over, putting an arm around my shoulder and pulling me in. "I promised I wouldn't lie to you again."

"I give you permission. Just this once."

"Renegade's good. A hundred percent."

"Thanks."

Raider rubs the side of my arm, and I relax into him. I'm so afraid for my friend. Without Raider's calming presence, I'd be pacing the wall like a trapped cat. It's still a temptation since everything seems so big right now—Diggs is dead, Renegade's hurt, and Tyran is waiting for us.

We're just two people trying to prevent pain and death. But, really, what can two people do?

My wet clothes feel heavy, and I shiver beneath them. "What are we going to do?" I ask, unable to keep the despair from my voice.

Raider puts his chin on my head, holding me in place. "We'll leave Renegade in capable hands. We'll meet Tyran. We'll do what's necessary and stop a war."

"Is that all?" I can't help the small laugh that escapes. Even though nothing's funny right now, it still relieves the tightness in my chest.

"Those are the major points, but we'll accomplish the little things too. The more important things."

"Like helping my sister," I say. Raider nods, his chin bobbing on top of my head.

But it's more than helping Chessie. It's the rest of my family and Raider's too. Indeed, all of Adlumen and the Southern Territory. They're all part of this. Even Arrick and Chett will be helped if we succeed. I feel the burn in my chest, wanting to fix things for us all.

"We need to get you back to Caelum to be with Sage and Valore," I say, the burn setting my words on fire. I hear the determination in my voice.

"Yes," Raider says with a catch in his, and then I'm startled when he wraps me in a hug. He's shaking. "Yes," he repeats, gripping me tighter.

I understand the need for human contact when facing the unknown. I needed it desperately during those first years in Aunty's Cellar. It was Squatty who helped me before he was gone. And then Valore. And now, in the strangest of circumstances, it's Raider. So, I wrap my arms around him, and we support each other. It's more than comfort—it's an understanding. We're both facing the same terrifying obstacle—Tyran of Torquent—and we're committed to confronting her together.

We're still holding onto each other when Wick returns. I hear the soft shuffle of footsteps and look up to find him watching me as he takes a seat. Raider releases me, and I sit up to wipe my eyes, unaware I was crying.

Wick's clean, wearing a new uniform and sporting wet hair—the strands are nearly black instead of their usual dark chestnut. I'm envious since I'm rain-damp with a chill, even though it's muggy hot. It's the adrenaline, as much as anything, making me shiver. My brother leans forward, putting his elbows on his knees. "Uncle Diggs was always a talker. Boasted he was never in Caelum. He had someone follow you to deliver the note."

"He has others working with him?" Raider asks.

"With him or for him, but yeah. I need to return to Adlumen and tell them what happened. I don't believe his death eliminates the threat to the governors."

"Agreed," Raider says.

"But what if it's the wrong move?" Wick asks, running a hand across the freckled bridge of his nose. "Is it better I go with you to meet Tyran?" I reach to grip my brother's wrist, knowing he's suffering the same fear and confusion I am.

Raider shakes his head, leaning back in the chair and running both hands over his short hair. "You need to go. Someone needs to tell Geric about his dad, and I'd rather it was a friend."

"There's still no update. I asked before coming to you," Wick says, nodding toward the mysterious area where they took Renegade. "I'll get a few soldiers and leave now. With luck, I could have Geric back here in four hours."

"Don't push your luck. Plan on five," I say, biting my lip.

"Maybe I'll try for three." Wick grins weakly, rising to his feet and pulling me up for a hug. "This is a mess, Shar," he whispers. "Please be safe. I just got you back."

"I'm not going anywhere," I say fiercely.

He squeezes me tighter, dropping a kiss on my forehead before taking a step back. "Do us a favor and get yourself a shower. The men in your life will appreciate it." He glances at Raider and winks.

"Wick!" I exclaim, and Raider chuckles.

A second later, my indignation vanishes as my brother walks away. I hope machismo and luck are enough to make it so we'll meet again. He turns the corner and is gone, and I face Raider. "Diggs mentioned wishing he could be there for what awaits me in Torquent. What do you think he meant?"

"He was trying to scare you. Get in your head."

"You think?"

"It's what Tyran would do. I'm sure Diggs plays the same games."

Raider's sure, but I'm not. My uncle was never that clever. But observing Raider more closely, I'm not sure he believes it either. He shakes his arms, pulling his jacket sleeves over his hands while he's lost in thought. He's just as concerned about what Diggs said as I am.

"I think I'll get that shower," I say, and Raider makes a dismissive hum before I go in search of someone to point me in the right direction. I need hot water running over my skin—the hotter, the better—but I quickly learn a shower must wait when someone stops me in my tracks, and I blurt out, "Why aren't you at The Hearty Badger?"

"My entourage woke me with news of Renegade," Chett answers with a frown. "Is he okay?"

"He's alive, but beyond that, we've had no news."

Chett purses his lips, and if possible, his frown deepens—such a surly, unsatisfied man. I wonder if he was this way before Chadd died. I didn't interact with him enough back then to know. But losing a family member changes a person.

I can't help thinking he'd be entirely different if his brother were alive.

Curses! What would an upbeat Chett be like?

His steps continue toward me, stopping a foot away. The Hamo emblem is on his chest, and I point at it as I ask, "Some of the emblems are strange, aren't they?" Dropping my finger, I look up at him.

"In what way?"

"Adlumen's, for instance. It's different now that the governors took over, but the old one explained more about the place."

"Did it?" Chett asks, but he doesn't seem invested in the conversation.

"Maybe it's just that I don't understand the new one."

"Each of the six sunbeams represents an aspect of Adlumen—governors, councilors, judges, advisors, soldiers, and citizens. None is bigger than the other. They're all equally represented."

I nod, considering his answer and comparing it to what I know about the governors and how they lead. I decide the symbolism makes sense. I look again at the gray rectangle with the upside-down crown on Chett's chest. "And what about Hamo? What does your emblem mean?"

"To question everything because even those with authority aren't perfect." I look at it again, thinking about those in authority—Arrick, Raider, Tyran, Casmo, Captain Rhed, and the governors. They all have different backgrounds and issues, driving them to behave in specific ways that seem logical to them but may not be ideal for another group. It's a mess. And Chett's right—they're far from perfect.

"So, Hamo's emblem reminds you to be wary and untrusting."

"I guess it does." Chett moves forward, cutting the small space between us in half. "I was surprised to learn you're traveling with Raider. Last I heard, you'd be alone in that car."

"He came upon me when I was leaving and volunteered to accompany me. We decided we might have a better chance facing Tyran together."

"Together," Chett repeats. Hunched over, he looks at me through his lashes. He's upset. But also, there's something else. "Shar, there are better ways to position yourself for this conflict. Ways it will play out in your favor." He grips his neck, clearing his throat. "I mean, did you even give my offer fair consideration?"

Curses! We're back to this?

"I did, Chett. Truly," I say, hoping he'll see my sincerity and drop this. "But things have changed since Ora, and you were right to encourage me to contact my family. My brother's been supportive, and I can't tell you what it means to have one of them accept me again. I don't know where I'll end up, but I can't go to Hamo when you're at war with Wick."

Chett tilts his head, watching me. I feel dissected under his gaze. "I'm happy for you," he finally says. "But that's not the entire reason."

I sigh. "What do you mean?" I ask, exhausted by this recurring debate.

"I saw you together," Chett says, looking toward the room where I left Raider after we held each other in shared grief and worry. Chett's mouth twists, imagining romance between Raider and me. I'm too tired to explain or excuse anything. It's true things have improved between us—I respect and appreciate Raider—but anything more is not worth speculation or words.

I squint against the morning sun shining through a plastic window in the canvas tent and concentrate on bringing us back to what's important. "We've been up all night. The situation with Renegade is scary. We need an update on him and then some sleep. After that, we'll be ready to go to Torquent and meet Tyran. Wick arranged for us to stay in the barracks. Should we meet you at The Hearty Badger this afternoon or tomorrow morning?"

Chett hums his displeasure, realizing I'll not address his assumption. "We'll meet you back here, and the sooner, the better. Expect us at noon."

"I'll sleep fast," I say, knowing the response sounds hollow. "But before that happens, I've been told I need a shower."

Chett sniffs, but it has nothing to do with my comment—just a strange coincidence—but I still bite back a grin. The feeling dies when he reaches out and grips my arm, saying, "I'll not mention it again, but you're making the wrong choice."

The rejection he feels is plain on his face, and I'm sorry for putting it there. I take a step back, breaking his hold. "It's the only choice I can make," I say, thinking of my brother. "I hope you'll come to understand that."

He nods, and his perpetually sad face is even more morose. "We could have been good for each other," he says before turning his back and walking away. We still can be if he'd allow a different connection for a different purpose. Our relationship might not be as he imagines, but it could be worthwhile just the same. But I don't stop him to press the issue. Instead, I find the showers.

CHAPTER THIRTY-NINE

Thirty-One Days Free at 8:00 a.m.

Thirty minutes later, I'm clean and searching for Raider. The compound is confusing, so I'm glad a soldier walks me to the visitor barracks. I tap on the fabric flap, which serves as a door, and Raider invites me inside. It's a small space with two bunk beds—barely room to squeeze between them—a side table and a standard plastic window. There are no frills—not even a closet or chair. It's tight quarters, for sure.

"I saw Chett," I say, dropping the flap.

"Me too."

"What'd he tell you?" I ask, and Raider watches me with a curious expression.

"Maybe something of what he said to you." I clear my throat, imagining the uncomfortable tone of that conversation while Raider continues, "He offered to drive us the rest of the way. Mentioned meeting at noon and pushing on to Monitus."

Monitus—a city in the Southern Territory that was historically the gateway to the Torquent light bubble but now makes up a corner of the Torquent Expansion. I've never been there, though I've seen the dot plenty of times on the Wall of Maps in Consilio Locus.

"We have a plan, then," I say, already knowing it's what Chett intended, but now I'm wondering if I'll be able to sleep since I'll be back with Chett and his solemn gaze in a few hours.

"Not as such. I told him we'd rather drive to Monitus on our own," Raider says, watching my reaction. My shoulders relax, dispelling the tension I didn't even realize was there. Things are so different between us. A month ago, I would have picked Chett over Raider in a second. Back then, Raider was doing everything in his power to leave me behind, and now, he's keeping me with him—traveling with me willingly. It's not just his words but his actions that prove we're in this together.

He's sitting on the bottom bed, his elbows propped on his knees, looking up at me. "On our own, we look like visiting dignitaries. With Chett, it feels like we're prisoners. His group is more rested and can arrive ahead of us to get things rolling, telling Tyran we're on our way. I told him we'd meet in Monitus and drive with them through Torquent to Contund, but we'd stay in our car."

When I think of meeting Tyran, my stomach twists in knots, so I drop my suitcase on a lower bunk and look around the room. "I take it I'm sleeping in here."

"These canvas caves are all they have for accommodations." Raider smiles tiredly. "But they're not full-up, so if you want your own space, we just need to ask."

"No reason. Besides, after today, I feel safer together."

Raider grunts in agreement, scooting back on his bottom bunk, hunched over so as not to hit his head on the top bed. Leaning against the wall, his chin pushes into his chest—these beds sure don't promote good posture.

Instead of kinking my neck like Raider, I lie down on the bed across from him, thinking about all that's transpired since my liberation from Aunty's Cellar. "You know, prison was easier," I say, then snort out a laugh. "I sound like I'm longing for it, which is far from the truth. Nobody wants to be in prison."

"Just because you don't want to be there doesn't mean it wasn't less complicated. The more people involved in any situation, the more complex it becomes."

"True." I reach up, tapping the grid above my head. "Death surrounded me in my cage, and I feared and sought it equally. But there's even more death out here, coming at me from all sides. Now, it's threatening those around me."

"Yeah," Raider says while we both think about Renegade—stable for now, but his fate is mostly uncertain.

"Beyond the threat of death, there are people actually dying." I think about Diggs. "I still can't believe my uncle did that."

"You were amazing. The way you jumped in to help your brother was impressive. You had the situation under control in seconds."

"Until it spun completely out of control. What Diggs did—it was horrifying. Completely brutal." I drop my hands and roll to face Raider. "What if that's life now? What if the atrocities don't end, and things only get worse?"

"I worry about that too," Raider says, staring into my eyes. "But I also have a lot of hope we can stop things from escalating."

"You do?" Raider's chin dips. "Where do you find it? I feel depleted of hope."

"Sage. He gives me hope in everything because I need the future to be a safe place for him. He's what I use to measure every choice. That and refusing to concede to Tyran's vision because she's selfish, and I have no respect for that."

"Sage is a good guide. I guess Wick's become that for me. For a long time, it was your dad."

"I'm sorry about that, Shar. I know I pushed hard for you to disconnect from my dad."

"It's understandable and probably a good thing. It made me look for other opportunities I might have avoided." I smile. "Like my brother."

"I'm glad for you." He returns the expression. "And I'm

glad you're here with me. If any two people can figure this out, it's us."

"You really feel that way?" I ask, sucking in my lip and chewing on the tender skin. It's hard to reconcile this complete change in Raider's opinion of me. "You were quite opposed to me in the beginning."

Raider nods, bouncing his head against the wall. "You were opposed to me too."

"Yeah. I sort of was." I chuckle. "Mostly because you insisted on treating me like my old self."

"It was wrong of me. I see how different you are."

"Well, since you're willing to admit that, I'll admit you weren't completely wrong," I say, surprising even myself at the admission. "I've felt parts of that person trying to resurface, so maybe I'm not as changed as I thought."

"Look. For eight years, I thought of you in one way, but I've gotten to know you over the last month. Your core has changed, but there are remnants of the girl you were. And that's okay. You're worth knowing, just as you are."

I hold my breath while those words try to penetrate. The soft expression on his face and his calm demeanor back up his words, so I want to believe him. He's so different from the man I met in Adlumen. I'll be twenty-five this year, and he'll be thirty-one. We're older and experienced. We've been hurt, and we've loved. We're the same people but very changed from the hopeful youth we once were.

"The day we met," Raider starts, adjusting on the bed to rest his elbow on a pillow with his fist under his chin. "I was drawn to your fire. I loved Kally with everything I had, but I would have been interested in you if things were different. That's why I was so angry. I'd never do anything to betray someone I love. And when you acted, I wasn't completely repulsed. So, I doubted myself, wondering if I could commit that type of betrayal. I did nothing wrong, yet I felt like I had to right a mistake thrust upon me."

"I'm so sorry, Raider. I know this is too late, but I promise I'll never put you in that situation again. I'm not impulsive like I was back then."

Raider barks out a laugh. "What do you call running off to Torquent in place of your sister?"

"Well, I'm not impulsive to the point of destruction," I say with a smile. "At least, the destruction of others. My own destruction is another story."

"Don't talk that way," Raider whispers with an edge. "And no more apologies. I know you, Shar. I understand you now."

"Do you?" Raider nods, and I feel pressure in my throat from the things I want to say. Still, it takes a minute to push them out, and it comes out quietly. "I admire you," I say, feeling the force of my confession.

"I admire you too," he says, reaching across the void between our two beds.

His response is like a perfect dream. The forgiveness and acceptance feel like power, buzzing under my skin. I accept Raider's invitation and put my fingers in his. Our clasped hands hang between us as we lie in the little bunk room. I swear the beds seem even closer than just a minute ago. Raider's dark eyes behind his lenses don't leave mine as we stare at each other and settle into a new understanding.

"I feel like I should give you one more chance to back out," he says, startling me. "We've said we're in this together, but are you sure you want to come with me?"

"Why wouldn't I?"

"I'm nervous about why she wants a daughter of Endrack. And I'm not trying to sound cocky, but she wants me more than anything else, so she'd get over it if you're not there."

"I've never thought you were cocky. Far from it, which is

funny since you're so handsome, and you'd have every right to be."

"You think I'm handsome?"

I scoff. "*Everyone* thinks you're handsome."

"I don't care about everyone," he says slowly.

I grin, squeezing his fingers. "You're very nice to look at. I made that clear eight years ago." Too quickly, the smile slips from my face as I get back to the subject of Tyran. "I appreciate the option, but I'm committed to going. I expect Tyran to be angry when I arrive in my sister's stead, but I believe she'd be angrier with no Endrack at all, no matter how much she wants you. So, no, you're not going alone. I'm determined you will get through this unscathed."

"I don't think Tyran would actually hurt me."

And I don't think Raider believes that. He's saying it for my benefit.

"What happened to her learning to despise you and then disposing of you?" I ask, recalling his comment from the Ambitus stables.

"I was being funny. Sort of. Regardless, she may try to trap me into something, but I don't think she'd harm me. You, on the other hand, don't have that safety net."

"You've got to stop worrying about me."

Raider chuckles. "See, that's the thing. I'm only worrying more, and I don't see that reversing anytime soon." He repositions on the pillow but doesn't release my hand, his eyes never leaving mine. "Valore raised me to protect those around me, so keeping you safe is part of my job. And if there's one thing you should know about me, it's that I take all of my jobs seriously."

I chuckle, and Raider grins back at me. Then he rubs his thumb over my hand, finding the scar Chessie gave me so long ago. "You needed to know your options, but I respect your decision. I'm here for you, Shar. No matter what comes your way, you'll have me on your side."

It's no secret I have issues with feeling abandoned. Chessie said nearly the same thing to me before I tried to kill Evans, and afterward, she supported my removal to a Dark prison. But maybe I've reached the point in my life where my actions warrant such devotion. Maybe I've earned the right to have someone stick by me.

And so I accept it, knowing it's a two-way contract. Knowing I have to keep up my end to maintain the strength of those words.

"Thank you," I say. "I'll do everything I can to deserve it."

CHAPTER FORTY

Thirty-One Days Free at 9:00 a.m.

"I hope you enjoyed your power nap," Raider says, nudging me awake.

"How long have I been under?" I blink, then open one eye against the light in our little room.

"Thirty minutes, maybe."

I roll onto my back, willing away the ache in my muscles and the heaviness of my eyelids, wanting so much to relax and disappear back into sleep. But I push through the mental fog, asking, "What's going on?"

"Renegade's awake. Thought you'd want to see him."

I push until I'm sitting on the bed, and my feet hit the floor. "I do."

It's fifteen minutes until I'm ready, having splashed water on my cheeks, roused my mind, and gotten presentable for a visit. Raider's by my side as we peek past a curtain to find the injured man on a rolling bed with his eyes closed.

"You go first," Raider says. "Call me when you're done."

I step through the curtain. The hard dirt underfoot muffles my steps, but the rustling curtain fabric catches Renegade's attention.

"Hey," I say with a brief wave.

My companion lifts his chin in greeting, then grimaces.

"Take it easy. No aggressive moves." I grin, stepping to his bedside and taking his hand, before sitting down. Raider says the doctors believe he should be fine, though they have some concerns. He's more haggard than after our drive to Hamo when he let the wind turn his hair into a nest. I hate seeing him this way.

"You're taking her place," Renegade says roughly, and it takes a minute to comprehend his comment.

"I am." He simply nods at my confirmation. If anyone understands my motivation for going to Torquent in Chessie's place, it's this man. He knows what it's like to disappoint the people who are supposed to come first. I don't know what reparations he's attempted, but even if he's tried nothing, I know he wishes he had. In his own peculiar way, he's a good guy—loyal and kind—but for some reason, that's never translated into his family life. Maybe he's incapable of revealing those traits to those who should be closest to him, or perhaps he's afraid to be seen that way. Possibly, like me, there was someone in his upbringing who isolated him until he didn't know how to engage properly. I'm really not sure. I doubt I'll ever truly understand Renegade.

"Be careful," he says, looking down at our linked hands and squeezing. It's a strange gesture coming from him. Then again, holding his hand is unusual.

"That's the plan," I say, putting on a carefree smile. "And you get better." I pat his fingers, and he holds mine tighter. "Wick went for Geric. He'll be here soon."

His hand goes limp. "Doubt it. 'Sides, there's no need for him to come." He turns his head, swallowing—the sound is dry in his throat.

"It's true. You're as tough as they come and don't need anyone at your side, but I, for one, want to be here for you." Renegade's head turns, his tired blue eyes taking on a shine as he watches and listens. "And I bet Geric does too, if you'll let him." I lean in, unable to stop myself, and give the older man a light kiss on his forehead—browned like leather from the sun. When I sit back, his cheeks are red, and I'm sure he'd look less shocked if I'd slugged him. "But don't bother with what we want or need—Geric or me—just focus on healing up. You and I have more adventures to go on together—I'm sure of it—and I need you in full health for the task."

Renegade chuckles—glad of the lighter topic—but his eyes are tired, so I give his hand a final squeeze and call Raider into the room, leaving them to talk before the last bits of his energy wane.

◆ ◆ ◆

There's no point in Raider or me trying for more sleep. We're wide awake, so we quickly gather our things and hustle to the tent where we left the car.

I reserve only a small portion of my thoughts for Renegade, hoping my friend continues to improve. He still has some obstacles to overcome, but I've known few people who take on battles as he does. I'm sure he'll win this fight.

Mostly, my thoughts are on what's coming. Beneath the early morning sky, I note the cloudless expanse is as clear as my mind. It has me determined to leave my worries in Periculum, shed the insecurities of my past, and focus on meeting Tyran.

Raider's words from our canvas cave are convincing. Though I'm changed, a part of me will always be Sharade Endrack, and that's not a bad thing. At least, not unless I let it be. I'm determined nothing will take me down the path of treachery again. I'm confident in myself and my future. I'm confident in Raider's perception of me.

I secure the circlight around my neck, and Raider takes off his lenses when we enter the Dark. We take the Talpa Trail delimit trade route from when Adlumen and Torquent traded through the Dark. While lamlight allows people to travel in many directions, the ground here is level and convenient for driving a car.

We're quiet, and where silence usually makes me sleepy,

my mind is so active it's not a problem. Each time I glance at Raider, he's similarly engaged in his mind—both of us trying to solve the world's issues on the long drive.

But nothing gets resolved. I'm just stirring the same thoughts on a loop. The only way to resolve the situation's intricate issues is to stand in front of Tyran herself.

CHAPTER FORTY-ONE

Thirty-One Days Free at 4:00 p.m.

"What do you think?" Raider asks.

"I think I'm tired of riding in cars," I answer, and he chuckles, but his inquiry isn't regarding vehicular travel, so I add, "Truly, I think Monitus is fascinating."

It took seven hours—taking breaks to stretch, eat, and refuel—but we made our destination. I experienced the drive via lamlight headlights with a circlight around my neck, though passing travelers periodically expanded my vision. Traveling by lamlight can be dull, but the curious city of Monitus is enough to reengage my mind.

Monitus is significantly larger today than at any time in its history, having evolved from a South T city bordering the Torquent light bubble into Torquent-governed land under the expansion agreement. Raider has mentioned before that while the agreement isn't permanent, it would be nearly impossible to reverse it.

Having visited Sperne—another thriving border city—the difference between the two settlements is obvious. Sperne uses lamlight to attract business from those with light sight while serving the light blind equally. But Torquent citizens expanded Monitus solely for their use. They built it to cater to those with light sight, and it's lit up brilliantly—every corner is visible and packed with people, more of them wearing circlights than not.

"Fascinating, you say?" Raider asks, repeating my observation. "That's what I've been told. It would be interesting to see it the way you do."

I forget the lamlight makes no difference to his sight. While the abundant resource expands the distance of my vision, his is the same as it's been for the last seven hours.

We're quiet as we travel the main road in Monitus. The emblem of Torquent is everywhere—flipping in the wind on fabric flags, painted on building sides, and pressed into leather handbags sold in the markets. Unlike Hamo, the symbol isn't a mystery to decipher. The yellow background symbolizes their light bubble, and the blue stripe down the middle represents Lake Divido, which nearly divides their land in two. Spanning the colors is a black Torquent blade—a sign of strength and security.

Being surrounded by enemies born and bred to take up the blade should be heart-stopping, but they barely notice us. There are so many people here, what are two more in the crowd? Or four, as the case may be.

"You're early," Chett mumbles, glancing between Raider and me. We're at Felicitations, where Chett and Arrick are lodging for the night. Our hope is there are still available rooms.

It's been weeks since I saw Chett and Arrick together. On his own, Chett is commanding, but when he's back with the leader of Hamo, he withdraws and lets Arrick direct what happens.

"That's right. We expected you tomorrow for breakfast, not tonight for dinner," Arrick says to Raider before his attention turns to me. "And I wasn't expecting you at all. What are you doing here?"

The man is perfectly pressed with his fastidious posture and coifed black hair, but his question lacks its usual politeness. His expression is split—happy to see me but perplexed. I look at Chett, wondering what he's said. He maintains my gaze, staying silent, so I answer, "I'm here in my sister's place."

"In her place," Arrick reiterates, and his split expression changes solidly to worry.

I shrug and twist a finger in my short hair. "I'm a daughter of Endrack. Isn't that who Tyran requested?" Arrick rolls his eyes, but before conveying his displeasure, I add, "Chessie has reasons for not being here. Good ones. Ones… I don't have."

Arrick releases a slow breath, turning to Chett. "Did you know about this?" Chett nods without delay. "Did you explain in your missive to Tyran that Shar is here instead of Chessie?" Arrick points at the paper in Chett's hand while Chett shakes his head, making Arrick's brow crease. "You support this deception?" Chett leans in, whispering in the man's ear. He listens, nodding a few times, then straightens. "I hope you all know what you're doing. Tyran won't tolerate being made a fool."

Chett's always the more serious of the two, staring at people and things while considering them. He's doing it now, rubbing his lip thoughtfully while watching me. I wonder if he realizes he's doing it. I doubt it because more than looking at me, it feels like he's looking through me—his mind on too many things to focus merely on one. Then his gaze falls on Raider, and it's a similar expression. One thing's for sure, Chett's a man with deep thoughts and secrets. A lot is happening in that head, and I'm not sure I want to know even half of it.

After concluding the logistics conversation, Arrick returns to his boisterous self, but today, his easygoing attitude annoys me. Anxiety about meeting Tyran overrides everything, and his joy—careless laughing and joking—is too much. Chett was sure if I'd gone to Hamo, Arrick would have ensnared me with his charms. With our furthered acquaintance, I find the idea quite impossible.

I recall overhearing the two men in the hallway of

Arrick's home. While I hid in the shadows, they spoke in whispers—Chett's voice distraught and Arrick's demanding. They weren't subtle, talking about something they're keeping from Raider. Their conversation bothered me, and the same feeling lands in my gut now. Of course, Raider brushed me off when I told him—insisting it's the way of those in charge—but he may listen to me now. Then again, maybe the nervousness I feel about Tyran is transferring to these two, but I'm not sure that's the case. We're trusting them with a lot, and I can't help wondering if we should be.

Glancing at Raider, he returns my concerned look with a calm smile. He's not pressuring me like Chett or exhausting me with enthusiasm like Arrick. Instead, Raider's gaze turns my fears into steady alertness. I'm hyper-aware of what's going on, but I'm relaxed about it. He did that. So, I smile back, gratitude shining from my face. The corners of Raider's black eyes crunch curiously behind his lenses. His mouth softens contentedly, and he tilts his head, considering me. Like Chett, the look is intense, but while the other man seemed to look through me, Raider's observation stops at my very core—seeing only me.

And I see only him.

Curses! What's happening?

My eyes spin away before I can think it through. This isn't the time to acknowledge interest in a man. And to get attached to Raider, of all people! I shake my head, forcing an end to the flutters in my stomach and tingles in my limbs.

It's Raider, I remind myself. *Raider Roil!* Get it together!

I'm sure these thoughts are surfacing because Chett pressed the issue when we last spoke. The idea is stuck in my head, but it's not real. Besides, it's not the time to think romantically. And it's never the time with my best friend's son! Nope. Nada. Not happening.

"So, dinner then?" I ask, keeping my eyes down as I brush

past Chett. There's an eagerness to my steps that wasn't there before. It's absurd that focusing on Tyran of Torquent feels more comfortable than acknowledging what I just felt for Raider Roil—completely ludicrous yet undeniable.

I sigh heavily, purging my mind and body of thoughts and feelings. Pushing inside Felicitations, I'm determined to ignore the revelation.

My movement spurs everyone else into action.

Chett finalizes his missive and sends it to Tyran.

Raider secures us space for the night.

Arrick requests a table for dinner.

Our meal is a long, drawn-out affair. They all try to engage me, but I'm tired of talking. I stare at the bright paintings on the walls because I'm tired of listening too. I'm just… tired.

Fatigue overtakes me, and while the others continue their debates, I beg off before Arrick's ready to let me go. I don't care. It's approaching nine o'clock, and while that's early by most standards, I've reached my limit. So, I drag myself upstairs, take a quick shower, and fall into bed with wet hair.

CHAPTER FORTY-TWO

Thirty-Two Days Free at 12:00 a.m.

"I hope you enjoyed your power nap," Raider says with a chuckle.

"What?"

I'm dreaming. I must be. Because I've lived this moment before. Raider said the same thing in the Periculum barracks, but we're not there anymore. We traveled to Monitus, and we're staying in Felicitations.

The words aren't real. Raider's not here. My mind is playing tricks on me.

But then a warm hand lands on my shoulder, shaking me gently. "Come on, sleepy. We need to go."

"Go?" My eyes peek open. "What time is it?" I see no signs of the sun, but Raider is indeed here.

"Midnight. You got a good two hours this time. Maybe more, depending on—by the looks of your hair—how long you were in the shower." I reach up and find my hair sticking out in every direction, but at least it's dry. "Aren't you feeling refreshed?" He chuckles again while I groan.

"What. Is. Happening?" I push out, hoping I made a sentence.

"We've had word from Tyran. She's opened her schedule for an eight o'clock meeting. That's eight in the morning. And while it's a four-hour drive to Contund, the Hams insist we'll have plenty of security hurdles to take up the extra time."

"The Hams." I snort. "Where'd that come from?"

"Hamians sounds lame," he says, pulling my arm until I'm sitting.

I rub my eyes tiredly. "This makes me hate Tyran even more," I say with a yawn, then shake my head, trying to wake up.

◆ ◆ ◆

The *Hams* are right about security hurdles. It's likely that—even with the Hamo symbol on their car—Arrick and Chett would have no issues traveling through Torquent. But add in Raider, with his light-blind lenses, and we're immediately under suspicion. Upon learning he's from the Southern Territory, we're searched thoroughly. Explaining Raider is Tyran's beloved nephew eases them some, and Arrick vouching for him helps more, but it's ultimately Tyran's letter that gets us on our way.

The problem is, it happens half a dozen times. Chett tries producing the letter from the beginning to speed up the process, and while the order of things is slightly different each time, we're still detained while they perform all the same searches and ask all the same questions. I wonder if they're playing with us, completing these repetitive security measures to drive home who's in charge. One thing's for sure—they turn a harrowing day into a miserable one.

Traveling through Torquent, I'm reminded of when the governors came to Adlumen, and they talked about the overcrowded conditions growing up in Harwell. Tyran claims they're in a similar situation, although—unlike the secluded Harwell light bubble, which had no contact with the outside world—the Torques trade heavily in exclusive items needed throughout our area. The east side has a profitable mining operation, and the west is oil-rich. And while the massive Lake Divido nearly splits Torquent in half, the abundant water in a predominantly warm area creates the opportunity for excellent produce. The robust population provides an extensive labor force to process their exports, making them very wealthy.

It's hard to feel sorry for them, especially after seeing the prosperous Torquent Expansion around Monitus. No, the Torques have done very well with what they have. The streets are clean and wide. The buildings are tall and well-kept. Nothing is in disrepair, and every corner could only be labeled as beautiful.

The citizens are upbeat and finely dressed, and there's no poverty to be found. Anywhere. It's as if the concept itself is against the law—no one in Torquent goes without.

I'm envious and wary at the same time. They seem like a spoiled people interested in little besides their own success. And while I understand their desperation for space to grow—indeed, I applaud their drive to expand—it's how they're going about it I find issue with.

CHAPTER FORTY-THREE

Thirty-Two Days Free at 7:30 a.m.

"Tyran lives *here*?" I ask on a gasp. It took seven hours after leaving Monitus to reach Contund—the capital of Torquent—and then another thirty minutes weaving through the bustling city to reach Tyran's home. Like other light bubble leaders I know—the governors and Arrick—she works and lives in the same place.

"Yeah. Spent a few miserable summers here," Raider says on approach, squinting at the place from behind his lenses. Chett steers the lead car, and Raider follows, parking in front of the main doors.

"Miserable?" I ask, looking across the manicured grass toward Lake Divido. Tyran's holding sits on a large cliff high above the waterline. The lake is enormous. The morning sun makes it difficult to see the land on the other side, but thousands of houseboats bob mildly on the flat water—the little vessels, glinting gold and brown, are stunning.

"Miserable," Raider repeats emphatically. "My aunt's goal in life is to make sure no one has too much fun. Herself, especially. Happiness means we're not focused on what makes life dissatisfying."

"Hmm," I say, staring at the structure and trying to imagine his experiences here. The place is nothing like Fiducha, with its layered balconies and high walls. I'd call Tyran's place a castle based on size alone, but in style, it's boxy, not cylindrical, and sleek, not ornate. It oozes authority—the stern, unwelcoming kind. Overall, it's beautiful, but primarily because of how it looks in its environment. Two dozen hilltop palm trees with thick polished trunks surround and dwarf the structure, and the green foliage sways melodically in the unrestricted breeze. It's intimidating, though only partly because of its appearance. Truly, it's because of what's inside. It's a perfect shrine for a powerful woman.

We're expected, so we exit the car and approach the tall, black, metal doors with Arrick and Chett. Raider falls in next to me, and we're followed by six Torque bravados, making me feel like a prisoner again.

Guided inside, we enter a room too large for what it contains—the balance is off in every respect. The walls are twenty feet tall. Three sides are white—the ceiling too—with no interruption in the expanse except the door through which we entered. The west side is one giant window—appearing seamless—where we can look down on Lake Divido's sparkling water. The floor is dark gray cement, polished to reflect any light hitting the surface.

In the corner, right off from the door, are ten chairs. They look more rigid than the famously uncomfortable chairs in Fiducha's Consilio Locus during my dad's time. It's quite a feat to outdo him and seems indicative of how welcome Tyran's guests are in her domain.

"You've arrived at an inconvenient time," one of the Torque bravados says as we sit.

Inconvenient? But Tyran chose the time.

My tailbone aches against the unforgiving chair, and with that one comment, I wish I were back in the car on the bouncy seat, driving away from this place.

"Tyran's in the middle of her breakfast and won't be disturbed," the bravado finishes.

"She probably needs a moment to sharpen her teeth," I whisper to Raider, and he chuckles.

"We'll wait," Arrick says, seeming unsurprised by the development, and wait, we do. We're in the room for hours—

well past our appointment time—with two bravados posted at the door. They don't move, barely blink, and don't offer food or drink—a neglected courtesy my stomach complains about.

Eventually, tired and bored, I pick the floor over the chair, lying on my side and curling my arm under my cheek. I stare out the window onto the brightening day, and soon enough, I'm asleep with every joint on one side of my body pressed against the cold, unrelenting floor.

CHAPTER FORTY-FOUR

Thirty-Two Days Free at 6:00 p.m.

My sleep is short and restless on the cement floor, and soon, I'm back on a chair beside my companions. We watch the sun traverse the sky. It's low now and a stunning yellow gold, lighting up the clouds. Nature is the best thing about this place. I'm about to express that thought when the bravados part, and the door opens.

Two more bravados enter, carrying a padded chair between them, which they place in front of us before exiting the room without a word. It's ten minutes before the same bravados return, but they're not alone. The click of heels announces her, and I swear she drops a heavy foot to overemphasize her progress. The sound echoes, pinging from flat surface to flat surface, and gets louder when she finally enters our room.

Tyran's tall—made taller by the shoes—with broad shoulders and a tiny waist. Her hair is long, hanging free, but doesn't move naturally as she walks. It's thick and wiry, which I'd guess is from chemical treatment more than genetics. It's on the yellow side of blond, and the color makes her pale skin look almost purple. She has a nose that's too big for her face, though it strangely suits her, and there's a solid shine to it—enough that I want to request a cloth so she can wipe it off.

Curses! Wouldn't that be awkward?

She wears a boxy tank in blue and fitted pants with flared legs in a darker blue. The noisemakers on her feet comprise two narrow straps crossing over each foot with a thin slab beneath her toes. The height of her heels is a mystery since the pants cover them. There's a long chain around her neck, suspending a small glass box. Inside are locks of hair from her mother and sister. I know this because Valore told me about the sentimental charm.

"You're late," she says, sitting in the plush chair provided for her. She tucks a pillow under one arm and leans into it comfortably. Her voice is lower than expected, and when she talks, her teeth look too big for her mouth, as if her lips can only just contain them. But they're straight and white, though she doesn't show them off—certainly not with a smile.

"A review of your communication with Hamo's emissary would reveal *you* are the one who is late," Raider says, nonplussed.

"I expected you years ago," she says without inflection, staring at Raider—her eyes awkwardly large. It's strange because her individual parts lean toward being unattractive, yet put together, she's rather pretty—though it only takes the slightest movement or adjusted expression, and I'm reevaluating that conclusion. I can't decide what I think of her.

"And you," she says, her attention falling on me. "You're different."

Different. Yeah. And if her tone is anything to go by, I'm not different in a good way. I don't respond but fist Squatty's necklace for strength and keep my eyes on her while she continues, "You're disgustingly thin. Are you sick or something?"

I glance at Raider, who gives me an encouraging look. We knew this would happen—that I would need to reveal my identity—but after hours of sitting in this awful room, the prospect of an explanation sounds exhausting. Still, I open my mouth to start what I came here to do, saying, "No. I'm actually much improved."

"Improved?" Her lip curls. "Marrying a Dirby did little for you."

Arrick clears his throat, and her eyes flash to him. Gaining her full attention, his eyes widen, and I watch his expression change as he hesitates to reveal the truth. But, like me, he's resolved to what needs to be said, and he starts, "About that," but Raider cuts him off.

"Are we here to talk about fashionable diets and marriages? Or can we discuss the abatement?"

I don't dare look at Raider, confused though I am by him delaying my identity reveal. It's a momentary relief but only postpones the inevitable. Still, Tyran bites, focusing on Raider and saying, "I get first choice of any abated land."

"I said discuss, not demand," Raider returns, narrowing his eyes behind his lenses.

Tyran's not deterred. "I get first choice," she repeats.

Raider sighs. "Leaders of the Dark territories and light bubbles will need details before we can agree. What are your parameters?"

"I require additional land equal to the size of Adlumen."

My eyes widen. The Adlumen light bubble is at least five times the size of Torquent. And that's if you include Lake Divido. If you're talking land alone, it's even more.

Raider's jaw tics before he says, "Keep going."

There's more? But then I remember it's Tyran we're talking about. Of course, there's more.

"I require the option to decline if the land isn't ideal. If land borders another light bubble, I don't want it excluded from my choices. I want the right to claim multiple areas, not just one, to equal the land I'm owed. And others may not claim land until I've secured the entirety of my area."

I stare at the woman, amazed by her audacity, before looking at Raider who watches her identically with a ticking jaw. "Your requirements aren't all terrible," he grits out what I suppose is a concession while betraying his true feelings. "Of course, we must assign a deadline for making your decision."

"No deadline." Tyran lifts a blond brow.

"You're not the only light bubble who will require abated land, and having no deadline hinders those wanting to make land deals. It could impact future generations for decades or even centuries." For the first time since she entered the room, there's a small smile on Tyran's mouth.

Raider folds his arms and glares at her. "If you were feeling uncommonly spiteful, you might leave a single square foot of your contract unclaimed forever."

Uncommonly? How Raider delivers that word without sarcasm is beyond me.

"We can work toward resolving the details," Raider continues. "But as to your main point—that Torquent receives first choice of land equaling the size of Adlumen—the South T has no issue. Neither do the Coastals or Adlumen governors."

Tyran sneers as Raider mentions Adlumen's leadership, and her eyes flash to mine. Arrick sees it and quickly says, "Hamo agrees." Her eyes move to him.

We wait, none of us breathing, until finally, with a wave of her hand, she says, "Consider it a contract, determinate on satisfying the details."

Raider jolts in his seat, a stunned expression on his face as he slowly asks, "So, we're all in agreement about abated land?"

"What about Casmo?" Arrick asks, looking between Raider and Tyran.

Tyran inhales, the nostrils of her big nose flaring. "He'll do whatever I tell him."

Raider looks at each person—even the four bravados in the room—and again asks, "So, we agree?" He's tense, anticipating a denial, and when none comes, his shoulders relax. "Does this mean we can end talk of war between us?" He speaks slowly as if it's too good to be true, and rushing the words will spoil everything.

I decide he could be right when Tyran answers, "That all depends."

"On what?" Raider's mouth works, worrying the skin of his upper lip, and I wonder if he's adopted my habit.

"I have three problems," Tyran says, dropping one leg over her other and turning sideways in her chair. "Torquent is out of land, and I admit, the abatement helps fix the issue, but not until many years in the future. Besides, it's still a gamble. Who knows what condition the land will be in? Torques need solutions now."

"Which is where the Torquent Expansion comes into play," Raider says. "We'll make sure your people have the space they need. In fact, the Southern Territory will sign over the areas you've expanded into. It won't just be borrowed land but fully yours. And with the lamlight, your people can live comfortably while we await the abatement."

"Well, that's the thing. The lamlight is another of my problems."

Raider squints. "How's that?"

"Adlumen controls the production of lamlight. They produce all the cars too." I press my lips together, remembering my time with Chessie touring her car factory. My sister was right—Tyran is jealous of Adlumen's success. How can we resolve anything when Tyran keeps piling on more discontent?

"They also make the advanced Dark lenses and have a superior zucchini crop," Raider mocks, though I'm not sure it's wise to add to her complaints, even in jest.

“Torquent isn’t interested in depending on others for our resources. Especially Adlumen, who’s getting fat with prosperity.” Tyran glares at me, which is silly because I’m far from fat in any sense. I look at Raider, who’s crossing his arms and scowling.

“Meet with the governors and discuss your concerns. They’ve offered multiple times.”

Tyran rubs her bottom lip, hiding her too-big teeth. “I have a better idea, but first, let’s talk about my third problem.”

With a sigh, Raider scoots back in his seat, saying, “Let’s hear it.”

Tyran’s stare intensifies on him. “I informed you of your father’s location. You made me a promise in return—one you didn’t fulfill.”

“But, it is fulfilled. I’m here now.”

“I wanted you sooner.”

“That wasn’t specified in the agreement, and I had other pressing matters—”

“I’m always the most pressing matter,” she grits between clamped teeth, pushing her index finger into the soft leather chair. She leans forward, the charm filled with her loved one’s hair suspended in the air. She’s poised to launch herself at Raider and force him into submission—physically if necessary—but attacking Raider won’t get her what she wants. Soon enough, her composure returns, but the rigid set of her back remains.

“Fine,” she bites out. “You’re here now.” She lifts her chin. “And if you want to avoid a war, *here is where you’ll stay*.”

The room falls into painful silence. Raider’s expression is one of anguish but also acceptance. He expected this, and while it’s not a surprise, I hate seeing him consider her deal. We have a war to prevent, and to that end, there are many things worth sacrificing, but this is going too far. Does she mean to imprison him in Torquent? What exactly does she expect from this arrangement?

As if reading my thoughts, Tyran says, "I'll do anything to keep you here. *Anything*. With or without your cooperation."

"Aunt, *please*." Raider begs, using the familial moniker to draw on her tender side, but I doubt she has one.

She shakes her head, tapping her heeled foot on the hard floor. "Your stay will be as pleasant or nightmarish as you make it, Nephew."

"I have a family. A home. A people. I belong in the South T."

Tyran lifts her pointed chin. "I'm your family. This is your home. You spent time here too."

"Two decades ago!"

Tyran surges to her feet. "I'm tired of doing this alone!" She grips the box around her neck, and the desperation in her words is frightening, as are her wild eyes and full body tremors as she rages. "Mom and Sivil are gone. You're all I have. I need you here with me." Tyran lowers her arms, adopting a relaxed stance while observing the rest of us. "I promise I'll let them all go. The threat of war ends now if you give me your word you'll stay."

"This isn't the way to get me on your side. Quite the opposite."

"I've tried everything else. This is all I have left."

Raider releases an unamused laugh. "You've tried nothing! What about asking me here for a visit without an ulterior motive? What about asking to meet my son?"

Tyran's eyes narrow. "I don't need visits. I don't care about your son." She pauses, and I wonder if she realizes she's gone too far when Raider sucks in a fierce breath, but then she continues, "I just need an heir for Torquent."

"Well, then get yourself a family," Raider says harshly, no sympathy present in his tone.

"I have no interest in children."

"Well, that's obvious," Raider says, curling his lip and looking her up and down. "You have a narrow view of the world and a polluted way of seeing the people in it. We perceive things in a completely different manner—you'd hate me in a week. I don't understand why you want this so desperately."

"It's not fair that I'm alone."

"Not fair? Then make a friend. There was a time when I felt very alone, but it was my choice. Choose to be different."

"I don't want to be different. I just want you. Here. With me. And if you deny me, you know the consequences."

They're locked in a stare-off, each postured for attack —physical or verbal, it's hard to guess. I don't dare move because they might mistake me for a threat and launch my direction. Arrick, however, doesn't have the same survival instinct.

"Let's take this down a notch," he says, standing and putting up placating hands—one aimed at each of them. "We're all friends here. We all want to work this out."

Friends? I recall using that word in Hamo in relation to Tyran, and the group laughed at me. But no one's laughing now, and Arrick seems quite serious. Who's he trying to fool? Tyran? Maybe himself as much as anyone, donning his disarming smile and glancing between the two of them.

Tyran releases a deep, irritated groan that sounds like a cat's low growl. "Your charms may work on simpering misses, Arrick, but after all these years, you should know better than to try them on me." Her eyes snap back to Raider. "What do you require to stay?"

"Nothing. I have no interest in living in Torquent."

"Ugh! Valore's poisoned you against me." Tyran kicks out her foot in frustration, and the thin shoe flies off her foot, sliding to a stop near the door. She bends over and tears off the remaining one, throwing it right at Raider. He catches it in the air, then surprises me by putting on a smile, leaning over, and calmly placing it on the floor.

"You are your own poison," he says, staring up at her from his hunched position. "It leeches from you, seeping from your skin like a festering sore."

Tyran drops both feet on the hard floor with a slap. "You can't say such things!"

"You have no control over the words I speak. I'm not yours yet."

That he says *yet*—putting a conditional clause on the statement—makes my stomach clench. He can't agree to the terms she's asking. *He can't!* But how can he refuse if it prevents a war?

Curses! What are we going to do?

I don't know Raider's plan—or if he even has one—but for now, he seems content to get in as many jabs as possible. "Your minion is dead," he says, striking again. I've become accustomed to his methods—how he drops a comment and waits for the reaction.

Slowly, her teeth appear in an oppressive smile. "I'm not sure to whom you refer, but I have plenty of minions to step into the spot."

"Diggs," Raider clarifies.

Her smile wanes, and she lifts her eyebrows with interest. "I see. However, I didn't control his actions." Raider doesn't even blink at the revelation, and then she asks, "What can I offer to tempt you?"

"I told you. Nothing."

"What if I give you Hamo?" She glances at Arrick, who can't hide his surprise. "I'll abandon the treaty with them, and we'll take them out together. Torquent and the Southern Territory would make great allies. You could control things from Contund instead of Caelum. It's a geographical switch. Barely an inconvenience."

"No," Raider answers.

"She's joking, of course," Arrick says with a forced laugh, but there's no validation from the room—none of us have ever known Tyran to joke. "We have a solid agreement," he continues, but his blue eyes have lost their arrogance and look mystified.

"What does Raider Roil want with a light bubble?" we hear in a boisterous tone, accompanied by a deep laugh.

I didn't hear the door open, but a man has entered the room. He's tall and slender with long dark hair and wears lenses over his eyes—old-school ones, not the transparent upgrade from Adlumen. His voice sounds like a young man's, but his face is tanned and wrinkly, making him look middle-aged. As it stands, I can't guess his age.

"We rodents have little desire for your light pockets," he adds, crossing the room. "Rats and moles like the expansive Dark." He grabs a chair by the neck and drags it with a screech across the floor, showcasing a long scar down his left arm. He stops when he's removed from our group, Tyran included. I get the impression this is how he perceives himself—separate from our nonsense.

He relaxes onto the seat, addressing Raider. "Next, she'll tell you she's breaking up with me." The man puts on an exaggerated frown that morphs into a grin. "Shame about this abatement business. Doesn't seem right them encroaching on our land."

"Casmo. Stop fooling around," Tyran commands. "I'm not pleased. You were supposed to be here hours ago."

Curses! It's Casmo Junius. Like we needed one more complication.

Casmo hears Tyran's complaint, then chuckles, shaking his head in denial. "You keep trying to press me under your thumb, but it will never happen." He turns his attention to the rest of us. "Arrick. Chett. Raider." He nods at each but stops on Raider to ask, "How's your dad?" He delivers the question with a smile, but Raider doesn't respond to the man who put Valore in a Dark prison for three years. I, however, give him the dirtiest look I can muster.

"Where have you been?" Tyran asks, drawing the attention back to her—she doesn't like being without it for long.

"I had business," Casmo replies, not looking her way. And like when Raider told her he had pressing matters, I expect Tyran to insist that she is Casmo's only business, but she stays silent while Casmo turns his head toward me. "Sharade Endrack. I heard you were missing from your cage."

"*Sharade*," Tyran releases my name slowly on a breath, turning her disapproving eyes on me. I expect her calm facade to deteriorate into a rage upon learning I'm not Chessie. Instead, her lips and eyes tighten, and she ponders me with a calculating gleam.

"I might just have to take you back with me," Casmo continues, and it suddenly seems he might be the more significant threat in this room—at least to me. I suck in my upper lip, scraping hard while a horrible chill runs over my skin. His words leave ripples in their wake, but he moves on, asking Tyran, "Did I make it before the big reveal?"

Big reveal? Curses! What more could Tyran have planned?

Her eyes stay on me while she answers Casmo, "You're just in time." Then she turns to Raider. "Would you agree to my terms if I turn over Adlumen's greatest enemy?"

"Right now, Adlumen's greatest enemy appears to be

you," Raider answers.

"I know you want to believe that, but it's not true." She faces one of her bravados. "Bring a table and send in the refreshments."

Curses! Refreshments? Does Tyran think this is a tea party?

We sit in nervous anticipation of what's coming next. Arrick and Chett are a matching pair—each wearing a ghostly pallor on their skin while Tyran's easy dismissal of the truce between their two light bubbles continues to shake them. Raider stares at the door, not making eye contact with anyone. It's a few minutes of silence before they bring in the table, setting it near the door.

And then, he walks into the room, and I nearly fall off my seat.

CHAPTER FORTY-FIVE

Thirty-Two Days Free at 6:30 p.m.

"Dad," I whisper, launching from my chair. Raider's by my side a second later, gripping my arm to keep me in place. I blink to clear my vision because it can't be him. Even so, I ask, "Is it really him?"

"Yes," Raider mumbles, pulling me back onto my chair and taking his too. The entire time, my eyes stay fixed on Dad. He's twenty feet away—not engaging with anyone but focused on his task—unaware his youngest daughter is in the room, freaking out.

Keine Endrack carries a tray full of tall glasses filled to the brim. How odd they're the same sea-green color as the bottle back home he gifted me in my youth. My mind gets stuck on the detail, but it doesn't stay there long because this situation is too weird. Too wrong.

He's dead! He's not supposed to be here, but there he is—across the room at the newly placed table, sliding the tray onto the surface while the glasses tinkle against each other.

"Serve me," Tyran commands, and Dad tenses briefly before picking up a glass, crossing to her, and passing it off to her fingers.

Curses! Not only is he alive, but she's got him acting as her servant!

Tyran nods. "Now, the others."

Dad turns on his heel, silently doing her bidding while contempt rolls from every move and gesture. Maybe the others don't see it, but this man is my blood, and I know his every nuance.

He returns from the table with a glass in each hand. The

gray hair that used to be at his temples and the base of his neck has advanced across his head. His once olive skin is lighter now, but the battle scars on his hands still stand out as he passes off the glasses, giving one to Casmo and Arrick but never making eye contact with them or looking down the line of chairs—never looking at me.

Chett and Raider are next to receive a drink, and I observe Dad's face when he gets nearer me—thin lips and a thin nose that are mostly unchanged. His gaze goes briefly to Tyran's shoe beside Raider's chair. A confused wrinkle appears between his brows, but then it smooths out, and he returns to the table for the final glass.

My glass.

"Your brother is dead," Tyran tells him as he approaches the table. Immediately, she has his attention, and mine too, as something connects in my head. This was the revelation Uncle Diggs wanted to witness. He knew my dad was alive—probably would have told me if I'd gone with him back in Bratus.

"Diggs," Dad says, facing Tyran with my drink held limp in his hand. "How'd he die?"

"I've yet to ask. Maybe they'll tell you."

And then, Dad's walking toward me. His eyes stay on the floor. He seems reluctant to look at any of us, but I can't take my eyes off of him. He lifts the glass when he reaches me, and I take it carefully, unwilling to fumble and bleed for him again. When it's secure, I tell him, "My uncle dove onto my sword."

Dad looks up. Light green eyes unlike any in our family meet mine. I don't know what I expect to see in them. Tears? No, because Dad doesn't cry. Happiness? Longing? He's done terrible things, but he's still my dad, and I feel all those things.

Moisture wells in my eyes, feeling overwhelmed that he's

alive. I yearn for our times together when life was simpler—when I was his little girl with no expectations. I crave to see affection radiate from his face. I ache to feel him rush to me with loving arms.

But nothing like that happens.

Instead, his eyes fill with confusion, and then his expression crumbles altogether. "Arrick!" He flings his hands out, narrowly missing my glass. He can't get away from me fast enough, stomping across the floor. "Your foolish emissary brought the wrong person."

"Well—" Chett starts, but I jump from my chair, rushing toward them and cutting him off.

"Hold up! I'm here because of *you*?" I ask, poking a finger in his direction. He ignores me, but I don't need an answer because the truth is sinking into my heart.

"This isn't the one we wanted. Explain yourself!" he demands of Chett, no longer sounding like the servant in the room but acting like the boss.

Curses! Was it him all along controlling this scenario? Is Tyran his servant, or is he hers?

A quick glance at Tyran finds her bristling at his commanding tone, making it seem less likely he's the one in charge. I'm just not sure, but one thing's clear—there are too many leaders in this room. This situation has the potential to explode if we're not careful. Unfortunately, I'm not in a cautious mindset—not in the least. I just found out I'm in this situation because of my dead dad.

My dead dad who doesn't want me.

It's no different from how it was in my youth. I thought I was over the pain of rejection, but having it established again by the man himself is too much. I fold over, holding my breath and squeezing my eyes shut to control my emotions. I'm seconds from losing it when Raider appears, rubbing my back in comforting circles.

"Tyran asked me to bring Endrack's daughter. I've done that," Chett says, and I lift my head to reengage in the conversation.

"Did you know he was alive?" I ask Chett, who shakes his head. I glance at Arrick, and he reacts the same, moving his head back and forth with surprised eyes. Neither of them knew.

Chett mouths to me he's sorry, though there's nothing to apologize for. His job was to deliver us here. I was the one who insisted on the trade. I'm the one who's not enough. If anyone should apologize, it's me.

A quick look at Casmo confirms he had firm knowledge of the situation. Of course he did. He undoubtedly released Dad to Tyran because Casmo's the closest thing she has to a true ally in this group. But their connection is thin, held together by their depravity. Tyran watches the scene, raising a glass to her tight lips and sipping casually.

"At least if you were going to mess up, you should have brought us a governor," Dad says, shaming Chett. "This one's useless!" He gestures at me.

Useless?

My jaw drops, and the tears I'd contained flow freely. A second later, Raider's tucked me behind him and stepped into Dad's space. "Hey!" Raider bellows, landing a solid punch on Dad's cheek. He staggers back, cupping his face where a trickle of blood runs.

"Raider, no!" I grab his arm, pulling him back. The last thing we need is for them to get into it. But Raider's stronger than me and more determined than I've ever seen him. He gets in Dad's face, and since I'm holding on, I move with him.

"Ten minutes ago, you were just a dead asshole," Raider says. "Now, you're alive and a bigger one than I ever remembered. I'd be happy to put the situation right—return you to your former state. And trust me, this time, it would stick. You'd stay dead, and your words would never hurt her again."

"Raider, please," I say, trying to pull him away. I can't let him get hurt—not defending me. His words mean the world to me—that he's furious about what my dad did, not that he says he'll kill him—and that's why I need him to back down. We still don't know what's happening between Tyran and my dad, and we need to keep cool heads.

Curses! Cool heads. How's that even possible?

I'm ready to punch my dad too. He was alive, and though he knew where I was, he never tried to get me. He abandoned me. Again. He's been out of prison all this time. Did he ever even think of me?

"All I ever wanted was for you to love me," I tell my dad, stepping around Raider, but he follows, refusing to leave my side, and I'm glad of it. I need him as I continue to expose my feelings. "But you only ever cared about Chessie."

"That's because she was the future of Adlumen."

It's not a shocking answer. Still, my heart cracks a little more. "I always knew my place," I mumble. Dad's preferences were never a secret, but I'm filled with a sudden need to understand how deep his indifference toward me goes, and I start by asking, "How did you get out? Was it Diggs?"

Casmo doesn't let my dad speak, laughing as he answers, "Your dad doesn't even know the details of his release. At least, not the real ones."

Casmo's satisfaction gets my dad's attention, but I'm not done. "Warden Ott relayed your request. He gave me a choice to end my life before my prison sentence began." Raider stiffens next to me, but Dad doesn't react. "And it didn't change how I felt about you. Isn't that crazy? For those first few years, I was still yours. But because I chose to live, I met two people who changed my life—Dell Denita and Valore Roil."

"Valore!" my dad spews, grinding his teeth. I knew the name would provoke a reaction, and I'd be lying if I said it wasn't satisfying.

"Yes. Valore Roil—my best friend and someone who opened my eyes to what a despicable man and father you are."

"Of course, he'd call me despicable. He hates me."

"He actually never called you anything. He just showed me a better example."

"You can call me names, but you're just like me," he says, genuinely believing it.

"Mom thinks so too," I tell him. "But even at my worst, I never reached your level."

"I'm curious what you perceive as my level."

"Someone more devoted to a cause than the people they claim to support. Someone who'll destroy everything to win. Someone I never want to be. It took time and suffering, but I can say with conviction I'm nothing like you."

"Your opinion of me is decidedly negative. I can't help but think it's coming from others more than yourself."

"Yeah, you never placed much stock in my mind." I glance away from him. "Though you were probably right. Chessie figured you out faster than I did. Wick had you pegged all along. I mourned you longer than either of them." I tilt my head, trying to see a different future from the one I'm in. "I'd be at your side right now if you'd taken me with you, so I guess I owe you thanks for leaving me in my Dark prison."

"You'd have weighed me down as I made my plans. I didn't need or want you."

My eyes flash to his, and I suck in my upper lip, licking off the tears and biting my skin to prevent more from falling. I take a step back, but then Raider's pulling me away—back to our empty chairs—but I watch my dad the entire way until we stop.

"Hey," Raider says, gathering my attention with a thumb on my chin. When he has my eyes, he tugs until my teeth let go of my lip. "Relax. His words don't matter. Remember? You're on my side, and I'm on yours. No matter what comes our way, we're in this together."

I nod numbly, resisting the urge to take my lip back between my teeth.

"If there's one thing you should know about me," Raider says, keeping his voice low and his black eyes level with mine, "it's that I never abandon those I care about, even when a long-dead relative resurfaces to create havoc."

I snort out a laugh while my chest swells from Raider declaring he cares about me. Then I break into tears, and he pulls me into his side. My head falls against his shoulder, and I let him take my worries. He can have them all. Because he's quickly becoming my greatest source of shelter and strength.

The hurt from my dad's words radiates within, but I vow to let it go. He's here—the man who, for so long, I wanted to love me. But no more will I pine for what could have been. No longer will I wonder why I didn't measure up. I'm moving on from our unhappy relationship. I'm letting it all go.

Twisting in Raider's arms, I look at my dad and watch his expression change. Before, he was angry, but now, he wears a disgusted sneer as he looks between Raider and me—Raider, whose fury over my dad's insults still radiates from his skin, and me, who just decided she no longer cares what Keine Endrack thinks or says.

But Dad never could read a room. He only knows to follow his inclinations, so he ignores the vibes we're putting off, asking, "Really?" He motions between us. "Another of my children has gotten involved with a mole? Where in the Dark did I go wrong?"

That almost provokes a laugh from me. If he wonders where he went wrong, I could surely tell him, but he'd never listen.

Dad spins away from us, going straight to Tyran. "How are you going to fix this?"

"It's not as bad as you're making it out," Tyran says calmly, sniffing her big nose. "I wanted Raider, and he's here. Your daughter was a side note."

"You're wrong. The plan won't work without my daughter—the *right* daughter. This one's not a weapon—she's a tool and barely useful at that. She's not the same caliber as Chessie."

Raider tenses, but I let the words slide off of me, running over my skin and landing at my feet, where I can press their worthlessness into the ground with the soles of my shoes.

Tyran tilts her head, watching me. "I'll admit, I'm slightly disappointed Chessie's not here. I've desired a blade rematch, but it can wait. And curiously, this one might be the better choice for my needs."

"Your needs?" I ask, surprised by the strength in my voice. Seeing my dad was a shock—enough to knock me off course for a bit—but I feel a resurgence of energy, and I'm done waiting to learn what this is about. "Whose plans are these? Yours or his? And what does my sister have to do with it?"

Tyran wears a tight smile while I talk. She pauses when I finish, then turns to my dad. "Refill," she says, lifting her glass and waiting for him to take it. He pauses, glancing again at me, before taking the glass to the table and bringing back a fresh one. Instantly, the dynamic has flipped, and Tyran's in control again. Though even through his tirade, I wonder if she ever wasn't.

"Sit," she commands him, and for the first time, my dad isn't standing, but he keeps his back stiff and eyes trained on her. Then Tyran addresses me, "I appreciate your candidness, and I'm willing to answer."

She lifts her hand and snaps her fingers. Instantly, there are two bravados on Dad, flanking his sides. He peers up at them with some alarm, but it doesn't last long as Tyran tips her chin at me, saying, "I'm glad you took care of Diggs." Dad clenches his jaw as Tyran continues, "Though I guess it happened inadvertently. While it's not in my nature to be grateful, if I were the type of person to give thanks, I'd do it. The man was a bug. I couldn't stand him."

Tyran takes a drink while Dad bristles in his chair.

"Keine Endrack is here because he negotiated his way out of prison. He's been living in Torquent these many years, providing me with information about Adlumen."

Dad doesn't look at me, which I take as a sign she's telling the truth. I'm shocked he's been living among the Torquent trash—the people he despised so heavily in my youth—but not only that, he's been giving them information about our home. Her words bring it all together. It's how she discovered Tesha is a beacon. What other information did he give her while hiding here? He's likely passed on heaps of military intelligence, increasing her confidence in going to war.

"It was valuable at first, but it was too obvious he was trying to lead me down a nefarious path." Dad scowls. "So, I let him think he was directing our course when, really, I guided him onto my path."

Dad's skills lie in forming and carrying out plans, not understanding human nature, so Tyran's words are a complete blow and confusion binds his tongue. Dad considers no one more intelligent than himself and never admits to being wrong, so he shakes his head in denial, but there's doubt in his light green eyes.

"He pretended to be my ally while secretly planning a takeover. He worked to get my bravados on his side, and I instructed them to let him believe he'd won them over." Tyran straightens, finishing triumphantly, "But none of them are with you."

Dad shakes his head some more, but not a word falls from his lips.

"Keine talked incessantly about Chessie, wanting her to come to Torquent so we could settle our differences with a blade challenge where the victor's terms would get instated at the battle's conclusion. Keine declared Chessie would lose to my superior skills, but he believed the opposite—that I would lose. He hoped to ingratiate himself with Adlumen by brokering the means of ending the conflict. Then, he'd lead Torquent, either with governor support or by using my bravados. And eventually, he would use force to take back Adlumen."

"No!" Dad says, trying to stand, but the bravados put heavy hands on his shoulders. "I never—"

"You always!" Tyran bellows, her yellow hair fanning out from her face. "In all your dealings, you seek to use others for your gain. But I was a step ahead and used you for my gain. You've lost while giving me everything I want."

Dad stares at his opponent, considering her words. I see it in his eyes—he's devising his next move—but for now, he's quiet, not wanting to be drawn into saying more than is prudent. Meanwhile, Tyran straightens in her chair. She's tougher than I imagined—more calculating too—making me nervous about delving deeper into her thoughts and plans.

"So, this was your goal?" Raider asks. "Fight Chessie Dirby for control of Adlumen?"

"No. That was his ridiculous plan," Tyran says, indicating Dad. "I let the word spread, but I have no interest in taking Adlumen."

"Did you ever want Periculum?" Raider asks, recalling her demand for that Adlumen city.

"No," Tyran replies, and my shoulders drop with exhaustion. I can barely keep up with her duplicitous stance. Her words and desires rarely match and change faster than Raider's infamous list of attributes.

Understanding her motivations has always been a problem, and it hasn't improved since arriving in Torquent. Bewildered, I ask, "Then, what did you want with my sister?"

"There are two reasons I wanted Endrack's daughter in this room. First, I'm not opposed to Keine's plan of renewing the old way of resolving a conflict, though I don't want Adlumen's land. I want rights to lamlight and car production. And, since my nephew mentioned it, the lenses. I'll let them keep their zucchini secrets for now."

"Which proves you're a fool, thinking this one could serve your needs," my dad says. "She's no soldier."

He has yet even to speak my name. It further proves how little I mean to him—next to nothing, really—and makes my revelation even more vindicating. "My dad's wrong in this as in so many things," I say, addressing Tyran. "Chessie's the better soldier, it's true, except in one discipline. Two weeks ago, I bested my sister with a Torquent blade. So, if you want a legitimate challenge from the Endracks, I'm the best you'll get."

Dad sends an abhorrent look in my direction, but I barely have time to think about it because Tyran nods before saying, "I accept."

Her flippant acceptance stupefies me. A fight with me includes no binding contract with Adlumen—it's not like I can surrender commodity production on the governors' behalf. Tyran knows this. Likely, when she planned a similar fight with my sister, she expected at least one governor in attendance to be Adlumen's mouthpiece. But that's not the case with me, so I'm shocked when she rises, her bare feet slapping the floor as she approaches a bravado, acquiring the Torquent blade sheathed at his waist.

Curses! We're doing this now?

"Wait! Hold up a minute!" Raider says, surging to his feet. "You said you wanted Endrack's daughter in this room for two reasons. What's the other one, Aunt?"

On the precipice of a fight, I don't care about her other reason for wanting Chessie here. It's probably shortsighted, but my mind is on one track—fighting Tyran. I'm willing to do it if that's what's needed. I can defeat her—I know I can—and maybe it will end this mess.

Raider fidgets, waiting for Tyran's answer. I wonder if he's invested in his question or if it's a stall tactic while determining a way out of this fight. Regardless, I stand and move next to him because he promised to be by my side, and there's no way I won't position myself the same for him.

But Raider surprises me, taking my hand and linking our fingers. Tyran and my dad watch, wearing polar expressions of impassivity and loathing.

"I'm glad you asked about the second reason. Your timing is perfect," Tyran says with a smile, and for the first time, there's absolute joy behind her show of teeth. "You see, I wanted a daughter of Endrack to witness her father's death."

Tyran's words don't register. Her firm grip and the mighty swing of the Torquent blade doesn't connect in my mind. Not until it's done, and I'm staring at my dad's head, noting the jagged cuts along his severed throat, and a scream leaves my lips.

CHAPTER FORTY-SIX

Thirty-Two Days Free at 7:15 p.m.

Tyran's death blow is instantaneous.

Dad's gone.

Almost as soon as he reappeared in my life—shocking me to the core by still living—he's gone again.

Only this time, there's no wondering about his fate.

"He's not coming back from that," Casmo says with an unrepentant tilt to his mouth. The bravados push Keine Endrack from his chair, and I blink my attention away, staring at the wall instead of his lifeless body falling to the floor.

The scene is disturbing, but so is my reaction to Dad's death. Where's the sadness and outrage over what's transpired? I feel nothing. And it's troubling because the nothingness feels right. There's no unfinished business between us—nothing I need to know or ask—because his actions were clarifying, and his words evidenced his long-held indifference. I meant nothing to him.

Despite that, I consider the man who, at many points in my life, meant everything to me. Dad gave it all to his cause and got nothing in return—not even people to mourn him. No one in this room is crying. That's what happens when you go after the wrong things. It's where I was headed eight years ago when I followed his plan. But I realized my error, and now, I have meaningful people in my life instead of self-aggrandizement. I've feared abandonment, but I understand now that even alone, I can keep what's paramount—respect for myself.

There's an expanding pool of red on the gray floor.

Seeing what powered Dad's malcontent life draining from him sickens me, so I face Tyran to keep the image from my peripheral vision.

"Finally. A reaction," she says, narrowing her huge eyes on me.

"Is that all you were after?" Raider asks, his hand still holding my limp fingers.

"And you were right," she continues, ignoring him. "You were, indeed, the ideal choice to witness this moment. I'd dare say you're the last of his children to have loved him."

"You're a terrible person," Raider says, lip curling distastefully.

"The man was a pathetic sort who used every cloying trick to enter my good graces. But his dispersal of Adlumen's secrets was exasperating. He distributed information like candy to a child—small rewards for pleasing behavior, but only after long deliberation and much performance by the child. In case you're wondering, I was the child in this scenario." Tyran slaps her bony chest angrily. "It was intolerable. No information was worth maneuvering that man's machinations."

"And in a final display of irritation, you offed him." Raider sways aggressively toward her, and I tighten my fingers to keep him grounded beside me. "Should we all let our emotions lead? Brandish Torquent blades and take each other out?"

"It was more than emotions. He was guilty of many things, both in and out of Torquent—a fact you well know. After all, wasn't Valore's purpose in meeting with Casmo to arrange Keine's death? And yet, you're upset I finished the task?"

"It's your methods I find deplorable. It's your motivations that are disgusting. I hated the guy, and maybe his death was long overdue, but he deserved a formal process through the law."

"I've had years to process his guilt. Today, we held court, and you witnessed his execution."

"While you disguised your purpose? While you secured his family member to feed your vengeance? You call it an execution, but what you did was perform a spiteful murder."

Silence reigns as 'spiteful murder' echoes throughout the room.

Arrick clears his throat. "I agree with Raider," he says, surprising me by going against Tyran. "I have little hope for relations between Torquent and Hamo if this is how you treat your allies."

"Keine was never an ally," Tyran says, passing the bloody sword off to a bravado.

"He lived in Torquent under your protection," Arrick says. "He collaborated with you on common goals. It was an alliance."

"He played me, and I played back. Just don't fool with me, Arrick, and things will be fine."

"Unless the Southern Territory decides they want Hamo and you come after us together," Arrick challenges. I've never seen him articulate his points so clearly—never imagined he'd dare speak to Tyran this way—but she's agitated their pact, and he's doubting her.

"You've murdered another ally, Aunt," Raider says, considering Arrick. "At least, for now, it's only a symbolic death."

"He'll come around." Tyran wipes her hands on a wet towel provided by a bravado, then lowers onto her high-back chair before facing Raider with a mordant smile. "And as for Keine, you can label his death however you like, but I truly see no reason for your discontent. I removed a threat. I provided an opportunity for his daughter to seek your comfort. Accept those gifts and abandon your hypocritical sensitivities."

I jerk forward—for what purpose, I'm not sure—but Raider's grip on my hand tightens, keeping me in place. "Enough!" he yells, his shoulders tense, vibrating with fury. If there was something to kick, he'd surely do it, but instead, he takes a breath, relaxes his fingers, and says, both deep and menacing, "Your callousness makes further negotiations pointless. I doubt you'd comply with any points we agreed upon."

"If there's the slightest chance I would, you'd take it. No one wants war." Tyran tsks. "Least of all me."

"Is that true?" Raider releases me, walking until he's in front of Tyran, towering over her. The bravados tighten their formation, but Raider's not intimidated. "You antagonized Casmo. You threatened Arrick. You murdered an Adlumian. It seems all you've done since our arrival is push for a fight with no real preference for who your opponent is." Raider shakes his head. "But alright, I'll take you at your word. Let's have this out. Full transparency without embellishment. *What do you want*?"

"You."

I wait for elaboration that doesn't come while that single syllable dangles like a noose.

I consider her demand from the viewpoint of the light bubbles and Dark territories. If Raider joined Tyran, would it improve their situations, or would he become another minion under her control? Would he be a symbol of her influence more than a contributing leader in her land? The answer seems obvious—I doubt it would end well for him—but I can understand how the others might hope he'll accept.

Raider releases a heavy sigh. "And in return?"

"I'll let you have the first option on the abatement."

He shakes his head. "I'm a mole. I don't care about abated land."

"You might someday." Tyran shrugs. "Plus, I can protect your family."

"I can protect my own family."

Tyran narrows her eyes. "I'll open gas trade with Adlumen," she offers next. "It's something they've always wanted."

Raider laughs. "We figured it out. The South T provides them with plenty." Raider's response time is impressive. He has a reply available the minute she fires off each offering.

Tyran huffs. "I'll discuss a season of peace with Adlumen."

"A season of peace? Does that mean you'll postpone war or end the idea entirely?"

"I'm undecided."

"I'll not bring the South T under your umbrella to rule."

"Okay. Then just you will come. Leave the South T to someone else."

"Abandon my people? What kind of man do you think I am?"

Raider's doing so well debating her points. I want to stand up and cheer until Tyran's eyes fall on me. "I know what kind of man you are." She pauses, tilting her head to look down her big nose at me. "I'll withdraw my challenge from Endrack's daughter and discuss options for lamlight, lens, and car production with the governors instead of fighting it out." Then she draws out, "If. You. Stay."

Raider goes silent. I figure he's preparing a real putdown, but it goes on too long, and when he looks back at me, I hate the conflict in his eyes. I remember his promise to stay by my side and realize he's considering doing this. He doesn't want to back out on his promise to me. But this isn't what the promise was about! He's supposed to stand in my corner while I fight—not prevent the fight entirely.

"No! He has no right to overturn that agreement," I say, surging forward and stopping at Raider's side. "The deal is between us. You threatened my sister by demanding she come here, and then, regardless of how despicable the man was, you killed my dad. It's my *right* to fight you."

Raider watches my impassioned speech, licks his lips, then turns back to her, declaring, "As she says." The words sound pained, and the emotion behind them transfixes me.

"Fine. Let's have it done so we can return to negotiations." Tyran stands, nudging us out of the way and showcasing her bare-footed dominance. "You have ten minutes to compose yourself, daughter of Endrack."

Suddenly, the challenge isn't only going forward but happening right now. I attempt to find a steady nerve in my body, but I'm shaken by all that's transpired. Still, I'm able to squeak out, "Okay. What are the rules?"

Tyran brushes back her yellow hair. "Where have you fought that you thought there'd be any?"

Okay, then, no rules.

"This isn't happening now. Shar needs rest," Raider says. "We were awake most of the night, and there's no point in watching her quick and needless death."

"Thanks a lot," I grouse.

Raider turns to me. "That's not—"

"I'm willing to postpone our meeting," Tyran interrupts, sounding as if we're gathering for a social event, not to rip each other apart with serrated swords. "But if we're not fighting now, I'd like to continue our negotiations toward your staying with me." She waves a hand at Raider. "That is, if *you're* not too tired."

"You're running out of things to tempt me with."

"No," Tyran says with a toothy smile. I'm learning to hate the expression. It's prophetic. It's what comes before she reveals something and everything falls apart. And I'm sure I'm right again when she adds, "I'm just saving the best for last."

"I'm overjoyed. You already offered me Adlumen's greatest enemy, then dispensed with his head before we struck a deal. Are you going to cut off Casmo's pinky? Then offer me his hand and promise five fingers?" Raider scoffs.

"Admittedly, the manner of Keine's death was primarily for my satisfaction." Tyran's eyes graze over me. "But what I'm offering now is something entirely different. And something entirely for you."

"Fine. I'll bite. What more could you possibly offer me?"

"What you've always wanted."

"Your resignation?" Raider asks wryly.

"The person who killed your beloved wife," Tyran says, knocking the wind from my lungs as my eyes turn to a stunned Raider. "What is that name worth to you?"

I imagine it's worth a lot, though Raider doesn't answer.

Death is Tyran's calling card. It's also her bargaining chip, only this time, she's using an old death—unfeelingly promising to seal Raider's never-healed wound in exchange for his compliance.

Raider claims that distraction and inexperience made him responsible for Kally's death, but I've always known his beliefs aren't entirely sound. Sorrow has a way of polluting memories. Guilt drives people to cling to blame. Even if a person's actions don't cause harm, inaction can be just as problematic.

I understand what this knowledge is worth to Raider, and the desperation on his face confirms it. Except for securing a safe future for his people and family, it's everything. Tyran knows it too—her teeth press against the back of her lips, tight with anticipation. She's so close to what she wants. I've seen this blind confidence in others. She's as sure he'll agree as she is that what she's doing is right.

Casmo waits on what will happen with aloof interest, staring at his hands while he picks the edge of his finger, but Arrick and Chett watch me. I don't fully grasp what this would mean for Hamo, but they look terrified and maybe hopeful. As is typical, Arrick's expression leans toward optimism, while Chett's is rooted in pessimism. The second man stares at me, unblinking, and I realize he's correct where Tyran is concerned—she creates plenty of reasons for us all to be afraid.

"So, what do you say?" Tyran asks, the silence proving too much for her. "Do we have an agreement?"

But Raider surprises me, pulling out of his stupor and shaking his head. "I don't trust you and wouldn't believe any name you gave me."

"Except I have proof. I have witnesses."

"Fine, then. Produce the witnesses."

"I want your agreement first." Tyran lifts her chin. "You must promise to stay in Torquent when the information I provide proves true."

Raider rubs the top of his head—fast and then slow. "What does your vision of 'staying' look like?"

Curses! Will Raider really do it?

Kally was his world, but is discovering the one responsible for her death worth risking the Southern Territory? In his right mind, Raider would say no, but he's not in his right mind. Understandably so.

"Since you're against combining our lands, you will turn the Southern Territory over to Imily or Stryke. You'll live here and prepare to take over when I'm gone. You can bring your son if you must. But you'll spend ninety percent of your time in Torquent, the expansion, or any abated land we obtain."

"You want me to leave my home and yank my son from his family?"

"This will become your home," Tyran says, stepping toward him. "I will become his family."

"I won't make you happy, Aunt. I'm not my mother. I can't replace her."

Tyran purses her lips, considering his words, but it doesn't last long. "Say yes," she tells Raider. "You don't want to see where this negotiation goes from here."

"How much further are you willing to go?" Raider asks, looking Tyran over and taking in the rest of the people in the room. "I'm sure you'd do almost anything to get your way. You've done quite a few things already."

Tyran clears her throat. "I'm a determined woman."

Raider nods. "When Dad disappeared, you offered to help me find him. But the offer was fake because you knew where he was, didn't you?"

While she doesn't admit to it, her silence is confirmation enough. I bite my cheek, appalled Tyran could do such awful things and hurt so many people.

"I can recall every time you reached out to assure me there were no new leads. The news killed me!" Raider yells, clutching his chest. "But all you cared about was advancing your plan. Did you think it would ingratiate me if you were instrumental in saving him?" He shakes his head. "I could have had him back sooner, but I never came to you. So, you left him there to rot."

"Valore took her from me," Tyran seethes, her bulging eyes framed by her yellow hair.

"So, you took him from me? And punished my family through our years of separation. Did it feel good to have your revenge?" Raider releases a mirthless laugh. "And your crowning achievement was positioning me to lead a phony prison rescue. Did you sit in your cushioned chair and laugh at my useless efforts?" He throws a frustrated hand toward the overstuffed seat before growling out, "No wonder I so easily found a willing guard."

"You should have been here with me all along."

"You made being here impossible." Raider radiates anger, and I'm afraid he's approaching his breaking point. "Mom tried to visit, but you pressured her, and each time was more hellish than the last. You made her hate this place."

Tyran shakes her head. "He did that."

"No. He didn't. Sivil chose a life with Valore."

Tyran stares at her nephew. "And she left Torquent and me behind."

"Yes. My mom didn't pick you. And now you're following the same pattern with me as you did with her—forcing us to stay near you. Is that all you know? Is your only approach for keeping us close to harm those we love until we fall into line?"

"Whatever is necessary."

"At least it's the truth," Raider says, shaking his head with remorse. "After all these years, the thing I remember most about you is how much you claimed to love my mother. But you trample your devotion underfoot. First, by imprisoning her husband, and now, by seeking to separate her son from his child."

"I said you could bring him!"

I wince from Tyran's shrill declaration while Raider leans into her. "I would never bring him here... to your light bubble of horrors." He shakes his head miserably. "How long have you known about the person responsible for his mother's death?"

Tyran opens her mouth, but nothing comes out.

"Trying to think of the best answer to get what you want?" Raider taunts. "It appears as if you had a hand in that too. Did you order her death?" He chokes out the question. No matter their differences, it's unthinkable she'd directly harm his wife. Then again, if it got her closer to her goals.

"No," she says, and the declaration is firm, so I want to believe it, but like Raider, I trust nothing she says. "Do you want the name?"

"No," Raider answers without delay.

"Wait!" My voice echoes through the room, and they all turn to me, but I look only at Raider. "You should do it."

"What?" he asks, staring at me with confusion.

"You need the name before we begin the challenge," I say, motioning between Tyran and me. "And we've yet to outline the terms of our fight. You must know I can't make Adlumen production agreements. I'm no governor and don't have their proxy." Tyran nods dismissively. "But I want it agreed that if I win, Raider's under no obligation to uphold his promise."

"No, Shar," Raider says, clasping my wrist while his dark eyes plead with mine. "Don't make this about me."

"It's not," I say, though my words aren't entirely true. "She took my father, threatened my sister, and imprisoned my best friend." Though, my relationship with Valore wouldn't exist without her actions, which is too strange to think about right now. "I want nothing for myself and merely hope to keep those I care for safe and happy. So, if I win, Tyran will leave Valore alone, not challenge Chessie, and void Raider's promise."

"What do you envision qualifies as a win?" Casmo asks, breaking his long silence.

I clear my throat. "Well, there are no rules, right? So, I think there's a clear indicator. The winner is the one who's not in a pool of blood on the floor." I can't look at my dad when I say it—though he's still right there—but I glimpse Raider and the horrified look on his face. Maybe it's a gruesome description of what will transpire, but no one can claim I'm naive.

Tyran looks me over—not with admiration, but there's subtle curiosity in her gaze. "You're awfully confident in your skills."

Am I? Enough that I don't plan on dying today? Enough that Raider will never need to submit himself to ruling beside her? Yes. I trust my skills enough to believe those things, but I'm not stupid enough to think she doesn't believe she's equally capable.

"As are you," I counter, and Tyran nods. "I guess we neither would be keen to battle if we weren't certain the outcome would go in our favor."

"Let's go then. Raider will give me his promise, and I will give him the name. After you're dead, he'll stay here with me."

"Sounds good. Except after *you're* dead, he's free to return to his family in the South T."

"We've already established you're not fighting now," Raider tells me. "You've barely slept the last few days. Shock and adrenaline are the only things keeping you going."

I twist my fingers together, tilting my head to look at him. "Maybe those are the best fuels for doing this." It's not like I want to do it, but waiting until tomorrow only gives me more time to freak out—for the reality of fighting Tyran and taking a life to sink in. Uncle Diggs falling on my sword was terrible. I can't imagine purposely doing that to someone. I tried it once with Evans and failed. Granted, I'm better trained now, but I'm not Tyran. I can't walk across a room and lob a man's head clean off.

Again, I avoid looking at my dad, but knowing he's there

is what gives me the courage I need. Tyran will not stop. It's not in her. Going through with this challenge is the best course of action, and I'm equal to it. And if, by chance, it doesn't go my way, maybe the connections I've made this last month will be enough to cast Tyran in a bad light. Perhaps I'll be the catalyst for Hamo turning on her.

"If it's rest she needs, I have no objection," Tyran says. "Tomorrow's as good as today. I've waited thirty years for my sister's son to be at my side. I can wait another day."

"I don't need another day. Ten minutes will suffice."

Her prominent nose flares before she pushes out, "Done. In ten minutes, Raider will have his name, and you'll get your fight."

"Oh. There's one more thing," I say. Tyran looks weary of my requirements. Even so, she waits on me without comment. "During those ten minutes, remove my dad's body and clean up the floor."

CHAPTER FORTY-SEVEN

Thirty-Two Days Free at 7:45 p.m.

"Shar, what are you doing?" Raider requested a place for the two of us to speak privately, so two bravados escorted us across the hall, shutting us inside a small room with a round table and no chairs. I lean against the table's edge and answer, "I'm doing what I came here to do. Fighting Tyran was high on the list of possibilities."

"Yeah. Because of Tyran's demented whims, not a wild bid on your part to keep me free."

"*Wild bid*?" I suck in my upper lip, frowning. I hate that he's accusing me of making errant choices on the fly. That's how I used to be, but not how I am now. This is a worthy plan, but maybe he doesn't trust I can do it. "You believe I'll die, just like Tyran does."

"I didn't say that." Raider tugs his sleeves, twisting the fabric between his fingers. "I came to Torquent to prevent a battle, but instead, I've created one—for you."

"You created nothing. I volunteered. Tyran's repeatedly hurt my family and yours, and today, she'll answer for it. I won't let it be otherwise. And additionally, she's going to tell you what you've long wanted to know."

"Shar, I can never agree to what she's asking. I can't live in Torquent! Even if—" he trails off.

"Even if it means finding out what happened to Kally." I bend to see his eyes. "Raider, I know it's important to you."

"It is, but—" He steps away, pausing before throwing his leg forward to kick the wall, leaving a dent. The divot makes me smile, even as he continues, "By the Dark, I don't like this.

I don't want you to fight her."

I approach, putting my hand on his shoulder. He's steady under my fingers, while there's a slight tremor in my hand. He can't know I'm nervous about what's coming, so I remove my hand and pace away from him.

"This is the way important things get decided, and I'm not opposed to renewing the old ways to resolve our conflict," I say, mimicking Tyran's low voice. She really is a ridiculous woman—ridiculously scary. "It's sort of true, though, isn't it? Whether in light bubbles or Dark territories, Dad was always going on about leaders battling for position. It's what they do."

"Yeah, but you're not a leader, and you're not the South T's paladin. Please withdraw."

The title makes me smile again—my levity an odd by-product of this discussion. "But in a way, *I am* your paladin. I pledged myself to you and your dad's cause. Remember?"

"I release you from your pledge," he says stiffly, refusing to feel light about this.

"Well, Adlumen was once my home, and it's where my family lives. Also, they're your ally. So, think of me as *their* paladin."

"I think you need to forget that word." Raider rubs his eyes around the edge of his lenses. "Chessie wouldn't like you taking her place."

"Chessie would agree with me."

"No, she—"

"Yes, Raider, she would. It's better I'm here and not her because—" I pause, but there's no reason to keep it a secret from him. "Because she's pregnant."

"Pregnant?" He runs a hand over his short hair. "I mean, that's great, but—"

"It doesn't make her a ready warrior."

"No, it doesn't." He groans. "Knowing that, many things over the last few weeks make a lot more sense."

"I bet. Anyway, no one knows."

"Evans doesn't know?" Raider asks snarkily.

"Of course, Evans knows." I roll my eyes. "But no one else does. Well, except Chett." Raider gives me an impatient look, and I throw my hands up. "Oh, my word, he guessed!"

Raider grins, and then, a chuckle breaks from his lips. I grin back, wanting to pump my fist for finally breaking him. Maybe now his mood has lifted, we can get somewhere.

Heading to the corner, Raider leans against the wall and slides down until he's sitting on the floor, his arms braced on his knees. "Oh, Shar. This sucks."

"We knew it would." I join him, sitting sideways and facing him. "You understand, don't you? I couldn't let her come here—ride that bumpy road and face this stressful situation. With what happened to my dad, I know I made the right choice. I'm glad she didn't see that gruesome sight."

Raider twists to face me, cupping my shoulder. "Yeah, but I'm sorry you did." Placing his hand behind my neck, he pulls me forward and surrounds me in his warm arms. "I don't like this one bit."

"You've said that before," I say, my words muffled in his shoulder. "It's not ideal, but I'm oddly calm about it."

"Please understand, I'll do whatever is necessary to keep you safe, even if it means jumping into the fight myself."

"I don't think that's in the rules."

"Tyran says there are no rules," he adds, and his grip on me tightens. His words relax me, and I soften against him.

"Trust me, Raider. Valore trained me well."

"I trust you explicitly, which is something I never considered when pulling you from that pit a month ago."

"Because you don't forgive," I say, remembering Hamo when he told me he was dependable but unforgiving.

"I think I lied about that," he says, pulling another smile from me. It's a pleasant moment, and then, the door swings open, revealing our two bravados. Raider helps me from the floor, and they escort us back into the great room.

My dad is gone. The blood is gone, but a pink circle remains. I guess when something ghastly happens, you can only make so much of it go away.

I've been in a bubble with Raider, so it's strange to be back with the group. Chett and Arrick look distraught, as if everything is already lost, including my life. I want to reassure them, but Chett won't make eye contact, and Arrick watches me with sad eyes, shaking his head in dismay. Casmo looks detached. I doubt he even left the room during Dad's clean-up. The thought makes me shiver. Tyran no longer wears her formal outfit with the click-clack heels she threw at Raider, but she paces the room in white athletic gear that matches the walls.

"We still doing this?" she asks, but the question isn't for me. She's asking Raider because he's the one who matters. It makes me eager. I can't wait to teach her something about myself.

We still doing this? Yes, we are.

But Raider's response differs from the voice in my head. "Shar says we are," he replies, giving me ownership of what's about to happen.

"But you'll abide by the agreement?" Tyran presses, petting her yellow hair, which hangs over her white shirt.

Raider all but growls, "Shar says we will." It nearly makes me laugh, but I'm suddenly sober because, with the contract in place, Raider's owed a name.

I wonder if she'll demand more from us before giving it

—like signatures on a written contract or Raider in chains so he's physically bound to keep his word. I wouldn't put anything past her. I'm also concerned we may have to coerce her to speak, repeating our promises or squeezing the information from her in increments. We're headed into the unknown, so imagine my shock when the secret is revealed through one simple statement—and not from Tyran.

"It was me," Chett says, finally lifting his eyes to the room.

"Uh, what?" I pause, my brow dipping in confusion. "It was you?" I ask, trying to figure out what I'm missing because Chett's words make no sense.

"It was me," he repeats, quieter, and then, there's silence.

Curses! What's happening right now?

My eyes move around the room. Only Raider and I seem surprised by the comment. Tyran and Casmo look smug about their pre-knowledge, but my attention sticks on Arrick's sad, knowing expression. This isn't news to him, and things click together in my mind. "This is what you were talking about in Hamo," I say, processing the thought out loud. I look at Raider. "When I overheard them in the halls late at night. Remember?"

Raider doesn't acknowledge my question but continues staring at Chett while displaying an array of emotions: confusion, loss, hurt, anger, and betrayal.

I recall the conversation—a secret that was too much for Chett, and Arrick's encouragement to stay silent. Chett felt guilty about what happened to Kally. That he *killed* Kally. I swallow hard because the puzzle is together, but now the picture is coming into view, and it's ugly.

"You heard us?" Chett asks me, and I nod. I mean, yeah, I heard, but is that the most important thing right now? He just admitted to killing Raider's wife. Didn't he? Needing to clarify I haven't gotten something wrong, I ask, "What exactly did you do, Chett?"

"I'm responsible for what happened to Kally," Chett mumbles, tucking his chin and eyeing the floor.

Responsible. Okay. Maybe it's not as bad as it seems. This could be a misunderstanding.

Raider makes a noise deep in his throat that I can't quite identify. If he was dumbfounded by Chett's declaration, it only lasted a moment. There's no array in his expression now. It's pure rage. "You killed my wife?" he asks, and it sounds like he's in a tunnel—his voice quiet and far-off.

"I didn't mean to, but yes." Chett nods. The motion is slow but sure, and then, he looks toward the bravados. Oddly, I think he now views them as a source of safety.

"No." Raider shakes his head and begins pacing in place before stopping and pointing at Chett. "We mourned together. We lost them... *together*."

Them. Chadd and Kally. Their respective losses during a similar timeframe cemented their friendship.

Chett inspects the gray floor while telling a stunned and angry Raider, "It was supposed to be Valore, but Kally... Kally... well..."

Curses! Supposed to be Valore?

Chett can't find his words, and while I have some, Raider has absolutely no problem with his. "You son of a bitch!" He lunges forward, but the bravados are primed to intervene and move in fast, grabbing Raider's shoulders and holding him in place. "You pretended to be my friend!" Raider struggles to get free.

"The friendship was real," Chett says. "I never meant to harm Kally."

A disgusted sound spews from Raider's mouth. "No, you meant to *murder* my father!"

"It wasn't—" Chett tries, but Raider snorts, turning his

head away. Chett takes a few breaths before trying again. "There's more to it." His eyes plead for understanding.

Raider shakes his head, unwilling to listen. Unwilling to look at Chett. I can't blame him. Chett's eyes move to me, and I can't hide my disappointment. He offered so much during a time when I needed it. He seemed heroic, willing to take in the unworthy Endrack daughter without a home. I thought him selfless, but his purposes were selfish, clinging to me since he felt we were kindred spirits.

But the thing is, while I've done horrible things, I did them with complete transparency. Meanwhile, Chett operated in the shadows, and his cruel secrets destroyed him from within. He's a broken man, and I don't know if anything can fix him. I'm not the answer, though he believed I was.

"Let me tell you why," Chett says to me since Raider won't look at him. His eyes beg for a chance, but I'm honestly not sure what to say.

"They've heard enough," Tyran says, lifting her hand to declare the conversation finished. I don't argue for more of Chett's explanation, and Raider remains quiet. The desire to learn more comes from the most unlikely of sources.

"No," Casmo says, standing up. "I want to hear what Chett has to say."

"I say we're done, so we're done!" Tyran exclaims.

"You don't decree my choices. I've supported you through many campaigns, but you don't hold court over me, and I won't have information kept from me."

"Then we'll discuss it privately."

Casmo tilts his head, taking in Tyran's defiant stance. "This gets revealed now for us all to hear." His tone is such that Tyran doesn't utter the slightest complaint. Casmo turns away from her. "Go on, Chett."

Chett nods, and a glimmer of relief flashes over his face.

"I always believed myself a moral person, but I ignored my ideals out of fear. I made terrible choices and lived with the aftermath."

"Don't ease your conscience through confession. If you're going to talk, give us the facts instead of a whimpered tale of woe." Raider tugs against the bravado's grip, but it does no good. I'm sure if he could reach Chett right now, he'd tear him apart.

But Chett's in his head and continues talking with no regard for Raider's demand. "I've lived too long with fear. Fear of being discovered. Fear of what I've done and what kind of person it makes me. Fear of Tyran and her reach and influence. And now, I've lost one of my best friends."

I feel Raider's agitation as he fidgets beside me, knowing Chett's words can't mend anything. All they'll do is cause more anger and trigger more feelings of betrayal.

"Chett," I say, hoping to direct the conversation so he'll reveal what's needed. "I understand your regret. It's awful to live with the choices we make that hurt others."

"I know you understand. That's why we would be perfect together, but even that's ruined now." He runs a fist under his nose.

We would in no way have been perfect, but his statement confirms the reason for the kinship he felt toward me. It's true, I tried to kill Evans, and I know what it's like to be led by another—I bite my lip, hating the reminder of who I was—but Chett's grasping for a lifeline, and I can't be that for him. I need to be here for Raider. Raider's what matters, and I need to help him through this.

"Please, Chett, tell us how it happened."

He nods, dropping his eyes to the floor. "Tyran knew I had special training with poison. She wanted Valore dead and said she'd kill my dad and brother if I didn't do the job."

"Tyran," I repeat. She's been blunt about her hatred for Valore, so when she doesn't deny Chett's claim, it's easy to determine he's telling the truth.

"And then I failed," Chett adds.

"But, you didn't *fail*. You just messed up." Raider's growl accompanies another worthless yank against the bravados' hold.

"You're right." Chett rubs his chin, fingers quivering. "I returned to Hamo and learned Valore was still alive. I was afraid but also relieved. Then, I heard about Kally, and I felt sick. I never wanted to hurt anyone, and learning I'd hurt someone innocent—"

"Killed!" Raider yells, and Chett flinches.

Fingers dropping from his chin, Chett's big shoulders hunch over as he continues, "Yes. That's what I did. And then, Tyran punished me for failing to kill her intended target."

"By killing your brother," I say.

Chett nods. "Dad should be dead too, but he was larger, and the poison didn't work as fast. Tyran had them use the same poison that killed Kally, and I knew the counteractant. My father lives, but he's a fraction of who he once was. He'll never live a full life. Because of me."

The pessimism. The sadness. I understand it now. Chett's dad is not the only one who'll never live fully. My heart aches to sympathize, but I can't, knowing about his attempt on Valore and his part in Kally's death. Chett's actions are a betrayal of the highest order, especially after feigning ignorance all these years. I wouldn't blame Raider for anything at this moment.

I'm surprised Raider's voice remains steady as he says, "Tyran's always hated Dad for taking away her sister. She always wanted him dead, but at some point, her goal changed because the only thing better than killing him was using him to get closer to me." Raider's attention moves to Casmo. "And, I'm guessing at this next part, but Tyran asked you to detain my dad when he came to the Desert Territory. It wasn't that he offended you. Putting him in prison was a favor for Tyran."

"Not a favor," Casmo says. "I owed her for something else, but yes, that mostly sums it up."

"Were you supposed to kill him?" Raider asks.

"No. Just put him away for as long as she needed."

"Yeah. And keep your mouth shut about it," Tyran says.

Casmo shrugs his slim shoulder. "It's nothing Raider didn't figure out on his own. It's not my fault your obsessions have caused you to operate transparently."

The word Casmo uses strikes at something deep inside of me. How many times did my love turn into an obsession? My dad. Raden. Chessie even accused me of doing the same with Valore. It's easy to be blinded when you get in so deep. She and I have acted similarly, and the realization makes a chill run up my back.

"When did you find out?" Raider asks Arrick.

The ordinarily energetic man looks exhausted, grimacing. "About a year after."

"And you thought it was better not to tell me?"

"You were both suffering. I didn't want to add to it."

"How noble," Raider says, glaring at Arrick, who's wise enough not to react. Emotions are high, and we're all poised for the next painful revelation—whatever it may be.

"Well, now that everyone hates each other, are you satisfied with Chett's explanation, Casmo?" Tyran asks.

"I am. It's better this way."

"Not for me," she says, her big eyes bearing down on Raider. "But we've struck an agreement. You got your name, and now, I get my fight." She brushes past Casmo, going to one bravado who holds a long box storing a set of Torquent blades. "You could have prevented this situation years ago by coming to me when I asked."

While Chett committed the repulsive deed, Tyran spearheaded it, and Raider is furious she's blaming him for the results. Rage emanates from him as he declares, "I need no more didactic lectures from you. I'd rather just kill you."

"Well, stand in line!" Tyran bellows, approaching me with two blades. "After she's dead, we'll decide how to resolve our differences."

"If she dies, there will be nothing to resolve. I'll hate you with my last breath."

"Raider!" I gasp, breathing heavily and silently begging he says nothing he'll regret.

But, instead of going quiet, he adds, "I'm nearly there already."

"Regardless, you'll be in Torquent. I don't care how you feel about me."

Stepping up to Raider, I put my hands behind my neck to remove Squatty's necklace. "Hold this for me?" I ask as much for a distraction as necessity.

Raider takes it and puts a hand on my arm. "I don't want you to do this. I can make a different deal with her. You don't have to fight."

I'm grateful he's not telling me what to do. He's not demanding or using anything I care about to force me to change my mind. He's stating his opinion. He's giving me options. He's respecting me, and I love him for it.

I put my hand over his and squeeze. "I came here to fight for my sister, but I'll gladly fight for you as well."

"It should be me, not you."

"I don't think that option's on the table. Your aunt wants

you too much to fight *you* to the death." I smile and step forward, putting my hand on his cheek. "You really are a beautiful man, and it's more than how you look. You're good to your very core. And not just because you'd stop this if there was an honorable way to do it, but because you'll let me fight because it's what I need to do. You really are more like your dad than I ever imagined."

I lean in and kiss his cheek. When I pull back, I smile. "I kissed Raider Roil. Again. At least I didn't attack you this time."

Raider puts his hand on the spot and rubs as tears gather on his black lashes.

"Hey," I say, dropping my hand and stepping back. I can't get bogged down by his emotions. I need my swagger for what's coming. "I'm not afraid. I have a purpose for being here. Whether it's helping Chessie or you, it makes no difference. I'm honored to fight for you both."

I spin, finding the others watching me curiously, but my eyes settle on Tyran as I ask, "You ready for me to show you a thing or two?"

"Your confidence borders on annoying," she responds.

"My dad was an easy target," I say, my voice turning hard. "You'll find I'm not."

Tyran gives me a Torquent blade. Unlike Sivil's, hers has the hand hilt guard I'm accustomed to. She doesn't allow me to choose my preferred weight, but this one's no C. The sword is heavy with a wide blade, and I'd guess it's an A. My muscles will feel every strike two-fold.

I take my first posture, holding the stance through the instant ache that appears in my shoulder. I'm determined Tyran won't see me flinch. I'll stay in my battle stance until I pass out if need be, but that's not what happens. Tyran chooses her posture, and a second later, we fly into motion.

CHAPTER FORTY-EIGHT

Thirty-Two Days Free at 8:30 p.m.

Tyran comes down hard with the heavy sword. I block her swing but can't counter since I barely have the strength to lift the blade. She grins at another win. She's three to my one, but my mind clings to the one. If I can best her one time, I can do it again when it counts. I mean, as it stands, we're both bleeding, though neither of us is in danger of dying.

I have the knowledge and skill to beat Tyran—this, I know—but I had more confidence in my weary body than is warranted.

It's my turn to choose the starting posture, and although it shows weakness, I pop my arm and lift the sword in the San Vive. A smile twitches on the edge of Tyran's mouth, and she takes a moment—making me suffer in waiting—before matching my posture.

With a relieved sigh, I turn my back on her and walk to a chair. Dropping the sword, I bend over and gasp for breath. I needed the break. I don't know what I'd have done if she'd rejected San Vive.

Died probably, a voice in my head tells me.

Great. Just great.

I glance at Tyran from my bent position. She's barely breaking a sweat.

"You okay?" Raider asks, crouched next to me.

"The sword's just so damn heavy," I puff out.

"We'll get you a lighter one."

"No!" I grab his arm so he can't move. "A lighter one will

give me even less of an advantage."

"Maybe, but at least you'll be able to pick it up," he says, not hiding his frustration.

My eyes tighten to keep his words at bay. I can't let them in. They'll only hinder me.

"Dammit! I'm sorry," he says, pulling me against him. I'm slick with sweat, but he holds me close. I'm so tired I could fall asleep right here without issue. It's not a fantastic realization. Maybe Raider was right—I'm too worn out to be effective. Or maybe Tyran's right—I'm not good enough.

No. No! I'm capable. I just need to catch my breath.

And then I look over, and in the doorway, I discover something I never imagined seeing in this Torquent room: my brother, Wick, my brother-in-law, Evans, and in the middle of them is Chessie.

Curses! What are they doing here?

My fatigue evaporates, replaced with an urgency to get them out of here as quickly as possible. I'm in a position to keep them from harm, and they've just walked into it!

I push from Raider's arms, abandoning him and the Torquent blade to advance on the Adlumen group. Absurdly, I note my sister has shown up with her ever-present jacket. In this tense situation—and in the sweltering heat—she's arrived in the enemy's lair with a jacket slung over her arm. Yep, that sums her up nicely.

Stopping before her, I demand, "You need to go home." Chessie's brow rises, and it only takes a moment to realize why. I sounded like the Sharade of our youth, ordering my sister around like no one else dared. And strangely, right now she feels more like my sister than at any other time since we've reconnected.

"I'm the one who was actually invited to be here," Chessie counters, bringing me back to the moment.

"Things have changed. You should have stayed away!"

"Chessie Endrack," Tyran croons, sashaying toward my sister.

"Dirby," Chessie corrects blandly.

"How pleasant. After I'm done with your sister, I can discuss commodity production and abated land with my new Adlumen emissary."

"Your fight is with me," Chessie says, tightening her fist to keep her hand from moving to the scar on her shoulder. I've seen my sister do it enough to know it's a habit, but she refuses to fall prey to her tell in front of the one who bestowed it.

I appreciate her bravery. I do. But Chessie doesn't know what she's walked into.

"I'll meet you another time since I already have a willing and capable opponent. Just let me finish up."

"Finish up?" Chessie asks.

"Yes. When your sister's dead, we'll talk."

"Dead!" Chessie shrieks, her brown eyes widening. "What kind of fight is this?"

"An unpleasant one," I deadpan.

"Are you finished with San Vive?" Tyran asks. "You seem to have gotten your spunk back."

I don't reply but go for my blade.

Tyran's right. As much as I hate that they're here, Chessie's arrival has given me the energy resurgence I desperately needed. But maybe it's more than needing energy —possibly my sister's a reminder of my purpose. Many people are depending on me, including the little secret in Chess's belly.

I feel the sword's weight in my hand, willing it to be lighter—if not a physical change, at least a mental one. I close my eyes, returning to my time in Aunty's Cellar, listening to Valore's voice telling me how to move and what to expect.

In the Dark, I lost my eyesight, but I also lost my fear. I learned to battle my demons in the Dark, and now I've returned to fight a real-life demon in the lighted world. Vowing to keep my focus, I lift my eyelids, and the light returns. Turning around, I imagine the metal in my hand is feather light—a beautiful tool to carve a safe place for us all.

I move my limbs, taking on the graceful form of the Lomax. Tyran quirks a brow and drops into a crouch with the sword above her head in the Mengele. I narrow my eyes, knowing she believes I've never seen this before, while her lips twitch eagerly.

Tyran has first move, and I know what she's waiting for. It's the same thing Valore taught me—to look for the barest shake of a tired arm. A glance at Chessie shows she remembers too, after experiencing this posture on the training field when I disarmed her with a blow and a kick. But I never revealed how to counter this posture, though Valore drilled it into my head.

And so, I fake the quiver in my arm, triggering Tyran's call to action.

She fakes left, expecting me to follow, but I don't. The sword is slack in her hand, and knowing she'll go right before she winds the blade into a mighty arc, I follow her. Before she builds any power in the sword, I throw my blade into hers, the serrated edges catching while forcing it to the ground.

Tyran doesn't release the sword as hoped, but she stumbles backward, barely staying on her feet before lowering her sword submissively.

Three to two. Now we're getting somewhere.

I bite back a grin as she straightens, saying with some awe, "You know the Mengele."

"I trained with Valore Roil. There's not much to do in prison, but six hours a day for three years... well, training passed the time. Though nothing compares to the weight of a blade in my hand."

Mention of Valore sours her expression. "You're better than I imagined, but you'll still not last long."

"We'll see. Choose your posture."

Tyran assumes nothing now, which takes away a significant advantage of mine. Still, when she goes into the Renquat, I know she's expecting the Fendeer—both are postures Valore taught me. Instead, I do something different. I get into an unfamiliar posture that has Tyran scowling and, more importantly, hesitating.

I have first move and perform the quick flick-and-slice the posture's intended for, leaving a solid cut on Tyran's forearm. And while it's already bleeding, it's not deep—certainly not enough to prevent her from making her move—so I'm unguarded against the Renquat.

Though I lunge, I don't get far enough away, and Tyran's blade connects. The serrated steel scrapes the tender skin of my upper arm. I twist to escape the edge, gritting to stave off the acute pain even when the cutting stops. But there's no time to focus on the injury, knowing I must guard against a second attack, but when I turn back, Tyran's out of battle stance, watching, shocked, as blood drips from her new wound. It's worse than I thought, but it doesn't merit lowering her sword and giving up the round.

Huh. I guess we're even at three.

I contort my arm, observing my cut of four red lines. It stings, but I could have lost an arm, so I'll take it. One thing I've always known to be true: Torquent blades are messy.

"Where'd you learn that?" Tyran asks.

I look back at her with a grin. "It's a technique

of my family. My dad taught us. We call it the Endrack."

Tyran ignores protocol—abandoning postures and moves—and surges forward in attack mode, fury behind each swing. Purpose fuels my every reaction, and determination pumps through my body, but matching her punishing onslaught takes everything I have. She's operating without thought. She's passion and instinct behind a weapon that's as familiar to guide as a limb.

I seek an advantage as we battle, but the path to victory eludes me. Evans once told me I sucked at killing, and he couldn't be more right. Not only am I afraid to do it, but I seem incapable, even when it's necessary.

I get in my share of good strikes, but Tyran's a formidable opponent, dropping the serrated blade in a heavy curve that bumps and hacks against the edge of mine. I have just enough strength to keep her from taking my head off, but no more.

And then, as I'm guarding against her crushing blows and formulating a countermove, Tyran suddenly stops, stepping back and lowering her Torquent blade. "You lasted longer than your sister would have, that's for sure."

I don't understand what's happening, but she keeps her eyes on me, watching as I straighten and lower my sword from a defensive stance. It's then she faces Raider. "You care for her. And if I kill her, you'll never be content in Torquent. I'll let her live if you stay here with me. It's a simple choice. Submit, or Sharade dies."

Tyran's avoided saying my name, but she does it now. Not out of respect for an opponent but as a tool against Raider, reminding him what's at stake. As if any of us have lost sight of the goal here!

"But it's not his choice," I say, interrupting her latest speech—I've heard too many of them today. I'm catching my breath, alternating from foot to foot as adrenaline rushes through me. Still, I keep my voice even as I continue, "It's better to die trying to prevent Raider from getting shackled to you. I want everyone in this room to understand my conviction. For them to see that, while I'm no leader, I'm willing to stand between you and your lust to take what's not yours. Maybe they'll remember what it's like to do the right thing." My breath heaves from my chest, but the weary state of my body is nothing compared to the scorching fire coursing through my veins, and I remember Raider's words.

Serenity will transform into fire when the fight is in you. I'm eager to watch it happen.

I hope he's watching now.

"Choose your posture," I demand, taking up the Supure. It's not the flashiest of postures. It's not a commonly used one. But it's the closest thing to a feint without actually using one. Tyran said there are no rules, so it's not like a feint isn't within my rights, but when the goal is death, it seems like cheating.

Tyran paces before me, straightening her yellow hair and swishing her blade back and forth. She doesn't speak but huffs her displeasure, likely waiting for me to crack. She's a determined person in a terrible position, but she put herself there. I die, and Raider's pissed. She dies... well, as far as she's concerned, that's unimaginable.

I'm eager for her to choose her posture and get going, but she's still processing the situation, and her anxious pacing is wearing away my resolve.

So, I close my eyes.

I concentrate on breathing through my mouth.

I hold my posture and feel a breeze run across my skin. It's warm like the air in Aunty's Cellar, and I imagine I'm back there, practicing with my bedpost sword while Valore instructs me on how to improve. *"Listen to everything around you. Your ears will tell you every bit as much as your eyes. Don't discount a single sound."*

And so I do as Valore instructed, and I listen.

Arrick moves his lips nervously. Chessie shifts her jacket from arm to arm. Casmo whispers to a bravado that he'd like a glass of water. Raider rubs the top of his head. Meanwhile, Tyran moves into position.

"The Cinkin," she says, announcing her posture, and I picture the stance. I hear her feet—the left heel lifting and her toe pressing into the cement. She raises her arms—the slick white fabric distinctly betrays her motion—and I envision her with the Torquent blade aimed to slice me in two. When I don't respond to her declared posture, her breathing becomes frustrated and unsteady before demanding, "Open your eyes and fight me."

One side of my mouth lifts, but I keep my eyes closed, telling her, "There are no rules here."

Tyran growls low, and the air shifts as her blade moves on its prescribed course. The Supure dictates I move my sword on a direct course with hers until the metal clashes between us. Then, it's up to the swordbearer's strength and craftiness with a serrated blade to name a winner.

But there's another direction this posture can take, and so I twist away from the force of her blade, hers following directly behind mine but never touching. My body spins, and when I reach a full rotation, my eyes fly open, finding Tyran with a wavering sword and a confused expression.

I step forward and throw my foot into her waist. She stumbles backward, staggering to keep her balance. I extend my sword and snag my blade against hers—the serrated edges screech as they slide together—and I yank, pulling the hilt from her fingers. A second later, she's without a weapon, staring back and forth between her bare hands where my Torquent blade hovers between them.

"Dead," I say, wishing I could look at Raider as I speak the word I used on him during our practice on Caelum's beach. I wish I could tell the room how I shocked him that day. I wish I could laugh about the memories, but Tyran's made this a day void of laughter.

"Only I'm not dead," Tyran responds, finding her voice. "Or did you forget, Endrack's daughter? This fight only concludes when one of our lives is lost."

"Is that the only way? You stopped mid-fight to give Raider a choice. Why should you get that privilege and I don't?" I step forward, touching the sword to her chest. "You said you'd spare my life if Raider gave up everything he loved and stayed in Torquent with you. Now, it's my turn to provide a similar offer. I'll spare your life if you give up everything you love: The war you so desperately want, your greed for objects you had no hand in creating, and Raider—a relative you don't truly understand whom you'd rather destroy than lose. Are those things worth dying for? Tell me they are, and I'll make it so. I'll take your life right now and end all our misery. Or back off and live. The choice is yours."

Tyran stares at me for so long that I wonder if she's gotten lost in her head. But finally, she looks around the room, taking in the nervous faces. I'm surprised the bravados haven't stepped in, but they respect the blades and what a challenge with them means.

"You're a selfish person, Tyran," I say, drawing her attention back to me. "I can't believe you'd choose death over the opportunity to connive another day."

With the Torquent blade still aimed at her, I finally feel the difference between now and eight years ago. Back then, I stabbed Evans in the back to gain my dad's approval. My motives were entirely selfish. Leading up to this moment, I wasn't sure if I was capable of killing Tyran, but everything is clear now. I'm not hungry to take her life, but I'll do it for the people she's had a hand in manipulating, hurting, or killing.

Curses! There are so many.

Their names run through my mind like a memorial: Chessie, Chadd, Kally, Valore, Renegade, my dad, and Raider. I'm sure there are others—names I don't know—and the thought infuriates me, so I tighten my hold on the Torquent blade and await the answer that will decide our next move.

"I am selfish," Tyran admits. "And you're not like me," she adds, stepping away from my sword to pace thoughtfully. Then she stops, putting her hands on her hips and facing me. "And there's something you givers don't seem to understand about us takers." Her mouth, with those teeth that are barely contained, spreads into a feral grin. "We never yield."

Tyran's hand flies from her waist. I barely register the glint of a knife she's pulled from her waistband before the sharp edge slices my arm. I scream, dropping the Torquent blade and gripping the open wound, releasing blood in a steady flow.

"That's cheating!" my sister exclaims while Tyran retrieves my sword. A second later, it's pointed at Chessie. "No rules!" Tyran yells before putting her focus back on me.

Locating the sword I yanked from her fingers only minutes ago, I scoop it up. Blood runs down my arm, between my fingers, and drips onto the floor. My grip is slick, so I hold the weapon with both hands. I lunge the sword at her, trying for surprise, but she's ready and knocks it off course. Simultaneously, I lose my balance and slide to the ground—taken down by my own blood.

Lifting the blade protectively, I scramble backward. Tyran moves with me, looking like a prowling tiger. A tiger who speaks. "You Endracks are a disgusting set," she says with an animalistic growl. "I'll rejoice for many months, knowing I dispensed with two of you in one glorious day."

Her eagerness to finish me is blatant in her rabid expression. Going on the offensive is impossible from the floor, so while it's still an option, I struggle to stand. I've barely gained my footing when she reaches me, and I jerk my weapon into a defensive stance. I'm ready for her and equally invested in ending her and rejoicing over it.

Tyran lifts her box necklace, kissing the glass. "For you, dear sister," she says before dropping it to her chest. While I don't understand how destroying me honors her sister, I know all prelude is over. This is our moment.

This is the beginning that will determine our end.

I step backward, giving myself space to maneuver. Tyran follows. One second, she's stalking toward me—and I'm ready to defend all I love—and the next, she freezes. My grip tightens on the sword—unsure of her game—as I watch her face morph from fierce determination to surprise and finally to pain.

Her fingers slacken, causing the Torquent blade to crash to the floor. The noise resounds off the walls, and with it, I hear in a voice both deep and defiant, "Tyran said no rules."

And then, I see Chett, standing behind Tyran like a large shadow, and the barest hint of a knife protruding from her chest.

CHAPTER FORTY-NINE

Thirty-Two Days Free at 9:00 p.m.

Tyran's legs buckle, and she drops to the floor. The glass box around her neck hits the ground—the small noise sounding as loud as a scream. Briefly, I note the impact caused the glass to crack, and then, everything falls into chaos.

"Secure him!" someone shouts, and I'm jostled to the side as bodies fly past me.

"By the Dark, Chett, what have you done?" someone asks while I lower my sword, staring outside at the twinkling houseboat lights on Lake Divido—such a peaceful scene compared to what's going on in here.

"What a mess! An absolute mess!" someone exclaims as my fingers loosen and the Torquent blade slides through my bloody palm, landing on the floor with a clatter.

"Sharade!" Chessie yells, barreling down on me while I catch my breath and relish in no longer being on the other end of Tyran's death blade. But my sister's ignorant of those things, grabbing me and declaring, "I'm so mad at you!"

"You're mad at me?" I ask, exhaustion settling in as I turn my gaze on her. "There's nothing unusual about that."

"Well, I'm not just mad. I'm furious!" she cries, smacking my shoulder and making me wince. "I can't believe— I mean, what were you— Ugh! Just tell me if you're okay."

"I'm fine," I say as she yanks me into a hug, holding me fiercely against her. It's a mothering gesture, and I don't mind it. In fact, I lean into the hug, adding, "Although, I could do with some sleep."

"Sleep!" She pushes me back with a grip on my shoulders.

"Now's not the time to be funny."

Curses! I'm being serious here.

"I can't believe you put yourself in danger like that. What were you thinking coming in my place?"

I recall the day Chessie fought Evans in Ambitus. When the battle concluded, I didn't investigate her condition—something she's doing now, cataloging my injuries with her fingers. Instead, I was upset she lost the fight, and I launched insults and issued challenges. I'm ashamed of the memory. Still, it provides me with an answer.

"What was I thinking? Oh, I don't know, Chess. Why did you challenge Evans?"

She squints. "That was a long time ago."

"It was, but I doubt you've forgotten your motivation. You were protecting us. Because you loved him, and you loved me."

"So, that's your reason?" she asks, throwing out her hands in exasperation. "You replaced me out of love?"

"Given our history, I can understand why you'd doubt it, but yes, I did it because I love you."

It feels great to say, and for the first time in so long, I feel hopeful. Maybe expressing love for Chessie through words and actions can build back the trust we've lost and enable our relationship to mend.

"It's a pretty good reason," Chessie says, increasing my hope as she pulls me in for another hug. "And I love you too."

"I'm getting you all bloody," I say, but she holds me tighter, mumbling, "Don't care." I bury my nose in her shoulder, feeling high on sisterly affection, and then, the moment gets better when Chessie admits, "And you really are better than me with a Torquent blade."

"I know," I say, biting back a laugh, but I quickly sober because proving my skills in a battle with Tyran wasn't fun.

It was ugly. My eyes drift toward Tyran but stop on the pink stain. I didn't realize, but she died in the same spot as Dad, and the physical reminder of his death looks like a rug beneath her body.

"Don't look at her," Chessie says, misreading the reason my muscles have tensed and spinning us to block my view.

"It's not that." I look into my sister's brown eyes and pause before shaking my head. There will be a time to tell her about our dad, but it's not now. Instead, I link my arm through Chessie's and pull her across the room where Wick and Evans have been watching us reconnect. Immediately, the four of us fall into a giant hug.

"You didn't suck too bad out there," Evans says with a teasing glint.

"That's high praise from the Lordly Prince," I return with a smile.

"Sharade!" my sister complains—and I don't even mind hearing my name—while Evans snorts out a laugh followed by, "You're getting us bloody, little sister."

Little sister. Who ever thought I'd enjoy Evans Dirby calling me that?

"Chess doesn't care about blood. Why should you?" I check him with my shoulder. "Did you notice I don't pull punches like my sister?" I ask with a playful grin, remembering how I accused her of that when she fought Evans.

"I've never—" Chessie starts, indignant.

"Burn," Evans interrupts, chuckling while his hazel eyes light with mischief.

"Hey! Be nice to my sister," Wick says, pulling me against his tall frame and kissing the top of my head. "I don't want you chasing her off again." He points at Evans.

"Burn!" Chessie and I call out together, dissolving into

laughter. I'm more like my siblings than I ever imagined. I want to think I've gained some of Wick's wisdom and Chessie's fight while learning how to use those traits for good.

Wick releases me and reveals a strip of cloth, wrapping my arm to contain the flow of blood. Watching my brother fix me up, I tell them, "Well, if you're going to chase me off again, please make it a beach town not a Dark prison. That's all I ask."

Chessie and Wick look shocked when I mention my prison, but Aunty's Cellar is a part of my life—not one I want to relive, but one I'll always acknowledge because I learned who I was in that place. Evans, however, doesn't look surprised. He hooks an arm around my neck and gives me a shake. "The good thing is, I'm in charge now, and I take requests."

I've never had a big brother, but the way Evans is acting, he's slotted himself into the role. I can't believe I'm thinking it, considering how we started, but it feels awesome.

I'm wearing an enormous smile when I spot Raider across the room, crouched beside Tyran. She did a lot of messed-up things and wasn't his favorite person, but she was still family. And now she's dead. I know how that feels.

"Excuse me a sec," I say, leaving my siblings to join Raider.

"Hey," I say, squatting beside him. "You okay?"

"I am," he says, facing me and brushing his thumb across my cheek. "I'm glad you're okay." I'm not sure what was on my face, but he wipes it on his pants. "I mean, you're not really okay, but you're alive," he amends, nodding at my arm. The blood's already seeped through Wick's wrap—red lines looking like I got scraped by a giant fork. It's obvious I need stitches.

"I feel okay," I say while he rubs his bottom lip

thoughtfully. "And I'm sorry about your aunt."

"She brought it on herself." Raider stands from his crouch, and I straighten to join him. "I'm truly more shocked by what Chett did."

Curses! I knew Chett had secrets, but I never guessed him capable of all he's done.

"It's hard to pick which of his crimes I'm more shaken over," I say, and not wanting to add to Raider's grief, I don't mention Kally or Tyran by name.

"Yeah." He sighs.

"Where is Chett?"

"The bravados have him secured." Raider nods toward the corner of the room, but I can't see Chett past the barricade of bravados.

"What will happen next?" I ask. It's an exhausting question because it encompasses not only today but tomorrow.

How do we get out of this room? Out of Torquent? What happens to Chett? What about the war? Is it off because Tyran is dead? Is it on because Hamo's citizen murdered Torquent's leader? Are we redrawing the alliances? The abundant issues fill me with trepidation.

And, selfishly, what happens to me? I'm still unsure where I belong. More than ever, Hamo is out. I'm sure Raider would allow me in the South T, and settling near Valore is tempting, but there's Adlumen to consider. With my sibling relationships stabilizing, going back home seems feasible. And while citizen acceptance—and even my mother's acceptance—may take time, I'd have family love there.

But when I consider where I feel the greatest pull—desires I've barely acknowledged for fear of disappointment—I know, if I could choose, I'd stay near Raider. The realization is startling, but I can't deny it's what feels right.

And while I won't resolve the issue today, I at least want to hear Raider's take on things.

"What's next?" He reiterates while a disgruntled laugh leaves his lips. "Honestly, I'm surprised they haven't put us in cuffs and locked us up, though maybe they're confused about protocol with a room full of Dark territory and light bubble leaders."

"Or maybe this is our cell," I say, looking around the stark room.

"Maybe."

"Well, in Adlumen, if something happened to the governors, they'd summon the next in command—General Pruden or Judge Statera. Maybe we're waiting on Torquent's equivalent of those people."

"You're on the right track, Shar," Arrick says, startling me as he enters our conversation. "But it's not a general or judge we're waiting on."

"Who then?"

"The next leader of Torquent," Arrick answers, and I hear Chessie's gasp from across the room. It seems Arrick isn't the only one eavesdropping.

"Do you know the next leader? Are they as unreasonable as Tyran?" I grip my throat, not liking this development in my pursuit of what's next. "Will they, too, make us wait hours for their arrival?"

Arrick chuckles. "I know them, and they're not unreasonable." He pauses. "And there's no need for concern about a wait. Torquent's new leader is in this room." And then, with full purpose and meaning, Arrick's eyes slide to Raider.

CHAPTER FIFTY

Thirty-Two Days Free at 9:30 p.m.

"What?" Raider barks, his eyes widening incredulously behind his lenses.

Curses! What's happening right now?

"That's right. Tyran's death makes you, Raider Roil, the leader of Torquent," Arrick clarifies for any who may have missed it—Raider included.

"Me? Torquent's leader?" Raider emits an unamused laugh. "I think Tyran's second-in-command might have something to say about that."

"You are her second," Arrick says. "Tyran had dozens of individuals reporting to her on political and military topics but never a single point-person. She left the position vacant because it was yours alone to fill."

"You're serious?" I ask while Raider shakes his head.

"Today isn't a day for joking," Arrick answers.

"But, I'm a Souther!" Raider exclaims, pacing a path in front of us. "I haven't stayed a night in Torquent since my youth."

"That doesn't discount the facts."

"I don't belong here! I can't lead these people. It's not going to happen."

"You can voice every denial, but it doesn't change what is. The responsibility of Torquent falls on you."

"Let it fall on the person in line after me."

Arrick folds his arms. "Tyran declared that's your son."

"Great." Raider runs his hands over his short hair in frustration. "You must see I'm the worst person to step in.

I'm light blind and the leader of the South T."

"There are worse people."

"We'll have to figure out something else because I must decline," Raider says with a swipe of his hand, wanting to end the conversation, but it's not going away.

"It's not something you decline," Arrick says, fighting the instinct to talk down to Raider and curbing his arrogance as he continues, "It's something that... *just is*."

"When my dad disappeared, the South T job went to me, but I followed the governors' example and put it to a vote to make sure it's what my people wanted. I think that would be best in this situation. We let the Torques decide who they'll have lead them."

"And what if they chose you?"

"By the Dark," Raider draws out, releasing a long breath. "The Torques won't want me. They'll want one of their own."

"And if they want you?" Arrick presses.

Raider groans. "I guess, in that case, I'd have to consider it more seriously." I hear in Raider's voice that he doubts a vote in his favor. Yet, I don't doubt it. The Torques may consider other options but could easily choose the leader their beloved Tyran wanted for them.

"You're sure about conducting a vote?" Arrick asks.

"I have a territory to manage, and it's the best thing for us all."

There's a beat of silence where we let Raider's declaration settle, but then the tempo of the room changes—even the air becomes unsettled—when Casmo inserts himself into the conversation. "The best thing for us all?" he asks, his voice laced with irritation. He steps in front of Raider, too close for a casual conversation. "That could be the dumbest thing I've ever heard from the mouth of a Roil."

"Your lack of support is shocking," Raider deadpans.

"Your lack of vision more so," Casmo returns. "Will you hear me out, or are you too stubborn for sound advice?" There's a pause before Raider nods, and Casmo continues, "Tyran's dead, and for all her craziness, the people loved her. You are, *without argument*, her successor because she made succession clear to anyone who knows anything. So, you can take over, and we'll have peace. Or, you can allow a vote, and we'll be at war."

"How do you figure?" Raider asks, annoyed at, once again, getting boxed in against his will.

"How do you not?" Casmo groans. "The Torques will look into Tyran's death. Seeing as Arrick's man did the deed, they'd cut off Hamo." The bravado barricade has moved, so I have line-of-sight to Chett, whose eyes are on the floor. "A governor is in the room, connecting Adlumen to the conspiracy, and as Adlumen's ally, the South T would get implicated. I'd likely escape blame because of my unwavering alliance. Still, I'd get forced back into a situation where I'm on the cusp of war. Only this time, it's with some unknown Torque leader who could be stupider and, with my luck, more unhinged than Tyran. It would ruin everything I came here to do—namely, stopping a war. Because I have no interest in fighting. Do you?"

Casmo knows the answer, so after a brief pause, he points at Raider. "You're positioned to facilitate a stable future for us all. None of the rest of us can do it. Only you. By choosing to lead Torquent, you make all our problems go away. It's perfect."

"Perfect?" Raider scoffs. "Perfect, except I've never wanted to live in Torquent. Perfect, except for Tyran getting her way even in death. I'd be caving to what she schemed for all along."

"But are you, really?" Casmo shakes his head. "Ruling Torquent isn't the prison sentence Tyran made it out to be.

Not with her gone. She has no control over your choices or whereabouts. You can set up things here, put trusted people in place, and divide your time as you see fit."

"Leading Torquent and the South T?"

"Why not?"

"It seems... complicated."

"No. It makes everything *less complicated.* For example, the Torquent Expansion into the Southern Territory. Suddenly, negotiations between two parties are no longer necessary because you control both pieces of land. It's the same situation regarding the abatement. Suddenly, the people are expanding into land controlled and made available by their leader. Raider, you are hands-down the most ideal person to take on this challenge. And is a new era of peace not worth such minimal inconvenience?"

"Hey, buddy," Evans says, stepping up to Raider. "I'm sorry this is happening to you, but it's worth considering. What Casmo says seems pretty legit."

"Look at it this way," Casmo continues before Raider can talk. "This plan would merge the alliances. For the first time in our history, Adlumen and the Desert Territory would be allies. That seems a rather monumental byproduct. With the Coastal and Southern Territories, Hamo, and Torquent rounding out our coalition, who would ever dare challenge us? We'd have long-standing peace. You mostly leave me alone, and that's all I want. Tyran kept sticking her fingers in and distracting me, but I've got enough problems contending with Circes. Captain Rhed can tell you they're an ongoing trial. At least the Northern Territory people keep to themselves. Well, Evans knows." Casmo gestures to Captain Rhed's son, who nods in agreement.

"And I'm just supposed to forget you imprisoned my dad for three years? We're just going to move on from that?" Raider asks.

"Can any of you say you or your predecessors haven't done similar to my people? Hell, Captain Rhed recently detained and threatened Mal within my borders."

"You're suggesting we forgive the past and operate on a different level going forward," Raider summarizes.

"Yes."

"Just that easily?"

"It can be that easy if we allow it to be."

"Evans, what would the other governors say to this proposal?" Raider asks.

"Are you joking?" Evans rocks excitedly on his heels. "Of course, they'd agree. My dad too."

"But I'd have to stay here," Raider says, trying out the words to see if they're something he can agree to.

"Until you get things in place, yes," Casmo says. "Get established, resolve the overcrowding issue, then divide your time."

"What about Chett?" Raider asks, not looking at his friend sitting silently in the corner.

"I can't decide that for you. But we've all wronged each other, and the biggest wrongdoers are now dead." He motions to Raider's aunt and the stain left by my dad. "Maybe we should take final stock of the abuses and forgive each other."

"Forgive Chett?" Raider asks, shaking his head profusely.

"Why not?" Casmo asks, and Raider clenches his jaw, grumbling. "For decades, we've perpetrated sorrow between us. It's time to acknowledge the hurt and let it go. And, yeah, you should forgive Chett." Raider moans, tightening his lips. "And maybe you should forgive your sister," Casmo continues, looking at Chessie. "By the Dark, that one's overdue, don't you think?"

My sister gives me a slight nod, seeing as we've already

made strides down that path. Amid Casmo's speech—wise though it is—it's heartening to remember he doesn't know everything. Interrupting my amused thoughts, Chett blurts out, "I don't deserve forgiveness."

"You're right about that," Raider mumbles.

Casmo huffs in Raider's direction before marching to the corner, pulling Chett to his feet and getting right in his face. "By the light, Chett, you've moped around the last few years, mourning your brother and despising Tyran for the position she put you in. It was a vicious move, to be sure, but many of us have controlled the political sphere similarly. So, let's liberate ourselves! Let's let it all go—not just the actions brought against us, but our regrets for what we've done to others. Let's agree we deserve more and move on. We'll shed that shit."

"Shed that shit?" I ask, and Casmo looks back at me. "Is that going to be the motto for our new undertaking?"

Casmo chuckles, seeming less sinister. Releasing Chett, he walks back to us, answering, "Maybe it should be." Casmo's smile is the first real sign he's got a human side and isn't merely a calculating, manipulative leader. It's the first time I've considered trusting him.

Maybe. Sort of.

Because even as I contemplate a change in attitude, logic tells me someone who so easily condones that level of forgiveness must have executed heinous acts of their own. Still, Casmo's plan is worth trying, even if we proceed with caution.

Raider stares at Chett, processing all Casmo laid out. I'm unsure where Raider's head is, but I decide to offer an opinion, even if it isn't my place. "Chett's well-known among the Torques," I say. "He'd make a leadership transition more successful."

Head jerking back, Raider wears an instant frown. He

doesn't look angry at my suggestion. I'd say his expression is more one of disgust. It's an uncomfortable solution —possibly a terrible idea—but it surely supports Casmo's suggestion of moving forward with forgiveness.

"I don't know—" Raider starts while Chett motions to Tyran, asking, "What about the fact that I killed her?"

Casmo's attention goes pointedly to Raider. He's turning control over to him. The rest of us follow his lead, remaining quiet. While my exhausted legs want a chair, I don't move. We're waiting for Raider to take the reins, which, after a resigned sigh, he finally does.

"Apparently, I'm the new leader of Torquent," he says, and for the first time, the words don't sound like a burden on his lips. "Gathered in this room are leaders from the surrounding Dark territories and light bubbles, but more importantly, we have four bravados—loyal Torquent citizens —who've seen and heard all that's transpired today. I'd like to hear their thoughts?"

The bravados look stunned, so Raider encourages them, adding, "Please. I really want to know what you think. Positive. Negative. Let's hear it."

One bravado quickly finds his voice, stepping forward and saying, "My name is Rowden. Every action I witnessed was according to Torquent law, except one—Emissary Chett murdering our leader. But Raider is Tyran's chosen successor, and if he forgives Chett, I'll act accordingly, keeping quiet about what transpired. Torquent's new leader has my support as he sees fit to employ it."

Rowden steps back, and another bravado steps forward —a young woman in her early twenties. "My name is Sivil," she says, and learning this Torque shares the name of Raider's mom doesn't go unnoticed. "I don't want war. I'll stay silent and serve." She bows her head and steps back while I'm still reeling from the coincidence that adds a personal touch to this circumstance.

Next is another woman who looks younger than Sivil. "I'm Bell. I agree with my fellow bravados, except in one regard. Rowden said all was done according to Torquent law, but Tyran's actions didn't align with our laws. She admitted to coercing Chett to do terrible things—not for the safety of Torquent but for her own gain—and revealed the gruesome punishment for his failure. If any Torque committed a similar deed, leading to innocent deaths, they would be tried and executed. Tyran of Torquent met the fate of her actions. That the individual she blackmailed was the executioner only solidifies my opinion. Her death is no one's fault but her own, and Chett requires no punishment, or even forgiveness, in association with her death." She glances at Raider. "I will leave judgment of his other crimes to our leader."

Bell tips her head and steps back while the last bravado remains rooted to his spot, saying, "I have nothing to add."

I'm confused by the magnanimous opinions of the Torque bravados. I never imagined they'd be so content to move forward under new leadership, but maybe it's as simple as Raider being the one Tyran wanted and her dying through no fault of his.

"We're making excellent progress," Casmo declares with a clap of his hands. "I'll send Mal to the next meeting of emissaries and promise he'll make no move against Captain Rhed, no matter how wounded his pride."

Evans chuckles. "Well, at least Dad only hurt his pride."

"Ahh, but you don't know Mal. His life and his pride are one and the same. You may as well have killed him for the vengeance he feels."

"Great. You're encouraging forgiveness, and you're doubting your own man," Evans points out.

"I've given my word," Casmo says, taking objection to Evans's comment. "There is no doubt."

"You think you can convince him?" Evans asks. "Control him?" I've never met Mal, but the man's reputation has Evans on edge.

"Hell, yeah, I do. Because Mal will understand the benefits. Because we're damn well invested in this working!" He pounds his fist. "And we're damn well not going to let it fall apart. Because we're sick of this shit."

"The shit we're shedding," I say, making Casmo smile and simmers right down. I barely know the man, but I'm learning he's excitable.

"I like you, Sharade Endrack," Casmo says with a complimentary nod before stepping toward the door. "I should have plucked you from Ott's hole and brought you to Windway."

"I was a different person back then. You'd not have liked me as much," I say, and then I think of him holding Valore and add, "Just like I don't like you very much right now."

Casmo chuckles, not at all bothered by my summation. "I figure we can hate or like each other all we want, as long as we're peaceable about it." He rotates his head to give us all one last look. "I don't know that you need anything more from me. You know where I stand, and I'll expect us all to operate under what we've decided here today unless you say differently. For now, I've got plenty of people back home who will rejoice to learn we aren't picking up weapons come tomorrow. And I'm eager to return to Windway to sleep in my bed tonight."

With a brief wave and a soft click of the door, Casmo leaves the room. I suck in my upper lip. I should feel calm, but there's a knot in my stomach, though I'm not sure if it's fear or anticipation. Whatever it is, the feeling increases as Raider addresses the room. "Casmo's gone," he says, clearing his throat. "But the rest of you aren't going anywhere. We have work to do."

CHAPTER FIFTY-ONE

Thirty-Nine Days Free at 6:00 p.m.

Watching Raider step into the role of Torquent's leader is mesmerizing. His bias toward declining the job seems absurd after only a week of him performing the duties involved. Simply put, he's terrific at it.

The Torques were naturally upset over Tyran's death. I can't help but think they never truly knew the woman since I've not been tempted to shed a tear. Though they feel the loss, no one questions Raider stepping into the position. Casmo was right—Tyran made everyone aware of her plan, and the people are eager to support Raider.

Without the looming threat of war, a collective calm has settled over Torquent. Even the sudden alliances with the South T, Coastal Territory, and Adlumen don't offend the people. They know Arrick and Casmo support the new coalition, which reinforces that things are moving forward positively. Add the promise of more expansion and abated land becoming available, and the Torques are optimistic about the future.

Raider's pleased with how they've responded, but more so, he's relieved because it reduces questions surrounding Tyran's death. He calls what happened a terrible accident—corroborated by Arrick, Casmo, and the four Torque bravados in the room—and encourages the people to remember his aunt's dynamic life, not her untimely death. Altogether, it seems to have done the trick.

Tyran's funeral took place this afternoon—a massive event honoring the woman who led their light bubble through years of great prosperity. They held it outdoors at a large sports facility, and while it's been a long, hot, tough summer, there was finally a break in the heat. The cool breeze across our skin, as the leaders spoke, was a gift and hopefully a sign of better times to come.

Casmo and Arrick both spoke, and while Arrick did a perfectly fine job, Casmo excelled. He's a difficult man to understand—his words shadowing a ruthless core—but he sure knows how to inspire a crowd. He left the Torques singing the praises of their longtime allies in the desert and adoring their new leader in equal measure. It was quite a feat.

Raider spoke last, and his beautiful words about his aunt made me think he must be talking about someone else. But he focused on the early years of their acquaintance —when he thought slightly better of her—and highlighted her accomplishments toward making Torquent great. It's unfortunate the woman knew nothing about cultivating relationships because she could have built something real with Raider if she'd tried.

After the public event, the light bubble and Dark territory officials gathered at Tyran's cliffside estate for a meal. The expansive lawn and lush gardens behind her home, which overlook Lake Divido, hosted hundreds of dignitaries. Yellow tablecloths with blue runners—to mimic the Torquent flag—covered each table, before being set with crystal glasses, silver utensils, porcelain dishware, and fresh-cut flowers. It was a lavish affair, and while everyone enjoyed themselves, I imagine Tyran would have found it lacking.

The scene looks less opulent now, as the aftermath of a pleasant time often does, but there are lessons in the disarray. The dulled crystal and sauce-marked linens visually represent moments between people. Messiness brought about by connection is beautiful.

The sun is low and hints a vibrant sunset isn't far off. It was a good day—all things considered—and now everyone's leaving for home.

"It's been a privilege," Casmo says, approaching and shaking my hand.

"Has it, though?" I ask with a raised brow, and he chuckles.

"You're always welcome in the Desert Territory."

"It does sort of feel like a second home." I smile, and Casmo surprises me by looking sheepish—an expression easily observed since he's wearing Adlumen lenses, exposing eyes usually hidden behind dark glass. I shake my head and laugh. "Don't mind me. I'm just testing your plan. You know, the one where we mend old hurts by forging new relationships. How am I doing?"

"It's... an effort, for sure," Casmo says with amusement.

"I'd try harder, but there's very little to mend between you and me. After all, unlike Valore, I was in your prison for a reason."

He lifts a slim shoulder. "Well, there was a reason in Valore's case too, though maybe not one so well deserved."

"We can agree on that."

"Take care of yourself, Sharade," Casmo says, walking away to meet Mal, who's still a mystery to me. He's been perfectly polite over the last week, but I detect an undercurrent of *something*. He makes me nervous, and I won't be upset if I never see the man again.

Arrick approaches next. "You promised to attend my birthday celebration next month. I will not forget."

"I'll be there." Arrick pulls me in for a hug, and I catch Chett watching from across the grass. "Is Chett staying here, then?"

Arrick pulls back, staring down at me with blue eyes and a lock of black hair hanging between them. "Actually, with things going so well in Torquent, he's returning with me. He plans to tell his dad what happened."

"What part?"

"All of it. What transpired last week, along with Tyran's part in poisoning Chett's dad and brother. That she did it because Chett failed to kill Valore. That Kally died because of Chett's mistake."

"Chett's dad doesn't know?"

"They barely speak. While Chett sought redemption, guilt kept him distant. Meanwhile, his father clung to a sickly life, wondering why his remaining son was so changed." Arrick shakes his head. "I wonder how many of us have acted similarly, leaving important things unfixed." I nod, knowing we each have things to work through.

"I'm sick of secrets," Chett says, appearing at my side, and from his expression, he heard much of what Arrick said.

Arrick releases me, and I face Chett, saying, "I hope it works out for you and your dad."

"Thanks. It can't turn out any worse than things between Raider and me."

"It's that bad?"

"Yeah." Chett heaves a breath. His eyes are still sad, though he's lost some of the darkness that dwelled in them for so long. "It's not easy working with him, but I'll help for as long as he'll allow it. And then, when my help is no longer needed, I'll ask Raider about a trial."

"A trial?" My eyes widen. "What kind of trial?"

"That depends on Raider. I'll turn myself into Hamo, Torquent, or the South T, whichever he feels is best, and I'll divulge what happened to Kally. Of course, I'll have to leave out some details." *Tyran*. He won't be able to speak about Tyran's part in things, which would uncover the truth of her death. "But I'll resolve the situation lawfully and finally start living an honest life again."

"You're sure about doing that?" It's a frightening prospect. People will hate him, especially since so much of the story must remain hidden behind a secret that could harm the coalition. "There's a lot to consider with such a step."

"It's the right thing to do, and I have good people to help navigate the finer points." Chett smiles, and I'm shocked when his eyes actually match the expression. "Besides, I see what wonderful things prison did for you, so I have a lot of hope for my future."

A gasp leaves my lips, unbidden, which has Chett laughing. Soon, I am too.

"I wish you all the best," I say, pulling him in for a farewell hug.

"That means a lot." His body is stiff in my arms, and he's quiet for a moment before whispering, "Everything happened how it was supposed to, but I'll always regret the life we could have made together. It would have been good."

"I'm sure it would have," I say, though I don't believe my words. We were never meant for each other.

Releasing him, I watch Chett and Arrick walk away, looking like shadows in the late afternoon sun. It feels like once I have meaningful people in my life, they just as quickly go away. Maybe that's how the real world works, and I forgot it in the monotony of my Dark prison.

I'm deep in thought when Chessie appears, asking, "Have you decided?"

My sister wants to know if I'm going to Adlumen with her. We had a long talk about it days ago. It was the same day I told my siblings about our dad—that he was in Torquent these last years while we thought him dead. I took Chessie and Wick to see his body, and we held onto each other while we stared at the remains of the man who raised us. They'd done a brilliant job laying him out so his head looked attached, for which I was extremely grateful. Then I apologized again for following Dad's plan, and they insisted the situation was behind us. I feel more ready than ever to move forward from my past, but I'm still not sure Adlumen's the place to do it.

"No, I haven't decided yet."

I run my finger over the old scar Chessie gave me. It's a constant reminder of her, and whether I go to Adlumen or not, a piece of her will always be with me—something more significant than an old scrape but a feeling that my sister knows and loves me.

"Mom will want to see you," she says, pushing to get her way. It makes me smile.

"That's what you said last time. It didn't go so well," I remind her. At some point, I'll try to fix things with my mom, but I'm not ready to do it now. Until then, she and my sister will just have to be patient.

"The Adlumians will accept you more readily after everything that's happened here," Chessie says, trying again to convince me. "And I'm going to petition to get your citizenship reinstated." That's a surprise, but I don't react because—while I appreciate it—citizenship won't affect my decision either way.

Chessie spots our brother across the grass, and continues, "Then again, Wick's staying in Contund. Maybe you'll do the same?"

Just today, Wick discussed this new arrangement with Evans. Raider requested Wick stay in Torquent and my brother expressed his desire to do so. Similar to Chett representing Hamo, and Mal the Desert Territory, Wick will represent Adlumen. Unlike the others, he'll do it based in Torquent.

I shrug, staring at my brother as I say, "Wick was invited to stay. I haven't been."

"Maybe it's assumed."

I tilt my head, putting my attention on my sister. "What do you mean?"

"Growing up, you'd come to a determination, then draw an invisible line. You stood on one side—ready to battle the world—while everyone else stood on the other. Crossing that line and coming to any kind of understanding was nearly impossible. But you're not standing alone anymore. You're standing beside someone now, and I think he figures you're there to stay."

"I'm not comfortable assuming anything."

"Then maybe you should talk to him."

"There's not been much opportunity for that," I say, lifting my arms and motioning to the constant movement around us. Raider's busy, and I don't want to be in the way.

Chessie nods, but I don't like the smirk on her face. "Well, we leave in an hour, so you have that long to decide. No matter what you choose, know I'll support you. And remember, you have a nephew back in Adlumen who's desperate to know his aunt. At the very least, we need frequent visits."

"That I can promise." Chessie hugs me, then leaves.

Alone, I'm grateful for a moment to think. I walk across the manicured grass and onto a path of cobbled stones, leading to a bench under a group of ash trees. Sitting, I bend over to scoop a handful of rocks, and with my eyes closed, I imagine I'm back in Aunty's Cellar, though it's a hard sell with the sun flickering through the trees and a fresh breeze blowing the scent of lavender. I count the rocks, thinking about Squatty and wishing he were here to experience this moment with me.

"Thinking about old times?" Valore asks, and my eyes pop open. I smile at his accurate appraisal and invite him to sit, brushing the rocks—the blatant clues—from the bench. They clatter to the ground, joining the rest of their kind. "Things with your sister are good?" he asks, settling beside me. I can see Chessie through the trees with her arm linked through Evans's while she laughs at something Raider's saying.

Raider looks exceedingly handsome in his dress clothes —a Souther-gold shirt and a Torque-blue suit—honoring both of his homes. Adorable, young Sage grips the side of Raider's pants while the adults talk about things that bore children.

"Yeah. She wants me to go home with her." I chuckle, then add, "Again."

"What are you going to do?"

I shrug, tempted to pick up the rocks and count them again. "I'm undecided. I know what I want, but I'm not sure it's possible."

Valore clicks his tongue, always the first sign he's disappointed in something I've said or done. "Have you looked into it?"

I don't know if it should surprise me when Valore doesn't ask me to name my desire but inquires what I've done to get it. It makes me think he already knows my mind, and that's just two scoops of embarrassing with a giant side of mortification.

"Not yet, but I will," I say, rubbing my tired eyes. Maybe I'll call it an early night and get some sleep. I could use it. Besides, even if I decide to go to Adlumen, I don't need to go with Chessie. I can find a ride. A few days of quiet could be just what I need to make some decisions.

"The boy will miss you if you leave," Valore says, motioning to Sage, who's running circles around Raider and slapping his hand with each rotation. I've spent a lot of time with the little man over the last few days. He arrives at my room early, knocking on my door before leading me to breakfast and teaching me games on the lawn. In the evening, he climbs onto my lap, requesting stories with his intense expression, and I tell them until my brain goes blank. Raider was worried about Sage feeling accepted in this place —feeling safe in a way he hasn't in a long time—but he's adapted better than expected. Indeed, from everything I've seen, he loves it here.

"I'd miss him too," I say, crossing my ankles and straightening the hem of my dress. In Hamo, they put me in a green dress they borrowed from somewhere handy. I was newly free—still weak and bruised from years of mistreatment—and the fit was off. But this dress was made to fit me, something I haven't experienced since I was sixteen and living in Ambitus. It reminds me of the dress I wore to the governors' reception—the night I met Raider. Indeed, it's the same bright yellow. Chessie said it's how she always pictured me during my imprisonment, wearing the fancy yellow gown with my hair pulled up. This dress is a summer cut—knee-length and sleeveless to accommodate my still-healing arm—but my hair is too short to put into a beautiful twist. While I love the dress and feel comfortable with my appearance, I feel like an imposter trying to relive a memory.

I'm still smoothing out the dress as Valore says, "I'm sorry about what happened to your dad."

"He hasn't been my dad for a long time." I've observed many fathers over the last month—including Valore, Stryke, Evans, and Raider—and it took minimal study to determine they all learned the role better than Keine Endrack ever did.

"That's unfortunate," Valore says, stilling my restless hand with his. "He missed out on knowing a remarkable daughter." The compliment settles warmly in my chest, and while Valore knows I care about him, I doubt he understands the depth of my devotion or the prime reason for it. It's likely time I tell him.

"Did you know I wouldn't be here today if it weren't for you?" Valore considers my question but doesn't answer, so I continue, "And I don't mean just sitting in Torquent. I mean, alive at all."

I rotate, facing him, for what I say next. "On my first day in prison, Warden Ott said he'd take my life if I asked. My dad arranged the option for me. I said no because, when I first got to prison, I was still fighting to live, but the time came when I was ready, and the warden wouldn't honor the agreement. Actually, he insisted he wouldn't have even done it that first day, but who knows?"

Valore pushes up the edge of his lens, wiping away a tear. I feel terrible for making him cry, but he needs to know the rest. "I felt cheated. Until you came. In the last three years, you've behaved more like a father to me than he did my entire life. If it weren't such a bad idea to appropriate you, I'd have started calling you Dad ages ago."

Valore grins. "I'd really like that."

"You're sweet, but I'd never do that to your real family."

A thoughtful hum rumbles in his throat. "Maybe things will be different someday, and you'll change your mind."

"Different? How so?"

"Can't you feel it? The good things coming our way? The speed at which things are changing?"

"Maybe." It's easy to get caught up in his energy.

"It's almost a flavor I can taste in the air," Valore continues, eyes twinkling with excitement. "And it tastes like watermelon." I wrinkle my nose. "Or maybe cherries, in your case." He nudges my shoulder, making me giggle. "The details don't matter. The point is to enjoy the result."

"The result of tasting air," I recap, bewildered by his illogical debate. "So, you're saying the flavor of cherries in the air will make me change my mind about calling you Dad?"

"Yes, Shar. That's exactly right," Valore confirms, which only confuses me more. "You'll see. Sooner than you think possible, you'll not only appropriate me but feel perfectly at ease doing so."

CHAPTER FIFTY-TWO

Thirty-Nine Days Free at 6:30 p.m.

A happy laugh escapes my chest—a mixture of uncertainty and contentment—because while Valore's viewpoint is resolute, I still don't see what he sees. But I'll not argue his point. He's my best friend, and I'll let him hold close to the ideas that bring him joy.

My skeptical reaction has Valore ready to debate his point further, but a squeal followed by, "Hurry up, Dad!" steals our attention. A moment later, Raider arrives with Sage. Or, more accurately, Sage arrives with Raider since the boy is impatiently dragging his father toward us.

Sage escapes his dad's grip, glancing between Valore and me before making his choice. A second later, his chest is against my knees, and he's strangling my legs in a hug.

Valore ruffles his grandson's hair while telling Raider, "You did well today, Son."

"Thanks, Dad," Raider says, straightening his suit and giving me a tired smile before instructing his son, "Ease up on your grip, Sage. Shar would like to feel her feet."

I laugh, rubbing the boy's back. "Hey, buddy. You have a good day?" He nods. "You enjoy your dinner?"

Sage loves food, so the happy sound he makes is no surprise. He licks his lips, dreaming of the chocolate cake they served—I'm sure of it—so I lean in close to whisper, "I saved a piece of cake just for you. You can eat it for lunch tomorrow."

He giggles, looking at me with irresistible eyes and gifting me a perfect smile. This kid has my heart.

I glance up to find Raider watching our interaction.

"Have a seat?" I ask.

"Sure," he says, taking my offer. "Did I just hear something about secret cake?"

I open my mouth—unsure what will come out—but Sage speaks before I find out. "You heard nothin'," he says, releasing my legs and scowling at his dad. Raider chuckles at his son's cheekiness, and then the boy's attention is back on me.

He moves to my side, bending backward to lie across my lap with his feet touching the ground on one side and his hands on the other. It exposes his belly, and I know exactly what he wants. Lifting his shirt a few inches, I run my fingertips across his bare skin in light strokes. He squirms slightly, but mostly, he lies there, smiling. I don't get it. I hate being tickled, but it's Sage's thing, and I'm happy to oblige.

Raider and Valore fall into a discussion about the successes and failures of the day, agreeing there were more of the former. Sage goes from lying on my lap to sitting on it. He has my arms around him, inspecting my hands and following the lines on my palms with his finger. I rest my chin on his shoulder, as my thoughts turn to the course of my life. There are still moments when the reality of freedom overwhelms me. Moments when I'm amazed the wider world surrounds me and not Aunty's Cellar. Moments when I feel undeserving of the happiness I feel.

"You okay?" Raider asks, and I nod, blinking away my weighty thoughts. "Come here, Son," he says, patting his lap. "I have a surprise for Shar, and she needs her mobility."

"My mobility?" I squint at the strange comment while Sage shifts from my lap to Raider's, but it's only a moment before Raider's words have meaning. "Renegade!" I exclaim, surging to my feet and rushing the man. Wrapping him in a hug, he fidgets uncomfortably—likely from embarrassment, though I loosen my arms in case I'm hurting him.

We'd heard Renegade's recovery was going well, and he planned to come to Torquent, but I didn't know if I'd be here for his arrival—if I'd be in Adlumen or somewhere else.

"I'm so happy to see you!" I'm overjoyed to reunite with my friend. It's another step in putting the fear, loss, and disappointment of these last weeks behind me.

"I can tell," Renegade says, while I lean back to get a good look at him. He won't quite meet my eyes, and his cheeks are tinged pink.

"It's fantastic having you back," Raider says, arriving beside us. "We scarcely managed on our own." Raider winks at me, making Renegade groan.

"How are you here?" I ask. "We were told it would be weeks before you could travel."

"Got the boy to bring me," he says with a jerk of his head.

The boy, meaning Renegade's adult son, Geric, who's settled at a table fifty feet away. He's slouched in a chair, legs outstretched, while visiting with someone wearing Coastal boots.

"How's it going with him?" I ask.

"Pretty okay," Renegade answers, slightly baffled. "Which is weird."

I grin, easily relating. "And how do you feel?" He looks thinner, though I don't know how that's possible.

"Alive. Barely." Renegade grumbles like he's unsure if it's a good or bad thing. "Bored."

"I can fix that." Raider chuckles.

"Hey, let's slow down," I contend, putting a soft hand on Renegade's wrist. "Give yourself another week before you go disappearing on me at Raider's whims."

"*Whims*?" Raider sputters, making Renegade laugh.

"Hey, all," Valore says, pushing from the bench and

approaching. "This old man's feeling his age. I'm heading in to rest my eyes. Shall I take the other old man with me?"

"I'm far from old," Renegade snaps while Valore laughs heartily. "But yeah, I'll come with."

"What about you, Sage?" Valore taps his grandson's shoulder. "Want to join the old men?" Sage shrugs.

"You'll need something better than a nap to entice him," Raider says with a headshake.

"How about chocolate cake?" Valore asks.

"Yes!" Sage starts dancing around us.

"You're all going to make him sick," Raider complains.

Valore chuckles. "It's bound to happen. He's too cute not to indulge." He puts his hand on Sage's head, stopping him in his tracks. "Let's leave the young people to enjoy the moon and stars."

"I'm young." Sage scowls.

"Fine, then. Let's leave the medium-aged people."

Sage considers the distinction, and then he waves goodbye and walks away while asking the men if they have any cool scars. He's excited to go with his grandpa and Renegade—cake aside—skipping and swinging his arms while he listens to their stories. Oh, how I wish I were fearless and carefree as a child.

"It's a bit early for moon and stars," Raider says, and I turn to find him posed with a bent elbow. "Care to join me for a walk instead?" I nod, taking the crook, and we start down the cliffside path before he asks, "Did I see you talking to Chett earlier?"

"You did. I didn't know he was leaving Torquent." Raider nods, so I ask, "How's it been working with him?" I got Chett's take, but I'm curious about Raider's version.

He shrugs. "Awkward."

"Yeah." That he even tried is huge in my mind. "Have you forgiven him?"

He sighs heavily. "I don't know if I can."

"I think that's okay."

"You do?" Raider glances down at me, surprise and sadness mixed in the expression.

"It's your right to decide when to take that step. If you never do, well, that's your right as well. In the meantime, you have plenty of things to keep yourself occupied."

"You think?" He grins, but it's strained. He looks exhausted, which is further corroborated when he says wearily, "This week has been intense."

"Yeah. I haven't seen you since Tuesday," I say with a laugh, but the words don't sound as funny when they leave my mouth.

"Sorry about that."

This time, I laugh for real because I won't be *that* person—the one who says one thing and means another, manipulates until they get their way, and lies to everyone, including themselves.

"There's nothing to be sorry for, Raider." I kick a larger rock and watch it bounce along the path we're taking. "You run an immense territory in the Dark, and you've taken on a light bubble overflowing with people. You're charged with integrating two vastly different groups while helping them keep their cultural identity. You've shown sincere respect for the passing of someone who tried to take every piece of your life for herself. And you're managing it all splendidly. It's quite impressive."

"And in the process," Raider says, stopping our progress to face me. "I've ignored you."

"I haven't felt ignored. Sage has kept me company. Valore too. And my family."

"Don't let me off the hook." He covers my hand that's still gripping his elbow. "It only makes me feel worse."

"There is no hook. I'm proud of you. And you owe me nothing."

Dropping my hand to break our connection, I continue down the path. I hear his footsteps behind me, but it's a minute before he calls out, "Hey, Shar. Hold up."

I stop, feigning interest in the limited view of Lake Divido, hidden behind a group of ash trees. A second later, Raider's there, taking my hand so our palms rest together. His eyes are on my face, but I don't look up—too caught up in how much I like the look of our entwined hands. The wind rustles the tree leaves, and another burst of lavender scent crosses our way. The smell calms me and clears my mind. It's time to tell him what I've been thinking this week while he's been working so hard. It's time to ask him if what I want is possible and if he might want it too. I open my mouth, vowing to release the words, but I merely exhale before taking another breath.

Curses! Why is this so hard?

It shouldn't be. The words come easily to my mind.

Raider, I care for you and don't want to leave. Can I stay in Contund while you figure things out? I can give you space, but be around to provide support. I'll find ways to be productive and help you in this transition. I enjoy construction and would like to learn that trade. I'll help the people with new housing as they expand beyond Torquent's borders. I'll continue to help Sage get settled and be with Valore when he visits. But mostly, I'd like to stay to be close to you.

I've repeated the speech in my mind every day for the last week, and now—here, under these ash trees—it's my opportunity to say it for real. I'm ready. *I am!* So, I open my mouth to communicate my desires.

And a bug flies in.

Sputtering, I pull from Raider's grasp, spinning away from him. "What's wrong?" he asks, following me to where I'm spitting into the bushes.

"Bug!" I manage between blowing air through my mouth and wiping my tongue with my hand.

It takes a minute, but I'm soon confident all insect remnants are gone. My composure is gone too. As are the beautiful words that were in my head. I'm mortified, desperate to leave for Tyran's sterile home where I'll crawl into the bed I've used this week.

The feeling triples when I turn around and find Raider's face red with laughter. If our roles were reversed, I'd find humor in the situation too, but I'm humiliated after going from being ready to confess my feelings to choking on an insect.

Stepping forward, I brush past Raider, intent on a quick escape, but he reaches out, snagging my arm and whirling me around to face him. For a moment, the bottom of my yellow dress flares like we're dancing, and then he locks me in his arms, looking down at me.

"I'm sorry for laughing," Raider says, not looking all that sorry, so I snort and roll my eyes at his feeble apology.

He begins swaying us back and forth, and other than my pinned arms, it feels like we really are dancing. If I freed my imagination, I could envision us back in Consilio Locus the night of the governors' reception. Only today, Raider has the upper hand. Where I fought for it that night, eight years later in Contund, I'm glad to surrender it to him.

"Your sister did a great job on your dress."

"Is she the one who picked it out?" She didn't tell me.

Raider nods. "I just told her it should be yellow. It's not a traditional color for a funeral, but I couldn't bear to see you in drab colors. In Hamo, Arrick dressed you in green, but that's because he didn't know you radiate in yellow. You're stunning."

My cheeks glow red, but I nod, accepting the lovely compliment but trying not to dwell on it too heavily.

"Something is missing, though," Raider says, releasing me and reaching into his jacket. "I've had this in my pocket all day." Holding Squatty's necklace aloft, the orange jewel twinkles.

"You've had it with you all day?"

"All week, actually." I'd been curious about the necklace's whereabouts, after giving it to him during my fight with Tyran. I'd never have guessed he had it with him all along.

"It was like having you with me," he continues, and my cheeks burn. "Every time I felt anxious, I'd reach up and feel it pressing against my chest." My eyes widen, having seen him do exactly that on multiple occasions. "It gave me the courage to keep going. Because I thought of your courage."

Curses! He's talking about courage like it's my constant companion, while all it's done today is elude me.

I clear my throat. "Thanks for taking care of it for me."

"Thanks for trusting me with it. I know what it means to you." I nod while Raider leans in, clasping it around my neck. I run my fingers over the bumpy surface. Thoughts of my friend always make me melancholy, but Raider's content expression keeps me from delving deep.

"It's too bad they had to leave," Raider says, running his hands over my shoulders before resting them on my lower back.

"Leave?" I repeat, trying to find the conversation in my mental fog.

"Chessie and Evans. It was hard to see them go."

"They're gone?" I jolt in his arms—releasing Squatty's necklace—but Raider keeps his hold on me.

"That surprises you?"

"Well, yes," I say, gripping his arms to turn and look behind me as if to catch a final glimpse of them. "Chess was supposed to talk to me before she left. She was—" I stop because Raider doesn't know she asked me to return with them.

"She was expecting an answer from you?" he asks with a gleam in his eye.

"Yes," I say, startled by his knowledge. I twist the short ends of my hair thoughtfully, then drop it because my hair looks nice today, and I don't want to ruin it with my nervousness.

"About going to Adlumen," Raider clarifies, tilting his head. "You needn't worry about it. I gave her an answer, so they left."

"You gave—" I squint at him. "What did you tell her?"

Raider grins. "I told her you're my girl, and you're right where you belong."

"*Your girl*?" I snort out an anxious laugh. "And she believed you?" I mean for the question to knock the smirk off his face, but it goes nowhere.

"Come now, it's not that shocking of a notion. We've even kissed before."

"That was a long time ago, and it was more of an attack than anything."

Raider chuckles. "Yeah. It was."

"This is a bizarre conversation."

"Is it?"

"Yes," I reply firmly.

"And you need it to be less bizarre," Raider surmises, and that finally has him losing his smile. "Because you've been through a lot, and I've put you through a lot, and you will assume nothing."

"Did Chess tell you that?"

"She didn't have to, Shar. Because, like you, I will not assume. I don't want to guess what's on your mind. I want to know." His words are soft but his shoulders are tight beneath my fingertips. Undoubtedly, if he weren't holding onto me, he'd be rubbing his hands over his freshly shorn head. After all, I'm tempted to suck on my upper lip until it's chapped and red. We're both searching for something to soothe our nerves. But instead of returning to old habits, it seems like a better idea to talk it out. To help each other over this bump. After all, we've conquered mountains together, so a bump shouldn't be any big deal.

In contrast to Raider's posture, I suddenly find myself very relaxed, and then, Raider releases his hold on me and takes my hands. "Look, what it comes down to is this," he says. "I admire you."

"I admire you too."

"I said that to you in Periculum. We were in that tiny canvas room on those bunk beds with our hands linked across the void. Then and now, the words are genuine but serve as camouflage, hiding what I truly mean."

My heart beats double-time, and I step forward, crushing our hands between us. "Tell me," I whisper.

"There are only two things you need to know about me, Shar."

"Just two?" I ask with a light laugh.

Raider grins. "Yes. But I promise these are the most important ones." He releases one hand, putting his fingers on my cheek and running the length of my jaw as he says, "When I love, I love with everything I am." He places a soft kiss on the edge of my mouth but leans back and finds my eyes when he adds, "And I love you."

I smile up at him, feeling a tingle from the bottom of my feet to the top of my spine. "You're right. Those are the most important ones," I say, taking a deep breath and telling him, "I love you too."

Raider erases any room between us, bringing his lips down on mine.

Curses! The beautiful Raider Roil is kissing me!

And it's not because I've manipulated my way into his good graces. And I didn't attack him with my lips. All I did was be myself, and through some miracle, over the last thirty-nine days, he's discovered I mean something to him.

Me! Just as I am.

He wants me to stay in Torquent.

He wants to kiss me.

He loves me.

When Raider leans back to break our kiss, a tear escapes my eye, rolling down my cheek. But it's a tear of joy, and they're my favorite kind, so I let it be.

"Sage is going to freak out," Raider says with a beaming smile.

"What about Valore?" I ask, laughing while my eyes brim with more happy tears.

"He'll want you to start calling him Dad," Raider says, brushing my cheeks with his thumb. He's smiling down at me with no thought to the comment, but all I can think about is what my best friend said not even an hour ago.

Sooner than you think possible, you'll not only appropriate me but feel perfectly at ease doing so.

It's like he knew. Maybe Raider told him. Or maybe he's very observant and watched it happen.

"Hey. Where did you go?" Raider asks, leaning into my vision.

"Sorry. It's just all sort of surreal."

It's then I notice his fingers stretched toward me. "Take my hand?" he asks. "It's our favorite time of day, and I don't want us to miss it."

With my hand in his, he guides me from the ash trees and farther along the pebbled path until we reach another bench overlooking Lake Divido. The sun is just reaching the horizon, and the clouds are burning pink while the sky flashes orange. I look down at my dress, brilliant under the setting light, and I marvel at the color.

"I do love this dress," Raider says, pulling me close. "You look sixteen again."

"Hah! I was dangerous at sixteen."

"It's possible you're dangerous still, but I know how to handle you."

"Yeah? And how's that?"

"Like the little prisoner you are." Raider laughs, brushing the hair on my forehead. "Only this time, you're stuck here in Torquent with me."

"Is that a condition of my sentence?" I ask, and his brow dips in confusion, remembering how those words hurt me in the past. But life is different now, so I smile because confinement in Torquent sounds perfect, and I tell him in all seriousness, "Because if that's the case, I wouldn't have it any other way."

THE END OF THE DARK SERIES

BOOKS BY THIS AUTHOR

AUTHOR'S NOTE

It's 10:00 p.m., and I just finished the final edits on The Prisoner. In ten days, the digital book will go live. (I'm not cutting it close or anything.) Even after the first draft, I was super happy with how this book turned out. That said, during the edits, I realized I rushed the ending. After writing five books, I knew all the pieces that needed to go into the final chapters to wrap things up, and I just plonked them in there. Don't get me wrong—I liked much of it—but some parts felt like a checklist I was getting through.

Cut to now, and I've spent fourteen days massaging the checklist chapters (chapters 46-52) on repeat. Tonight, I went out for dinner to celebrate being nearly finished, and I just zoned out because my brain felt like mush. But I'm ecstatic with the end product and glad I took the time to get everything the way I wanted it.

It's done! And it's bittersweet. I'm excited... to finalize the story. I'm sad... to leave these characters behind. I'm relieved... that the pressure is off. (Well, it will be in another week or so.) I'm scared... at the prospect of doing it all again. (Galactic DJ is coming next!) I'm amazed... that I accomplished what I set out to do. Like Sharade in Chapter 52, it feels pretty surreal.

SPOILERS AHEAD. (So, skip to the three diamonds below unless you've read The Prisoner.)

Something unusual about this book... Sharade has TWO character arcs. When the idea came to me, I didn't know if it was proper, or even possible, but I liked the challenge and decided to try it, regardless.

The Aunty's Cellar chapters are her positive change arc... Sharade comes to understand herself and makes core, fundamental changes to her nature. The main character arc spans the entire book and is a flat arc... Sharade goes through a genuine change but must bring others to trust and accept her transformation. I placed objects, actions, or dialogue at matching arc points to connect her two arcs, including the bottle, water, hand scar, apples, taking her hand, Torquent blade, blood, and promising not to abandon her. I doubt anyone would ever notice, but it was a lot of fun, giving that hidden depth to the story.

When naming Chessie's siblings, I thought Sharade sounded edgy and figured I'd lean into it—make her a person who's not as represented. It ended up working symbolically in The Prisoner when she insists on being called Shar—like she's shedding her former persona. (Note: Choosing to call her Shar was a bit of a struggle because people sometimes try to call me Char... a nickname I've never liked. You might have noticed Shar didn't like it either at first.)

Raider... Is he a liar? I still don't know. Haha. Honestly, it's pretty stupid how much I pondered that through each read. He insists he's not, and for the most part, I think he's an honest person, but he sure does tell a lot of non-truths... even down to insisting that he never forgives. But he does forgive! This is probably terrible of me, but I think he gets away with it because he's handsome. Do you ever feel that way? That people who are nice-looking get away with more? Maybe it's a book/movie thing and not a real-life thing. Regardless, I used it to my advantage and decided I didn't want his truthfulness to be confirmed one way or the other.

Squatty... Oh, man, I get choked up just thinking about Squatty. I wish things could have been different so Sharade could have known him outside of prison.

Valore... One of my favorite scenes is when Sharade's talking to Valore about wishes, and she realizes her wish puts her exactly where she is... in a Dark prison with him. The realization set her up for doing good things going forward —like willingly give up Valore if it was best for him and his family.

Renegade... We've had snippets of Renegade in all five books, but I liked getting to know him better. I liked that Sharade could empathize with his complicated family life. I liked that he's found fulfillment working with Raider. And I liked that Geric, approaching thirty, might finally make a place in his life for his dad. "It's weird." Haha... it's not that Renegade doesn't enjoy connecting with his son, but it's new and uncomfortable, and he's not sure how to adjust to it or maintain it. After all, he's programmed to go off on his own at Raider's whims.

Tyran... You got that her name is short for tyranny, right? Of course you did. I had a perfectly boring name picked out, but it wouldn't do. I really had to cut back on descriptions during her chapters because she created such a strong image—a pretty woman with all those awkwardly large features.

Keine... I mentioned previously that Keine's relationship with Chessie was complicated because he loved her, but it was a strange love, and he was mean about it. Keine's relationship with Sharade is less complicated but sad because he doesn't love her. He used her, but she failed, and he figured she should die rather than endure prison because she's weak and would fail at that too. I don't think I ever explained it to that extent. But I was glad that during their reunion—one chapter is all he got—she got to expound on her strengths, even though it meant nothing to him.

Chett... He was interesting to write because I didn't like him much. Haha. And it's not all because of the Kally/Valore thing. He often felt like a festering sore... a bit painful and irritating. While he was legitimately trying to be Sharade's friend, his past overshadowed his efforts, and their relationship felt wrong. He was keeping so much from her, and their interactions had an edge of dishonesty.

Casmo... After five books, we finally meet Casmo. He's a character I'm pretty conflicted about. I like him, but he's not a good guy. I mean, he legit imprisoned Valore for no *good* reason. But even though he's on the page so little, I feel like he packs a punch.

Torquent blades... It was fun making up a system of organized fighting. A couple of beta readers requested more, so I added an entire fight scene and extended another one. Serrated knives are scary enough... I can't imagine fighting with a serrated sword.

I struggled with the final battle and how to make Sharade strong without her killing Tyran. Because I really didn't want her to kill Tyran. Sharade is not a killer. She proved that with Evans and Diggs. She was sick after her involvement in those acts, and I didn't want her to live with successfully taking a life on purpose. Chett, on the other hand, had every reason for retribution. Tyran manipulated him into committing terrible acts—against innocent people—by threatening the lives of those closest to him, and he lived under a dark cloud for years. It was so obvious that Chett should be the one to take her out. This scene is very altered from the original draft because I kept at it, balancing strength, mercy, and motivation for Sharade and Chett. Fingers crossed that it came together.

One more note... Raider forgiving Chett. Yeah, that's a big ask. When Casmo suggested it, I thought it was pretty gutsy of him (which tracks well) to ask that of Raider under the circumstances. I understood the motivation for wiping the slate clean, but... yeah... Chett walking free was hard. I'm a firm believer in forgiveness, but forcing it doesn't work. Sometimes, all you can manage is believing that someday it might be possible. Maybe forgiveness isn't always a final state of being but a goal you're working toward.

Ultimately, I couldn't let Chett off the hook entirely. He told Sharade her prison time was an inspiration to him, which came across as a joke, but there's a lot of truth there, and he's content if that's his destination.

My readers: You made it to the end. Thanks so much for giving your time to this adventure. It's such an honor and means more than you'll ever know. If you have a moment, please leave a review on Amazon or Goodreads.

To Matt: Love you! Yay, it's done! (Until the next one, but I'll be smarter about deadlines next time.)

To Matt, Sandi, Tara, Kirsti, and Fish: Many thanks to these awesome beta readers for their time and interest. (And a special thanks to Aunt Diane for her after-release catches. Appreciate you looking out for me!)

To the Instagram bibliophile community: I've enjoyed connecting with so many of you over the last year, and appreciate your words and inspiration. Keep posting!

To any prospective writers: If your dream is to write, do it! Go to NaNoWriMo and join a writing group during Nov, Apr, or Jul. Check out Novlr as a great place to put down your story. Grammarly can't be beat for getting your words right. Go to Canva and make your social media shine. Happy writing, everyone!

And happy reading too!

www.ingramcontent.com/pod-product-compliance
Lightning Source LLC
LaVergne TN
LVHW041052080826
845145LV00007B/1547
* 9 7 8 1 9 6 2 6 9 5 1 7 6 *